Threaded Secrets

K. Malady

To my husband, who supports these books even when he finds them completely baffling.
To my daughter (age 4), who said this is the 3rd best book cover of all my books.
And to the readers, who picked up this book.

Also By

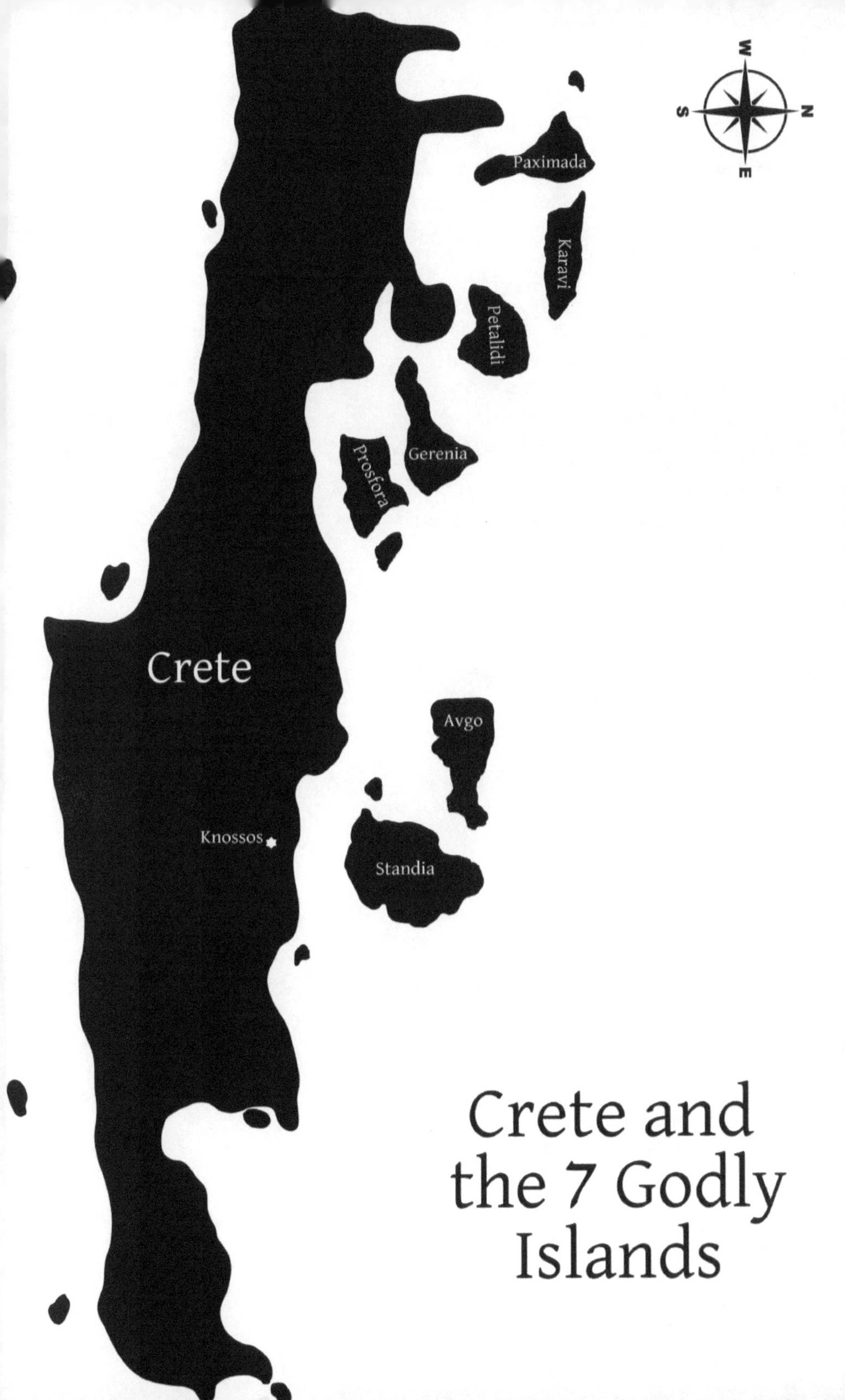

Paximada
Karavi
Petalidi
Gerenia
Prosfora
Crete
Avgo
Knossos
Standia
Crete and
the 7 Godly
Islands

Chapter 1

A bull stood on a tall hill, wrapped in a cloak of serpent's skin. Thunder and lightning boomed and flashed around him. A crack appeared in the earth below and he tipped his horns to the side, allowing a crown to fall into the hole. He snorted and shook his head until the vision faded away to nothingness.

"The Labyrinth was vast and unfathomable, its architecture a boundless braid of undulating pathways. When the Beast's unfathomable gaze focused on Naid, her lips quivered—"

A snort interrupts the presentation, and my head turns to find the woman with the guts to laugh at Lyra's oral reading. I agree with the mystery woman—using unfathomable twice, the repetitive phrasing, not to mention *venerating* those poor women—but Lyra's pride has created more than one bruised face among this group of women. She behaves like a younger daughter, someone who needs to be scrappy to survive the Collection, and not a clever twenty-one-year-old eldest of nine.

My view of who interrupted Lyra is limited. I sit in the first row of the amphitheater in the center seat, pin straight and focused on the presenter. I place a magical illusion on my body, something that looks like a golden net only visible to me that creates a feigned Thalia, one who mimics my respectful posture and position. Except fake-Thalia's hair has more luster than my dull brown locks, and I may have removed some of the frizz around my temples.

Using the illusion's cloak, I crane my neck about the room to find the pseudo-heckler, but the mystery woman doesn't present herself to my gaze. *Smart*; it's not as though I'd stand in her corner when Lyra struck. Governors can't take sides in private squabbles, they must be neutral and appear as firm as granite.

My search ends when I realize all eyes are, for the first time since childhood, pointedly ignoring me. All my life someone is staring at me: curious about the power I'll someday wield, comparing me to my godly ancestor, judging whether I deserve to be heir. If not for the magical illusion making it appear like I'm staring placidly at Lyra, I'd likely never notice the change. But now, there's no subtlety in their disregard—necks are craned towards the darkening sky above and the plaster below. I expect someone to whistle nonchalantly. Only Lyra's sparking gray eyes glare in my direction.

Drat. I'm the accidental heckler, my hidden apathy for these yearly presentations making an unanticipated appearance. Future Governors don't laugh at the Collection; they don't speak out of turn in front of constituents. And my connection to Athena may be long-removed, but a bit of her spirit still runs through my soul and her blood through the heart of the Island. And she didn't 'joke.'

"Did you have a comment, Thalia?" Lyra's full lips twist into an angry pout. "Surely you mean no insult to my rendition of our most treasured tradition? Especially since neither of us will ever have the joy of participating in the Collection."

My cheeks heat, my skin blotching in complete contrast to the beautiful, but angry, blush on the porcelain skin of Lyra's face. At least the illusion hides my unbecoming reaction and how I slink down in my seat.

The Collection demands one of the youngest daughters from each of the seven Islands, who are taken to Crete every seven years to meet the Beast, the monster that appeared after King Minos won the war. Once, we were eight separate civilizations: Crete where most of the Gods' half-mortal children live, and the seven Islands grown from the lifeblood of the Olympians' most powerful children—Apollo, Ares, Artemis, Athena, Hermes, and Hephaestus. Only Aphrodite was a child of Titans herself, sacrificing herself instead of her eternally youthful niece.

Each God offered their soul and life to an Island, creating additional barricades against the titan Typhon. To keep the world from losing the *benefits* of their gifts, they infused their spirit and body into a single heir: that human who would carry on their legacy and rule the future inhabitants of the Islands. But power, divine or mundane, always seeks more, and after several centuries of infighting between the Islands, the new King of Crete brought forth a war against us.

As the ultimate victor, he united us all under a single flag but demanded penance from the Islands by creating the Collection. Some, like Lyra, believe it a blessing to be Collected. Considering none of the women ever come back and that Lyra's *own* parents mate like rabbits to keep their youngest daughter below the age cutoff of fifteen, the truth is probably closer to what I hear my father whisper to my mother when the staff leaves us for the evening.

"Are you deaf as well as mute, Thalia?" Lyra snaps.

A gasp goes through the room at her audacity. My status as heir to the Governorship means I'm usually left alone and unquestioned. With an inward sigh, I square my shoulders, readying myself to appease an angry citizen. I've seen Father do it enough; he switches from a placid advisor to an enlightened advocate as easily as breathing. I've only managed it when my illusion covers the nerves shining from my eyes. I drop the illusion like a cloak slipping off my form and shake my long bangs from my face, chin rising.

As I lift from my chair, the moderator scuttles from her seat in the highest tier towards the flat stage. She nods in my direction, and I reseat myself. A thirty-year-old fifth child, Regan runs our age group's culture class, where we discuss and create art, literature, music, and anything the non-youngest daughters need to learn to be well-rounded citizens. Today, we're presenting dramatic readings on a historical event of our choice and the offerings are dismal.

Sometimes I wonder if the youngest women would be better served joining us in addition to their classes learning weaponry and defense. At least they are more likely to know what the Labyrinth entails, unlike Lyra. But from age eleven and up, we separate into our little castes: the learned and the warriors, the safe and the imperiled. Only if one of the girl's mothers gives birth to another girl child do those women switch to our track and begin their formal education, or if they age out without being chosen. But by the time the youngest daughters turn forty, they rarely want to spend the rest of their unregulated life studying. It's a pity, truly.

"Lyra, this is a culture class, which involves both experiencing and sharing our truth." Regan gives me a strained smile. "Thalia found your writing... humorous, and we thank her for the expression of her truth."

Lyra pouts. "Her truth shouldn't mock the Collection."

"We thank her, Lyra," Regan says, eyes twitching.

"Thank you, Thalia," the theater echoes. Lyra's voice is only a beat behind.

Regan claps her hands. "Let us adjourn for the morning, ladies. Do not forget the Scrimmage will occur this evening after dinner." A thunderclap sounds and Regan flinches. "May the Gods allow us to do so while keeping dry."

After class, I race home to avoid the sky's inevitable opening. Perched in the center of town, the white marble Governor's house is a beacon for the village, its facades adorned with intricate frescos depicting scenes from ancient legends and the exploits of Athena before her demise. Vines and ivy creep up the sides and trail around windows fitted with simple wooden shutters kept open to invite the gentle breeze and sunlight. The main entrance is flanked by two sentinels: gilded owls with eyes that follow those who pass beneath the archway.

As I pass the columns marking the entrance, I whip off the overtight belt cinching my waist and toss it onto the tile fresco. For its valiant, if unsuccessful, effort, I lob it towards Zeus's godly head instead of his still-godly-but-less-impressive ankles.

The mosaic in the entry is one of twenty-seven in my house, and I pass six of them on the way to the library. The Governor's house has been in my family since Athena pulled the Island from the water and gave her legacy to a long dead ancestor. Each new generation has expanded the house's footprint, including adding to the library where we now boast thousands of volumes. With Athena as our ancestor, we could do nothing less.

The seventh mosaic lies between the library and my brother's playroom. I trail one hand over the grouted mica. It's a rendition of Athena bursting from Zeus' head fully grown. I designed and installed that mosaic, not because of any interest or talent in the artistry, but because it was a puzzle. Mother gave me mica sheets and a set of heavy shears and told me I needed to fill the space with a picture. Each piece, each shape, each color, they all fit together perfectly. It simply took raw materials and the ability to see the puzzle to be formed.

Before entering the library, I change directions to peek my head inside Cleon's playroom. Cleon sits on the floor with a lump of sewn cotton in his hands. As I watch, he transforms the cotton into a stuffed owl, then a living bunny, then a clay doll with snakes for hair. A faint golden mist of magic coils around the fabric with each transformation.

I stroll into the room and drop to the floor in front of him. "Did Anike tell you the story of Medusa?"

He holds out the doll. "Yes. You play?"

"For a bit." I crane my neck searching for Anike in the giant room. "Where did Anike go?"

Anike had been my nurse and Father's. Though I outgrew her, she remained living at the house as an unofficial member of the family. When Hera unexpectedly blessed Mother with another child almost twenty years after her first, Anike stepped back into her role.

"Anike eat," Cleon says seriously. His sky-colored eyes, the same shade as mine, widen. "Anike no dinner."

I take the doll and Cleon scrambles up into my lap. I'd almost forgotten we're dining with Lukas and his parents before the Scrimmage tonight. Anike will be responsible for Cleon the entire evening, as we'll leave from dinner straight to the Scrimmage.

This is yet another in a long line of dinners to discuss our future marriage and the combining of our families. Lukas' father, Argon, is the Second Councilor, the next in line after the Governor with high ambitions. Only if no children of Athena remain could he or one of his children rule Standia. Marrying us would be politically beneficial for both families: Lukas would be Second Councilor and husband to the Governor, and his future child the next Governor.

I rest my chin on Cleon's dark hair. "How about I tell you another story?"

He wiggles in my lap and takes the transformed Medusa doll back, changing it back to its natural form: a puff of fabric for him to practice the magic he received from Athena, transfiguring physical items. He looks at me expectantly while I consider which story to tell.

"A long, long time ago, the Islands were at war…"

Anike returns after I've finished telling Cleon the story of the Collection. Only then do I kiss him goodbye and head down the tiled hallway into our public library to study.

I select the history book my tutor will review tomorrow, placing the gold leaf bookmark aside and curling up in my favorite chair under a tapestry woven by another dead ancestor. Part of being the Governor's heir is knowing the history of our people and I've read almost every book in this room to prepare myself for my inevitable future. It helps that I prefer the company of books over almost everyone else in Standia.

But the recounting of the most recent olive famine can't hold my attention, no matter that my family helped create olive trees. The incident in culture class pulls my attention inward.

The Island views me as a learned and perfectly composed future leader, a facade I wear through magic and will. With expectations the size and weight of the Island on my back, how I'm perceived is just as important as the future decisions I might make. Better they think I'm a still pond, one without weaknesses or frustrations to be exploited, than a rolling ocean. Oceans cause tsunamis, something too turbulent for a good leader.

Lyra's last words echo through my mind, something she hissed to her various sycophants when she didn't know I was also hiding in the orchestra, gauging the timing of the dark clouds that rolled in earlier that morning.

"And the one time she acts like a human, she mocks me!" No surprise who the 'her' in that sentence was. Lyra's voice was muffled, like she'd been sniffling into a handkerchief. *"Doesn't she know how lucky she is? Her life is mapped out, with no surprises or disappointments. She gets Lukas, and she gets to lead. She could have been Collected. She—she could have gone in place of Serai."*

The others ushered her out of the room before I heard anything else.

Serai had been Collected during the last Collection, a sixteen-year-old whose mother couldn't bear more children. Out of the dozens of eligible women around the Island of Standia, the Councilors voted to send Serai to Crete. I was fifteen, the youngest daughter in my family and only just age eligible. But being the youngest also makes me the eldest, a silly bit of wordplay my father fed the other Councilors. He may not have been the first to think of it, but his status as Governor meant it worked. And with me a descendant of Athena and next in line after his death, no one would vote for *me* to disappear to Crete. Even if my leadership skills remain untested.

But Serai and Lyra had always been close. I caught them embracing behind the school more than once. Perhaps Lyra's adulation of the Collection is false, to protect her heart. Perhaps she wishes she could have joined Serai wherever she ended up.

A loud boom of thunder shakes the window behind me, a colored mica sheet depiction of the three major deities: Zeus who rules the sky, Hades who rules the Underworld, and Poseidon who rules the sea. Between them is the Earth, ruled by none but herself. The storm that threatened the village all day bursts free, echoing through the mountains that mark the borders of my village from the next. Lightning illuminates the window, casting eerie and unnaturally colored lights over the wide room.

Serai is dead, most likely. The Councilors talk as though it is an honor: be a part of the Collection, provide glory for Standia, succeed against the Beast, and come home a hero. No one explains what happens when the girls don't return, but I doubt King Minos is housing four centuries' worth of women who failed to defeat the Beast. Crete is already overpopulated with the living Cretans. Although he, and all the others on Crete, aren't deities, they have magic that keeps them immortal and more powerful than the rest of us. But power rarely metes mercy. Power isn't generous with those that lack it. My circumstance is evidence of that.

Thunder booms, almost covering the sound of the copper balls clanging on the library clock, the alarm for our afternoon meal, and I replace the unread book. My thoughts still swirl, but I blink them away, composing my face into its usual mask. I need no illusion magic to create it, though this morning's incident has taught me that I can't rely on my will alone. Not when my own body might betray my inner thoughts.

And some of those inner thoughts must remain hidden, for my own heart's protection. As I walk down the long outer hallway from the library towards the formal dining room, sliding against the cold marble walls to avoid any possible rain splatters, warmth spreads in my stomach, holding off the chill. I may not love Lukas romantically—I've never let myself—but I've admired him since childhood. He's my closest friend, immediately understanding why I wear the mask and not teasing me for it, even if he disagrees. "Thalia saves her words for those people she feels are important," he'd say if people asked him when I wasn't around. Given he was the only one I spoke to, the joke left us laughing.

I slide into the chair next to his at our long dining table. Only six of the twenty seats are filled, the table crafted to hold a larger family than ours, one that would have as many children as needed to avoid sending a younger daughter to the Collection.

Lukas' own family boasts five children, all boys. Now our table only seats that many on holidays when my many cousins and their parents take turns visiting.

Lukas grins at me and presents a plate of roast duck as if he's offering me some glorious prize. The dimples that frame his caramel cheeks blossom.

After I've served myself dinner, his grin turns sly. It's a smirk that made several girls agree to meet him under the docks when we were younger. Lukas is objectively handsome, and he knows it. But those grins never worked on me; it's not as though he was truly flirting.

"Did you have a good culture lesson?" he asks.

Nothing in his face shows he knows what happened, or that I spoke out in front of them, that my still pond had a pebble dropped in it. I shrug and remain silent.

"Take some more duck, darling," he says as he doles out another portion on top of the one I've yet to eat. "Expressing one's truth takes a lot of energy."

I groan, turning my face towards the back of the room to scowl at him without being seen by the others. "Who told?"

"Nephele."

Nephele's older sister is in our class, while she is a youngest daughter and only studies combat. That she already knows means it made the rounds in the village.

"The *one* time I don't use my illusions," I grumble.

"It was bound to happen sometime."

"Not likely. I went twenty-two years with complete poise and composure, then for no reason I can't hold it in at culture class." My eyes roll skyward. "It wasn't even a dignified laugh or a stately murmur. I snorted, like a pig."

"Don't insult pigs," he says. "They're noble, intelligent creatures." I elbow him in the chest, and he laughs, full and deep. "Good thing you have no strength, or I'd be covered in bruises from your so-called composed persona."

I sniff imperiously. "Leaders are made through discipline and study, not brute strength."

"There's brute strength and then there's—"

"I will elbow you again."

He wraps an arm around my waist, squeezing gently. "Perhaps it's time to hang up the mask, let the 'snort' lead you into, I don't know, actually *speaking* to someone other than me."

"I speak to people," I protest. "You act as if I'm mute."

He hooks his chin over my shoulder, his mahogany eyes gazing at me. "With the illusion up, sure. When was the last time you said something of substance to someone outside this room? Something other than 'excuse me,' 'good morning,' and 'indeed, your position has merit.'"

I stay silent. He sighs, the warm air tickling the gentle curls by my nape. I don't close my eyes, or I'll start thinking things about Lukas that he doesn't want and that will do us no good.

"I'm not trying to criticize you, Thal. I simply want—" He makes a frustrated sound. "You know, the ice-queen persona will need to thaw at some point. You can't hide behind an illusion *or* a mask forever."

This isn't a new argument. But Lukas is charming and handsome; he'll smile and our people will trust in his decision. But me? The only magical skill I kept from Athena was the ability to create illusions. I have nothing to offer but a significant education and no other appeal beyond being born into the position—one wrong move and no one will trust me. Better not do anything.

I tilt my chin challengingly. "Calm waters spill—"

"Spill no secrets, I know. Calm waters don't inspire loyalty in your people either. They don't show Standia your incredible personality."

I pull back, forcing Lukas to loosen his grip on me and slide his hand to my hip. "So, what are you suggesting? I spout poetry?

Something like: Lukas, my Lukas, standing as tall as a ficus, with a voice like a squawking ibis."

He laughs again and I can't help but smile. "It's a good thing I'll be your Second, as I have little faith in your speech writing abilities. But you picked the perfect subject."

"What joy it gives me to see our children so content with each other." The deep voice of Father interrupts the byplay between Lukas and me. Father and our mothers beam at us, while Argon eyes us flatly. Lightning flashes along the windows that run the length of the table.

"Have you considered a wedding date yet?" Lukas' mother, Ariadne, asks.

Lukas removes his arm from my waist as the dimples disappear from his expression. His apparent unhappiness at our future union makes the duck swim unpleasantly in my stomach.

"Not yet, mother," Lukas says. "But we're in no hurry. Our lifespan may not mirror our Cretan overlords, but we have decades to marry."

"Do not speak against the King and his people," Argon says, scowling.

Lukas picks up a glass of wine shipped in from one of the other Islands and lets the liquid inside spin. "I'm not speaking against them, just offering my truth."

Mother snorts but composes herself as Father lifts his glass. "And all truth should be valued," he says as he tips his glass in Argon's direction. "I, for one, have no plans to resign my position soon."

Argon grunts. "Nor I, but a wedding might distract from any unrest related to the Collection."

"What unrest?" a voice asks. For the second time today, I'm surprised to learn it's mine.

Lukas' parents are as well, since I rarely speak directly to them, and never try to engage them in discussions about politics. Argon recovers from his shock quickly, which on his sharp face looks like nothing more than an eye twitch.

"Most of our eligible women have become… ineligible because of a surprising bout of fertility within the last year, making their youngest girls below the age requirement," Argon explains.

Lukas and I share a glance. The population of Standia is already enormous, meaning the numbers of eligible women should be dozens, if not hundreds. *How many women recently bore children?*

"I wouldn't call it surprising," Father says, touching Mother's shoulder affectionately. "Having experienced our own gift of unpredictable fertility. Though that over three quarters of their mothers gave birth in the last six months is remarkable. Had I not met each babe herself, I wouldn't have believed it."

"They, or the Goddesses of childbirth, must have realized that being part of the Collection isn't the honor you make it out to be," Lukas says mildly.

Argon stands as Aridne presses a hand on her cheek, but Lukas rolls his bright brown eyes.

"Come off it," he says. "It's not like I'm saying anything you haven't said over dinner in our own home. Everyone in this room will be family someday, and our opinions don't differ. We have no secrets from our truth here. And we all know the Collection is no prize."

I nod my head as if I agree, but even the murmuring of my parents hasn't been half as treasonous. The Collection isn't a choice the Governor can stand against publicly or privately. There are a lot of us, but none with the might of King Minos, the Cretans, or the Gods they can claim direct kinship to. It isn't as if we can *decline* because the population finally realizes it is a reparation of the war.

Lyra's earlier statements and the memory of Serai float through my head. "How many women are eligible?" I ask.

Thunder chases my question through the long room, lightning streaking once, twice, thrice outside the glass windows. But rain has yet to slam into my home. Only the threat of it waits above us.

"Four," Argon says as he sits. *Five with you* hovers silently over the table.

I slump against the back of my chair. Of our entire Island, only four, *five*, women can partake. *Will there be any in ten years, when the Island is so overpopulated we can't feed ourselves? At what point will King Minos demand us all instead?*

"Do you expect any volunteers?" Lukas' voice is tight, as if he's realized what I have.

"None of the women are zealots, if that's what you're asking," Father says. "They're all from less conservative families, who feel as we do about the sacrifice."

I suck in a sharp breath. That's the first time my father has admitted what the Collection is: a sacrifice, a death to all those women. He's hedged around it alone in our home, but the bluntness of the statement, his agreement with Lukas' opinion, creates a stifling tension. Something dark *is* in the waters today. Perhaps Zeus and his threatened storms affected our usual restraint. It isn't unheard of for the Gods who remain above to give direction and lessons through their powers. Zeus speaks through storms and the air. And sometimes I have dreams that feel God-touched, with flashing images full of their symbols that I must interpret in the morning. If only they could hop down from the clouds and give us messages directly.

"Without volunteers, the Councilors will vote and make their selection," Father finishes.

"Are any of them from our community?" I ask.

"Nephele," Lukas answers in Father's stead.

Nephele: strong, sweet, and simple Nephele. *Is there a Lyra that she will leave behind?* Another set of lives affected by a Collection that will never touch me.

No one speaks, only the sounds of silver tines on porcelain plates clinking against the backdrop of what the future might bring.

Chapter 2

Lukas has shaken off whatever frustration he carried at lunch by the time we descend the flights of marble towards our seats in the stadium. The rows ascend like a colossal staircase, accommodating thousands of spectators, but our seats are directly above the sandy arena and overlooking the spectacle to come. The Scrimmage is a pageant of skills that the candidates for the Collection present to the community. As Athena's Island, the candidates should show more than strength, and display a cunning and clever mind to overcome the brute challenges provided. But the presentations in my lifetime have been nothing but physical feats.

Little is known about the Labyrinth, except that the Beast stalks the center. But battle strategy, the interconnection between war and wit, is ignored. The candidates receive no formal education, learning none of the arts and culture and only the bare minimum of war tactics. Standia only includes it as an homage to Athena, not because they expect the candidates to use the teachings. I don't even think the candidates from Avgo, whose patron is the Goddess of Love and Beauty, include it at all. I've reviewed Standia's Collected candidate curriculum, and it leaves much to be desired in terms of *actual* knowledge.

"You're scowling," Lukas says as he slips into the seat beside me.

The thirty visiting Councilors and Lukas' parents file in around us. A burst of lighting skitters across the sky. The murals of former Scrimmages encircling the arena flicker in the flash, the images of long dead women vanishing and reappearing in the light.

I place an illusion on my face like a golden matron's veil, but Lukas tsks. He's stared at my face enough to catch when my expression changes as the illusion shrouds over me. He told me once it looks like a gust of wind blowing down my face.

"No illusions around me, remember?" he says, mouth barely moving.

I roll my eyes and let the illusion drop, relaxing my expression to a mirror image of the illusion I'd tried to use. "This is a waste," I say from the side of my mouth. The aisles are filling behind us and many eyes keep their focus on me. "They learn archery and swordplay, but not how to think. For once, I'd like to see a Scrimmage where they must do something strategic."

Lukas huffs. His father plans the events, but I know he doesn't agree with everything Argon does and why. "Your elitism is showing, Thal."

"It's practicality and wanting our citizens to survive. At least have them pretend to run a Labyrinth, to show they can *get out* and not just get inside and start slashing the Beast with swords."

A sniff sounds behind us, and I stiffen. Lyra and her eight siblings slip into the seats behind us. Lukas places his hand palm up on his knee and I slide my fingers through his.

"When you're Governor," he says, leaning close. His breath caresses my ear. I restrain a shiver, conscious of my many watchers, like Lyra. "When you're Governor," he repeats, "perhaps you can correct the deficiencies in our potential candidates."

"Or stop the Collection entirely," I say idly as the four candidates march towards the center of the field, kicking up the fine sand that makes up the arena floor. Thunder rumbles above us, but the rain we heard earlier hasn't reappeared.

Lukas opens his mouth to speak but stops himself to glare at our conjoined hands.

Thousands of onlookers sit in rapt attention to watch four solitary women prove they are an asset to Standia. With only a handful of candidates in a field where dozens have stood before, the event looks farcical, a poorly managed spectacle. But even knowing that the Collection is barely more than a death sentence, no candidates have ever skipped the display.

When the audience is a mass of colors instead of empty marble, Father stands and claps. Magic allows him to be heard through the massive space, magic and science, his gift from Athena being the ability to transform parts of his body combined with the knowledge of how to effectively construct the stadium.

"Welcome, good people of Standia," Father begins, his voice booming out over the crowd. The strain on his face is barely present under his beard, something only Mother and I would notice. "We have been given a gift. Not the Collection, and not our Great King, but these four women. They stand here willing to represent our community in a challenge with little opportunity for success."

He claps his hands a second time and dozens of banners fall from the outer edge of the stadium like a wave of red, covering the older murals. A small snake wound together in the shape of an ouroboros decorates the center of each banner, instead of the more common owl symbol Standia presents. Four banners also have images of a feat of strength behind it: wrestling, fighting a beast, boxing, and trapping an animal.

"As you know, one symbol of our patron Goddess is the serpent, an emblem of duality. Serpents are both creators and destroyers, their venom a poison and an antidote. Much like Athena, we must understand that duality, in our pursuit of wisdom and war. As the ouroboros shows us, they are symbols of transformation and unity. They live by the grace of our nourishing earth and, as they shed their skin, they emerge reborn. They are our Island's hope for regeneration and immortality."

He nods to the four women. "No matter what may happen, you are more than our protectors, our honored candidates. You show us the unity in all things, our Island with our King, our hope with our fear, our lives with our deaths. You are the infinite and finite, the endless cycle of creation and destruction, birth and death. Thank you for the lessons you teach us, and I pray to the Goddess we heed them."

A murmur goes through the stands as Lukas and I trade glances. No one seems sure how to react, whether Father made a political statement about the Collection, or merely a gracious speech to comfort these women and their families. I suppose that was the point. It can be everything and nothing.

Argon stands in a bluster and scowls at the women. "With that, we shall begin!" he shouts.

A woman from Tros goes first; the drawn lots show she must fight some kind of beast. She's young, gangly and with that unfinished coltish look teenagers have. This is probably the first year she's been eligible. Though I can't gauge her expression, she raises her bony chin with confidence.

A braying sound echoes from beneath our feet, in one of the underground pathways into the stadium. A barred gate under us creeps open and a rumbling creature comes forward. It looks like a pig, but only in the loosest definition of the word, as it resembles nothing seen on Standia. It stands higher than her shoulders, with tusks as long as my forearm. Like a child of monsters, foam drips from its overgrown fangs. Coarse fur ripples down its towering back, ending in a whip-like tail that flicks with agitation.

"What a *noble* creature," I murmur to Lukas. He wheezes out a laugh that sounds forced, his attention too focused on the Scrimmage before us.

The young woman crouches low when the animal clears its cage. The pig barrels towards her, braying an inhuman roar. When the tusks look close enough to pierce the delicate skin on her arms, she leaps upward, her skirts flying overhead in a flourishing display that has both men and women tittering. She lands on the pig's back, her hands grasping the short tuft of hair at the scruff of its neck and around one ear, as if she was riding a wild horse.

"That was clever," Lukas whispers to me.

I agree. Perhaps these girls have a chance if they use strategy and wit like this one.

The pig bucks its back legs, intent on throwing her off. The audience shouts both suggestions and jeers until the woman pulls a dagger from under her skirts and swipes at the pig's neck. I pinch my eyes shut. Though I know academically how things die, even the precise location on that pig to slice its primary artery, seeing it is another matter. If only I could place my illusion, then I could cower until it ends without one of the populace judging my squeamishness. Lukas keeps a tight grip on my hand until safe to open my eyes.

The woman stands with one foot on the sow, her dress splattered with red. The crowd cheers, except for a small section to the left of us, which may be the delegation from her home. Groundskeepers quickly remove the carcass and throw sand on the blood, preparing the arena for the next candidates.

We sit through two more feats of strength until it's finally Nephele's turn. The only remaining event is wrestling, which must be her task. Lukas leans forward so far that my hand is the only thing keeping him from tumbling out of his seat and into the arena. Nephele slinks forward, her gaze searching until she finds Lukas in the crowd, and she stiffens.

An uncomfortable swooping whooshes through my stomach at their focused stares, but I shake it off. Lukas isn't mine, no matter that we are betrothed. He can show interest in other women, so long as it is kept private. I could do the same if anyone else had ever caught my eye. If I'd ever let myself look.

A hulking beast of a man ambles from another underground tunnel below our feet. I vaguely recognize him as Peithon, one of the sparring tutors for the younger daughters in our village. He stands two heads above Nephele, and were he to wrap his hands around Nephele's waist, his fingers would touch. Nephele may have studied with him, but the entire audience seems to realize she is outmatched. Lukas' hand starts to sweat, and even Lyra sucks in a sharp breath from behind us.

Nephele ties her skirts out of the way, displaying the firm muscles of her bronze legs. Then, they bow to each other, and the match begins.

They circle each other three times, both bent on their haunches, although Peithon still towers above her. Though he is massive, he moves like an oar cutting through water, patient and still. Nephele looks nervous as she leaps towards him, hitting his stomach with four sharp punches. Peithon doesn't react beyond a tightening of the muscles in his back as he rams her backward, knocking her to the ground. She attempts to kick him, but he grabs one ankle and twists it around his back, leaning over her to pin her shoulders to the sand. From afar, they look like entwined lovers, but the fear on Nephele's face shows it to be a lie. She yanks her knee upward, hitting Peithon between the legs. The crowd jeers at the action, some shouting about fair play. Lukas winces beside me.

"It's good; she's using everything she has," I tell him. I'm secretly delighted by what Nephele attempted. It shows, like the girl from Tros with the pig, that *some* strategy will be used. The better to make Athena proud. The better to keep them alive against the Beast.

The hit distracts Peithon long enough for Nephele to stand, while he groans and curls into himself. But the moment doesn't last as he shakes off the pain and charges forward again. His shoulder catches her stomach as he grabs her thighs and flips her over his head. She lands on her back with a pained whimper and a loud crack. I wince; she could have broken her spine.

"She'll never pin him," Lukas says, squeezing my hand until it aches. "They need to stop the match." He looks around wildly for his father, who sits next to Mother down the row. He hisses his concerns, but Argon ignores him. Lukas' caramel face pales and he snaps his attention back to Nephele. Peithon stands above her again and is about to hold her down and count out his victory when she regains her breath and flips onto her stomach.

"She needs leverage," I murmur as Nephele claws the ground to scrabble away from Peithon. "She can't beat him in strength, but if she can get something under him and lift, she can topple him to the ground."

Lukas inclines his head, his gaze focused on Nephele's form. "What do you mean?"

"Leverage," I say, dropping his hand and rummaging through the purse at my hip. I find enough implements to act it out. With Athena's spirit running through me, handicrafts and inventions are second nature, though the model made from my pencil and a balled-up piece of parchment isn't the quality I normally present. Lukas stares in rapt attention as I show him what I meant. He stands, knocking my makeshift display to the ground.

"Leverage, Neph! Get under him and knock him off balance," Lukas shouts.

That isn't quite what I said, but Nephele wasn't close enough to any giant slabs to hoist Peithon under anyway. That she can't lift him is the entire point.

At Lukas' cry, Nephele stops fighting and lets Peithon drag her back towards him. As he pins her shoulders, she sits up, bashing him in the nose before crawling towards his ankles. With Peithon distracted by the blood gushing down his face, he doesn't notice her stealth approach as she slips between his open legs, spinning to yank on his ankles. Peithon loses balance and topples to the ground face forward, allowing Nephele to leap onto his prostrate back. Peithon could easily buck her off, but must have hit his head. Nephele brushes the wisps of blond hair that escaped her bun, then raises her hands to count. As soon as she reaches five, the number needed to end the match, she slips off him, her knees buckling.

The crowd cheers wildly for her. Groundskeepers race out to catch her as she dizzily stumbles, and to help Peithon stand. They're followed by an ambassador from the Island of Generia, one of the many daughters of the current Governor and a descendant of Apollo, who came to act as a healer for the Scrimmage using her magical medicinal skills.

Lukas vibrates next to me while Father stands and makes his closing remarks about the four girls. He remains in his seat while the audience shuffles from their seats, so I stay beside him. Probably he's waiting on Nephele to reappear, but the candidates haven't reemerged from the space below the arena.

When the last of the crowd trickles from the arena, he hoists himself over the barrier and hops into the arena.

"What are you doing?" I ask as I peer over the edge. He stands just below me, but at a distance that is the height of two full-grown adults stacked on top of each other.

"Just seeing what it's like from this side of the arena." He sounds nonchalant, but his voice shakes. "Come down," he says, lifting his hands as if to catch me.

My lips purse as I confirm the arena is empty. Lukas can talk me into much, but I only let him if no one can catch us. I'd once attempted to put an illusion over both of us to hide from Argon, but it broke, and I'd learned we needed to be unseen in other ways. Groaning, I sit on the edge and let myself fall into Lukas' waiting arms. He misses, and we tumble into the sand. I land on his chest and a wheeze pulls from his throat. I shuffle off him quickly. What I felt of him was sharp and muscular, a poorly designed pillow, though I imagine other women who have lain on top of Lukas weren't interested in sleeping.

"Show me the leverage thing," he says after helping me stand.

"Why?" I brush the sand from my skirts, but what the fall did to my hair is unfixable.

Lukas sidles close and tucks my unruly locks behind my ears. "Because I'm curious. Can I not be curious?"

With no real reason not to, we heave the top of a wooden bench to the ground. Or Lukas heaves it while I look like I'm doing more than I am. In minutes, we build a large-scale version of the model I showed him in the stands.

"Now, stand on that end," I say. Lukas obeys at once, though the corners of his mouth tilt upward in a smirk. "This is what she needed to do," I explain, using the bench to lift him into the air. "She needed to get under him."

Lukas hops off the wood. "It wouldn't have worked. What would she hoist under him to lift him up?"

"I know that. I was just thinking through ideas."

He shrugs and walks to my side. "Not very helpful ideas in the moment, though."

I bristle and cross my arms over my chest. "What you shouted out had a low chance of working, too. If she couldn't lift him, getting under him would do nothing, unless she tripped him."

He displays his palms to the sky. "I don't know, it appeared to work. She flipped him, just as I suggested she do. It was clever. More than brute strength, at least."

"It only worked *because* of strength," I retort. I can't explain why the conversation irritates me, but it does.

"Let's try it," he says. "I'll plant myself here, and you grab my ankles as Neph did and try to toss me to the ground."

"Fine. But when I have stains on the knees of my skirt that I can't explain to the laundress, I'm blaming you."

Another smirk unfurls. "I'd love to hear what she says when you do."

I restrain myself from slugging him. Instead, I offer him a glowering scowl as I crouch. Just as Nephele did, I reach for his ankles and try to keep hold of them while I crawl between his legs. My shoulders get caught in the space, as he hasn't widened his stance, but he otherwise remains stubbornly in place.

"See? Strength, not leverage," I say peering at him. The sky darkened during the Scrimmage and only the moon illuminates the arena. Lukas looks like a god above me.

"Why don't you try to pull the other way? You'll make me lose balance, and then it will work."

This time, I don't withhold rolling my eyes, though in the darkness I doubt he can see it. Instead, I dutifully grab his ankles again and yank him forward. It works, he topples over, but instead of falling away from me like he should given the direction of his feet and the direction I pulled, he falls forward, tripping over my hunched back and causing us both to career into the sand. His elbow connects with my temple as his knee pummels into a hip.

We land on the ground again, me lying on my back staring at the moon as a dull pain travels through my body, him landing on his front above my head. He drags himself up and crawls over to me.

"Are you hurt?" He kneels and leans over me, running his hands from my head to my hips to check for injuries.

"Only my pride." I wince as he pokes my head. "And a few other things."

"I'm sorry for suggesting it. Though you have to admit, it worked, strength or no."

"If you'd fallen backward like science *says* you should have, it would have worked *and* only one of us would have bruises tomorrow morning."

His face falls as he trails his fingers over my cheekbone to the tender spot on my temple. "Then I'm doubly sorry, Thal."

He remains in shadow, but I can just see his tongue wet his lips. I try to suppress the shiver that blooms through me, but

I can't. Only Zeus knows how I've dreamt of this in the quiet nights before. He leans closer.

Then, there's a sound from the underground entrance behind us. He leaps off me, running his fingers through his hair and over his mussed clothes. He holds out a hand to help me up, but I wave him off.

"I'm going to rest my head for a bit longer," I tell him. "Can you make sure no one comes outside?"

"Of course, Thal. Anything for you," he murmurs, looking at me with an odd expression. "I'll see you tomorrow at the Council meeting."

He leaves as I blanket my body with my golden illusion magic, becoming invisible in case Lukas isn't successful. Then, I have only the stars for company until the pitter-patter of rain begins again, each drop landing on my still form like a warning from Zeus.

But of what, I don't know.

Chapter 3

An owl flies overhead. He drops full loaves of bread into the waiting arms of faceless children on the ground below. One child sits astride a horse wearing a crown of serpents. When her fingers touch the bread, a flash of gold transforms it into small seeds. She plants the seeds and eight flowers burst from the cracks, one capped in braided laurel.

With one day before the selection for the Collection, my morning begins by following Father to the Council House in our family's carriage. If not for the rain, we'd walk the thirty minutes to the tall stone building that sits at the edge of town. Instead, we pass dozens of houses and businesses, including a sacrificial pyre to Hera, Goddess of childbirth, women, and family. Even in the rain, a handful of men and women offer tithe. They must be preparing for the next Collection.

The carriage stops over the tiled pathway to the steps of the Council House entrance. My ceremonial dress robes are dark enough to hide the water splatters from the short walk, but my frizzing hair hides nothing, the thick waves no match for both my heavy gold adornments and the surprise shower. Father laughs at my plight while I place an illusion over the chaos of my hair but sobers when we cross the threshold of the door. He immediately becomes the Governor, introspective and quiet.

Decades of practice has honed his version of my mask, one that never needed magic; he appears competent and inviting even when saying or expressing little.

The chamber of the main public room is a circular amphitheater that can hold several thousand people, with balcony seats built into the walls, and semicircle stands that rise from the floor and span the length of the spacious room like concentric ripples in a pond. The size is to accommodate petitioners on Petition Day, the workers on Production Day, and the families of candidates on Collection Day. Elaborate engravings illustrating Standia's history and traditions cover the balustrades. Sunlight filters through narrow windows decked with linen curtains, casting soft patterns on the worn mosaic floor depicting constellations and geometric designs. At the heart of the sanctum is a circular dais where the Council members sit, decorated with a mosaic tapestry of Athena's life.

The Council scheduled as many meetings today as they could, taking advantage of having all the Council members already gathered in place. The thirty Council members mill about the chamber until my father takes his place at the center chair on the platform at the bottom of the arena. He slips into his chair and interlocks his hands on top of the long wooden table in front of their chairs.

Today is a normal Council session. Only the bored would attend the budget reconciliation session on the schedule this afternoon, meaning the cavernous chamber is empty but for the thirty Council members, various heirs who sometimes attend, and government staff.

I sit behind and to the right of Father, with Lukas doing the same behind Argon. Usually, he makes faces when the presenters aren't looking, but today his gaze stays firmly focused on the long wooden table in front of us. Bruises paint the golden skin under his eyes and his normally pink lips are white from the pressure of pursing them together.

"Do you agree, Thalia?" Father's voice is authoritative and loud enough to echo around the vacant room. Lightning streaks overhead from the wide skylight.

I blink and peek at Lukas, but he doesn't give me any hints as to what was being discussed. I pretend to stare pensively at the table, to stall for time. The first time Father asked my opinion in a Council meeting, I was twelve and finally old enough to attend as an heir. It was Petition Day and the family of a worker who died requested an extra allotment since they could no longer produce their own supplemental income. After running through every feasible option I could think of, I presented my suggestion and Father took it. Even though it's been ten years, every time he asks my opinion, I feel that little bolt of nervous excitement like I did that first time, that my opinion is wanted and helpful.

But something is in the air today, and that bolt doesn't come, only the damp from the rain sticking to my skin and the worry for my friend.

"That position certainly has merit, Governor," I finally say.

Lukas snorts lightly, the stress releasing at the corner of his mouth.

"Indeed," Father says, as if I said something enlightening. "With that recommendation, I agree with the line request. All, we will break for the day and reconvene—"

"Wait," a heaving voice calls out from the rear of the chamber. A reedy looking man scurries towards the Council table, holding a slack rope that trails out the door. Once he stands in front of Father's place at the table, he yanks the rope taut and pulls. After a few more, the rope rises and a smirking man breaches the back door, the rope tied around his stomach. Age bends his back and the traditional Retribution Day cuffs circle his wrists and ankles. He walks towards us as though he isn't bent double and being dragged by his waist.

"This is not Retribution Day," a senior staff member says, frowning. "Is there anything on the schedule?"

The junior assistant next to her runs ink-stained fingers over several pages of the schedule book until he pauses and shakes his head.

"I do not have an appointment, Governor and Council," the reedy man says. "I was traveling from Redweld for the Collection tomorrow and came across this man, who the locals caught tricking travelers and pushing them off the cliff."

Redweld is an hour inland from us and located deeper in the mountain range that surrounds us. As a smaller community, it has no Councilor of its own, but Father and Argon represent it.

Father's lips thin. "Why did you bring him this day rather than wait until Retribution Day next month?"

The reedy man bows and directs his answer to the floor. "The townspeople could not hold him until you could hear his case, and I was already on my way."

Argon crosses his arms. "And?"

"And," he says hesitantly, "I had hoped the Council would compensate me for my time."

Argon leans back to speak to Lukas just as Father turns to me. I force myself to focus on my duty rather than Lukas' sadness.

"Should we hear his case, Thal?" Father asks.

"There's no downside," I whisper back. "If the elder is innocent, he won't wait in custody until Retribution Day. If he isn't, he will have surety in what happens to him now."

"And giving the other a prize for bringing him?"

The reedy man wears threadbare clothes and appears tired. An opportunist he may be, he still may have done some good in helping Redweld with their alleged criminal problem. Refusing to compensate him might keep him from aiding in the future, and the risk that he would fabricate a situation is worth the benefit, given Redweld is under our direct jurisdiction. I tell Father as much.

"We will hear your case," Father announces. Pride colors my vision, as it does every time I prove myself. The staff quickly fill the clock basins, creating various timers. They fill every basin, hinting that this will be a trial for death.

The reedy man presents various secondhand accounts and crumpled letters that a staff member reads aloud. After he finishes, Father stands.

"We have heard blood verified statements of your crimes. But now, with the time allotted, I would hear any defense you may give."

The man leans his head back to stare at us, his bedraggled appearance not making him less intimidating, but more.

"I would admit it," he says.

"Who are you?" a woman named Magda asks. Her tag shows she rules over the small province of Bae. She's newly appointed and here for her first meeting.

"The son of royalty and more, which is better than any of you at this table, the Governor included."

The table bristles as one, all but Father, though a muscle twitches in his jaw.

"Have you no shame?" one of the inner Island Councilors asks.

The criminal's relaxed posture is at odds with the severity of the discussion. "I live my life without regrets. Those who passed by me, made their choice."

Lukas growls. "They washed your feet as an elder, recognizing your status with the time-honored tradition of our people. You took advantage of their respect by... by killing them." Argon places a steadying hand on his shoulder, but Lukas knocks it off.

The criminal shrugs, though it looks more like a flinch. The gloating expression on his face proves it isn't. "That they gave me such respect without merit is no fault of mine."

Disgust fills me and a look around the room confirms I'm not alone in my thoughts. We are given a responsibility by birth, our positions provide us respect, but we must prove we're worthy of it by deed.

Lukas slams his hands on the armrests of his wooden chair. He moves to stand but Argon cuts his hand across his throat, stopping Lukas mid rise.

"We will now deliberate," Father announces. Several staff members escort the two men from the room.

Father doesn't ask my opinion. He sits with his fingers interlocked and lips pursed.

"Father—" I begin, but he shakes his head.

"Toss him from the same cliff he used to murder his victims," Lukas rasps.

The room stills.

"A brilliant idea," Argon says smiling. The other Councilors echo him. Still Father stares at the space where the criminal stood.

"Father—" I start again. Had he asked me, I would have suggested the customary punishment of ostracism and exile, coupled with marking his skin with a criminal's tattoo, so all who meet him will know what he is and stay wary.

"That is acceptable," Father says.

The assistant scurries from the room to bring back in the men. Only then does Father look back at me.

"Deciding his fate is a duty for which you are not ready."

My stone face prevents me from scowling, but Father knows me well enough to know I would. I almost consider using an illusion to glower in secret. "He exerts his will on others, and we exert it on him. Why is *my* will not valid here?"

Father's expression softens. "I would save you from making these hard decisions."

"I should be given the choice," I whisper back. "If I am to prove myself, I cannot be coddled."

Lykos, a Councilor from Tros and the uncle of the candidate who fought the sow, snorts. I don't need Athena's spirit within me to know he's alluding to the Collection, but Father doesn't have the chance to respond as the men return. There's nothing

I could say to ease the Councilor's worries anyway, even if I wanted to. I will remain coddled as Athena and Father's heir, and no one can choose me for the Collection.

But the reaction must have affected Father, as he doesn't pronounce judgment, instead gesturing for Argon to do so. Glee fills Argon's expression when he sentences the criminal, but the man marked for death doesn't cower. Instead, he smirks.

"Life cares not for how you live, only that you do," he says, almost idly. "I've lived mine freely, by my own choices, the consequences be damned. Any punishment you give me cannot take that away from me."

"Your choices had you deciding your life had more value than theirs," Lukas says seething. "Who are you to choose yourself over others?"

It feels like lightning under my skin, a prickling that scurries from my wrists to my neck. I blink away the unwelcome similarities in my situation, ones the room must recognize as gazes focus on me. Even Lukas seems to realize what he's implied and shifts in his seat.

Father clears his throat. "In this case, the consequences will kill you, meaning your advice is less valuable than you think." A few Council members titter and the budding tension eases.

The session ends and the staff take both men to another room, one for payment, one for the gallows.

I leave before Father can attempt to give me more excuses, hoping to speak with Lukas. But he slips out a back hallway before I can catch him. I chase him through the antechamber, to the tiled square outside. He disappears around the bend in the road, just as a lightning strikes one of the surrounding trees.

The resounding crack feels as if it hit me directly, the singe sharp enough to burn. Zeus must have something specific in mind, but I hesitate to guess what. A second crack hits the portico of the Council House. I swallow violently, echoing the surrounding thunder.

Whatever he wants me to understand, I need to discover it fast.

Chapter 4

When night falls, I can't sleep. I leave my house before I can second guess it, my rain cloak held over my head like a blanket. It isn't sneaking out; a grown woman can't sneak out of her own home. But I haven't left my bed in the night since before my majority, when Lukas convinced me to leap in the ocean in my nightclothes as a dare.

The flat stone pathway reflects the light of the moon peeking behind the rain clouds as I walk to Lukas' house. The worst of the storm is over, but not in my heart. As my best friend, Lukas can quiet the thunder within, that churning feeling of guilt and unease I can't explain.

The Second Councilor's home is behind ours, but the distance between them is as long as a tree is tall. The walk is solitary, though there are at least four guards hidden in the brush bisecting the path. I've learned to ignore them, and their presence is almost seamless in the surroundings.

Quiet voices reach me before I arrive at Lukas' window. I duck into the underbrush and place my illusion, shuffling until I'm no longer next to a guard. Apparently, adulthood doesn't remove the instinct to avoid getting caught.

Crouching uncomfortably, I peer through the openings in the brambles. Two people take cover at the base of a tree. They hold each other, closer than anyone has ever held me. My status as heir means no potential scandals, so I'd never sought it out. Lukas would be my only choice, but his teasing jokes were never serious.

And they *were* only jokes, as he's never attempted to embrace me as he does Nephele now.

"You'll be fine, Neph, I promise." Lukas' voice sounds strained.

"You can't promise that."

He presses her closer. "I'll make it happen. I've the ear of the Council, you know that. I just—I—I can't lose you. I love you."

Something pierces the space between my ribs. I can't tell if it is rejection—the ultimate proof that Lukas didn't want me, that I wasn't his choice—or sympathy for my friend, whose choice may be taken from him. His reaction during lunch yesterday, his pained expressions, the bleakness that fell over him when we discussed who might be Collected, his anger at the Council meeting—yet again I'm reminded that the Collection takes more than just one woman.

"We'll leave," Lukas continues. "Tomorrow before sunrise. We'll quit the Island. We can start over at one of the outlying settlements on another Island."

Nephele snorts, a derisive echo of the one I made at Lyra not two days earlier. But hers sounds soft and feminine, pained. "What about Thalia, Lukas? Your *betrothed*."

"She'll come with us." His immediate response lessens the throbbing still attacking my chest.

Lukas tightens his arms around Nephele's lithe frame. She isn't wearing a nightdress and cloak like I am but a tight robe that's painted on her form from the damp. She's spent eleven years preparing for the Collection, honing her body instead of her mind, and she looks beautiful in his arms.

"What a happy family we'll make. You, your wife, and your... mistress?"

"No." Lukas snarls the word, frightening a bird into abandoning the tree.

My eyes close to trap the moisture threatening to break free. The scene they make must rivet the guards. Their very own dramatic theater. If I showed myself, I could become the villain in the second act.

"Thalia," Lukas says, sounding frustrated. "She—we wouldn't need to marry if we left."

The words "painful truth" now have meaning. I can't begrudge his happiness, neither of us chose each other. But Lukas is sunshine and charm, I might have chosen him if allowed. My secret ideas of a happy future—quiet nights reading together, grumbling about our political positions, laughing in bed, Lukas holding me like he's holding Nephele—drown in the ocean.

"*She* should be taken for the Collection. It would solve every problem we have."

He remains quiet, hopefully in as much shock as I am, and not because he's considering it. My heart nearly stops beating as I await his reaction. A large part of me wants to leap through these bushes and shake Nephele until her teeth rattle, to berate her for such small thinking. But another part, one stung by the raindrops landing on my skin, wants to tell them things will be better, somehow.

"Never suggest that again," Lukas finally says, voice hard. "I will not sacrifice one of you for the other. Thalia is my best friend, my future. Don't resent what we were born for."

A few tears break free without my consent. I wipe them away before they might hear any sniveling.

"You're right. I didn't mean it," she says. "I'm just scared, Lukas."

They hold each other tight and then only sounds coming from them are sighs and soft exclamations. I slink away hidden by the illusion, back to my solitary home.

The sun reaches through my window as morning comes. I've still not yet slept, too preoccupied by the recent revelations. I spent the hours after leaving Lukas and Nephele in the library, reading over what we know of the Collection, of King Minos, and of the Beast.

My tutor, Plades, joins me in the library, shaking the rain from his overcoat. He limps towards the back corner, his worn robes swishing against his ankles and catching on his cane. I don't move from my table, strewn with books and directly under one of our oldest woven tapestries, a piece made by the first child of Athena born on the Island, about her sacrifice so that our family and Island might live. Plades blinks his pale eyes at the mess and, I'm sure, the crazed look on my face. But ever the professional, he whips out his record book and opens it to a page near the back.

"Now, we left off at our last session discussing the political actions that led to the olive famine of 236."

"Tell me about the Collection," I ask instead.

Plades blinks, unused to any demands from me. He glances at the spines of the books on the table. "I imagine you know everything about them. As I was saying—"

"What about something not in the books?"

Plades rests a hand on his chest, like a fainting maiden from a statue in Mother's garden, whether because of my uncharacteristic outburst or the suggestion that there is knowledge not within the scores of books in my library. "There is nothing not in books," he says, wide-eyed.

Something pushes the words from me, the requests I never make, the disruption I never create. "Plades, please. There are only fi—four eligible tomorrow. I would simply like to understand how it began."

"You know how it began. The King, in his excellence, offered a chance of glory to each Island, to rid the world of the Beast." Plades sounds like he's reciting a propaganda advertisement from the King, not speaking truth. Except... none of *that* is in any book.

"But why?" I tap my fingers on a book without a name, the words within it so faint I had to squint over candlelight to read them. "Ancient records believe the Beast turned the tides of the war, but the Collection didn't begin until sixteen years later."

I drag the next book to the top of the pile, another nameless tome that looks like it might disintegrate between my fingers. "And it was sons *and* daughters at first, a mix of them from each Island, not only the women." Now, only those children who identify as female are eligible. "Why the change? And why wait sixteen years to start? And, if the Beast must be destroyed, why does the King not simply destroy it himself rather than demanding we do it and fail?"

Plades opens his mouth and pauses. He turns a shrewd eye on me. "Will you refuse the lesson until I indulge you?"

"It isn't indulgence, but necessary information," I say firmly.

He sighs and drags a book towards him. After flipping through several pages, he stops and spins it back towards me. "What do you see?"

It's an illustration of a man with a crown kneeling before a golden being. The golden being holds a three-pronged trident in a muscular arm. Long blue hair trails down his back, touching the waist of his chiton. Like most depictions of Gods, he is shirtless. But unlike others, his skirted robes aren't made of silk or linen, but are the leathery skin of a bull, with the head and horns resting against his hip.

The man kneeling before him has shorn hair covered by a spiky crown. His chiton is dark, contrasting with the pale shimmer of his skin, shining like starlight. On his bare chest is the modern symbol of Crete- a winding circular labyrinth with one entrance and no exit.

"This is King Minos' devotion to Poseidon," I say. "How does this relate to the Collection?"

Plades closes the book. "Was that devotion given or bought?"

I blink. *Given*, I assumed. The Cretans are closest to the Gods, both in political and familial relationships. Most can trace their lineage back to some form of God, else they wouldn't be so long-lived, but they have none of the Gods' powers. Only the Governors' families on the Islands can boast those skills.

Plades doesn't wait for my answer. "We know the Gods provide for us based on our prayers, like your mother for little Cleon. But what if someone *asked* the Gods for something they weren't already intending on providing? What if someone desired a specific blessing?" He leans forward and lowers his voice. "The Gods aren't blessing us altruistically. It is a bargain, Miss Thalia. We give them offerings, and, in exchange, they bless us. If someone, a king perhaps, desired a very specific form of blessing, the key to winning a war, would a prayer alone be enough?"

"So, you're saying King Minos gave Poseidon something in exchange for him providing the Beast to win the Island War?"

Plades splays his hands upward towards the heavens. "Gave something or agreed to do something. The Collection, perhaps."

I slump in my chair and press the heels of my palms against my eyes. "Meaning the Collection is blessed." And meaning the Collection must continue and Nephele may be taken. The look on Lukas' face at the thought of who the Council might select, the memory on Lyra's face when she mentioned Serai—they play behind my closed eyelids like bad theater.

Plades clears his throat, and my gaze refocuses on him. He licks his lips and darts his eyes around the room. "Blessings, *bargains*, are individual. Your father could pray and give sacrifices to Hera his entire life and never would a child quicken in your mother. Only her request, *her* bargain, would do it. Perhaps the King's bargain includes terms that force others to do something, but that is... rare in any book or history I've read. King Minos would have been asked to fulfill the bargain himself."

"So, turning over the destruction of the Beast might be a deal breaker?"

"Assuming the terms of the bargain, yes. And assuming you have proof to present to Poseidon. Only if his eye turned to Crete would he have noticed the breach himself," he says ruefully. "Assuming one wished to, the easiest way to stop Minos is for whomever desires to stop it to fulfill the terms themselves and bring it to Poseidon's attention. Although..."

"What?"

He purses his lips. "This is all hypothetical, of course. If Minos *is* or has breached the bargain, he'd be an oath breaker, and the Erinyes would have come for him. That they haven't is a tick mark in his favor."

The Erinyes, the infernal Goddesses that live beneath Hades' domain, take vengeance on oath breakers and criminals. Something like lighting trickles up my skin again. But maybe Minos' deceit is hidden from Poseidon *and* the Erinyes. Someone simply needs to discover the breach and bring attention to it.

I cancel the session. Plades grumbles but an invitation to raid the library after I leave soothes his raised hackles.

I follow the phantom footsteps of my father to the Council House, where the Councilors will decide the fate of at least one woman. Yesterday's rain still threatens the village, an oppressive energy that drags me through the thirty-minute walk.

Something has rooted in my soul, growing not like a tree, but like a slowly building tidal wave, one that destroys villages when it crashes to the sand. Here, there is no chance it will disperse before ravaging the beach. At least the beach in this simile is only my life and not my people, not Lukas' future.

It's early enough that the few fanatics who wait in the antechamber and the opportunists who bet on the choice haven't yet arrived. The meeting room is modestly sized, with a low ceiling supported by austere columns. In a recessed alcove, a wooden shelf houses a modest collection of scrolls, as this room is normally for internal Council business only and not open to the public. With so few women this year, the usual pomp isn't needed. Only the eligible women, their immediate family, and the Councilors attend the selection. The Council sits crowded along a long table at the far end of the room, weathered by years of use. A small statuette of Athena stands behind them as a silent guardian, watching over the proceedings with a stoic gaze. Mismatched wooden chairs rest haphazardly around the open space, each filled with one of the attendees.

Nephele sits closest to the door, one hand clutching her older sister's leg, the other her father's hand. He remarried after his first wife, Nephele's mother, died birthing her. But any children he had with his new wife don't count for Nephele's line. She will always be the youngest. Lukas will always have to fear for her safety, assuming she makes it through three more Collections unchosen. Her frame trembles and shiny tear tracks run down her face.

I duck behind their chairs, unnoticed as the attention remains on the Councilors. I've arrived in the middle of the presentation of the eligible, catching the beginning of Nephele's. The preliminary votes are tallied along the wall and Councilors from other villages believe Nephele is the best choice.

"She's trained the longest and has the best likelihood of handling the Beast and bringing pride to the Island," a balding man from Neith says, the blue emblem of Standia covering his entire chest and making him look like an odd bullseye. He's been a Councilor my entire life and his word carries weight. That one of the few eligible is also from Neith might also explain his position.

"She also has the least to lose," says Magda.

My father clears his throat, a frown marring his face. "We do not consider the Collection in such a negative light, Councilor Magda." The words "*not publicly*" hover about the room.

Magda doesn't notice the slight twitch in his eyes that warns her from continuing. "She has only her sister and father to leave behind. Surely that should be a marker in her favor."

"Losses are not considered, Magda. I will not repeat it." He gazes warmly at Nephele, though I doubt she even notices. "Blood does not make a family. I know you love your siblings as much as I love my daughter."

That's as good a cue as I'll get. I allow myself one deep breath, as a small part of me considers abandoning my poorly devised plan. But then thunder sounds outside the walls and, like a bolt to the chest, my resolve hardens. I've made my decision, rolling it over my tongue like a sour candy, something bitter but still palatable. It's time to swallow.

I stand and maneuver around the chairs to the front.

"I would like to present," I announce, my mask in place.

The Councilors look confused, some haven't heard my voice unless it's a whisper in Father's ear: the staid heir who listens and learns but never outwardly takes part.

Only Father realizes why I'm there. His face—the one I inherited—pales.

"Thal, don't."

The words are quiet, whispered, but I can hear it like he's shouting. My steps falter at the nickname, but I don't stop.

"I wish to be Collected."

Chapter 5

They recess the presentation to consider my announcement, but it's perfunctory. That I volunteered means they must accept me. Even if I withdrew my consideration, I've confirmed for the entire room, full of the families of the eligible and Councilors, that I should be included in their ranks. I'd never avoid another Collection until I aged out.

As the Councilors whisper amongst themselves, Father stares at me. He doesn't cry; he doesn't yell. His attention doesn't falter on the conversation he's having, but his eyes stay on me. I offer him what I hope is a composed smile while we wait.

Sooner than I expect, Nephele leaves the sanctuary of her family's protection and zips towards me. She's no longer crying, but I can't place the expression. Not mad, not happy. Puzzled, perhaps.

"Why would you do this?" Her voice is shrill. The Councilors' low murmuring dies as they all turn to us. When they resume their conversation, she repeats her question in a whisper, "Why would you do this?"

I want to tell her about what I know, about Lukas and her, about Lyra and Serai. That it's unfair that I wasn't on the list. That the King may have distorted Poseidon's blessing to win the Island War. That there must be a way to stop this from happening to another woman, because every question has an answer. That I'm the best chance, out of all the eligible, to discover the bargain and present it to Poseidon. That this is a choice I should have been given and need to make.

I won't kid myself in thinking I can defeat the Beast, or even that I'll succeed in my quest. But I want the chance to try.

"It's the right thing to do," I finally say. "It solves many problems."

She doesn't roll her eyes, but I would in her place. I wonder if she's remembering what she said, if she thinks she brought this into the universe somehow.

"What about Lukas?" she asks suspiciously.

The placid smile slides off my lips. "He'll have you."

"He wouldn't choose between us. He's your future," she says, repeating what I shouldn't have already heard the night before.

Father calls our attention back to the front before I must answer her.

"As is our tradition, we accept Thalia—" He cuts off to clear his throat, not with frustration but to swallow tears. "We graciously accept Thalia's offering. She will bring great pride to the Island, no matter the outcome of her... trip."

With that pronouncement, I slip out the door before he, or anyone else, can approach me. My arms shake with the realization of what I've done, at what can't be undone.

I burst from the building, taking a side exit I hoped would lead to an empty tree line. The decision was made early, so the oglers still haven't arrived. My skin feels as though fire itches it, as Zeus' lightning storms made their way inside me, and I rub my arms frantically even as my face pales with nausea. If I misinterpreted Zeus' dreams and offered myself up as a sacrifice accidentally... I can only hope Hades will be kind to me in the Underworld for trying.

Strong hands catch me before I can leave the clearing. I elbow the person holding me and wiggle wildly, but they don't budge. The arms grasping me shuffle my body until we're face to face.

"Thalia, what are you doing here?" a familiar voice asks.

My neck snaps upward. Lukas stares at me, now holding me as tight as he did Nephele last night. After a moment, he releases me, instead clutching my shoulders.

"Thalia, focus. What are you doing here?" His eyes aren't the color of polished mahogany but of old leaves, grim and full of death. "Did—did they choose Nephele?"

I force my face into a semblance of a grin. "No, she's safe."

He hugs me tight, but his normal brightness is still missing. He knows, as I do intimately, someone must be Collected.

"Neph mentioned the names of the other eligible women. I didn't think we knew any of them?" It's a question, a request to explain my presence and the reddening of my eyes.

My mouth opens but no words come, only a sharp breath bursts out. Lukas tightens his grip.

"Come on, no illusion now. Do we know the Collected?"

But he's wrong, no illusion covers my face. I'm immobilized by what I've done, that I'll have to explain it to him, to Father, to Mother and Cleon. That my plan goes no farther than 'try to stop it' while hoping that the mind Athena gave me will give me a chance no one else had. I can't force myself to do anything but nod.

"Who?" He shakes me hard. "Thal, who? Is there some geas on your throat keeping you from telling me?"

As if that was the key to break the spell on my silent tongue, I speak, whispering into the air. "I volunteered."

Lukas' mouth drops open. A beat of silence goes by before he smirks shakily. "Bad joke. I know your sense of humor is untested in the real world, but it's too soon for something like this. Start by speaking in culture class and *then* let me help you with your comedy act."

My hands pat against his chest, and I try to commit his face to memory. "I'm not joking, Lukas. I volunteered. I'll be leaving tonight."

The door behind us creaks open and Nephele's face appears from within.

I inhale his scent—sea air and wood—before releasing him. "Be happy, Lukas."

Nephele slinks towards us and I use the distraction to place an illusion and slip into the trees, far away from Lukas' shocked stare.

I don't run home, where I'd be expected, where I'll have to explain myself to my parents. My mother, the woman, will understand, and my father, the man, will be disappointed, but they'll hide their fears to support me. But my parents in their official capacities, as Governor and Lady, may never understand what I may accidentally sacrifice. Even I don't understand it, or what it might mean for the history of my family and our people. If I don't return... Each potential consequence of my actions hits the base of my stomach like rocks.

But I can't regret my choice. Not when there is no turning back.

I run to one of the tall mountains surrounding our village while forcing away the shaking tears. I remove the illusion to give the patrol guards notice that I'm present, and then I climb a mountain peak alone, leaving them at the base. The rain is gone, the skies above completely clear now. It's like a sign, the confirmation that I've made the right decision.

It's never been harder to lie to myself than right now.

I'm winded by the time I arrive at the peak, chest bursting and limbs shaking. I can only see the little mountain through the curls of my hair as I lean heavily on my knees to catch my breath.

The summit I choose isn't one I've visited before. Lukas and I used to play on some of the other clifftops, but I want to avoid the memories they'll invoke. This peak is nothing special, not the largest or the smallest, with no beautiful view of the ocean or our inlet harbor. The terrain is sandy, with few trees and bushes dotting the rock face and no soft greenery upon which to rest.

With no comforts, I'll be alone for as long as I desire. At least until Lukas comes looking for me.

I stand near the edge to better breathe but the view knocks the air out of me again. It looks out towards the whole of Standia. With the sun reaching its zenith, I can make out cities that are hours away. If I squint, I can almost see the ocean on the far side, with Crete behind it.

I spend precious seconds staring at the Island, attempting to memorize the terrain. The ship that will carry me to Crete will arrive at sunset. We're the closest Island to Crete, and the last woman taken. The early decision means the Collected woman—me—has almost an entire day to prepare to leave. I can stare at my Island as long as I want.

Sooner than I expect, footsteps trudge up the path, interrupting my solace. But the body appearing from the slope isn't Lukas, it's Father.

"You hiding is not how I would choose for you to spend your last day here," he says, voice cracking.

"I'm not hiding," I say, not taking my eyes off the land before me. As soon as I do, and I see his face, I'll start crying too. "I've never visited this cliff before. I'm glad I found it."

"You never were much for the outdoors, not unless Lukas could tempt you to explore." He stands beside me and spreads his hands out in front of him. "But I've seen every rock, every blade of grass, every being living and dead on this Island since I took up my father's mantle. This was my favorite place to be when I was younger. Now, because it shows me my responsibility, the people I'm entrusted to govern. But then, I cared not for the view but for the secrecy of this place."

If this summit holds a secret besides the view, it refuses to tell me. I open my mouth to respond but Father's attention is elsewhere.

"In fact," he says, leaving my side to crouch near the base of a scraggly tree. He digs his fingers through the sandy earth until he's created a hole a foot deep. With hands dirtier than I've ever seen them, he pulls out a dusty and faded travel bag. He beckons me closer and gestures to it. "Open it."

Groaning, I kneel beside him to open the small bag, As I undo the laces, several roaches skitter through the tied opening. My inhaled breath is my only reaction. With what I might face, I can't let something as benign as bugs bother me. Father huffs, no doubt remembering my silly phobia. I dump it upside down and out falls a pair of shoes and a thin knife. The knife looks like a miniature version of the ceremonial blade he wears to Council meetings.

Father ignores it to reach for the shoes, running his fingers over the frayed leather. "No one knew to look for me here. It was my place to hide. When my father demanded I first sit in on one of his Council meetings, I hid here instead. In a fit, I also hid my shoes and blade, thinking that if I didn't have them, no one could force me to be the Governor, that they would choose one of my younger brothers instead."

"What happened?" Given my father *was* the Governor, I know the ending of the story, but not the middle.

"Your grandfather threatened my guard until he gave up my location and he dragged me to the meeting by my ears, barefoot and weaponless. He never considered that one of my siblings might have been better suited for it." He closes his eyes tightly. "I love what I do, and I love serving my people. But not then. I resented my lacking choice." His eyes open and he pins me with them. "Is that why you volunteered? There are other options. I can renounce you as heir and make you regent-in-waiting until Cleon is old enough. You have a choice."

"That wasn't why. I want to help the Island," I say, unwilling to describe the many steps that brought me here, particularly when one reason was because I already *had* choices not offered to others. "I believe this is my purpose, that Zeus led me on this path. To make sure no other woman has to experience it."

"You intend to stop the Collection, then?"

I nod. There is no other path for me now.

His deep blue eyes, the color of an ocean storm, assess me. No expression runs over his face, his true mask even better than my magicked one. He sounds mild when he asks, "Have you determined how?"

"Only partially," I admit. "King Minos did something to win the Island Wars, we know this. Plades told me it could have been blessed through a bargain."

"Plades would know," Father murmurs.

"The Beast turned the tides, and the Collection was born, meaning there is something that must be done about the Beast or related to him. If Minos... distorted the blessing by not completing his part of the bargain but passing it on to the Collected instead, perhaps I can stop it, break the bargain perhaps."

"What will you do if there is no bargain, simply a violent game demanded by a tyrannical sovereign?"

I can barely restrain the flinch threatening to make an appearance. "Then I'll try to make Standia proud in the Labyrinth."

"You have done so every day since your birth," he says, cupping my shoulder. "Do you believe you have the skills to break this bargain?"

"You've been training me to govern, to negotiate, to learn what I can and make conclusions based on the facts I have and extrapolate what I don't. You've taught me to listen and never assume a piece of information is irrelevant."

"You will need more than an inquisitive spirit," he says. "Remember what I said about the serpent. We recognize the duality of all things. Knowledge is not enough. Steel will be necessary."

I shrug. Brawn will never serve me. Steel, assuming he means being prepared to make hard choices like he believes me unable to do, is in my blood. If only he'd have let me prove it before. If only the first *true* choice I had wasn't one that took me away from all I loved.

He smiles faintly, discomfort crinkling the corners of his eyes. "I do not tell you this as an aphorism, but because of what you might face in Crete. There is a geas on the populace to keep the circumstances of the Collection and the Beast a secret. *And* King Minos has many supporters. Choices will need to be made."

"How do you know there's a geas?"

"I do not willingly send our Standian children to a fate unknown. I attempted to glean information through an agent's concealed trip to Crete but the geas could not be overcome."

My own eyes widen. That was a diplomatic way of saying Father sent spies into Crete.

He purses his lips, the smile long gone. "Do you intend to kill the Beast?"

"No." The word leaves my throat before I realize the truth of the statement.

To his credit, he doesn't laugh or scoff at my decision. I have no weapons training, tripped twice on my walk uphill, and have never left my Island. He could have, *should* have, railed at how unprepared I am physically. Gaining information to halt the Collection is irrelevant if the Beast murders me.

"For what it's worth, I too believe there is a bargain. If the Collection came from it, then…" he trails off, staring at the interior of Standia. "Everything that begins must end."

Chapter 6

F ather doesn't need to convince me to return home for lunch with Mother and Cleon. Not only must I say my goodbyes, there's only one other person I need to see before I leave, and I expect him to storm through our house before sunset.

Father shoves the knife in my hands, secreting the shoes somewhere else in our vast home, leaving me alone in the library to await lunch. His blade and the clothes on my back will be the only things I carry with me. Once we arrive in Crete, King Minos provides anything else we need.

Until he doesn't.

I can hear my parents speaking softly through the walls, but I don't strain to hear the words or press my ear to the walls this time. I can guess what they're saying. Instead, I move the books I tore through during the dawn hours from their teetering piles back to their homes. A conspicuous hole in the mathematics section tells me Plades took advantage of my offer.

After twenty minutes, the door opens and I turn, wiping my clammy hands on my skirts, mentally preparing myself to diffuse Lukas' sadness that will have mutated into anger.

He slinks through the door, which he closes behind him with a soft snick. His eyes are sunken and his hair wild, as if he's been running his fingers through it. When he sees me, his expression turns from grim to enraged.

"What were you thinking?" he spits. He doesn't let me answer, instead spinning back towards the door and leaning against it.

His head bangs against the wood. "Of all the foolish ideas. How in Zeus's name could you even imagine this was a good—"

I try not to smile at how predictable my best friend is. "Is it not possible Zeus blessed this path? Are you truly going to malign something the Gods agree with?"

His turns, his jaw falling open. "You would blame Zeus for your poor decision-making skills?"

I tease him, hoping to distract him from his hidden sadness. "I *would* blame you, but I haven't figured out how." The words die in my throat. I *could* blame him, and I know why. I quickly change tacks. "Just calm down. Please don't let our last conversation be of you whining."

"My betrothed has abandoned me to get herself murdered. I'm entitled to some whining," he says, scowling.

"Of course, let's make it about you again." I roll my eyes dramatically, happy the tempest of his anger and my sadness have stilled. "I'm reminded of when I caught the shock, and you couldn't stop wringing your hands over my sick bed. Hades could have taken me, and you would have been more worried over losing your escort to the solstice celebration."

He stalks across the room, his finger pointing at my face and his eyes narrowed. "Hades *was* going to take you and if not for my constant vigil, he'd have spirited you to the Underworld before anyone knew to call the healer. That you would bring it up to *mock* m—" He cuts himself off, heaving above me, his breath causing a few of my wavy locks to blow into my face.

"Go on," I say, "I'd love to hear you blame *me* for getting sick."

Before I can blink, he wraps his arms around me, squeezing my chest into his. His hands settle at the small of my back.

"Are you teasing me?" he croons, his eyes intent. One hand leaves my back to brush the wayward strand back behind my ear.

"I meant what I said." My voice doesn't tremble, but it's a near thing. I allow my hands to travel up his chest to touch his shoulders. "I'd certainly prefer our last conversation be us as we were, not fighting or troubled."

"Is *this* how we were?" His arms tighten around me.

It isn't how we were, but it is a look at what we could have been; it's what I thought I saw in his eyes after the Scrimmage, before he remembered Nephele. "We've always been friends."

"Friends and engaged," he reminds me, squeezing gently. I can see why Nephele enjoys being in his arms. Even though I'm not as lithe as she is, Lukas almost makes me feel delicate. "You were to be mine. And now..."

I sigh. "I was never yours, Lukas. Just as you were never mine."

"You could have been," he says as pain crinkles the lines by his lips usually made by laughing. And this his face washes of expression, as though he's puzzling something out.

Birds take flight in my stomach as he leans down and kisses me. On instinct, I adjust my head and allow us to slot together, our lips dragging against each other lightly, softly. The touch is tentative, on mine because of my inexperience, on his perhaps because he's thinking of Nephele.

That possibility has me stiffen and draw in a heavy breath. When my lips open to draw back, his tongue dips into my mouth.

I should protest and withdraw from his hold, but to the Underworld with Nephele. She will have him for life, while I may give mine for his happiness. Although the thought is uncharitable and untrue, I let myself have this, at least for a moment. *Who knows when I'll ever feel cherished like this again?* I slide my arms around his neck and melt into him.

In our years of friendship, Lukas has never pursued me like he does others. We kissed once, one of those silly games children played. But by the time I found men sexually attractive, my reputation as 'untouchable and dull' was cemented. Lukas was the only man who wouldn't have risked a scandal had I taken him, but he never showed a genuine interest. But the low rumble from his chest as I press closer tells me I might not be as good at reading him as I thought.

I tug on his hair, and he grunts in response, pressing his hips into mine, proving just how interested he is now. My stomach flips at the realization.

"Thalia," he groans, backing me up to one of the many wooden tables scattered around the library. We part only long enough to hoist myself onto the table where Lukas follows, moving into the open vee of my legs.

Minutes pass, hours, days surely. His interest continues pressing against me, my head swimming at how good he feels. His hands roam over my back. With Lukas, that familiar feeling rushes through me much quicker than when I'm alone in my bed, my entire body warm and soft.

A thought forces its way through the haze of Lukas and his arms. *Days can't have passed*, my mind finally remembers. *I have only this day.* I pull away, leaning on my arms behind me, chest heaving. Lukas isn't deterred as he moves to kissing beneath my ear and nuzzling my neck.

"You can't go," he says between light nips to the space above my collarbone.

The question is rhetorical since I've volunteered; there is no "can't." But I answer him anyway. "I must, Lukas, you have to understand that." My voice is breathy, like I've scaled a mountain we used to play on.

That stops him, his head dropping onto my shoulder. His arms slide behind me to cover my hands resting on the table. "If we'd have done this earlier, would you still be leaving?"

I huff out a laugh, more at the continued feeling of his lips on my skin when he speaks than at the question. I'd like to say 'yes,' but I shouldn't lie to myself. "You think highly of yourself, don't you?"

His head lifts and his brows raise. "I've had no complaints."

"Not everyone can be as discerning as I am," I say imperiously, though the waver in my voice ruins the effect.

He releases me slowly and moves to my side, sitting close enough that our bodies still touch. "Why did you volunteer? You've trained your whole life to be Governor, not die for a King who will use you as a toy."

"I have a plan. Or something of a plan," I say, leaning my head against his shoulder. "You're right that this is what I was raised for. I can do that by stopping the Collection. Somehow."

His hands tear through his hair in agitation as he stands and faces the mica window. "*Was* there something in that storm yesterday? Did Zeus whisper through it and let his voice breathe through Standia? Everyone is behaving erratically."

"Everyone?"

"Yes! You, my father, Neph—" He cuts himself off, blinking and avoiding my gaze. He's quiet when he continues, focusing his words to the floor. "Have you even considered what your loss will do? To the Island, your people? To your parents and Cleon? To—to me?"

I cross the room and grab his forearms, running my fingers down to squeeze his hands. The action doesn't differ from something I've done hundreds of times, but the knowledge of what those hands feel like on my body has me shivering. Our friendship is forever altered; it's probably an exceptionally good thing I might never see him again.

"I did this for the Island," I tell him. "For you."

"How can you say that? I'm losing my best friend, my betrothed, my—my future." His voice cracks. "I had plans for us. How to make you happy. Even though I wasn't your choice. In a few years, when our parents forced us to wed, I would have done everything I could to please you."

I duck my head to catch his gaze, but my eyes swim. "That's the point, Lukas. It wasn't your choice. It's none of these women's choices. If I can stop the Collection, I can give them one. I can—I can give you your freedom."

"What are you talking about?" His own eyes are red rimmed and glistening.

"Part of why—why I did this, was for you, so you could have the future you want, with Nephele. She's safe and you'll be happy."

He withdraws from me as if I've slapped him, dull spots of color rising on his cheeks. "What—Nephele?"

"She was likely to be the woman from Standia. I heard you last night, and I realized how unfair the Collection was, that I could stop it and make you happy too."

"Nephele was a—a *lark*, Thal. I—I care for her, but she was nothing more than an unwritten possibility."

The words sink like rocks in my stomach. But... I remember the look on his face last night.

"If only you'd said that before," I say with a wet growl, but it has no heat. Perhaps he and Nephele aren't meant, and they'll never have their future. But if he became mine because she was dead, that burned out love would leave ashes and scorched earth behind. The plans he made for us would never have fertile growth.

"Don't tease me, Thalia," he says, sounding desperate. "I wouldn't give you up for another."

I take him in my arms. There's nothing carnal in this embrace, but me holding my best friend like I have since we were children. I'm comforting him again instead of the opposite, but it keeps me from thinking about what will come for me. "You're not giving me up, you're getting a choice."

"Maybe I didn't want a choice."

My eyes close. Lukas has always been stubborn. "How about this? We will not foreclose our future for a month. You won't be bound to me, but the door will remain cracked. If I've not returned by then, you can start writing that possibility. With Nephele or whoever you choose."

"A month?" His voice has a strained quality. "Either you be-lieve you will ferret out the solution to stopping the Collection that quickly or..."

Or I'm assuming I will die. "We don't know how long the Collection lasts, since no one has returned. I may be tossed into the Labyrinth the night we arrive."

He rests his cheek against my head. "Six months, then. That will give you more time to come back to me after."

I hum but stay silent. There's nothing more I can say. I'll either return successfully, or not at all.

"I'll panic at the sight of every ship, you know," he whispers into my hair.

"It isn't as if I can warn you that I'm... not returning."

"Black sails," he says. I lean back to look at him and he repeats himself. "Black sails. Beg them to send word of you if the worst happens; the black sails will tell me before the messenger does."

I snort into his chest. "I'm sure King Minos will grant that request. 'Good evening, Your Majesty. Thank you for including me in this Collection, which we secretly know will kill me unless I stop you through my secret agenda. Although you've never admitted it and the fate of hundreds of women is unknown, will you send a note to Standia when I inevitably die? And do have your shipmaster gather black sails for the trip.' Brilliant idea, Lukas."

"I will never repeat this," he says, his tone turning serious.

I look back up to see an intense expression on his face and I can only imagine what he intends to confess now.

"But you're *actually* quite convincing, Thal. I can't count how often you've talked me out of something I wanted to do."

I pinch his side and he yelps. "That's exactly how I wanted to practice my fifteen years of policy classes."

He laughs, but it sounds clogged, and wrestles my arms back around him. After another minute of silence, he speaks again. "What will you do if you succeed and find your own possibility in the next six months before returning?"

My lips flatten. The likelihood of that has never been smaller. "Then I'll ask King Minos for green sails."

Chapter 7

A single ship towers over the fishing and trading boats in the harbor, covered in aged dark wood and gleaming gold fixtures. The setting sun behind it only adds to the ominous quality, like a shadowy sea monster rising from the depths, holding stories of death and despair in its body. The deck is empty save for a single man in white staring at the empty harbor. The sun behind him shadows his face and he looks of nothing but a death-spirit Ker taking me to my doom, as though Hades is taking me to the Underworld instead of Crete. I blink and the man shuffles, the image vanishing with his unsteady steps.

Mother stands beside me, with Cleon in her arms, staring at me instead of the thin gangplank that rises high off the ground to carry me to my future. Lukas and Father stay away, both having told me they won't be able to watch me leave. *Men.* Clearly there's a reason they select women for the Collection.

Mother fusses with the pin at my shoulder, a silver owl that designates me as a part of Athena's bloodline and then bundles me into her arms, her soft limbs wrapping around my waist squishing Cleon between us. He grumbles but doesn't wriggle free. He doesn't understand what's happening but knows I'm leaving.

Mother stands a head shorter than me, but it's a fact I forget until we hug. Her personality is bold and big, taller than her slight height. I squeeze my arms around her and Cleon, tucking my chin over her shoulder.

"Any last words?"

She pulls back and runs her fingers over the hair closest to my face, dark brown waves she gave both Cleon and me, though hers are threaded with gray. "Only that I know we'll see you again soon, my love."

"Bye-bye, Thal," Cleon says, waving a chubby fist.

With a grim smile and a last kiss to both of their cheeks, I march up the gangplank.

The shuffling man from the deck is the ship master, Perry, who gives me a brief tour when I arrive. He's thin and waiflike, with short red hair, and green eyes that look older than his face, which appears as young as mine. Perry has been the shipmaster for six Collections, meaning he must be Cretan, with ancestry connected to a God through blood that allows him a lengthy life. It's a tradeoff—those with godly blood receive a longer life but no access to magic, whereas the Island Governors touched by the spirit gained magic and the ability to inherit the domain but only for a mortal life. Perry is proof that age and experience doesn't always give confidence.

It's discouraging.

The tour winds through the ship while he explains that, though it will take all night to arrive at Crete, I'll want for nothing on the trip. As we descend into the body of the ship, I pass tables of food, delicacies from each Island, picked over from the few Collected that have sailed for the last two days. Luxuries stack up the walls, anything we could want to keep us entertained and happy on the journey. Blankets and books litter the floor, an easel is tucked behind a pile of swords.

A dozen men and women with overly bright eyes watch our descent from the top and first lower deck to the middle of the ship, each holding the end of a long wooden oar. One man with black hair cut tight against his scalp and warm olive skin scowls and bares his teeth at me. He looks near my age, but if he is Cretan, he could be anywhere from eighteen to a hundred, depending on his parentage.

"Pay them no mind, they're only necessary if we lose the wind," Perry says as he shakily cups my elbow and directs me through a narrow path between the oars. "Or if Zeus interferes again," he says in a sotto voice.

If not for my habit of eavesdropping at doors, I wouldn't have been able to hear him. I consider telling him I believe Zeus *wants* the ship to make it to Crete, but keep my mouth shut.

He ends the tour by gossiping about the other Collected until we arrive at the space where I'll remain until we arrive in Crete tomorrow. It's the lowest deck, normally used as storage but converted into a cozy nest. There are furs and soft blankets on seven cots, colorful tapestries tacked to the wooden walls, and jewel toned pillows covering the floor that the others lounge on. Perry introduces me to the other women as if introducing heads of state.

He bends at the waist, one arm pointed outward. "Ladies, may I present Thalia of Standia, heir to the Governorship, spirit daughter of Athena, and a venerated Collected."

None of them introduce themselves, nor does Perry give me their names. But he told me what he knew on the walk, and I committed my new knowledge to memory. My overwhelming impression is that they're all merely children.

The Collected from Prosfora, the Island that sprang forth from the God of War, is Elara, who stands and points at the door until Perry leaves the room. Her black hair is bundled tight against her head, and she wears a tightly woven wicker vest over her red chiton. She reminds me of a cliff's edge, her skin tawny like the dry sand but sharp and jagged. Perry told me Elara is the oldest, aside from me, but she is still barely seventeen. At twenty-two, I'm an old matron compared to the other women—girls.

Elara eyes me before sniffing the air. "Don't think I'm giving up my cot just because you're some kind of heir," she says, gesturing to the bed farthest from the door. Blankets sit haphazardly on it, piled higher than any of the others. "I was here first."

I let my actions answer for me, walking to the barest cot and slumping on it. With a sniff, Elara sinks to the ground and the others return to their quiet conversations.

Mina, the Collected from Paximada, only fifteen and the youngest of us, sits closest to my feet. Like me, she adds little to the discussion, some conversation about King Minos' sons in Athens. Her bronze face, still round with childhood, puffs with silent tears as she curls into herself on the floor. Something maternal swells in me and I imagine holding her and running my hands through her hair, like Mother does. But I'm not her mother, and I've comforted no one but Cleon.

This will be a long trip.

The girls settle a few hours after my arrival, leaving the nest in pairs to grab small plates of food from the upper deck. They eat in silence until one by one, they sleep.

I sit on my cot, leaning back against the tapestry covered wall behind me. Though the tapestry reminds me of home, and of the skill Athena created and gave my family, it doesn't comfort me. The design across the hull depicts Zeus and his Olympian brothers gaining control over the world. Zeus holds a lightning bolt with an eagle perched on his shoulder, while Poseidon sits astride a seahorse and brandishes a trident as a bull dances between the two deities. Hades stands slightly apart, a black helmet with ram's horns on his head, the helm that gives invisibility, while he holds a bundle of narcissus flowers with a serpent peering between the petals and a bident, a two-pronged spear.

The tapestry *behind* me is a story I don't know, something about Poseidon tossing a baby into the water surrounding our Islands. An owl soars through the sky, watching the child submerge beneath the depths.

I thought our library was world-renowned, but this story was missing. My hands cover my face as a pang hits my stomach. I've barely begun, and already my one advantage in discovering the specifics of the bargain—my knowledge—fails me. And I'd forgotten how many symbols the brothers share. What if I've misinterpreted the dreams and the storms? What if Zeus didn't pull me here, but Poseidon was warning me away?

Before I can work myself into a good sulk, a long thump sounds above me, followed by two more in quick succession. Elara jumps from her cot as if the sound landed directly on her. She rouses the other girls, who leap to attention, bodies coiled for whatever threat is above us. Even Mina, with her doe eyes still red rimmed, looks like a warrior, scraping her brown curls up and bundling them on her head. With a finger to her lips, Elara motions them towards the door. They give my cot a wide berth as all six creep up the stairs.

It takes longer than it should for me to follow, but I stumble up the stairs after them. Half the men and women on the middle deck are asleep while the other half ignore me, except the scowler from before who drops his oar when I shuffle past him.

"Planning on being a hero like the rest of them?" His voice is deep, but biting. Pale blue eyes squint at the corners.

The exhaustion from lack of sleep removes the filter I usually keep on my mouth, and I scowl. "Do I *look* like a hero to you?"

He blinks and quirks his lips, drawing attention to the sharp cut of his jaw and cheekbones. "Well, the ship gossip says you volunteered for this sui—" He cuts off with a wheezing cough.

After rubbing his throat with a golden skinned hand, he says, "You volunteered for the King's Collection."

I don't owe him an explanation, but there's no reason to lie. I've already opened my mouth, meaning the seal is off. "I did, but only to help my friend."

The gleaming teeth he bared earlier in the evening reappear as he grinds them audibly. "Hero, then. And an idiot just like the rest of them, leaping after something you don't understand."

I ignore his insults. "Do you know who is out there?"

He looks towards the wood ceiling separating us from the upper deck and the loud thumping that hasn't begun again. "No, but don't worry, Hero. They won't let anything happen to you until you get to Crete."

"Why not?"

His lips thin like I'm missing something obvious. I might be, but that's what questions are for. "I can't tell you, but suffice to say, you have value until you meet the one who stands at the center of the Labyrinth."

"The one who—do you mean the Beast?"

He scratches his throat with one long finger, the tendons in his wrist flexing all the way up his muscular arm. "I can't tell you."

"Thanks for all your help," I mutter sarcastically as I slip past him.

"Good luck, Hero," he calls as I ascend the final staircase.

I stay in the shadows when I arrive at the top deck, ducking a few steps below the landing to inspect what I might walk into, placing an illusion for added protection, letting the golden net cloak me from danger.

The six girls stand in a row, Elara in the front with her teeth bared. Perry cowers behind her, along with several other men in white coats holding long knives.

A one-eyed man stands across from my shipmates, towering over even the tallest crew. He holds a club in one meaty and golden hand, while the other curls menacingly around a dagger near his hip. None of the armed men on our side make any move towards subduing him.

"You've picked the wrong ship to plunder," Elara hisses, her long black tresses whipping about her face in the night wind. Even sleep rumpled, she looks like a soldier—no, a commander, ready to lead her troops into battle and die alongside them if necessary. I let out a heavy breath and shut my eyes. That man has no chance against six highly skilled, if young, women. I could go back to bed, and it wouldn't even matter.

"I've the luck of the Gods, girlie. Been doing this for longer than you've been alive." The man shakes his club, which glints in the moonlight, and raises his gaze to the whimpering Perry. "Longer than any of you've been alive. Never picked the wrong ship before."

Elara sticks out her chest, as if his boasting is meaningless. "You've never boarded a ship of those heading to the Collection either."

Instead of retreating, the man shrugs and removes his grip on his dagger to grab the club with both hands. "No matter to me. Don't scatter now, 'm too tired to chase you 'round the ship. Rather bash in all your heads with only one blow."

He shuffles forward as Elara and the girls crouch into defensive positions.

"Wait!" Perry cries, slipping beside Elara and wringing his hands. "You mustn't. Have you no idea who they are?"

Elara smirks as the other girls loosen their stances. But the man doesn't withdraw or lower his club.

"The girls for the Labyrinth? Don't rightly care whether Poseidon gets his cr—"

"Hold your tongue." Perry eyes the girls before looking almost surprised he interrupted the would-be-thief. He gulps before continuing. "The fate of all of Crete depends on these girls. Please, have mercy."

Chrysa, the short girl from Karavi, elbows Mina and whispers in her ear before Elara holds up a hand. They immediately close their mouths.

The man lowers the club until it hits the wooden deck with a metallic thump. "As I said, Poseidon's—" Perry squeaks, and the man rolls his eye. "Poseidon's *business* with the King don't change my intent to knock heads 'round and loot your corpses. Imagine there's plenty to be had here, if these girls are who you say."

"But—"

"If Poseidon wanted my support, he'd a done somethin' when my sire got dropped in his domain."

My head thunks against the side of the stairs. The girls can surely wallop a normal man, even one with a metal club and dagger. But this man isn't normal. Perry's already implied this stranger is at least Cretan. And the only being I know who was tossed into the sea is Hephaestus, the child of Zeus and Hera with power over metallurgy, who later sacrificed his lifeblood and spirit to create the Island of Petalidi. Which means this man is likely his child, and half-mortal at best, stronger and longer-lived than any of the Collected. Even Perry's lineage is three times removed from the Gods. None of them can out-match the man tormenting our boat.

"Please, sir," Perry is saying when I refocus on the threat. "One of your own stands on this ship," he says, gesturing to Eriphyle, from Petalidi, a golden skinned blonde woman that stands a head taller than everyone on the ship.

The stranger snorts. "Not mine, never stepped foot on no Island that killed my sire."

Perry kneels on the deck, while the half-deity stares at him in disgust. "Can we do nothing to change your mind?"

"Get up, boy. Feel like 'm at temple." He leans against his club. "Need to rob somebody, makes the labor worthless otherwise."

Elara steps around the still kneeling Perry. "Perhaps only one," she says, lowering beside Perry in offering. A frisson of respect runs through me that Elara would so quickly give her life for others.

The man heaves his club to his shoulder and walks around Elara as if inspecting a slab of meat, one leg dragging behind the other. "Shirt's dingy, girlie. Not sure you'd be enough. One'd be fine if the quarry's worth it."

"There's Thalia," the small Mina squeaks, blinking guilelessly.

"Quiet," Elara hisses, but the damage is done.

My eyes close again, this time in resignation. Maybe if I'd tried to comfort her earlier, Mina wouldn't be throwing me on the man's dagger.

I could still stay hiding, but he'd inevitably come for the rest of us when he finishes 'bashing' the people on the top deck. And I owe a duty to those on the ship. I should have been out there with them already. I agreed to become a part of the Collection with my role as heir in mind. Hiding in the darkness and letting others hurtle towards their death is not what a leader does. If I can't do this, I may as well walk into the Labyrinth and let the Beast devour me. I pull my shoulders back as I remove the illusion and march out from the stairs.

"Good evening," I say. My voice only trembles once before I force my heir mask back onto my face.

All heads swivel in my direction. Perry looks pleased, while Elara looks annoyed. Mina's cheeks are dark in the dim light as she bites her lip, and the other girls watch me with varying expressions, though I see *where in Hades' name have you been?* on more than one face.

"You Thalia, then?" the man asks, one bushy white eyebrow raising. Head on, his face and neck are crisscrossed with pink scars that disappear under his tunic only to reappear in thick raised lines along his arms.

I nod my head as my mind races towards a plan. "I am. And you are?"

"Periphetes," he says, one corner of his lips turning upward as if amused. While Periphetes' one-eyed gaze focuses on me, Elara yanks Perry to his feet and drags him back towards the other shipmates. "You got goods enough to keep the others with their heads whole?"

The plan cements, a stupid one, but not my worst, volunteering for the Collection takes that title. If it works, Lukas would certainly appreciate it.

"At home, yes. But you heard our shipmaster, we are this year's Collection, and carry nothing but the clothes on our back." And my dagger, but I *might* attempt to fight him if he demanded it. "If you go to my Island, you'll have plenty of goods to take from my father and the other Councilors."

Periphetes considers this as he leans on his club again. "Sounds like a trick. Send me away and some guard bothers me on your Island. And don't get my bashing."

I trudge towards the railing on the opposite side of the deck until I can lean against it. The sea behind me is dark and choppy. Elara still stands at the ready while the other girls appear puzzled. Perry appears to have fainted and the other men try to hold him up.

"It's no trick. You can still bash my head in." I'm careful not to word this like a bargain. He could bring the Erinyes' eyes upon me. It would be bad luck to survive Periphetes' threats only to be dragged down towards the Underworld to experience the Erinyes' vengeance against an oath breaker.

Periphetes follows me to the railing, dragging his club in time with his limping foot. "And the guard?"

"Put black sails on your ship. That would distract them long enough to do your... bashing before grabbing what you can and sailing away."

His one eye narrows as he towers over me. "Why black sails?"

I can't restrain the wince that pierces through my stony expression, but hopefully Periphetes takes it as proof of my sincerity. "That will tell them I'm dead."

Periphetes smiles, showing off his straight white teeth. "Clever, girlie. Worthy quarry you be. I accept. You in exchange for them others, and all I can carry off your Island."

I shift until I'm standing parallel with the railing, silently praying no oath is made on my side. "Wonderful." *If I don't outwardly and specifically agree, does it count?*

He bares his teeth before planting his feet and raising the club over his head. In my periphery, Mina flinches.

"What fine craftsmanship," I say before he can swing that weapon towards my brain. His grip on the club falters and I barrel on. "You must be Lemnos' son to carry such a piece of metallurgy."

"That I am." Periphetes puffs out his chest, the club still poised to strike. "Made me this club, you see."

"Is it gold?"

The club swings towards me and I fear I've miscalculated, but it neatly misses my head. My breath leaves me in a lurch as he holds it chest height.

"Not gold, girlie. Too soft. Bashes fine but takes too many hits. This here's bronze. Stronger than gold, can bash many a head before wearing out." He gestures to a dent near the crown of the club. "My twelve-hundredth hit."

I nod with the same feigned interest I used to give at my culture classes. "It appears sturdy, though I'm sure it is incredibly heavy if it is true bronze."

He snorts. "As if Lemnos' son would carry false bronze." He holds it out towards me. "Try it, girlie. You'll see."

Biting my cheek to hide my eagerness, I take the club from him. Although it is heavy, the weight is distributed as I hold it two-handed. Hopefully I'm strong enough for the next step in my plan. I haven't tried an illusion on anything but myself since my failures in hiding Lukas. I grab the base with two interlocking hands and squint at the scratches there. "Is that an inscription?"

Periphetes leans over me, but I shift so the base is lit by moonlight. He stands in front of the railing.

"Look right there, isn't that an inscription?" I nod towards it. "Something about fire?"

Periphetes ducks farther to see the symbols I magicked onto the metal. "What?"

With speed only fear can give me, I heave the club towards his head as hard as I can, hitting his skull with an audible crack. What I lack in strength, I make up for in leverage as Periphetes loses his balance and tumbles over the railing. His head strikes the ship's wooden side before he plummets into the dark sea.

A quiet splash and surprised exhalations are the only sounds of the ship.

My limbs lock, the club held aloft, as I realize what I've just done. Blood that splattered on the club runs and threatens to drip onto the skin of my neck. I lower the club until it lands with a thunk beside what look like three of Periphetes' gleaming teeth.

The girls rush towards me, Mina at the front, crying again and blubbering apologies. Elara blinks twice before picking up the club.

"Could have been worse, Heir," she says as she wipes the blood off on her pants. She hands it to Eriphyle who cradles it against her chest. "Could have pissed yourself and passed out like Perry, or—"

Before she finishes, I gag and heave bile onto the floor by our feet.

She scoffs. "Or you could have done that."

Chapter 8

A crow swoops over a golden blanket. It scratches and picks at the seams of the fabric until the threads burst into a magical flame. Hiding under the blanket is a blooming lotus.

We arrive in Crete only a few hours later, after an uncomfortable nap, landing at Heraklion, where all the Islands' and mainland trade is focused.

The Palace is in Knossos, an hour's walk from the coastline. There is no procession to greet us, but an empty dock leading into a sparse forest that trails upward into a low mountain range. From the sea, Crete looks identical to Standia, which gives me strength.

Perry and the other men from the top deck stay on the ship. Elara is first off the boat, followed by Eriphyle with my club. After her comes the milky pale Diomede from Gerenia, whose flaming red hair falls to her hips. Then follows the stunning Thyia from Avgo, her ebony hair twisted around her head like a crown and a secretive smile on her pink lips. Finally, Chrysa and Mina trudge down together. Just as my feet step onto the slippery gangplank, the man from the lower deck knocks into my hip. He winks as he passes me to stand on the dock with the others.

"Hurry, Hero. It looks like rain," he calls. I look to Perry who shrugs and turns towards the stairs to the lower deck.

"Not that talkative this morning? Did all the heroism tucker you out?" His pale blue eyes twinkle, the belligerence from last night gone.

That he's a morning person is of no consequence to me or my goals on Crete. I ignore him to tentatively make my way down the wet gangplank.

"You're coming with us?" Thyia asks, standing beside the man and gazing at him with shining eyes. I slip in beside them.

He smiles at her, displaying perfect teeth. "Consider me your guide to Knossos."

"You were on the ship too?" That comes from little Mina, whose dark brows furrow.

"A rower," Elara says from the end of the dock where she waits with Eriphyle.

Mina turns to Chrysa. "Do rowers double as guides on Crete?"

"They do when rowing doesn't pay the expenses," he says.

Chrysa sighs dramatically, heaving her head back and letting her short black tresses fall over her back. "And here I thought all the Cretans lived like kings." She looks at me and smirks. "Or was that just Standians?"

Elara frowns. "I have no need for a guide, but feel free to help the stragglers." She pointedly stares at me before turning and stalking into the trees.

The others follow, until Thyia, the man, and I are the only ones on the dock. Thyia bites her bottom lip charmingly. If I tried that expression, I'd look like a toadfish. Her cheeks turn pink, and she spins and rushes after the others.

"A fan already," the man says as we watch her go.

I ignore him and follow the path the others took.

"I'm Dolion," he says, his long legs catching up to me and walking by my side. We breach the trees when he speaks again.

"This is when you introduce yourself. And then I say it's nice to meet you, and you say the pleasure is all yours, and I agree because I'm wonderful. It's part of the social contract."

He reminds me of Lukas in that moment and a huffing laugh bursts from me before I can stop it. I purse my lips to hold in further reactions.

"Come on, Hero," he pleads. "You spoke to me last night. There was even some fire to you. This will be a dull walk if I must talk to myself the whole trip."

I consider telling him to walk with Thyia, as she'd give him the attention he so clearly desires, but don't want to encourage him. I then consider placing an illusion to hide from his company, but don't want the questions.

A loud crack of lightning, followed by the rumble of thunder, saves me. Thank Zeus for his timing, and for whatever purpose he has in storming over me now. The sky opens and buckets of rain pour down. Dolion grabs my hand and drags me deeper into the trees. I wrestle it away from him and he snags my sleeve instead.

We find the other girls hiding under a small tree canopy. Elara is attempting to persuade them to follow her into the rain, but only Eriphyle looks like she might agree.

"It's only rain," Elara is saying, her hands planted on her hips. Her long black hair fell from its bun and sticks to her face. The rattan armor looks like it will mold.

"I'm not sure of the custom in Prosfora," Diomede says. "But we take cover from the rain, lest Zeus strike us down." She holds her hands up in supplication. "We rest and appreciate the gift of the water he offers us."

"We all live on Islands, it's not like we're lacking in water," Chrysa says under her breath. Mina snorts next to her.

They bicker until I clear my throat.

"None of us are on our Islands. We don't know how things might behave on Crete, or whether the storms here are messages or warnings. We should wait out the storm," I announce, channeling Father and his authoritative tone.

Dolion smiles in my periphery, murmuring, "You can still speak."

Diomede looks thankful I've almost agreed with her.

"You're not in charge of us, Heir," Eriphyle says, looking to Elara for support.

My blank mask hides my frustration. People listen to Father without question. It should be no different with me.

"Hero's right," Dolion says after eyeing me speculatively for a moment. "Zeus does like to play with Crete. The waterline will rise, and we're more likely to drown than be hit by lightning, but this area could be underwater in another five minutes."

"Where can we find higher ground?" I ask him.

He points towards the trees to the left of us. "There's a hill that way. I know a compatriot who may offer us shelter. If she's unavailable, we can always climb a tree."

I grimace inwardly, and Dolion's smile widens as if he can see it.

"Fine," Elara says, jutting out her chin. "Lead us there."

We're drenched when the land rises upward into a steep hill, the water already covering our sandals. I fell twice on tree roots or other obstacles; as did Thyia, but she kept from slamming onto her knees. I'm sure I look like a drowned and muddy cat compared to her. After the second fall, I didn't refuse Dolion's arm again.

A building appears from the haze of rain, near the tops of the incline. The building turns into a windowless hut with a straw thatched roof. Elara pushes to the front of us, knocking into my and Diomede's shoulders as she passes. She bangs the heel of her hand onto a scratched wood door.

A rail thin woman opens it, and stares unseeing out with milky eyes. She looks Mother's age, only the thin lines at the corners of her mouth and creasing her forehead showing her long life. Dolion smoothly steps beside Elara and grasps the woman's hand.

"Hecaline, it's Dolion. We need to hide out from the rain."

She runs wrinkled fingers up his shoulder onto his face, trailing them over Dolion's features. She smiles brightly in recognition. "Dolion! You've come. Is it time then?"

He stiffens before offering a flat smirk, something that appears forced. "Time to let us dry out, of course. The women from the Collection join me and I must get them to the Palace."

Hecaline's expression clears, and she nods. "Come in, come in."

She ushers us in and we stand in a clump by the closed door. Thyia shifts until she stands next to Dolion and beams at him, who ignores her.

A comforting heat wafts from a metal stove near the middle of the room, next to a thick gray mat that covers the heaps of ash that make up the floors. Thick scratches cover the walls in a haphazard pattern, like curved claw marks. The hut is small enough for us to stand side by side and touch the opposite walls. Dolion disappears behind a blue curtain near the back corner.

Hecaline shuffles to the mat and lowers onto it, creating a cloud of dust and feathers that catch in her short black hair. "The fire's not much, dears, but it will warm you."

"It's fine," Elara says. "The rain isn't the issue, it's the water level."

"Chill will kill you before a flood," Hecaline sniffs. "Water level, she said. The water has never risen to my door in the years I've lived here."

Dolion pops out from the curtain, wearing dry clothes. Elara scowls in his direction.

"If there's no threat from the rain, we should return to the path," she says, pushing her way between us towards the closed door, forcing me closer to Hecaline's spot on the floor. Eriphyle nods and follows closely behind her, knocking into Mina with the bronze club.

"There's no threat here, girl, but below my mountain..." Hecaline scratches a finger over her throat, in the universal symbol of death. "Though the water won't be the culprit there."

Dolion clears his throat. "There're a few blankets, but you'll need to share." His gaze lingers on me. "I volunteer to share with Hero once I get her out of those dirty clothes."

Thyia sighs as Mina titters. Hecaline smiles indulgently at him while I restrain an eye roll, settling on ignoring him completely again.

"I will not be idle," Elara announces. She searches the room. "I will gather more wood for your fire." She nods to the other girls. "You five, your help would be valuable," she says, before marching out the door.

Diomede is the only one who doesn't follow, instead grimacing. "Zeus will not mind if we work in his storms?"

Hecaline snorts. "Does Zeus mind? Zeus, you said? Zeus cares plenty, but not for the—"

"You'll be fine," Dolion interrupts. "Tell the others—most storms last only an hour. When the sky turns green, it is near the end, and you should return. The bossy one may think she knows the way, but she will need my guidance to avoid what will have washed out."

Diomede tips her head and steps over the threshold.

"Be careful of the boar, dear. Don't let him hide or pass the line," Hecaline calls. Diomede pauses briefly before trudging into the deluge.

When only the three of us remain in the room, Hecaline pats the space on the mat beside her.

"Deary, don't make the blind woman get up and drag you to her."

Dolion watches us silently, leaning against the wall behind the stove. After a brief hesitation, I join her, trailing water droplets as I go. From my new vantage point on the floor, the gouges on the wall appear to depict daggers and triangles, with a single winding serpent directly above Dolion's head. The serpent reminds me of Zeus and Athena, of home, and I release the tension the morning brought me.

"Dolion never brings me visitors, you know," Hecaline says.

The fire cracks as Dolion tosses another piece on kindling onto it. "Because you're my favorite, Lina. Why would I bring someone who'd pale in your light?"

She giggles, making her sound younger than me now. "Flatterer. Dolion only likes my words. When the earth cracks, words will be all we have."

I peer around Hecaline and raise my brows.

"Hecaline has seer blood," he explains. "Sometimes it bleeds into unrelated conversation."

"He means being blind opened my other sight and I'm old enough not to care for social demands. Now, come here." Her hand darts out to grab my face. I repress a flinch as she runs her fingers over my features, rubbing away the mud from my first crumple to the ground. "You must be important," she says when she finishes her perusal.

A spark jolts through my stomach. I can only hope that's a prophesied claim and my chances of success here are high.

Dolion clears his throat. "They are the women for the Collection, as I told you when we arrived."

Hecaline blinks three times in quick succession. "You did say that. Did you say that?"

"I did, Lina."

Her unseeing eyes roam over my face with enough intent that I'd believe she could see me. "And it's time then?"

"Not yet, Lina." He pushes off the wall and strides towards a box near the door. "Let me get us something to warm us."

Hecaline snaps her fingers in my face. "Are you mute, deary? Or deaf? Dolion, is she —"

"I'm neither, ma'am," I answer.

"Speaking only when spoken to. That's the fear in you." She leans forward. "What if you're the only one who can speak the right words?"

I try not to bristle that she's discovered my self-doubts so quickly. She *is* a seer. "I speak. I simply keep my thoughts to myself until necessary."

She shakes her head. "That won't work. She needs to speak. Did you hear me, Dolion? I said that won't work."

Dolion hands us mugs of warm drinks that smell like honey and lemon. "I heard you, Lina. I'm sure that Hero did too and will take your words for what they are."

Nonsensical ramblings, something prophetic, or another Lukas-like complaint about how I behave. I know which one I *want* to be correct.

"Hero? Is your name Hero? That's convenient," Hecaline says before slurping her tea.

"It's Thalia actually, daughter of Galenus, Governor of Standia," I correct, staring at Dolion who bares his teeth in a hungry looking smile. I curl my fingers around the steaming mug and take a deep breath. I'm not afraid to speak. God's teeth, I'm a *leader*. Even so, I place the illusion over my face to hide my hesitation. The illusion projects something calm and commanding in my expression that my face can't create. I almost fix the streaks of mud traveling down my chiton but decide it would go too far.

Hecaline blinks her milky white eyes in my direction. "That may bring more attention than your name."

Dolion peers at me, confused. "What?"

But Hecaline doesn't answer him. "Be careful with that, deary. Magic calls to magic. They cannot see what I see, but the walls of the Palace are painted with blood."

"She means that literally and metaphorically, Hero," Dolion says, no longer looking curious about Hecaline's cryptic statements. Befriending a seer must mean he's used to it. "The King updated the Palace after winning the Island War. He used certain... benefits they gave him to spell his domain. Blood sacrifices imbuing magic," he finishes, holding his throat.

I take a sip of the tea, tucking the knowledge and warning away and drop my illusion. It's simply more practice in keeping my mask without magic. The burn of the tea feels as though it fortifies me. "Is there anything else you might tell me about the King, or the Collection?"

"There is much I would tell you, if I could," she says. Behind her, Dolion conspicuously taps his neck.

I nod; this must be the geas Father mentioned. "Is there anything you *can* tell me?"

Hecaline smiles, baring brilliant white teeth. "What do you wish to know?"

"Can it be stopped?"

She grasps my hand and squeezes. The intensity in her face burns me. "*Everything* has an ending, deary. Some things simply take longer."

I glance at Dolion who is staring intently at Hecaline. "How do I stop it then?"

She blinks, her expression clearing, and she takes a deep sip of tea. "Stop what? Dolion, what is there to stop?"

Dolion grimaces.

I swallow my disappointment and answer in his place. "Nothing, ma'am. But thank you for your hospitality."

"You're favoring me," she says with a wave of her empty hand. "I can't gather wood as easily as those colts out there."

"Not with your boar underfoot," Dolion says, slumping to sit against the back wall.

I remember the ease at which they all faced Periphetes and sigh. "They're strong, I can't imagine something as simple as a boar will cause them grief."

"The boar," Hecaline says, staring into the fire. "The boar. There's something about the boar. Something... something to tell but can't speak."

Something churns through the air, an expectation or energy. Dolion slowly stands and walks towards Hecaline.

"Be careful, Lina. You'll—" He cuts off as his eyes dart to mine and he raises his eyebrows expectantly. "You'll hurt your throat."

"That's the key, you see. He's always been the key." She drops her mug and grasps my hands. My mug falls, and the tea spills between us. "You wish to stop it, then don't let him hide. He must not pass the line. Save the boar, Alis."

I look to Dolion who offers me a grim smile. "It's Thalia, ma'am," I say in a soothing voice.

She coughs, squeezing until my finger bones grind uncomfortably. "The boar, Alis. You must—"

And she screams.

The door bursts open, the sky outside green and hazy. Eriphyle comes in backward, dragging the body of a boar by its tusks. Elara follows her in, the bronze club resting on her shoulders, the blood dripping down the head replicating how it looked earlier this morning. The others straggle in behind them, carrying wet kindling and leaves.

"What did you do?" Hecaline demands, grasping her throat.

Dolion places a bracing hand on her back. My hands flap uselessly in front of her before I drop them to my side. I'm out of my depth with Hecaline's panic.

"We got your boar," Mina says proudly. "As a token of our appreciation for letting us wait out the storm."

"It attempted to pass the tree line, but we didn't allow it, as you said," Thyia says.

Elara spins the club, sending blood droplets around the room. "It was easy, good practice for the Beast."

"No no no," Hecaline rasps, milky eyes gazing around the room fearfully. "He must not hide. He cannot pass the line. You're to save him. The boar, Alis."

Diomede drops to her knees. "What's wrong with her?"

"The boar. It... it meant something to her." Dolion coughs and shakes his head. "It was like a pet."

Elara thunks the club onto the dusty floor. "She should have been clearer. It's not our fault."

"She didn't say kill it," I snap, glaring at Elara's mulish face.

"Like you'd have done better," she says, scowling.

"She killed Periphetes," Mina says. Thyia silently slips to the floor as her lower lip trembles.

"It was just a misunderstanding," says Diomede, reaching out one hand to rub Hecaline's knee. "We didn't mean to harm your pet. We could not have known otherwise."

They could have in another life. Logic says that "be careful of the boar" and "not to let him pass the line" has multiple meanings. At the very least, it wouldn't mean *murder*. Of course, the girls who have never taken comprehension classes wouldn't consider anything other than brute force.

Hecaline's eyes stare in my direction, as if she can see what I'm thinking. *Is this when only I can speak the right words?* If I had made sure the girls understood exactly what Hecaline said, and demanded they use their heads before traipsing out into the woods with murderous intent, would the boar still be dead?

I stay quiet and Hecaline's stare moves to the wall behind the fire.

"Can we do anything to make it better?" Chrysa asks from her space behind Thyia. She squeezes Thyia's shaking shoulders. I wonder when they became friends.

Hecaline shakes her head. "Save the boar, Alis."

Chapter 9

We leave soon after. Dolion and Diomede calm Hecaline *and* Thyia, until finally the tension drains from the room like an emptying tub. Hecaline doesn't bid us farewell, not that I blame her given we killed her pet.

The trip is somber as we trek through the marshes and puddles that remain from the sudden storm. The green sky hangs over us like a sickness, an omen for what's coming. I've never been suspicious, not in the way Gerenia, Diomede's home, teaches their citizens to be. But beginning this journey with a death doesn't bode well. I can almost see the wings of Keres, *the Darkness*, the starved children of the Goddess Nyx that feast upon death, waiting in the shaking trees. Waiting for us.

But Nyx's most treacherous children haven't been seen since Zeus, Poseidon, and Hades were born. The memory of an early lesson comes to me: there are no records that they were killed, only that they disappeared into Hades' domain. Now, they sup on the souls that died violently in the Underworld but... *What better opportunity for the spirits to reappear to slake their desire in ravaging those that die in battle than to follow the Collected and their massacre by the Beast?*

I blink away the shiver that thought produces. Better I imagine the flash of wings are the Erinyes, the Keres' sisters, watching Minos and ready to drag him into the depths of the Underworld for oath breaking. Dolion, who walks between me and Thyia, places a hand at the small of my back, just above the knife holster.

He offers what I imagine he believes is a comforting smile, but I slide out of his reach.

We breach the city limits an hour later, still silent and filled with either anticipation or expectation. Dolion directs us down a long thoroughfare. A dozen other entrances to the city span to the east and west of us, like the spokes of a wheel. Knossos creeps forward, crawling upward until it hits the base of the mountain. Behind that is what must be the Palace, a tall stone structure that appears to jut out from the rock behind it. In comparison, it makes my village look almost rural and abandoned.

Aside from its size, the buildings of Knossos look no different from any of the ones I've seen on Standia. But instead of the Council House at its center, the Palace acts as the center of the half circle wheel. And instead of the homes of our most important citizens acting as the far spokes of the wheel, the houses farthest from the center and closest to the port we arrived from are the poorest. Crumbling and abandoned facades meet us until we get more than a block inside the city.

We walk at a snail's pace through the main street. The girls' eyes focus on one treasure or another—a market stall selling what looks like baked fruit, a cobbler holding out the shiniest leather shoes I've ever seen. The Cretans wandering the road have a gauntness unseen on the Islands but otherwise look no different from us humans, the increased lifespan their ancestors gave them not apparent in how they dress or move, unlike the other half-gods living elsewhere, like the mystical and hidden Atlantians. Perhaps like Perry, if I got close enough, I'd be able to see the age in their eyes not present in a cursory scan of their forms. The only difference appears to be in the fashions—instead of men wearing long chitons that match the shape of the women's, theirs are cut to the knee and they traverse the street shirtless, which only emphasizes their thin chests and emaciated forms. The women's clothing looks like Standia's, except they all have hair shorn to their shoulders or chin instead of the long trailing locks that is the Island style.

I expect to see the many creatures that live amongst the godly, like those that live with the half-gods in Athens. A nymph, a satyr, perhaps a centaur roaming the streets. To my knowledge, none of them live on any of the Islands. But none appear on the streets, or even the forest we just walked through.

And given the pomp the shipmaster displayed and Dolion's cryptic statements about keeping us safe until we arrive at the Palace, I'm surprised no one stops to gawk at us. There are no bystanders desiring to touch us and experience "our luck" at being Collected. The thought strikes me—they could feel as my father and Lukas do, and they know our selection is no prize.

The stone buildings increase in size and decoration the closer we get to the center of Knossos. Buildings closer to the sea, those that weren't abandoned and broken, were modest, with no tile designs on the walls, and either windowless or only open to the elements. But stories rise with the incline until the largest houses would dwarf my own. Colored mica designs reflect into the street, more histories of the Gods I know. Diomede and Chrysa stop at one that depicts Zeus, in his white robes with a sun halo-ing his head, standing side by side with a man wearing a white bull as his robe. But instead of Poseidon and his trident wearing the bull, this shows King Minos, using Poseidon's symbols and stance.

Finally, we arrive at the square of the Knossos Palace complex. The Palace itself is four stories, looking no grander than Standia's own government building. But our Council House is a single structure, and the Palace complex expands as large as our town square. To the east are several long and lean buildings that must hold Knossos' magazines, the supplies given by the citizenry that are doled out at Minos and the Court's direction. To the west are thinner buildings that sit two to three stories tall, perhaps where other aristocrats live when not living inside the Palace.

The Palace itself looks to be the edge of Knossos, with the city bound by the mountains behind it. But knowing what I know about governmental architecture, the area drifting up the mountain will hold other necessary buildings and supplies, like an armory, any permanent barracks, and magazines for those goods that have less of an immediate need. Tile covers the Palace facade in a kaleidoscope of bright colors, no picture depicted but starbursts of light.

Dolion stops us in the center of the square. "You'll need to pass that to me," he tells Elara, gesturing to the club she and Eriphyle took turns carrying.

She hands it over without complaint. My fingers flex to touch the knife resting in its holster against my back, though the layered folds of my chiton should hide it. If there is a ban on weapons, no one told me. I don't invite trouble by bringing it up.

A woman in a long red chiton-style gown saunters towards us from the few steps that mark the entrance to the Palace. Her skirts sway against her legs, the golden tone peeking through a daring split up the side. She's stunning, her face symmetrical and painted with rouge on her milk pale cheeks. The skeletal figure found on most of the women we saw isn't present on her curves.

Several of the girls look thunderstruck, Dolion included, though his perusal of her figure appears more cataloging than appraising. Only Elara brusquely strides forward to kneel at the woman's feet. As if she was on a lead attached to Elara's waist, Eriphyle immediately follows, and bends at the knee. The others mimic them, and self-preservation forces me to do the same. Dolion remains standing beside us, a small smirk gracing his lips.

"Lady Deianira," he calls. "What a pleasant surprise we would meet you this day. You have grown even more beautiful in the time I've been away."

Deianira smiles something soft and sensual, an expression that would never fit on my face. The jewel encrusted pin at her right shoulder—a bull's head inside the Cretan labyrinth—reveals she is of some importance at the Palace, but not what position she may hold. She doesn't spare us a glance and I shuffle on my knees ready to stand when the moment presents itself.

"Dolion, you wonder," she says huskily. "I knew the girls were coming, but not you! Have you truly spent the last fifteen years working as a simple rower to gather the Collection?"

"There's nothing simple about it," he says, flexing his arms and showing off his powerful muscles. "And with my account no longer overflowing, I'm resigned to taking on such tasks. Unless you have another idea?"

She sidesteps around us to link arms with him, and they whisper to each other. I stand and brush the dust of the stone square off my dark skirts, though it fits in with the rain, seawater, sweat, and mud that developed on our jaunt from Standia.

Diomede, Mina, and Chrysa stand beside me, and we watch the lady in red simper for what must be ages, given how the shadows begin to cover us. Objectively, I suppose Dolion would be considered handsome, but on principle people who annoy me have no pleasing physical qualities. But I'm alone in my assessment. Blushing, Deianira touches Dolion's chest while he leans close and whispers in her ears, twice tucking a pale blond lock behind her ear. Thyia remains kneeling throughout the entire teasing byplay between our guide and Deianira, quiet until a sniffle comes from her delicate nose. At the sound, Elara huffs and stands, along with Eriphyle.

I clear my throat. The others are too meek or impressed by whatever station this Deianira holds, making me our only choice to move this along and begin what we came here to do. I'm used to handling dignitaries, or at least being in their presence. This is where Hecaline's first admonition must matter. Out of all of us, I am surely the only one who can handle this.

"At what point do we begin the Collection?" My voice rings out over the square, the hidden irritation threatening to overtake my blank mask.

Lady Deianira drags her hands from Dolion's body to trail her gaze over mine. "Are you one of the matron tutors?"

Chrysa chokes out a laugh but covers it with a cough.

"I'm one of the Collected."

This time Deianira laughs, the sound like ringing bells. "Truly? At your age?"

Twenty-two is old for the Collection, but not ancient, not when women up to age forty could be chosen. Unless she's implying something else about me that I don't understand.

"I believe she has *your* years, Dei," Dolion says from behind her.

"Perhaps." Her nose twitches. "But with my father's blood running through my veins, I will have this face for another century, while hers will wrinkle within another ten."

"Who can say? Perhaps our Hero has an unknown history." He smiles, though it looks like a sea spirit's shark teeth. "Even aged, I imagine those soulful eyes will still see to the heart of us."

A scowl forms on Deianira's pretty face. "Soulful eyes, Dolion? I suppose that's all she can offer." Her eyes travel over my form. I know what she's seeing: my wavy hair plastered to my head, my chiton coated in dried mud and sweat. The slit in one leg shows my scratched knees, and my face must look pinched and tired. "That and confirmation that her Island overfeeds their candidates."

I straighten, attempting to hold as much confidence as I can with muck covering me. Dolion's smirking words may not have held an insult, but Deianira's certainly do. "My history is known, at least to you," I say, lifting my chin. "I am the heir to the lead position in Standia's government."

"Were," Deianira says snidely, her delicate nostrils flaring.

"Excuse me?"

"You were the heir," she explains, offering me an insincere pitying expression. "I doubt you'll remain so after entering the center of the Labyrinth."

"Now, Dei," Dolion says. "Surely, you're not implying something might befall Thalia?"

She simpers. "Of course not, simply that her choices *after* her jaunt through the Labyrinth may not allow her to return to her heir status."

"And she will have many choices, won't she?" Dolion's eyes narrow.

"Indeed, especially if my father has anything to say about it."

The two stare at each other in weighted silence, something unsaid running between them. Dolion strokes his throat with one finger. The girls shift behind us.

"I haven't had the pleasure of meeting your father, Miss Deianira," I say politely, hoping to ease the odd tension developing in the open air.

Her head shakes, as if waking from a dream, and she pins her hard focus on me. "You know him as King Minos. And as you are so eager to begin the Collection, I will take you to him."

Arm and arm with Dolion, Deianira leads us through the first floor of the Palace, passing the many statues depicting King Minos's deeds. The crowning glory, given its position beneath the main staircase, is a marble rendition of him defeating the Islands to become the oligarch over us all. His statue form stands alone, long hair flowing behind him. In one hand he holds Poseidon's trident, in the other a knife. At his feet lay two men cowering, the symbols of all seven Islands chiseled into their bare backs.

The path winds through the second and third floors, as if Deianira wanted to show off the grandeur of the Palace. But the rest of the design scheme, which is no less chaotic than the exterior, overwhelms the many tapestries and busts of King Minos.

Colored stones and tiles blanket every surface, deep cobalt blue on the floors, brightening to azure walls as the stones rise until it meets the whitewashed ceiling.

I might find the gradient style pleasing if Deianira gave us a chance to appreciate it, but she directs us past each hallway at a breakneck speed. The circuitous hallways are a reminder of the Labyrinth below us, except the layout of the Palace is akin to a rabbit's warren, interconnected pathways with many openings and back exits. The Labyrinth has only one entrance.

I'm the only one winded on the trek and I struggle to hide it. I'm also the only one not awed by the sights we pass. But that isn't because my home is as pleasing—I'm not so delusional to think my home could compete with a Palace—but because each step brings me towards something I'm not prepared for. If not for the ramblings of supposed seer implying there was a way to stop the Collection, I might have slipped down a distant hallway and ran far away. If not for my commitment to this path, I might remind the King of my status and ask for an exception.

The confusion building from our winding march must show on my face, though I could swear my mask was in place. But when we ascend the stairs to the fourth floor, Dolion slows to walk beside me. When we make it to the top, his hand lands on my low back as if he's delivering me in the correct direction.

"You'll meet with the King first," he whispers. "Then you'll be inspected, and your time will be your own until things begin tomorrow."

I shuffle away from his touch, excusing it as attempting to catch my breath. But I'll need to gather allies where I can find them, and my behavior has done little to aid me. I offer him a small smile, one that barely lifts my lips.

"Thank you," I murmur. "What is the inspection?"

Diomede, who had already crossed the hallway, slides beside me. "They will inspect our health and confirm we didn't bring any contraband that might make our meeting unfair."

I purse my lips. That explains the club, which Dolion must have stashed when we entered the Palace. But that meeting the Beast unarmed is somehow *fair* creates an angry heat in my stomach. Only Hades has ever demanded true fairness from mortals, as each soul has an equal chance in his realm. It wouldn't surprise me if Poseidon's version of fairness was askew.

"You'll also be outfitted with the proper dress," Dolion says as we turn another corner.

Thyia joins our little huddle. "If only they'd let us prepare for our introduction," she says, pouting and holding onto the limp locks at her collarbones, ones that this morning were full and curled.

"It shouldn't matter," Chrysa says blithely from in front of us. "We look better now than we will as corpses."

Diomede gasps. "Chrysa!"

Finally, our long walk ends at a statue-filled hallway with two guards flanking large wooden doors, which are thrown open when Deianira's soft footsteps land on the carpet leading to them.

Now I'll get my first look at King Minos and the risk I've forced upon myself.

Chapter 10

The doors open into a massive meeting room covered in stark white stone. The ceiling, painted with celestial motifs, gives the illusion of an infinite expanse overhead. At the center sits a colossal ebony throne with arms that end in claw-like grips. A canopy of deep purple silk, embroidered with silver thread, cascades from the ceiling above it. A man sits atop the throne, shirtless like the guards, displaying thick muscles and long golden hair that looks like it's twinkling in the dim light, a braided coil that trails down his chest and lands in his lap. It must be King Minos, who resembles one of the many statues on the first floor, hard and cold, but in color rather than white marble. An oversized pin rests at his hip, displaying the Labyrinthian symbol of Crete in gold. The torches that line the walls cast flickering shadows that dance ominously across the room, landing on the King, who stares down at us, as if cataloging our very souls.

His gray eyes drag over us as we parade inside, and they appear to rest longest on me. I may not look stately now, but as Father always said: poise comes from within. Still, I raise my chin and angle my left shoulder forward to better display my shoulder clip. Deianira slinks across the room, inclining her head in a mocking bow before moving to stand on the King's right.

Guards slam the door behind us and corral us closer to the center of the vast room. There's no question about kneeling this time, and I'm among the first to fall to my knees.

After a minute of silence, the sharp expression melts off King Minos' face. "Good afternoon, dear girls. I have heard the distress you suffered while at sea and I am thankful to Poseidon and his brothers that you are here unharmed and prepared to meet He who lives at the center of the Labyrinth."

He who lives at the center is an unusual way to describe the Beast. I glance at Diomede to my left to see if she also finds his statement oddly worded, but she doesn't react. The King snaps his fingers and a short man with a shaved head scurries out from one corner behind us, appearing like a ghost against the white walls and in his white robes. He introduces each of us, starting in the order in which the ship picked us up. When the bald man comes to my name, he pauses for a fraction of a second. His gaze dart towards the King, or perhaps to Deianira, before he stutters through my introduction.

"Finally, coming to us from the Isle of Standia, Thalia, child of Galenus, Governor of Standia, first in line."

I don't lift from my knees but raise my head.

"Are you an heir, child?" The King's voice has a smooth quality to it, not soft like silk but slimy like oil.

"I am, Your Majesty," I demure.

Deianira shuffles beside her father, derision in her gaze.

Minos leans forward. "And you are the youngest daughter of Governor Galenus?"

"I am," I repeat, swallowing the lump that forms at the thought. "I am his only daughter."

He stares for a moment longer, before smiling and straightening his back. As someone who has spent nearly her whole life hiding behind masks and reading the expressions of others, I can see the cracks in it, a slipperiness he can't hide.

"You must be tired, girls," he says with a smarmy smile. "But before I release you and you begin that which you were Collected for, we must address certain formalities you will be required to follow. After all, without the rules of sport, we are no better than the beasts."

Deianira laughs as if he's made a great joke and the others in the King's employ join in. He lifts his hand, and all sounds cease.

"You will be inspected. This is for your own safety and the safety of my people." He looks at me when he continues. "Although I have no reason to believe there are any conspiracies to overthrow my reign or harm my citizens, we must confirm that you are not a danger to my people, personally or politically." He snaps his hands and two willowy women in white robes with billowing sleeves and long skirts appear from somewhere behind him. They look identical, but only in how strikingly beautiful people do, that hint of knowledge and confidence behind their driftwood-colored eyes. One's face is more angular and wears her dark hair loose while the other's skin is more olive and has her hair bunched high on her head.

"Kyra and Kynna will be your caretakers while you are present in my Palace. They will also undertake your inspections."

Dolion clears his throat from behind us and Deianira steps forward. "Father," she begins, "given the constant odd number of girls, I thought, starting with this Collection, we should have three caretakers. Such a change would allow Kyra and Kynna to—"

Minos indolently waves of hand. "I have no concerns with your suggestion, daughter. You will arrange it."

She bats her eyes almost aggressively. "I have, Father. I'm not sure if you recall Dolion, son of Cleades. I would recommend him as a caretaker."

King Minos purses his lips and stares at Dolion with the same intensity he gave me not moments before. Finally, he nods.

"Very well, see to the inspections with Kyra and Kynna." Minos directs his attention back to us. "They will show you to your rooms and provide you a meal. You're dismissed."

The girls all stand and Dolion moves to my side. His hand slides to my low back yet again. Only the King's presence keeps me from elbowing him.

The assistant squeaks audibly and scurries to the other side of the King and whispers in one ear. Minos frowns before thrusting his hand out towards the assistant, who whimpers and scampers back to his corner.

"My Minister has reminded me that I have yet to explain your task during this Collection. You'll forgive me," he says idly. "Each Collection runs together, while my focus must remain directed on my kingdom's needs."

Dolion's hand clenches the robe against my back, his fingernails like claws.

"You will remain here for seven days, with your last day culminating in your purpose here. You are to traverse the Labyrinth, find the center, and meet He who lives within. What happens after you meet him is within your capabilities to manage," Minos says, splaying his hands outward.

My heart thumps loud in my chest. *Seven days.* I only have seven days to break or fulfill the bargain and tell Poseidon of the deception.

Minos continues, "As your fair and benevolent King, I would not force you to meet him without first providing you the opportunity to *find* him. Thus, you will have three chances to study the Labyrinth. Outside of those three runs, your time is your own. You are welcome to any corner of my Palace. The city is also open to you, as are our magazines and even our coffers. As further proof of my generosity, you will also attend the Festival of Poseidon in the coming days. The only limitation upon you is that you may not enter the west wing on the fourth floor." He claps once. "You're dismissed."

Kyra and Kynna flutter forward and direct us outside the throne room. But this is my first chance to discover the existence of the bargain and how the Collection relates and whether I can break it. I've already learned there's something important about the west wing, but the vagueness as to what we can or should do after we meet the Beast pricks at my skin. Perhaps King

Minos is simply avoiding harsh words, not wanting to upset us by discussing the probable outcomes, most of which are surely dismemberment, destruction, and death. But the warrior king I've read about, and the man who sat ramrod straight with eyes that burned... he is not someone who would shy away from discussing a grim fate to avoid our *discomfort*.

I linger near the threshold of the door with Dolion, who apparently refuses to step foot outside the room without me.

My delay bears fruit, as a snapping of fingers sounds just as my feet breach the door frame. Dolion stiffens, yanking on the back of my robes to keep me from entering the hallway, ignorant of my intention and plan.

The few inhabitants of the throne room have vanished, except for Deianira who stands cross-armed beside her father and the bald minister. I quickly dip into another curtsy.

"I find myself intrigued that a woman of your—" Minos pauses and tilts his head, his blond braid tipping to the floor. "That a woman of your position would be... chosen for my Collection. I thought the children of the Island Governors spent their time on other pursuits."

"That's correct, Your Majesty. Though I believe even the youngest daughters of our Councilors studied weaponry and defense. As the heir, I did not." I drop my eyes to the ground to appear conciliatory. If Poseidon expects King Minos to eliminate the Beast, one of the Collection being unprepared to do so could disrupt his plans. "I hope my lack of knowledge on those subjects will not limit me here."

Deianira scoffs. "It *should*."

But... something in her tone tells me it won't. *Interesting.*

Minos leans forward. "Tell me, child, which of my comrades was the patron of your Island?"

"Athena," I say proudly.

"Goddess of Wisdom and War," he says, sneering.

"And handicrafts, Your Highness" the minister adds, his voice trembling. "And...one who is of horses and ships."

A silent conversation occurs between them, charged with a dark intensity. Poseidon is the God of horses, but Athena only invented ways to harness them. And though she taught ship-building and navigation, she isn't a Goddess of water. My lips thin in confusion. It isn't as though Athena could be compared to the King's patron, Poseidon.

"If this is to be a fair Collection, perhaps I might lessen my limitations through some study," I suggest.

Shadows lengthen on the walls as Minos stares again, that blistering gaze back. "I will consider any... limitations you may have and how to... fairly... reduce them. What a pity they selected you amongst the many, and now find yourself... inadequate."

Mindful of Hecaline's warning, I don't place an illusion to hide my annoyance. Instead, I mimic Father's smile when one of the older Councilors says something obviously dim. "Though there were only four other prospective candidates, Your Majesty, I volunteered."

Everything stops. Every sound, every movement: gone. Even the flickering candlelight appears to freeze.

"You... you volunteered." Deianira says, her hand clenching at the gaping fabric of her neckline.

Minos shoots her a harsh look before giving me that same oily smile again. "What a treasure you are. Rarely do we have volunteers, rarer still that they put themselves in a situation without the appropriate context."

"She wished to save her friend, Your Majesty," Dolion explains from my side, speaking through clenched teeth.

Minos leans forward, his long gray braid on coiling from its place in his lap and falling to the floor. "Tell me, child, what do you expect to meet in the center of the Labyrinth?

I blink, unsure of the relevance or if this is my first test. "The Beast, sir."

Minos leans back, replacing his hands on the side of his throne, repositioning himself into the statue he resembled when we first entered. "One of the spirit-born of Athena, coming here without the proper preparation, and doing it with benevolence in mind. I have much to consider, Thalia, child of Galenus, heir to the Governor of Standia. You are dismissed."

Before I can bow again, Dolion grabs my forearm and wrenches us both out of the room. He drags us through the winding hallways and down the stairs as if we're being chased. My thoughts swirl, his firm grip on me the only thing keeping me from tripping. The King's reaction already provided me with my first clue: whatever Minos bargained about the Beast, warrior skills aren't required. *If not to kill it, what else could the King need to do with the Beast?*

Dolion slows when we arrive on the second floor, stopping us near a door half hidden by a tapestry. The stone around the doorframe is a pale blue that matches his eyes, with a double-sided triangle crudely etched into the surface. After checking the hallway, he opens the door, and I traipse inside before he can push me.

It appears to be a storage room, wooden stools and chairs piled up near the back wall and several musty smelling rags laying on the floor. I could cross the space in four steps, and I do, selecting two unbroken stools and placing them in the center of the small room. This isn't my inspection, that much is clear, but the weight of Minos' gaze on Dolion, and his own reaction to what was said, tell me he is no supporter of the King or his Collection. I may have found my first ally.

I sit on the stool and motion to the free one. Dolion doesn't move, but studies me with crossed arms.

"Is something wrong?" I ask mildly.

"Not yet. Though your admission that you are only skilled in politics may make things more complicated."

Even though my quest will never provide me Minos' approval, and the history of the Collection makes me uninterested in having it, old insecurities—that I need to be a perfect heir—bubble in my stomach. "I never said I was *only* skilled in politics, but that I had no weapons or similar training."

"And you had to remind him you were descended from Athena!" He stomps to the opposite stool and sits with a loud thud. "If we're lucky, his god-sized arrogance will intercede, and he'll forget you're anything other than a normal Collected. Honestly, you'd think with your prior mute act, you'd not reveal information like that."

I ignore the implied insult. "It's true, then? The Collected women don't *need* to have only studied aggressive fields?"

He scratches his neck with his index finger. "I can't explain. But—" His teeth clench and the veins pop out in his neck. "It... may be a benefit," he forces out, cheeks red with exertion.

The geas. Unthinking, I grab his wrist, like I would have with Lukas, and squeeze. "I understand. Don't hurt yourself."

He coughs twice, his eyes wet as the pain drifts from his face. Nodding, he attempts to interlock our hands, but I pull mine back to my lap. The corner of his lips rises slowly. "I think we'll become good friends, Thalia."

"I'll only be here for seven days," I remind him. If I'm lucky, on day seven I can take his ship back to Standia, flush with the success of stopping the Collection.

He nods. "Yes. Only seven days. Then, we've no time to wait. As your caretaker, I suppose I must begin your inspection."

I take in the room's mess and raise my brows at him.

"Don't go silent on me now, Hero."

I roll my eyes and gesture around the room. "Is this the traditional location for the inspection?"

"I've never done one myself, though I know what is supposed to occur." The smirk drops in what can only be remembered pain.

After his reunion with Deianira, I assumed Dolion was Cretan. But perhaps he's from an Island and knew someone who went through the Collection. "Did you—"

"Traditionally, the inspection is done naked." Dolion's smile reappears as I blink in surprise. "What a lovely blush you have, much prettier than that constipated look you've been showing everyone else."

I stand, knocking over the stool and begin unfolding the sides of my chiton under my arms. I ease the silver pin from my shoulder and toss it on the floor. If Dolion thinks he can shock me into giving something away, he'll learn otherwise.

Now it's his turn to blink in surprise. The skin of my side is uncovered before he stands and puts his hands over mine, stopping my continued undressing. His hands are warm, the tips of his fingers grazing the side of my ribs. He stares at me with an unreadable expression.

"If you're to bare yourself to me, I'd prefer it in a more comfortable location."

I lift my chin. "This is the only circumstance where I'll bare myself to you."

A grin unfurls on his lips as his fingers twitch against my skin. "I suppose we can forgo the inspection then. Except—" His hands slide under my robe, dragging lower. My breath catches. Twice in as many days is a man touching me, after twenty-two years of nothing. A pity I might be dead in seven days and unable to decide whether I like it and want more.

The pads of his fingers are rough and catch on the softness of my skin. I open my mouth to stop him, shout at him, *encourage* him, when he hits his target. One hand slides the dagger from its holster around my waist while the other squeezes my thick hips. As quickly as it began, he withdraws.

He inspects the dagger, taking in the design on the hilt and the sharp tip. I prepare my arguments for why I need it and that he can't take it.

But he doesn't. Instead, he brandishes the dagger and reaches behind me to grab my hair. He fists it in his hand, wrenching my neck backward. There's that smirk on his lips again, but I'm not afraid. Not when he still stands close enough for me to feel how much he enjoys my proximity.

In a flash, quicker than I could have escaped him, the knife strikes, slicing behind me until he holds a long knot of my dark hair. My hands fly to my neck, the locks brushing my collarbones.

Dolion pulls a ribbon from somewhere within his robes and ties it around my cut hair, the wild waves uncooperative and sliding to the floor. Before I can think to stop him, he slips a bundle of my cut locks inside his robes.

"King's requirement," he says as he turns his attention back to me, where I still stand touching the now short strands. "No one can have hair of any longer length."

"Why?"

"Another thing I can't explain, but you should take care to remember it," he says. He brandishes the dagger. "Do you know how to use this?"

My brows raise. He did just imply the skill was unnecessary. "Are you offering to show me?"

"No," he says before presenting the dagger, hilt first. "I will replace it in the holster, if you'd like."

I snatch it and return it to its holster at my back, rearranging my robe to cover my bared skin.

"It was worth a try." Dolion purses his lips, oddly serious given his recent jokes. "Will you tell me what magic you received from Athena?"

"I thought that information was to be protected."

He shrugs. "Not from me."

I cross my arms about my chest and scowl. "And why should you be special?"

He leans in so close that my eyes cross when I try to focus on his face. "Because I'm your best bet at succeeding in seven days." He doesn't let me react, stalking the two steps to the door and throwing it open. "If anyone asks, you had a complete inspection, and I was a complete gentleman as a caretaker."

An uncomfortable snort bubbles out of me. I'm not sure either of those is true.

Dolion drops me off at the first door in a small offshoot hallway on the first floor, dragging me through the hallways as though we're being chased by something. It's only when he's about to leave that I grab the edge of his robe and hold him in place.

"I'd like to read. There are things I wish to study, texts that Standia may not have."

He examines me with an intensity I've only seen from Lukas, and only during our last goodbye. Heat coils in my stomach and trails up to my cheeks, threatening to burn me until he speaks and I drown it. He finally says, "The only public library is on the fourth floor, near the statue of Minos and the shark spirit."

And then he's gone, disappearing behind a corner.

The hallway where he left me has four doors, two on each side. Inside my room are two small beds, thin pallets raised a few inches off the floor with wooden frames and knobby linen sheets. A bland wooden wardrobe stands against one stone wall. It appears to have only the essentials for our time here—a few plain chitons and shifts and an extra pair of shoes for each of us. Two wooden stools sit near a small shelf carved into the wall that holds a single candle. Chrysa sits on one bed, staring at her hands. When she notices me, she rolls her eyes.

"They put the misfits together, of course."

After noting where my bed will be, I return to the hallway.

"Not wanting to slum it, Thalia? I'm better than the floor in some hallway at least," she calls towards my back as the door closes.

I ignore her. I've a library to find.

I find the library after an hour of searching, getting lost twice and ending up on a different floor than I intended only once. I'd assumed finding the fourth floor meant I needed to keep going up each flight of stairs I found, but I hit many blockades and stone walls, hallways that backtracked and twisted, until I couldn't be sure what level I was on.

By the time I drag the heavy door open, my stomach is growling from skipping dinner. But this is my first opportunity to check if there are any records about the bargain; food is a secondary concern.

Except, when I ignite the lights, there's almost nothing there. No magnificent and world-renowned library greets me, not what I'd expect from a Palace. The room is smaller than my family's library, with a dozen shelves spanning the length of the walls, hitting the ceiling that is only a few feet above my head. Instead of the dizzying height of the throne room on the same floor, it's petite and quaint, a single paned window revealing the mountain behind the Palace.

Though I begin my search, my stomach, and hopes, sink to the floor.

It takes hours, but much shorter than it should, had the library been what I was hoping for. In the end, I find two books that I don't already have. Two to hinge my life on.

The moon is high in the small window when I sit at the desk near the entrance and light another match to review my quarry.

The first book, a tome on Crete's military history, I skim, but nothing relevant jumps out at me. There is a map of the exterior Palace, which would only be helpful should I decide to flee. The second is a historical account of the deeds of various Gods. The compilation isn't one we have at home, but some stories are the same. Minos isn't included anywhere within the history. Only one story is even about Poseidon, an account of one of his consorts, Gaia, and that one of his titles was Husband of the Earth.

The Divine Mother is Kingmaker. It is through her blessing that her celestial issue hold power. Although her will was denied once, the Moirai confirm her chosen will once again rule over her body. But her patience is not unboundless and her child of the sea must inherit before she takes action.

I close my eyes to revisit my own studies, and memories of the Gods. The Moirai—the Goddesses of Fates and more of Nyx' children, who are tasked to make sure every being, mortal and divine, live out their predetermined destinies. And Gaia is speculated to be Poseidon's aunt, though never confirmed. I'd hope it hasn't been, if he had children with her. But nearly all of Poseidon's children are half-mortal and Cretan, as all have his blood running through their veins. Only a few are pure Gods, children begat by other Titans and Olympians. None of his Cretan children were born of Gaia as Mother Earth. *Unless Mother Earth is a metaphor for children born in this realm by the Sea God?* So perhaps any of his children could inherit, or any Cretan specifically.

But none of them are Minos. Meaning Minos will not hold his kingdom long, not when the Fates decree otherwise.

I consider the implications. Perhaps that was the bargain he struck, that *he* could be King and Poseidon is holding Gaia at bay? But how does the Collection relate, and who else did Poseidon give it to? And what children of Poseidon are children of Mother Earth?

I press my palms to my eyes until lights flash behind my closed lids. All the story does is give me more questions and my brain feels thick and honey slow. With effort, I replace the book and shuffle out of the library with my head hung low.

I retrace the four turns I used to get from the stairs but find myself in an unfamiliar and dark hallway. I continue down it, sure something recognizable will pop up, but the only thing that draws my eye is another double-sided triangle scratched into the azure blue tile. That it occurs twice in two separate areas of the Palace makes me pause.

A sound echoes behind me. I spin towards it, but I'm alone in the hallway. The sound repeats, a low muttering that must come from one of the rooms. I tiptoe down the hall until I come to a door that was left open, a sliver of light seeping into the empty hallway.

Shadows flicker against the light, and King Minos appears in the crack. He stalks around a seated figure, his braid scraping the marble floor under his feet. The figure looks as though they would dominate a room, tall and hulking with skin that looks mottled in the light, a prismatic array of metallic colors. Long black hair rests against the back of the chair, trailing to their waist.

"The time has come, yet again," Minos says, continuing his circular inspection of the figure. "Another opportunity that will end in another slaughter."

I wince at the confirmation. The figure does too, their head ducking.

"I wish things could be different," the figure says, a deep masculine voice rumbling from their chest. I squint but can't guess who this potential ally might be, this person who sounds pained at our potential deaths.

Minos pauses in front of the chair and stares at the figure with a sneer. I place my illusion in case they can see me from the crack. Minos falters, his beady eyes staring to the side as if someone is whispering in his ear. He must have an alert to magic. With an internal curse, I drop the illusion, and crouch on the ground, as out of sight as I can get without an illusion protecting me.

Minos refocuses on the figure. "One would assume after four hundred years, we could give up, after proving Poseidon's demand will never be met. At some point we will run out of women. Will *that* be enough for Poseidon's bargain?"

Anger blazes in the King's eyes, though it dimmed when he spoke of the women. For them, he sounded bored, like their continued deaths is an insignificant consequence, that it is *he* who is most affected by the bargain not culminating, whatever it may be. Rage licks at my skin like lava from Mount Ida, ready to erupt all over that room and the King who believes our deaths are inconsequential when weighed against his inconvenience. But that fury doesn't blind me, it focuses my intention like an aimed arrow: There *is* a bargain, he's confirmed it! If Minos explains what Poseidon's demand is and I learn of the breach, I will target his heart with it.

"The debt must be paid," the figure whispers. I must strain to hear them now.

"You think that fact escapes me?" Spittle bursts from the King's lips as he snarls. "I understand debt far more than you ever will."

The figure inclines their head again. "I meant no disrespect, Your Highness. With success necessary for us both, if the current plan is not working, perhaps we can change something. We could make the location more neutral, like one of the empty banquet halls. Or the Collected could be introduced much earlier, making it more likely that—"

"You've given this much thought," Minos says, cutting them off. His anger hasn't vanished but returned to a simmer, the heat behind his eyes searing in intensity.

"I have nothing but time between the Collections." They say it without seeking pity or praise. "Considering all avenues of the event and preparing for the meeting is my only occupation."

I wonder if he's the Keeper of the Labyrinth, or the Beast's master. No wonder he regrets the death of the Collected, if he must care for the monster that kills us.

Minos leans over the figure. The menace in his expression might cower another, but the figure tilts their neck back to stare into Minos' glower. "I am charged with ensuring the fairness of the event, and I have done so. Your proposals are unwarranted and would do nothing but create disorder, destroying any chance for success. After all, no matter where the girls are, no matter when it takes place, their fear will remain. Nothing will eliminate their horror."

My heart drops into my stomach, imagining meeting the Beast and what it might try to do to me if only terror awaits. The figure sits as still as a specter, no doubt imagining the same chaos that has led so many to their deaths.

"I understand," they say, ducking their head. "But the day is long and as you said, there is much to do to prepare for this latest opportunity. What need do you have of me now?"

Minos hisses a breath through clenched teeth. Then, he snaps his fingers, and another man comes into view holding a pair of scissors. "Nothing too demanding. It is simply time for your haircut."

Chapter 11

We begin our first full morning in Knossos by traveling down a weighted elevator near the back of the Palace. The elevator is nothing more than a platform resting in the air, with a long braided strand of flickering golden-white rope looped around it. The elevator creaks and rumbles as it descends deep underground. Mina holds one of Chrysa's hands while Thyia holds the other and leans against Diomede. The tiniest bit of envy at their immediate friendship curls through my stomach, but I swallow it in favor of remembering my purpose. I'm here for a reason, not to make friends.

They outfitted us with new-to-us chitons and our caretakers helped arrange the fabric in folds around our bodies and shoulders in the Cretan style. Dolion helped position mine, hiding my holstered dagger at the small of my back again and replacing my silver owl pin with one of the generic clasps all the girls wear. The high neck of mine needed to be cut to account for my chest and shoulders. The fabric slits flap against my skin but I hold my head high as though I wasn't squashed into a chiton tunic I will never fit. I'm pointedly ignoring the possible metaphor for my presence here.

The elevator continues its plummet into the earth as the air turns stale and the light fades. Soon, the shaft descends into total darkness. I shuffle closer to Dolion for protection from falling off and getting wedged between the concrete wall and the platform.

The rumbling ends when the platform lands at the base of the tall shaft, made more frightening by the darkness enclosing us, as if we've been sealed in a door. The caretakers shuffle us from the elevator platform as hanging candle wicks explode into light, taking us into a small room ahead.

Even Elara appears wary of the place we've been taken. In the flickering candlelight, it looks like the entrance to a temple, with symbols etched into the aged limestone. The double-sided triangle is there, along with a bull and waves. On the opposite wall are the seven symbols of the Islands—a rose, a spear, a moon, an owl, a hammer, a lyre, a laurel wreath—and the eighth, a maze, for Crete. It's a comfort no blood stains the floor, given what we can guess happens within the snaking passages of the Labyrinth. It's another comfort that I don't recognize the smell of death and can't connect the musty scent to murder and madness.

This is to be a perfect simulacrum of our future Labyrinth run, except the Beast is caged somewhere else. When we've all stared at the three walls long enough to memorize the symbols, Kynna whistles and the stone door before us rattles open. Elara is gone down the center passage ahead before the stone makes its full ascent, with Eriphyle following behind her. They both shudder the moment their feet touch the Labyrinth's stone floors, from the smell or fear or something else entirely.

"What's stopping us from remaining in the antechamber the entire time?" Thyia asks as the other three girls peer into the shadowy halls.

Kyra points to the threshold where the stone door once sat. "There is magic within. As soon as you cross the line, you cannot return until we call for you."

Chrysa turns from her inspection of the left passage, taking care not to let her feet touch the threshold. "That's once we start. What if we stay here?"

Kyra lifts one shoulder in an elegant shrug. "There is magic here too, a second geas boundary that will force your tongue down your throat. If you cross the boundary, it will reverse. If you don't, you'll swallow your tongue and die of starvation. It is your choice."

My eyes fall shut. *Some choice.* That the King's borrowed magic can prohibit someone from speaking and bring unspeakable pain means the entire Palace is more dangerous than I first imagined, with potential geas boundaries anywhere.

"I thought the Cretans didn't have any magic. That's what Perry said," says Mina perplexed.

"The Gods have much magic," Diomede says. "Their power and might is why we bow to them."

Chrysa rolls her eyes. "Gods do. Cretans aren't Gods, just related to them. Only the spirit-born have magic."

Mina nods. "Oh. Like Thalia." She peers over at me. "Does that mean you have magic, like my Governor? That doesn't seem fair when we're competing against you."

I stay quiet, unwilling to admit that my family *does*, though casting illusions won't help. With what I know of Minos, making myself appear fearless, or even invisible and hiding in the Labyrinth from the Beast won't work for long. No doubt a geas will grab hold of my ankle and capture me.

Chrysa snorts and is probably about to say something cutting when Kyra claps. "This magic is ancient, sacrificed by the blood of satyrs and centaurs," Kyra says. "You cannot escape it. Your time has begun, Collected. Only a minute remains before you will lose your tongue."

All but Diomede appear ready to ask more questions, though I feel squeamish myself. Dolion's earlier comment and Hecaline's description, that the walls are painted with blood, suddenly make terrifying sense. If Minos would sacrifice magical creatures without hesitation, no wonder our lives are meaningless to him.

Both Kynna and Kyra make throat cutting gestures to ward off any more discussion. The girls wander into the Labyrinth in pairs, Diomede and Thyia flank each other towards the left, and Mina and Chrysa hold hands as they chase the stagnant air towards the right. Like Elara and Eriphyle, they all tremble when they cross the threshold. Both pairs soon turn opposite corners and vanish from sight.

Kyra and Kynna return in unison to the elevator platform. Dolion stares at the three entrances by my side, something bitter growing in his pale eyes.

"How long do we have?" I ask. He drags his gaze from the dark entrance.

"A few hours, I imagine." He attempts a grin. "You need enough time to find the center and—" he coughs. "And try to get out."

I almost take my first step into the center passage, but stop myself, curiosity bubbling up where bravery should be. "Did you know someone who ran it?"

The insincere smile falls from his mouth. "I'm not from the Islands."

"That doesn't mean you didn't know one of the Collected."

"I—" He stops himself, and I imagine he won't tell me, or the geas prevents him. But then, he speaks again, in a low voice. "My mother died of illness fifteen years ago, and my father faded soon after, leaving me penniless and an orphan. I booked passage on a ship, not caring where it took me, ready to leave everything of my past life behind." A faint glimmer of joy flickers in his eyes. "I ended up in Avgo and met a girl."

"And she was Collected."

"I wanted her to win," he murmurs. "Even if it meant—" He flinches. "I took a job with Perry to stay closer to her, to say goodbye, and have remained working for Perry ever since."

Another person torn to pieces by the Collection. I rest my hand on his tense forearm, which unclenches at my touch. "Why did you leave the ship?"

He stares at where our bodies connect before snapping his gaze back to me. Calculation, not pain, fills his expression now but what he says is nothing more than a joke. "I'd heard there was a Hero on board."

I swallow a smarmy retort and instead roll my eyes. He huffs a laugh, and we step away from each other.

"The timer's running, Hero. Most of them don't care if you swallow your tongue, but I'd miss your banter, no matter how limited it is," he says, crossing his arms around his bare chest and smirking.

My throat doesn't yet feel the consequences of failing to take that first step, but I can't hide forever. Not if I'm to prove myself.

"I would hate to disappoint you." I adjust my posture, adding scant height to my frame and firmly affixing a still mask over my expression.

"So, my opinion *does* have value?" he calls to my back as I take one tentative step over the threshold.

I don't linger to answer, instead I stroll through the opening with feigned confidence. Nothing changes when I cross, no phantom wind or spectral fingers trailing down my back to make me shiver. If not for the long hallway in front of me, I could still be standing in the antechamber.

Dolion raises his eyebrows as I turn and inspect the threshold but he does nothing to distract my scrutiny. I raise my hands into the space where the stone door would be. A light buzzing stings my fingers, the same feeling the air has just before lightning strikes. It must be the magic, but had I not sought it myself, I'd never have noticed its presence. I've never felt foreign magic before, only seen it, and then, only my family's versions.

After rubbing the prickling feeling and my nervous fingers on the front of my tunic, I start down the center entrance, my feet touching the scuffed brick floors.

Within minutes, I'm lost. First, I ran like the other girls, but soon had no breath, and heaved myself around corners and through never ending passages. Out of spite, I will give no credit to Lyra, but her melodramatic description of the Labyrinth proved true. It is vast and unfathomable, a boundless braid of passages and doorways.

I don't find the center by the time a sharp whistle trills three times, which must be the cue to return to the antechamber. But that's easier said than done. Though I didn't find the center, I wound myself somewhere within the maze and can only find my way out by sound. The fetid air is dry; there is no draft to guide me back to the beginning.

But Kynna keeps whistling, each trill lengthening as a beacon. And each beacon feels like a shriek of failure. The Labyrinth is nothing more than a maze, a puzzle, but I couldn't find my way to the center.

Six turns later and I find Diomede and Thyia, who also didn't make it to the center. Together, we stumble our way back to the front, no doubt taking just as long as the time we had for the original practice. Without clocks marking our time, we'll never know how long we remained lost within.

Elara and Eriphyle have already returned when we cross the stone threshold towards the platform.

"Did either of you find the center?" Diomede asks.

Elara ignores the question, but Eriphyle nods and answers. "Yes, though only just when the whistle—"

Elara elbows her in the ribs, cutting off Eriphyle's confession. She juts out her chin. "I know I'll enter the center quicker next time, now that I know the way."

"But we didn't mark the route," Eriphyle says, puzzled. Elara elbows her again and Eriphyle pinches her lips closed.

"Why wouldn't they release us inside the center, instead of forcing us to spend energy in finding it first?" Thyia pouts as she speaks, but her question is sound. Dolion looks amused.

"To wear us out," Elara says, as if it's obvious. "Then only the best can make it to the center and engage the Beast."

Mina and Chrysa clamber out of the left entrance, chest heaving with exertion.

"We found the center," Chrysa says. She and Mina hold each other up. "We got distracted trying to come back."

Elara stiffens. "Before or after the whistle?"

"Before," says Mina, wrinkling her nose. "Was that bad?" She searches for the caretakers. "Should we not want to get there fast?"

Elara looks as though she swallowed something sour. Inside, I might look similar, since all four solved the puzzle I didn't. Although I assumed I would find it too, Mina and Chrysa locating it fast shouldn't be a surprise. Perhaps Elara's forgotten that Mina grew up on Paximada, the Island founded by Artemis, Goddess of the hunt, or that Chrysa came from Karavi, created by Hermes, the God of travel and speed. They aren't spirit-born, but their Islands would leave a mark on their upbringings.

"It won't be as easy when the Beast is chasing you the minute you enter the center," Elara finally says, balling her fists on her hips.

"I thought the point was to kill it so it couldn't chase you around the Labyrinth," Thyia says.

"And that wasn't easy," Chrysa says, groaning dramatically, making Mina giggle beside her. "Beginning with the uncomfortable prickles when we entered all the way to the rotten smell in the center."

"If the point is for one of us to kill the Beast, they should drop us all somewhere else," Mina adds.

"That's what *I* said," Thyia mutters.

Dolion strokes his throat. "No one ever said it wouldn't be hard. What matters is whether it is fair."

The girls all shuffle in place. Only Mina asks, "Who decides if it is fair?"

"Hades and Themis," Diomede says immediately. "They judge everyone."

But no one pays her any attention, too focused on the intensity in Dolion's stare as he turns to me and answers, "Exactly."

That night, I plan to intentionally find my way to the fourth floor. With no other public library, the only likely places for more information are somewhere *not* public. After my dismal showing in the Labyrinth and the magic binding us, death seems more likely than bargain breaking or fulfilling, especially when I don't know what the bargain even is. A game without knowing the shape of the board is a game I won't win.

I wait until the girls and caretakers leave for dinner. We aren't dining with the King or his court, but a cook let slip that we all eat at the same time. With everyone occupied at dinner, I can skulk into the west wing without many eyes watching me. I feign illness when Kyra comes to bring us to the dining chambers in the hall beside our rooms, claiming the exercise from earlier upset my stomach. I don't know whether to be relieved or insulted that they believe me without question.

I wander through multiple levels and hallways, the pathways uncomfortably similar to those in the Labyrinth, until I find myself in an area that feels similar to the one from last night. There's something humming in the air, magic perhaps. It might be the west wing, but the circuitous route I took to get there gives me little confidence. For all I know, I'm not even on the fourth floor. Even so, the minute I scale the final staircase, I take tentative steps in case the King placed a geas boundary like in the Labyrinth, holding my hands out hoping to feel the warning prickle of geas magic. I didn't walk through one last night, but with our schedule last night keeping us in our dorm area, he may not have set them until today.

Voices hum from behind me, guards no doubt. I tiptoe the opposite direction of the voices, hoping for a bout of wisdom that would tell me which door might hold a library, or at least which one can hide me. With each step, I risk passing a geas line, but at least that is a consequence I know. I could probably fashion a way to live without my tongue and sever the muscle from my mouth, but what the King might do to me if I'm caught is an unknown consequence.

After turning a corner, the voices rise in pitch. They're getting closer. I spin around the hallway, but each door looks the same, until candlelight reflects off scratched symbols beside the hinges of a door to my left. They are the same double-sided triangle design. With no time to decide whether the image was a harbinger of ill fortune, I slip through the door.

I'm just in time as voices echo and travel farther down the hallway. I lean against the door and let out a sigh, both at my escape and at my continued possession of all my body parts. The room I've found isn't the library I seek, but what looks to be a small study. A desk commands the space, leaving little room for any other furniture. But beside it, someone shoved a slim bookcase overloaded with books. The tomes spill off the shelves, sitting in precarious stacks on the desk and in piles on the floor. The only other furniture is a curved chair, which is also the only surface bare of books.

A smile blooms over my lips. I've no idea what I've found, but someone who enjoys collecting books is someone I'd willingly meet. I drag my fingers over the back of the chair as I lean closer to the mountains of books. One of them may be useful. There are so many, perhaps whoever they belong to wouldn't miss one or two.

Something shuffles behind the desk, and I freeze. In walks someone through a doorway I missed behind the bookshelf.

It's a tall humanoid shape wearing a black tunic that pulls against their muscular chest with no ornamental clasp over the shoulder, giving me no hints as to their position or affiliation in the Palace. The fabric trails snuggly over their arms, covering all but two long fingered and scarred hands. If they are a man, they're the first I've seen since arriving that isn't shirtless. And their kilt doesn't stop at the knee but hangs past their feet. They stand a head taller than me, but their face is shrouded in black gauze. In the dark, I'd never see them. In the dimly lit room, they look like a wingless and brawny Keres: a death-spirit ready to devour me and send me to my doom.

"Who are you?" they ask. Their voice is low and gravely, but no emotions color the tone.

There is no use running now, not with the guards behind me and the near-spectral figure in front. I square my shoulders, feigning confidence even as my neckline bulges more open from the run and I look nothing like a respectable heir. "I'm one of the Collected."

The figure remains as still as the spirit I imagine they are. The swath of fabric hides their face, a better and more permanent version of my mask. Theirs won't crack, as I can't read anything from their utterly motionless form. They give no clues as to whether they're enraged by my presence or bored of it.

Finally, they say, "I did not realize you had arrived in Crete already."

I nod. "Two days ago."

They look like a statue, standing still as the dead. "Two days, and you came to my study. But why are you in my study?"

I chance a half-truth. If this is an agent of the King, as I suspect everyone in the Palace may be, they can't know what I'm up to. "I was searching for something to read. The public library has nothing new."

They still don't move, but I catch their fingers flexing. Had I blinked, I would have missed it. *Spirits don't have skin*, I remember.

They leave the doorway, shifting forward as sleek as a predator, with a precision and evenness of movement that could only be explained by them rolling on wheels. Or floating. My eyes flick towards the floor but I can't see their feet.

"What do you wish to read?"

I swallow my initial statement of 'everything,' chastising myself for almost losing my chance to study one of these new books. *How I remained silent for years on Standia, but here I must catch myself from speaking is a mystery.* "I enjoy studying the histories, specifically around the Island Wars." Another half-truth, hopefully one revealing enough to get me the knowledge I seek.

Their arm shoots towards a book at the bottom of a stack on the desk. They extricate it with an economy of movement that keeps the pile from falling. No wisps of smoke pool from their scarred bronze hands, meaning they are no spirit. They hand me a tattered blue book, one that appears well loved. I hug it to my chest.

"Thank you." I hesitate before leaving. "May I know the name of the person providing me with my evening's entertainment?"

An exhale comes from under the black gauze. Silence seeps through the room for long enough that I assume they won't answer. Until- "Orion." Using the masculine suffix, he repeats in a silky voice, "My name is Orion."

I dip my head. "I'm Thalia. Thank you, Orion."

I turn to leave as he shuffles behind me. When I turn back, he is beside me, moving as quietly as a spirit. My heart rate quickens.

"Should you wish to read anything else during your next days," he says, raising a weathered key. He's careful not to touch my skin when he places the key in my open palm, but our fingers brush when I close mine around the key. His fingers are chilled and calloused but still a zing like lightning crackles where we touch, like magic. He inhales a breath and glides back through the doorway, leaving me alone in his study.

The key rests heavily in my hands, its spindle bronze and curving to a point that would fit into a keyhole. Designs decorate the shaft, with an inscription that's been half rubbed away. All I can make out is "Poseidon's glory." I shove the key between the folds of my chiton, slipping it under my twisted cord belt. Then I leave the mystery of Orion and his study behind.

Chapter 12

When I round the last corner in my journey, Dolion is leaning against the entrance to our shared hallway, blocking access to my room.

"I brought you something to sate your stomach," he says, brandishing a pomegranate.

I shoulder past him, but he slides backward to keep me from crossing to my door.

"Even heroes need to eat." He waves the pomegranate in front of my face.

It's ripe, the tart scent combining with an earthy perfume that makes my mouth water. That's what I get for skipping dinner.

I press the book tighter against my stomach, keeping the key in place. "Will you let me pass?"

"Not without the pomegranate," he says with a wink.

If not for Minos' eyes, I'd consider placing an illusion to avoid this encounter, but the easy banter makes me want to stay. It reminds me so much of Lukas, and a time when I was with my friend. "This had better not force me to stay with you for half a year," I say, holding in a smirk.

Hades had already stolen Persephone, else she might have made another Island. It was a story told to young girls on Standia, a warning about the trickiness of Gods. The teachers seemed to forget that Persephone was a Goddess herself, and none of them would catch a God's eye. Neither would I, of course, but our time should have been spent studying something more relevant than a morality tale. Persephone traveled to the Underworld through a cave, maybe teach us which one so we don't tumble through it. Or how to *escape* from a God or avoid one entirely. Maybe then none of us would be in this position.

Dolion's continued presence pulls me from my internal annoyance. He waggles his eyebrows. "Not *half* a year."

I smother a resigned laugh and snatch the fruit with my free hand. "Not even to win the Collection."

He laughs too, but it sounds strained. "If you won, not even—" he coughs and grasps his throat.

I almost drop the pomegranate to help him from falling to the ground. "That's three times in fewer days that you've almost activated the geas. You should stop," I tell him as I hold his forearm until he regains his breath. Only his eyes show the recent strain, pained tears gathering in the corners.

"I won't," he rasps.

I frown as he bends over, putting his hands on his knees. "Why not?"

He scowls up at me, his pale eyes narrowing. "This is our best chance in centuries. This is *my* chance. I've spent years letting my anger build while doing nothing of value, simply sowing dissension without a genuine chance, without hope. And now? I'll get my due, I'll finally—" He coughs.

"Don't—" I begin, reaching for him in case he almost falls again. But he shakes me off and rises.

"No, I must try." His hands pull at his scalp, dragging through the short hair there. "That's the point, Hero. I must try to bring this to a conclusion. Would you stop?"

The question catches me off guard. There's no confirmation we desire the same things, though his earnest declaration that he can help me succeed has battered through my brain like a storm. I'm only guessing that our interests align, that perhaps the desire for 'his due' demands revenge for the woman he lost, that the conclusion he seeks is an *end* to the Collection. Without a safe answer, I remain silent.

Dolion scrutinizes me for a tense minute. "I won't stop trying to help you. I wouldn't forgive myself if I lost this opportunity."

My eyes pinch shut for the count of five. I've no idea what I've done to earn his loyalty this fast. If I could figure it out, I'd attempt to replicate it with all those who didn't see me as the heir I knew I could be back in Standia.

"Fine," I say when I reopen my eyes. "At least be smart about it. There must be ways to tell me whatever it is you think I must know. Riddles, half-truths. You could write it."

He rubs his jaw. There's dark stubble that wasn't present this morning. It also looks like there's ash under his fingernails. "Can't write it. Can't even answer yes or no questions about it, if you thought of playing that game. But I'll think about it. Between the two of us, we can figure it out."

I offer him a strained smile. "Take your time, it isn't as though there's a deadline for my death, or anything altogether pressing."

He barks a sharp laugh. "You're funnier than I expected, for an heir. You should travel the Islands offering comedy performances. It might loosen you up more."

"Thanks," I say dryly as I gesture to my door behind him. "I'll think about it. Though, assuming I survive the Collection, it's unlikely a rival Island would welcome the heir to Standia with open arms." The treaties between us are tenuous at best. Only remaining under the banner of Minos' keeps one of the other Islands from becoming insurgent. My wandering family members can only visit those Islands under assumed names. If the Collection united us, halting it probably wouldn't tighten those relationships.

"If you succeed at the Collection, they'll have no choice. You'd be more than just Standia's heir, you'd be their—" He buckles at the waist to cough.

I scurry to his side again. "Was there a hint in there, before the geas took your voice?"

He blinks wet eyes at me before a corner of his lips tilts upward. "There was. That was unintended." He stands, pressing his palms to his eyes to wipe away the tears born of pain. When they're clear, he peers at me with an inscrutable expression. "Even just your presence has changed things in our favor."

Lifting a hand, he slides one of my curls behind my ear. My cheeks warm and I curse myself for letting him get a reaction from me. I bat his hand away. "Go think about another hint," I say, biting back a smile.

He bows low, overdramatically. "As you demand, my liege." He ducks down the hallway leading away from our rooms.

I watch him for a moment before sighing and shuffling into my room.

Chrysa looks up from where she sits on her bed, worn pieces of parchment covering her lap. She quickly gathers them and shoves them under her pillow.

I slip onto my bed and take a page from her book, hiding the key under my pillow. Setting the pomegranate aside, I open the blue book to the beginning, swallowing my curiosity at Dolion's motives. If he's willing to tell me things that Minos deems contraband, that can only help me.

"Are you going to eat that?" Chrysa asks. I toss her the fruit, which she catches one handed.

The book Orion gave me is another historical accounting of the Gods, but it appears to be focused on Poseidon, and not the Island Wars as I might have guessed. I run my hands over the worn spine and wave embossment found there. Lucky that Orion gave me this during my brief time in his study, rather than something on Zeus' lacking involvement in the Island Wars, or the like. Though given the inscription on the key and Minos' power, it might have been inevitability instead of luck.

A page near the back is bookmarked with a slip of parchment inscribed with that same double-sided triangle. Coincidences aren't truths, so I refuse to read anything into it yet.

That story starts out discussing Poisedon's heirs, most of whom I've heard of. The Olympic Brothers weren't known for abstinence or monogamy, meaning they all have dozens of half-god children. Most of their children with other gods created the Islands, meaning only a handful of full-godlike children remain living. Those that do are not to be trifled with, as they're incredibly powerful, being both long-lived and holding magic. My fingers trip over the list until I find Poseidon's name next to Gaia's, Mother Earth. I stutter out a surprised breath, remembering the book from yesterday. There is but one line, half stricken out, with only the letters "Bore" remaining. This could be the child that should rule. *Bore means winds, perhaps they blew away and that's why Poseidon backed Minos as King, but—*

Chrysa's voice interrupts my musings. "Are you and Dolion lovers?" She rips the pomegranate in half and tosses seeds into the air, catching half in her mouth. She doesn't look at me when she speaks, but her lips are curved upward with mischief.

A flush threatens to burn my cheeks, but years of practice keep my lips from thinning in irritation. "We just met."

She shrugs. "That doesn't matter."

"We're not," I say firmly. "Why would you think that?"

She bites a seed with her front teeth, spraying juice across the room. I curl over the book as she ticks off her fingers. "He wasn't at dinner, you weren't at dinner, you weren't in the room when I arrived, you both were speaking outside as if you walked together, he keeps watching you even when others are around, he only talks to you and you to him."

I blink away my surprise. Chrysa didn't strike me as that observant. "Coincidences. And we weren't together tonight."

She slumps, as if disappointed, before smirking again. "He wants to be yours though, I can tell."

I stare until she explains unprompted.

"Why else would he want to help you win the Collection and risk his tongue? He seems like the type that might want to use it."

Thin walls, it seems, if she's heard some of what he said outside the room. "Perhaps he intends to help all of us."

"Not Thyia," Chrysa says gleefully, dropping the pomegranate. "She asked him to join her for dinner and complained all through it that he wasn't there."

I reopen the book, now that there's no risk of pomegranate stains. "Thyia is sixteen, Dolion is at least in his thirties."

"Doesn't matter, we like who we like," Chrysa says, shrugging. "She didn't notice that you were gone too. Coincidences or not, I can't wait for her to make the connection. She might faint."

"That seems callous." And like something Elara might do to remove her competition.

"What's callous mean?"

I blink, reminded that Chrysa is a youngest daughter and all that it implies. "Cruel or insensitive."

She shrugs again and begins digging more seeds from the pomegranate, making a small red stained pile on her sheets. "No, it's funny, there's a difference." And as if she heard my thoughts on Elara, she continues, "If I wanted to be cruel, I'd tell Thyia before the next run so she fumbles the practice. But first I'd tell Deianira."

I forcefully shut the book. I won't get any reading done with Chrysa as my roommate. "Why would telling Deianira do anything?"

"Because she might slit your throat if she knew Dolion was flirting with you," she says giggling. "Or she'll make a servant do it," she amends.

I can't restrain the laugh that bubbles out of me. "Dolion is welcome to be attracted to who he likes, but she wouldn't believe he'd choose me over her, if she was interested in him."

"She's interested," Chrysa confirms. She picks through her bundle of seeds. "And I'd hope people can look past a person's exterior and choose based on heart, not body."

Her downcast eyes look heavy with remembered pain, something no sixteen-year-old deserves to feel. I'd like to tell her it doesn't matter, but beautiful people receive more. There's a reason Lukas didn't need to study hard in his policy sessions; there's a reason the Gods tossed Hephaestus into the sea before he joined his siblings in creating the Islands. I open my mouth to speak but can think of no comforting words.

But Chrysa doesn't stay mournful for long, shaking her short curls and smirking back at me. "Will you toss these seeds in my mouth and count how many I can catch?"

Chapter 13

An egg sits on a steel plate, not hard like a bird's but soft and malleable, like a snake's. The shell melts from within, fire bursting towards the sky. As a sprinkle of rain extinguishes the fire, a lily sprouts from the ashes.

I return to Orion's study the moment breakfast ends. The other girls scuttle off together to train, but I'm hoping I'll learn something from the other books, something that details Minos' bargain. When Chrysa slept last night, I finished Orion's book, but other than discovering just how many mortals the Gods slept with, I learned little else.

I try to retrace my steps unsuccessfully for twenty minutes. I'd turned so many corners to avoid the voices yesterday, it's impossible to follow my past path. Finally, I let myself meander, only ducking down new corridors to avoid the few roaming guards who would object to my presence on the fourth floor. It's only when I turn a corner or cross an intersection between two hallways that I tread with hands outstretched, still wary of geas boundaries. I also didn't chance any illusions, hoping to avoid Minos' interest. Best not die now when the Labyrinth may kill me in five days instead.

It's another half hour until I locate the door with two double-sided triangles above the hinges. When I drift inside the study, two chairs are placed on opposite sides of the desk, as if awaiting me.

There are at least two dozen books on the bookshelf that I've never read, but I intend to methodically run through them all from top to bottom.

After perusing an overly-enthusiastic biography of Minos—*born of Zeus and a mortal, gifted with 'illustrious golden tresses' comparable to none other*—Orion stalks through the doorway behind the bookshelf. He falters when he notices me, before appearing to fortify himself, as much as I can tell under the cloth costume, and sitting in the chair opposite.

"Good morning," I offer, focusing my gaze where I think his eyes must be.

He inclines his cloth covered head. "Did you have any issues returning?"

"I wandered until I found the study, as I got lost but otherwise no."

"I meant with the key." He clears his throat as the covered muscles of his forearm tense. "In this Palace, if the choice is given, always go left. You will not lose yourself on that path."

I tuck that helpful hint aside and close my book hesitantly. Nearly two decades of politics and manners won't be forgotten, no matter the urgency of my goal. "Thank you for letting me read here. You've amassed quite a collection. There are books here I'd never heard of."

He folds his hands over his lap. "I've had a prolonged opportunity to compile them. Nearly four hundred years to fill."

That's only somewhat surprising; most Cretans have direct godly ancestors and have extended lifespans. But even Cretans age, just more slowly than the rest of us. If he's been alive for centuries, he would sound elderly, or move as some of the aged men do, with creaking limbs and a raspy throat. He must have a more direct connection to the Gods, like Minos, to look so youthful. Perhaps one of his parents was the child of a God, or a God themselves.

"Did you enjoy the book?"

His question pulls me from my musings, and I motion to the one I've returned, sliding it across the desk to him. "I did. But I've already started another."

He cocks his head, a slight movement I wouldn't catch had I not been staring so intently on his clothed body. "I can find you a better book than that," he says.

The silky smoothness of his voice barely covers the revulsion in his tone. He may yet be another ally against Minos if he finds the propaganda as distasteful as I do. I slide my current choice across the table, and he drops it on the floor with a loud thunk.

"You mentioned you enjoy the histories surrounding the Island Wars," he continues. "Is there a particular subject within it that draws you?"

I shrug, my mask in place. He may be an ally, but like Dolion, it doesn't mean he'll support my goal in destroying the Collection. "I've always been interested in Poseidon and his relationship with Minos."

With nimble fingers, he plucks another choice from the bookcase and presents it to me. "We are alike in that," he says.

We sit in a comfortable silence. I read the histories left on the desk while Orion reviews the blue book he lent me yesterday. None touch on the Collection so far, but there are enough available that I won't lose hope. But as time passes, Orion doesn't advance the pages, his scarred fingers tapping the edges of the same page.

"Would you like me to leave?" I ask. I can't study with Chrysa around, but there must be other places in the Palace where I can read without inconveniencing him.

His hands still. "Not at all."

I motion to the book. "If you are uncomfortable with me sitting here—" And then I realize the issue. "Can you not read through the fabric?"

His fingers twitch before they slide out of view onto his lap. "I can. It is just difficult."

With a swallowed sigh, I gather the books I've chosen in anticipation of finding another space to read. "I've taken up enough of your time and space. Thank you, Ori—"

Suddenly, his hand rests on mine, stopping my lurching movements. Lightning doesn't strike again, but I can feel his muscles twitch. "Please, stay."

"Are you sure?"

"I know my mind," he says as he pulls his hand away.

I return the books to his desk. "So long as you tell me when you wish to read."

He nods and crosses his arms over his covered chest. His fists clench and unclench twice. Finally, he exhales. "You have no questions?"

"About?"

He gestures vaguely to himself and then makes a sharp circle around his face.

I do, but he doesn't need to know that. Finally, I say, "I understand wanting to keep parts of yourself from the world." After all, my mask has been both metaphorical and physical.

His neck moving upward is the only evidence that he's inspecting me. My cheeks threaten to flush at the covert appraisal, and I drop my head to stare at the table instead of the piercing eyes I imagine underneath that cloth.

"People expect things from me, and I'm frequently watched," I explain. That I can't see his face pulls the words from me, knowing I'll never see judgment there. And when the words start, they just keep coming. "They're waiting for me to fail. I can't show weakness; I can't be inadequate. So, I restrict my behavior, and what I share. Keeping things hidden means I'll disappoint no one."

"Does it work?" The question is mild.

I force myself into a nonchalant shrug. "They'll never know otherwise. Calm waters spill no secrets."

There's a huff from under the gauze. "Do you truly imagine what you decide to hide doesn't *reveal* as much as it protects? That you even need to wear a metaphorical mask shows more of your identity and temperament than any ripples from a rock dropped in your pond. I do not need passion and fire to see someone. How they react to the stillness, *why* they hide from the world, the fear within, that tells their story."

It's as though he's unclothed me, staring to the heart of who I am and finding the flaws, my self-doubt and anxiety that the mask is supposed to hide, and I shift in my seat. "And yet *you* wear a literal mask," I say, somewhat petulantly.

His shoulders flex, a shrug. "That has less to do with the thoughts and opinions of others, but because I prefer the sight of oblivion than my reflection."

My hackles lower with his confession, and I pinch my eyes closed. I can't escape my poor impulses even on a different Island. At least I didn't laugh at him. "I'm sorry," I offer. "That was unkind. Your reasons as your own."

He replaces his hands on the table, a mollifying gesture. "I apologize as well. I wasn't attempting to criticize you or your methods for protecting yourself. I don't converse with others often. There's been little chance to learn that words I speak might affect the feelings of those who hear them." His fingers twitch. "I would see those parts you feel you must hide, should you wish to share. I have no expectations for you but as reading partner, you see." He splays his hands; I'd never realized just how expressive hands could be. "You could be... safe here."

I study his figure, as if I can gauge his sincerity only through body language. I'd never expected to find a place to feel safe and unwatched in a Palace full of those who would rather I die. "I—thank you, Orion. I'll consider it."

He nods.

Hecaline's admonishment that I must speak runs through my head. Whether divine prophecy or advice for living, it can't hurt, not with the mystery of the Labyrinth still threatening my skin. I offer him a small part of the fear I've tucked under my mask. "It would be *nice* to have a safe place, given the uncertainty of my fate in the Labyrinth."

His entire body lurches, as if an invisible sword slammed into his stomach. "What do you expect to happen to you?" he asks gruffly.

I reopen the book I was reading before the interruption, unwilling to display the vulnerability that must show on my face. "I expect nothing. We know very little. That is what I wish to learn more of, the purpose and reasoning behind the Collection."

Orion jolts upward and stomps through the doorway behind the bookcase, no longer smooth as a floating spirit but like a child who just learned to walk. He careens back through the doorway seconds later, another blue book in his hands.

"This may help," he rasps, holding the book out like a present. Even from a distance, I can see annotations and bookmarkers. "I wouldn't—I wouldn't read it where others can see. But I hope you find it useful."

"Thank you, Orion." I slip the book under my belt. I'll need to hide it, if only to keep Elara from pushing me down the stairs for the assumed advantage.

"I would do more," he says, laying his hands on the table again. The skin turns white as he presses hard against the wood. "But I'm limited before the Collection, it's fairness that—I—"

"The geas. I understand." I rest my fingers on top of his until he exhales. There's no lightning this time, but I'm not imagining the heat racing from my fingers and up my wrists and elbows to settle in my shoulders. "Perhaps this book will explain why the need for the geas." I don't ask, because I know he can't answer, but specific phrasing might get me more information. It's all a game, a puzzle. One that must have an answer and a way to win.

He clears his throat a second time, something that sounds like a masculine roar, and withdraws from my touch. "If not that one, I have others."

I leave Orion just after the lunch hour, hoping to read the new book he gave me. At breakfast, the other girls agreed to practice together all day, meaning I should have the room to myself for a few more hours.

The book starts like any of the other histories, dull and unfocused on Minos, not Poseidon as I expected. I turn to Orion's notes. A looping script covers half the pages, penmanship more beautiful than what I can do after seventeen years of calligraphy study. When the stories advance past the Island Wars, his handwriting turns sharper, with more splotches.

I spend my time there, reviewing the history of the Island Wars, but no details of the Beast or the reason behind the Collection emerge. Only Orion's delicate writing decrying "Poseidon's blessing" slants across the margin. But given the favor Poseidon has of Minos, Orion's note could be a declaration of his faith and not evidence of the bargain between the two. After the section on the Island Wars comes several long passages about the Collection. The substance is nothing I haven't already learned, though it includes a brief paragraph about the construction of the Labyrinth. My breath stutters to learn there are two entrances. One must be the one we've used; but the other might be a way to leave. If I don't solve the puzzle, I can use it to escape.

Better are Orion's annotations, where he asks, *"why a Labyrinth?"* In a different ink, he answers his own question, *"must prove she has necessary skills, including focus, determination, methodical thought process, logic."* It's just as Dolion implied, I don't need physical skills. We must be attempting to prove something, to earn a victory for Minos. But why are those skills necessary? How does it relate to the bargain I hope to discover? And will logic defeat the Beast?

Before I can answer the questions I've discovered in response to Orion's notes, Chrysa stomps in the room, red faced and scowling. I hide the book under my pillow with the replaced key as she throws herself on the bed and shoves her face into her pillow.

She huffs a few times before I finally ask, "Are you well?"

She grunts into the fabric. "Do you even care?"

Better not to lie. "I don't suppose it matters if I do, so long as I'm a good listener. It's always easier to share if you don't care what the listener thinks of you." It isn't a tack *I've* taken, but I recognize the truth of it.

That drags out a small laugh. "It's silly," Chrysa says, pulling herself to sit cross-legged on her bed. "Thyia and Mina were supposed to train with me this afternoon. We were going to run to the top of the mountain and back. But Mina left with Diomede instead." She pulls on her short curls. "I shouldn't even care. It's not like this is a place to make friends. I'm lucky that I even got to come, whether Mina likes me shouldn't matter, especially not if we're dead in a week," she finishes darkly.

As we both expect, I have no comforting words. But one thing she said zings like lightning in my stomach. "If you believe you're going to die, why are you lucky to be here?" She didn't strike me as a fanatic.

She grimaces, her brown eyes squinting in remembered pain again. I'm about to make a rote apology for overstepping when she reaches under her pillow and tosses a stack of paper at me. I don't do more than hold it curiously.

"I wasn't... eligible at first," she says, staring at her hands. "I should have been, but Eileithyia and Hera did something wrong when I was born, tried to make me a son instead. My best friend Delia was the one who convinced our Councilors to let me in the youngest daughter classes. When this Collection came, she was going to be picked, so I put my name forward instead." With hard eyes, she offers an insincere smirk. "Don't tell Diomede I said that, though. About the Gods. She'd never believe they made a mistake."

"No," I agree. "We sometimes forget that the way we were taught isn't the best, or only way."

She laughs, clutching her stomach as though I've said something hilarious but won't explain why.

"You volunteered?" I ask when she stops giggling.

She nods and gestures to the parchment in my lap. "Just like you. Those were my thank you and goodbye letters. Delia was our Councilor's niece. He was grateful."

I look through the parchment. "Did you smuggle these in?" I stop myself before adding "*too.*"

"Under my girdle during the inspection," she says with a sly grin. The melancholy drains from the room at her smile. "Kynna missed it."

"I thought the inspection had to be naked?" I ask idly, more focused on the parchment.

Chrysa laughs. "Did Dolion make you do it naked? I told you he wanted you."

My cheeks heat involuntarily, and I close my eyes to push the embarrassment away. I clear my throat and hold up the letter that caught my eye. "This one isn't a thank you letter. These are notes."

Chrysa squints, as if she can read the small penmanship from there. Then, she shrugs. "Councilor Iros must have been very grateful."

The slanted writing says older records reveal the Beast to be a type of boar. *How odd that boars are so popular on Crete.* I skim the rest of the page, looking for any other tidbits of information Karavi had that Standia didn't.

"Anything useful?" Chrysa asks as she pads from her bed to mine and slips in beside me.

"Have you not read them yet?" I ask as I study the next few letters for anything of note.

Chrysa shrugs, her shoulder knocking into mine. "I can't read."

The letters drop from my hands as if yanked from me by a hook. "You can't read?"

Chrysa scowls at my scandalized expression. "Youngest daughters aren't taught that. It isn't like we need it."

I almost can't shut my horror-struck mouth to respond. "You need it for studying, for living. God's teeth, what if there was a door in the Labyrinth that said 'exit?' You'd never know!"

Her expression flattens. "I'm not dense. If I found a doorway to lead me away from the Beast, it wouldn't matter what was written above it."

"It would if it said, 'immediate death beyond this door,'" I mutter. Given the uncertainty of the second entrance, it's actually a possibility.

She bumps into my shoulder again. "Look at that, you're kind of funny."

"I learned it from all the reading I do," I say, but there's no heat to it. More than anything, I'm just sad. I'm sad for girls like Serai and Nephele, for Chrysa and Dolion's lost love.

But Chrysa isn't offended. "We learned important things. Like weaponry and how to scale walls."

"Weaponry and physical skills, yes. But you didn't learn how to think," I say, frowning.

She gathers her letters and returns to her bed, shaking her head. "You're so stuck up. That's why no one wants to train with you."

I cross my arms around my chest, burying the bit of pain that statement produces. "I thought I wasn't training with you by *my* choice, not yours."

"Not like you'd know, since you haven't spent time with us," she grumbles.

A faint smile plays over my mouth. "So tomorrow I should try to join you, so I can make sure you all can *intentionally* ignore me."

"Yes, exactly," she says, but her lips curl in the corners. She's quiet for a minute, before adding, "And you can't pick a lock without knowing how to think."

"That's better than what the youngest daughters in Standia learn," I admit. Though *they* can read, but I keep that fact to myself.

"Karavi is Hermes' Island. We all have to learn it, or else we'd be laughed out to sea and have to live somewhere like *Standia*," she says, smirking.

I offer her another metaphorical olive branch. "I learned nothing about weaponry or survival. I didn't take those classes. Knowing how to think but not how to escape from a locked room still might get me killed in the Labyrinth first."

Her eyes widen. "No wonder you're trying to leash Dolion for help."

"I am not," I say, affronted.

"How about this?" she continues, as if I hadn't spoken. "I'll teach you how to pick a lock, if you read me my papers and teach me the letters for 'exit.' Just in case."

The warmth in my stomach that began at Orion's offer for a safe space builds into a deeper well at Chrysa's deal. "You would have to spend more time with me," I remind her.

She shrugs. "I can manage. 'Stuck up but funny' is better than a lot of people I knew in Karavi. So long as we can agree on one thing." Her expression turns serious, her gaze pinning me in place. "Elara has to be the first one the Beast eats. She'll never shut up in the Underworld otherwise."

And I can't help but laugh.

Chapter 14

Chrysa bites her lip around a smile when I join them for breakfast. I actually *join* them, sitting across from her and beside Eriphyle in the small dining hall they set up for us, instead of shoving fruit in my mouth while standing next to the door.

"I've lost a shoe," Mina is saying as I grab a chunk of bread and cheese.

"A single shoe? Is it possible you left it under your bed?" Thyia asks.

Diomede nods. "You have a lot shoved under there."

"How? We came with nothing," says Eriphyle, puzzled.

Chrysa smirks in my direction, as if we have a shared secret about contrabands. "Mina is like a squirrel, always gathering things for a rainy day."

"Like rocks, and shells," Thyia says with furrowed brows.

Elara hums thoughtfully. I can just imagine what *she's* thinking: that perhaps Mina intends to bludgeon the Beast to death.

"I'm missing a shift," I offer. I thought a caretaker had taken it for laundering, but it didn't return with the cleaned clothes.

"As am I," Elara says, grudgingly.

Mina purses her lips. "We have so little, why would someone take things from us?"

"You think someone took it?" I ask, sharing a glance with Elara. For once, she doesn't roll her eyes and avoid my gaze but stares back as if considering Mina's suggestion.

"We can lose shifts in the wash. No one would have reason to take a shoe from our room except as theft," Thyia says reasonably. I'm not the only one at the table who raises their brows at her addition to the conversation. Thyia doesn't notice, turning back to her bread to dip in oil.

"If it isn't found, I'm sure the King will offer a substitute. He said as much." Diomede leans to peer at Elara and me. "For all of us."

Kyra claps her hands to let us know the meal is over, cutting off further conversation as she glides from the room. We follow, with Kynna in the rear, as we're led to the platform elevator that will bear us into the Labyrinth.

Dolion appears by my side before we turn onto the hallway that will take us to the elevator. "I have an idea," he whispers.

"About the missing items?"

He leans closer and lets his breath caress my ear. "No."

I restrain a shiver. Chrysa looks back and waggles her eyebrows. Dolion misses the exchange.

"We need to talk," I whisper back, remembering what Chrysa said about the inspection.

"That's what I'm trying to do. I have a riddle for you, something generic. I practiced saying it aloud all morning. No choking." His eyes brighten with the joy of success. "It was only a matter of time I discovered the solution."

I'm the one who suggested riddles two nights ago, but I don't spare the energy to remind him. I'll need it all to make it through the Labyrinth this morning and find the second entrance. But Dolion is almost vibrating with excitement.

"Go on," I say, letting the matter of the claimed naked inspection slip into the sea. "Tell me before you burst."

He grasps my forearm and stops me. The others continue ahead as he leans close a second time. "You might think to brush it or braid it, or even pull it. But I would always suggest cutting it."

My expression flattens while Dolion looks exceedingly pleased with himself. He doesn't let me react as he yanks me onto the elevator, which lowers into the darkness.

Hair.

The answer is obviously hair. I already *know* Minos requires everyone to cut their hair. Meaning the answer isn't prohibited by the geas, or else it would have been harder, making the knowledge almost meaningless. I stifle a frustrated groan. Unless...

Whispered conversations filter through the platform, the knowledge of what we're walking into no longer making the trip fear filled. I sidle up to Thyia, who is murmuring to Diomede.

I pitch my voice low. "Thyia, I have a question."

She turns and I can just see her expectant eyes before the light in the shaft disappears as we descend further underground.

"If I were to say you can brush, pull, or braid it, but I suggest cutting it, what would 'it' be?"

The darkness hides her expression. After a minute she says, "Hair."

And my heart plummets into the ground.

"Was I right?"

"I think so," I say glumly.

"What are you saying?" Elara asks from across the platform. "Did you get a hint that you're not sharing?"

Chrysa snorts. "If she did, why would she tell you?"

"It was a riddle," Thyia says, sounding proud.

"A riddle," Dolion says, his voice flat. He shuffles close to me and grips my forearm. "I didn't realize you enjoyed wordplay, Hero."

"Thalia only took culture classes, so she must be very good at wordplay," says Mina from behind me.

"And bad at everything else," Chrysa says cheerfully.

"Thank you, Mina," I say with forced poise, shaking off Dolion's grasp. "You too, Chrysa." *For sharing* that *with the group.*

"Don't worry, Thalia. Whatever happens will be the Gods' will," Diomede says.

"Death for us all," says Chrysa, still sounding gleeful.

"Speak for yourself," Elara mutters, echoed by Eriphyle.

Finally, the platform lands with a thump and we all file out and away from my deficiencies. As soon as Kynna's whistle releases the door, Elara and Eriphyle race towards the middle entrance. Chrysa and Mina head to the right again, followed by Diomede and Thyia.

"Riddles?" Dolion hisses into my ear.

"I don't have the geas preventing me from sharing," I whisper back.

"But you still shouldn't. We don't know their loyalty."

I don't know *his* beyond his claims of wanting to help me, but I keep that to myself. "Your riddle was too simple. If everyone can figure it out, then the geas won't matter and you may as well share with everyone, as it can't be important."

"Simple!" He says, indignant. "I spent hours with Hecaline on that, how to make sure you knew it in case the opportunity presented itself."

"It was a good first effort," I offer. "But surely that can't help me succeed in the Labyrinth."

He scowls, his chiseled jaw tensing. "It's... more."

"More as in more helpful than succeeding in here?"

His face reddens with the strain of clenching his teeth in anger. Or he's fighting against the geas again. He finally twitches out something like a nod and bursts out a gulping breath, as though he'd been holding it.

I squeeze his forearm. "I'm sorry for asking. If you feel like continuing to try, I'll listen to any other riddles you have."

He nods, his eyes wet and angry. "Enjoy your practice."

I release a breath as he stalks back towards the platform. Yet another person I disappoint. I brush off the puncture to my pride and walk through the antechamber. Armed with the confirmation that there is another way out, I vow to find it. With no better ideas, Orion's idle advice has me try the left entrance this time.

Before I turn the corner and leave the antechamber behind, Kyra's voice coils towards me.

"You're new at this but don't get attached. We all know what happens to them."

I don't stay to listen to Dolion's response, but my feet trudge heavier as I head down the next distant passageway.

My left hand trails against the stone wall, a physical connection to keep me always moving in that direction. Each time the path offers me a choice, I turn left. I count twenty-seven before the fetid air clears and the candles lighting the passages flicker. There must be an exit nearby. After one more left, the passage ends at what looks like a blank wall. The slight space could hold a doorway, but nothing else.

I run my fingers over the wall, searching for a seam, but feel the prickling sensation of magic, identical to the threshold leading into the Labyrinth. I touch the edges where the wall meets the passageway. There—that's a seam, the edges of a door, a track big enough for my fingertip to slide within it.

I squint, as if I can see the magic and discover what it's hiding. A faint gold sheen covers the doorway, looking like my *own* illusions, a curtain of iridescent gold stretched over the door. I allow myself a minute of pleased excitement. I found the second entrance; I'm not simply floundering here.

But the pride ebbs quickly. Since I've never come upon some-one else's illusions, I don't know how to break through it. I race through all I know of illusion magic. Several of the Gods possess a version, some magical creatures too. One must have placed this, or, I remember grimly, been sacrificed for it.

But... theoretically, if I can see and touch them, I can *disman-tle* illusions. I do it to mine daily. And the Gods did it all the time. Surely if Athena's powers allow me to create and change illusions, I can affect other illusion magic too. Like layering my magic on Cleon's. I've simply never had the opportunity.

I knock my forehead against the wall. Lukas would *love* my positive attitude, no matter that it's born of mortal peril.

I close my eyes and press my fingers against the seams to find the matrix of the wall's enchantment, its source. It's a winding twist of magic much like the Labyrinth with golden threads that were knotted together in a clump. With the vision of a cloth curtain still embedded behind my closed lids, I mentally pick apart the strands, starting with the left. A headache blooms behind my eyes, as the thin threads are only visible within me and are miniscule, more like golden hair than solid string.

Could this be what Dolion meant? By cutting through the illusion, I might destroy it. I create my own illusion, a sharp dagger, much like the one I still carry in my holster at my back, and slice through the strands.

But nothing happens. I try again with the actual dagger and do nothing more than create a slight nick in the wall.

After replacing the knife, I think very uncharitable thoughts about Dolion and his awful riddle while I continue disentangling the knot. I treat it as a puzzle, a mental skill, and solvable by anyone with illusion magic and intelligence. It takes hours, there's no telling without a clock. That Kynna hasn't whistled for our return is the only sign that I haven't wasted my entire practice run on this knot.

I'm woozy when I finish, leaning against the now magicless doorway, a blank piece of wood with a single twisted wire keeping it closed. I remember my admonition to Chrysa, but there's no warning of 'imminent death' over the top of the door.

Swallowing my fear, I walk through the door that will lead me from the Labyrinth.

After another trek in near darkness, the thin hallway beyond the door widens into a large space that is a mirror image to the antechamber at the start of the Labyrinth. Just beyond it is a platform with another long braided rope leading upwards into another dark shaft. Gingerly, I step onto the platform. I don't feel any magic from any geas boundary or illusion.

But the rope sparkles, just like the rope attached to the main elevator. For a brief minute, I consider cutting the braid as Dolion's riddle would have me do. One hand slides to the side of my robes to begin the meticulous process of unfolding layers again until the seams open on the side. As I reach back to the holster attached to my back, I lose my balance, stumbling and yanking on the rope to keep myself standing. And then the platform moves.

As the elevator ascends, I have enough time to adjust the folds on my robe and curse Dolion for putting bad ideas in my head. I never would have considered cutting the rope without him, and if I had, doubtless the elevator would no longer work. That can't have been what he meant when he told me the riddle, unless he wanted to desert me inside the Labyrinth. For all I know he does. He wants me to succeed but has never defined success. Success in the Collection could be dying *alongside* the Beast.

Those thoughts carry me upward, even as my skepticism descends lower into my stomach. The elevator takes longer than the earlier one. It must rise higher than the main elevator, to a higher floor. Candles ignite the hallways when the platform arrives, but instead of marble floors and gradient blue walls, it looks like packed dirt. I creep down the hall, taking hesitant steps to avoid any geas boundaries when the hallway veers to the left.

At the end of that second passage is a single door and I tiptoe towards it.

There's a taste of magic against my tongue when I peer through the doorway, a stronger version of that zip of lightning that marks the doorway to the Labyrinth. To avoid activating it, I duck away from the threshold and inspect it from the hall. It looks like a bedroom, but for someone who'd been forgotten years earlier. The walls are stained not with filth but with the discoloration of age. The floors aren't packed dirt, though it's hard to tell as they are covered with piles of books and wound string. The only furniture is a narrow bed with pilling sheets.

There are no windows but two doorways leading to the interior of what must be the rest of a small, sad, apartment. *Maybe it belongs to the keeper of the Beast, who must live near his monstrous charge.* I can think of no other explanation for why a room would connect to the Labyrinth. And though it isn't the simple exit I hoped for, it might be a way to hide from the Beast should the worst happen. The consequence of that zip of magic over the threshold would likely be better than death-by-monster.

Content knowing that there might be an alternate outcome to death at the center if I can't stop the Collection, I retrace my steps at a brisk walk, slipping back through the door I unraveled and throwing my illusion over it to appear as it did before. I don't think magic is traceable, but hopefully it will trick whoever is using it into thinking the illusion wasn't disturbed.

As soon as I'm back in the Labyrinth, Kynna's whistles pierce my ears and I pick up speed, dashing around corners and taking every right turn I can to return to the antechamber. When I round the last corner and hustle over the threshold, the others are waiting with varying degrees of patience.

"We thought you'd been eaten," Mina says as I cross into the antechamber.

"Elara was already celebrating her first win," Chrysa says, baring her teeth in a smile. Elara doesn't deny it.

"Don't worry, Hero. Five more minutes and I'd have come for you." Dolion smirks but worry hides deep within his gaze.

"Is that allowed?" Diomede asks. Elara looks curious in the answer as well.

Kyra and Kynna purse their lips in tandem. "You must have the opportunity to meet He who is found in the center," Kyra says begrudgingly.

"Meaning?" asks Mina, scraping her teeth over her lower lip.

"Meaning we need to stay alive until the official Collection, and then no one cares," Elara says. "I, for one, have no intention of needing help to remain alive, both inside and outside the Labyrinth."

Chrysa rolls her eyes. "We get it, you're wonderful and the greatest warrior the Collection has ever seen."

"She could be," Thyia says. "There aren't any survivors to ask, anyway. For all we know she's the best of the Collected. Only time will tell."

I stare at Thyia appraisingly, joined by the other girls intrigued by her sudden bout of competence.

Thyia shuffles closer to Dolion and stares at him, pouting. "Can we go back to our rooms? The darkness of the Labyrinth scares me."

The idea of *weaponized weakness* runs through my mind, another skill that isn't physical. Perhaps Thyia, and the others, are more competent than I thought, and able to wield other talents they hide beneath a facade.

"The dark just makes it easier for me to kill the Beast before any of you," Elara says, tipping up her chin.

Then again, maybe not.

Chapter 15

After the practice run, they bustle us back to our rooms to wait for the Festival of Poseidon tomorrow. Dolion disappears, but Kyra and Kynna stand guard at the hallway to our rooms, unwilling to let us leave as we need 'our sleep' for tomorrow. They refuse to explain what will happen at the festival, or why we need to sequester ourselves for almost an entire day. The cynic in me thinks they believe we might run to avoid whatever is to happen tomorrow.

Unable to abscond to Orion's study, I join the group for dinner that evening. Chrysa mockingly gestures to the seat next to her as if she saved it for me. We spent the afternoon working on her letters, after which she taught me to pick a lock. I don't know who had a worse time.

Mina makes shapes in the oil on her plate with a chunk of bread, not raising her head. "What do you think will happen tomorrow?"

"If it is anything like the festivals in Gerenia, we will wear our best clothes and offer a sacrifice. There's dancing and music, all our Councilors perform an original composition. Then we amuse ourselves with games and sports. The children make it a contest, with the winner the most likely to receive a blessing the next year," Diomede says, smiling. "I won last year."

Chrysa wrinkles her nose. "And the Collection was your blessing?"

Diomede shrugs. "If it was the Gods' will, I won't question it."

Chrysa looks ready to respond with something teasing but Thyia's hand on her forearm stops her.

"Our festivals didn't even focus on Hephaestus, but Athena." Eriphyle says, scowling at me as if it's my fault. "So I couldn't go."

"Festivals in Prosfora had no games or music," says Elara begrudgingly. "We sacrifice an ox and celebrate with food and drink. Though the men and women are separated during the event, we were never told what the men do." Her eye twitches.

Thyia straightens and clutches the fabric at her neck. "Will they expect *us* to kill the animal for sacrifice? That's barbaric!"

"You told us the first night that your weekly devotions involved bathing in the blood of a dove like Aphrodite," says Mina, dropping her bread with a wet plop.

Thyia shrugs. "Yes, but they're already dead when we bleed them."

Chrysa elbows me in the waist and rolls her eyes dramatically, like we're in on the same joke. An ember of warmth pools in my stomach at the inclusion.

"Maybe *we're* the sacrifice," she says, waggling her eyebrows.

A few of them look to be considering it. It's the feeling in my stomach that allows me to burble out a laugh and say, "Are you telling me that you believe Minos, after demanding you study weaponry and combat for *years*, dragged us here to shove us in the Labyrinth to practice not once but three times, and instead of requiring us to battle the Beast as we've been told, intends for us to act as human sacrifices at their Festival? That this long-standing event is nothing but a centuries' old ruse?"

Eyes have widened by the time I finish, though Chrysa hasn't lost her teasing grin. She splays her hands over her plate. "It's the perfect trick. No one comes back, so no one can ruin the joke."

Elara's fists land on the table. "If Chrysa is right, I will murder you all before tossing myself on the altar."

The table remains quiet, no one sure how to respond. Even Eriphyle looks a little pale at Elara's emphatic declaration.

Chrysa coughs to cover a laugh. "On that note, I'm missing a shoe now too."

The next day, we leave the Palace after lunch from a secluded side entrance wearing long tunics emblazoned with our Island's symbols. Dolion delivered them before dawn. I was already awake, attempting to read Orion's secret book by candlelight in the hall. He didn't comment on my actions, distracted and almost leaving the tunics for Elara and Eriphyle instead of mine and Chrysa's.

Mine is ill fitting, for a woman lither than I. The owl embroidery is picked apart in several spots, only half the owls have feet while various others are missing eyes. Even the robe clip looks reused, the brass tarnished. Mine isn't the only outfit that shows its age, but the waists on the other girls' robes at least fit. I could pass out from lack of air before even arriving at the Festival.

We trudge from the square courtyard through the main street until we head east to the public Knossos stadium. In front of the entrance are statues of renowned athletes who stand guard, their stoic gazes overseeing whatever spectacle Minos intends to put forward. Carved into the natural amphitheater of the mountainside, the stadium rises to a towering height. The seats are engraved with spiral waves that roll into carved bull horns and horses that dance across the tops of the twisting Labyrinthian symbol of Crete. It's the perfect example of the marriage between Crete and Poseidon. Or *Minos* and Poseidon.

We enter through the lower levels, much like the Standian candidates at the Scrimmage. Only silence greets us, not the roar of the crowd I'd expect from a busy Festival, and I wonder if we've arrived too early or few Cretans attend this mysterious ceremony. Through the darkness, we rise from the underground level to the main stage, shoved to the center by our caretakers. Kyra and Kynna stay in the tunnel next to Dolion, all with muted expressions. For the former, that's expected, but Dolion's seriousness is worrying.

But the silence was deceptive. The arena bulges with attendees, each sitting silently in their packed rows, rising into stands nearly touching the sky. Pillars line the periphery, draped in vibrant banners while wreaths of white and yellow narcissus decorate the base. Odd considering those are Hades' symbols and not Poseidon's. And there are no murals in sight.

We stand in single file, like animals inspected for auction. I finish the line next to Chrysa, with Elara at the front. I expect the pity emblazoned on half the audience, those that must understand how unwilling we are to be here. What I don't expect are the glares, the scowls curling the lips of the remaining attendees, as though we've sacrificed their favorite deer or slaughtered their pet.

"What did we do?" Chrysa asks through clenched teeth. Beside her, Mina shrugs. I'm sure I'm not alone in wondering if Chrysa has skills as a seer and we're in for an afternoon of pain. I consider withdrawing into an illusion to hide my wariness, or at least change my dingy and snug robe, but I stifle the urge.

Finally, the King saunters out, not into one of the lower levels but appearing above us in a high balcony that overlooks the center of the stadium. He remains shirtless, but he's traded his golden-threaded chiton for the skin of a bull wrapped around his waist, the bull's head and horns between his legs. His long braid trails down his muscular torso until it twines around the bull's neck at his waist, like a macabre noose. Deianira joins him wearing a silvery blue, shimmering like a wave cresting in the ocean at dawn.

"Welcome to the Festival of Poseidon." Minos' voice booms around the arena, much like Father's can, and I wonder what magical being was sacrificed to give him the skill. The crowd finally shows interest in what's happening as a hushed murmur rolls through the stands.

"Every seven years, from seven Islands come seven women, who have seven days to meet He who lives at the center of the Labyrinth. These are seven opportunities not for those women, but for all of Crete."

Diomede nods emphatically.

"Today we honor not your King, but Poseidon, as it is at his leisure that I stand before you. It is in his honor that we celebrate and undertake the Collection rites in three days."

My stomach drops to my feet. *Was that confirmation of the bargain? Or a denial of it?*

"The women before you do not differ from the many who came before them, who took their chance in our Labyrinth. Each woman met the one who lives there, and the Gods decided the outcome." Minos flashes a sly smirk. "For, had there *been* a concern, surely the outcome would have changed." A few in the crowd laugh longer than is polite, given we all know the unsaid outcome is death.

"And these seven women will have their equal chance," he continues. "Whatever may occur is God's will." He then sits, and stares at us impassively, as though we've disappointed him somehow.

The arena quiets again as the bald minister we met previously scurries out from under the arena and begins introducing us. His voice can't carry like the King's, but the silence allows him to be heard.

Until the hissing starts.

It begins quietly with Elara's introduction, growing through Diomede's, and becoming deafening at Mina's. By the time he shouts my name and title, the scant hisses turn into jeers. When the minister finishes, he abandons the arena and the clamor builds. Words are shouted at us and at the other agitators, but nothing I can understand. Chrysa slips her hand in mine, and I jolt at the touch. She peers at me wide-eyed, looking younger than she has before.

They all do. They all look afraid for the first time in this place. Even the ever-present sheen of confidence and competence Elara's face is absent. I squeeze Chrysa's hand, the only reassurance I know how to give.

Guards shove into the aisles and drag out the loudest aggressors. The words don't change but clash as a chant of "Minos" overlaps the unintelligible yelling.

Minos stands, and the arena silences as if their vocal cords had been cut. Maybe they were. "And now, the sacrifice."

Chrysa's fingers nearly break mine as the tension builds. But Dolion's expression hasn't changed. Surely, he'd look more alarmed if the Collection wasn't about running the Labyrinth but a way to lower our guard and then murder us for sport. Or... murdering us with an audience rather than murder by Beast.

Unless the 'success' he was after involved stopping the Collection by removing the Collected. The blood in my veins transforms to ice at the thought.

Elara leans forward to stare mutinously down the line at Chrysa.

"I didn't think I was right," Chrysa hisses at her, her nails clawing into my hand.

"You manifested it," Diomede says shakily.

"Don't start, Di."

I extricate my fingers from Chrysa's hand prison and loop our elbows instead, like I've seen Lyra do with her entourage. "It's fine," I tell her, using all my skills as heir not to show my fear on my face. Someone needs to remain calm and reassuring. "You've trained for whatever will come."

"You're not in charge of us, Heir," Elara says, though her voice wobbles, reminding me she is only a month past seventeen.

A shuffling comes from the lower entry and four men carry out a wooden altar covered in spiky pink sugarbushes wound with white narcissus. Behind it, another guard drags out a small boar. The group crosses before us somberly and we all exhale in relief.

But my relief doesn't last. Hecaline's warning churns through my mind. *Is this the boar I'm to save?* I stare out into the audience, as if someone there can give me guidance. But no allies present themselves, not with a stadium filled with agitators and syco-phants. And Minos smirks down at us, as though satisfied with the momentary fear we displayed. But his amusement quickly morphs to rage, as a man joins us in the arena, leaping from the stands. Perhaps *he* intends to save the boar himself.

Half the crowd seems invigorated by the stranger's presence as a gleeful cry rolls through the stadium. Even Chrysa gusts out a surprised laugh, echoed by Mina, Thyia, everyone but Elara and me. The shirtless man raises his fist to us and then turns to the audience, bellowing words the crowd's noise drowns out. I'm rooted in place; so too are the others, unable to stop whatever's happening but unwilling to try. Even the guards seem shocked into stillness before the King's shouted command forces them to act.

The four guards drop the altar with a thud, the garlands drift-ing down to the grass. The boar squeals at the sound and jolts back towards the entrance where our caretakers and the minister wait, dragging the fifth guard behind it, who refuses to release the rope. While the guards stand frozen, the running man sprints half the length of the arena. The guards finally chase after him, before he doubles back and zigzags behind the altar, grasping his throat with one hand and groaning.

"Long live," he rasps as he runs behind us, raising his free fist to the sky. On his back is a scar in the shape of two sideways triangles, the same symbol from the Palace. That he's tattooed confirms he isn't a man Minos and his government approve of; he's been punished and marked with shame. That the same mark is carved around the Palace makes his scar even more curious.

When the guards reappear, he feigns changing directions again, knocking into Chrysa and almost pushing her down. She clings to me and Mina, and together we remain standing. One guard breaks through our line to snatch the runner, barreling into Eriphyle but she's planted her feet and the guard stumbles to the ground.

A second guard shoves Thyia aside as he attempts to reach the runner, but trips on Diomede's extended leg. His fingers only graze the edge of the man's bare shoulder before he lands beside the first guard. Eriphyle and Diomede steady Thyia and hook arms to repair our line. Only Elara stays unconnected, crouching with fisted hands, as if ready to leap onto someone's back and join the fray. The entire event feels like a poorly choreographed comedy, especially when the boar arrives at the underground entrance and the minister clambers up Dolion's back to avoid it.

The man uses the commotion to sprint back to the front of the altar, shouting, "Long live the boar!"

Then the sound turns garbled as he cuts off, screaming in pain. The guards not tangled around our feet leap on him and the three slam into the grass. One of the fallen guards tries to use Elara as an anchor to pull himself upward until she steps sideways, and he trips again. They end up crawling away from us and joining the human pile in front of the altar. Finally, they all stand and flank the moaning man who has curled into himself on the ground. As they drag him from the stadium and he crosses our line, he bellows a mangled scream.

He's swallowed his tongue.

Chapter 16

After the guards return from wherever they've stashed the choking man and the minister climbs off Dolion's back, the fifth guard drags the boar back to the crooked altar. I look at Dolion and tip my head minutely at the boar, but he doesn't react. Chrysa remains hooked on my arm with Mina on hers, and on down the line until Elara, who stands rigidly with her arms crossed around her chest. I search for the King and what he might reveal from the incident, but he's vanished from the balcony. Instead, Deianira looks down her nose at the stadium with an unreadable expression.

The guards complete the sacrifice while we stand behind them, skipping the offerings and slaughtering the boar without ceremony, as if afraid someone *else* will leap from the upper arena. The crowd resumes shouting "Minos," though it's quieter than before. Half the audience sits solemnly but I can't tell if they approve or disapprove of what happened. The guards finish the sacrificial rites, and the rest of the ceremony mimics our Standian sacrifices. If not for the inevitable death of the man missing his tongue, and our rumpled chitons from our unintentional part in the skirmish, it would be comical how normal this part of the event feels.

When they finish, the guards remain in the stadium, hands covered in blood, and look around the stadium as if waiting for instructions. Deianira leaves, her scowl burning bright as she fades from view. Finally, the minister scurries back into the arena. He says nothing but twitches his arms towards the exits, an instruction that everyone should leave, and then flees back where he came. The audience files from the stands while we shuffle to the underground entrance.

Dolion slides to my side. "Could have been worse," he says.

I restrain myself from laughing in disbelief. "How?"

He opens his mouth and then grimaces. "I can't say. Though... what I expected to occur, didn't."

I mull that over as the guards pass by carrying the broken and bloody altar, and the other girls start up the incline that takes us from the building. When there's enough distance between us and the others, Dolion places a warm hand on my low back and directs me forward.

I lean close. From a distance, we might look like two lovers out for a stroll. It's a fine cover for my continued treason. "Can you tell me the significance of the boar, or is that something you need a riddle for?"

His lips flatten. "There was no significance to *that* boar."

So, I haven't lost my chance, assuming I need one. "That wasn't the boar I'm to save?"

He coughs and shakes his head.

"But... there *is* one to save?" I consider the notes from Chrysa's Councilor, and the claim that the Beast is some kind of boar. *Surely Hecaline doesn't expect me to save the Beast?*

"Something like that," he says before clearing his throat. "I hope the agitators didn't bother you."

I frown. "Why were they behaving that way?"

He scans around the tunnel and lowers his voice. "Some people would prefer the planned consequence of the Collection... not occur."

Maybe that was the problem, they didn't want the boar sacrificed for us, and that man wanted to earn Minos' favor. "What about the ones hissing and yelling in support of Minos?"

He scratches his throat. "*Those* were the ones I meant."

We join the crowds outside the stadium. Now it looks identical to the festivals on Standia, after we've completed the weaving competitions and turned to the celebrations. The sounds of excitement and music trill all around, the scent of meat and wine thick in the air. We could blend into the crowd if not for the ostentatious, if sloppy, embroidery on our tunics. That and the film of unease in our eyes from the ordeal at the stadium.

The streets are lined with vibrant stalls and canopies, each draped in richly dyed fabrics capped with golden tassels. Cretan merchants peddle an array of wares from rare herbs with healing properties to intricately carved artifacts depicting mythical creatures. Jewelers display sparkling amulets, their surfaces reflecting the sunlight filtered through colorful banners overhead. As we walk, we overhear storytellers captivate audiences with epic tales of gods and heroes, while musicians play enchanting melodies on lyres and pipes. It is a far cry different from the Knossos we walked through on our first day. Gone are the signs of poverty and malnourishment. In its place is an exhibition perfect for keeping Poseidon from thinking there's anything wrong.

Kyra and Kynna direct us to the twisting trunk of an olive tree, and we hide from the midday sun under the shade. They take off their matching cloaks and display stark white tunics that emphasize their toned arms. Kyra ties her black hair back and turns to whisper to Kynna. Noticing we're watching, she pauses mid word and stares at us with an annoyed expression.

"You're free for the day," she says.

Mina blinks as though she's forgotten where she was. "To do what?"

Kyra and Kynna trade glances before Kynna responds, "Whatever you'd like. Be back by sundown."

Chrysa crosses her arms around her chest, hiding her shaking hands. "Just like that? Like all that chaos from the stadium didn't happen?"

"Given our purpose here, I suppose no one would consider how we might feel about it," Thyia says reasonably.

I turn to Dolion. "Should we have any concerns about our safety?"

Elara shoves between us and stalks to the base of the tree, leaning against it and studying the area as though surveying for enemies. "No one would dare attack us."

"But that man from the stadium—" Diomede begins.

"Elara is correct," Kyra says, though she looks pained at having to further converse with us. "As we mentioned yesterday, you must have the opportunity to meet the one at the center."

I raise my brows at Dolion, and he shrugs. "No one *can* harm you, no matter if they want to," he explains.

A musician sets up not too far from our tree, strumming a lyre. She's soon joined by a man with some kind of reeded instrument. The space before them turns into a makeshift dancing stage as celebrants move in time to the music. Kyra and Kynna clasp hands and join the small circle, leaving us alone.

Kyra spins as Kynna snaps and whirls to follow her. They look like birds in flight, their long white chitons tangling and flying around their legs. Thyia slinks closer to Dolion, but Chrysa grabs her hand.

"Come on, Thy. Celebrating might help my nerves. I'll teach you and Mina how to dance to a lyre," Chrysa says before winking at me.

Thyia allows herself to be dragged away, only looking back at Dolion with disappointment for a moment before a smile grows on her face. The three twirl hand in hand as the music builds. An older man stands behind the musicians and begins singing a song about Poseidon's birth.

Diomede claps to the beat and knocks her hip into Eriphyle's. "Join me in celebrating the Gods?"

Eriphyle peers back at Elara, who is still scowling. She appears to steel herself and tosses her blonde hair over her broad shoulders. "You'll need to show me the steps."

Diomede beams. "The patron of music founded *my* Island."

Eriphyle nods and stalks out to the dancing circle.

Diomede turns to Elara. "Come with us?"

"I don't dance," Elara says, staring ahead.

Diomede's smile dims, and she shuffles to Eriphyle's side with less cheer than before. But when Eriphyle holds her hand and slinks close, Diomede blooms again. They remind me of a sunrise when Diomede's flaming hair mixes with Eriphyle's gold. Eriphyle smiles just as Diomede spins them away from my view.

We watch the dancers for another minute until Dolion cocks his head towards Elara.

"Dance?" he mouths. I blink back at him as he grins and nudges me.

I exhale and shuffle closer to Elara, inwardly cursing being the eldest and most responsible. She shifts against the tree trunk. "There are war dances too, if you're interested," I tell her. "I've never seen them but read about the steps. I can explain them, and you could join the others?"

Her lips thin but she stays quiet.

Dolion cups my elbow and pulls me out from under the tree's shade. "I was asking you, not suggesting you ask Elara," he murmurs as he slides his hand to my wrist. He yanks me sideways as if forcing me to twist to the music and I let him turn me.

"Can we not return to the Palace? I could use this time to prepare." With the attention on the festival, I could read Orion's book. Other than what I've read so far about the Labyrinth, the contents and Orion's notes aren't enough. I've also learned that the Collection will occur until "it" becomes impossible, but neither the book nor the notes tell what 'it' is. It must be the heart of the bargain, the 'it' that makes logical skills, not physical, necessary, whether that means saving the Beast or not. I've created the board, the foundation for the puzzle, but half the pieces are missing.

Dolion spins me the opposite way. "You still can, Hero. This is important too."

My breath catches from the sudden movement. "What, dancing?"

He pulls me in only to spin me away and wrench me back to him, but too close, our chests brushing. "Trying to remember what you're fighting for in the Labyrinth."

I peer around the circle, attempting to put some distance between us but he won't release me. Over his shoulder, I can see Chrysa, Mina, and Thyia giggling as they trip over each other while trying to leap in tandem; Eriphyle is smiling wider than ever as Diomede ducks under her arms in time with the music. Others have joined the dance space, laughter and music heavy in the air.

"I don't need to remember." I know what's at stake.

Dolion clenches his jaw; it flexes in time with his heartbeat against my chest. "Then yes, just dancing. Can that not be important?"

Heat bursts from my cheeks and trails downward to pool in the pit of my stomach. It's like what I felt when Lukas kissed me just before leaving, and I have a fleeting image of a boat with green sails. Dolion won't let me respond to his question, loosening his grip just enough to put me in the traditional dancing position in his arms. Then he spins me faster and faster like a balanced top, grabbing my waist and lifting me in time with the music, over and over again. There's no time to think about what he implied, or how I might feel about it, as we keep moving, dancing and dancing until we're nothing but a blur of conjoined movement.

His hands flit about my waist, my back, my shoulders. Mine aren't idle either, clutching his shoulders and swooping down his muscular forearms, as we come together and come apart in the dance. It's fast and wild and different from any dances I've danced in Standia, when only Lukas was my partner and I worried too much about what others saw when I moved. Even though I know my robe is tearing, and my hair blowing into my face, none of it matters. Here, there are no steps, there is no audience judging me as the heir. There's only Dolion keeping me from falling, and me propelling my body to the music.

And maybe he's right, that this can be important, a tangible feeling to hold on to in the Labyrinth: for this moment, for this dance, there's no Collection, there's no secret to discover, there's just me letting myself feel free. And freedom is the point, freedom for the youngest daughters, freedom for Crete from whatever geas Minos has them under, freedom for me to be without self-doubt for once.

The song ends and Dolion captures me in his arms. We're both breathing heavily as the other dancers clap for the musicians. The singer starts up again, something low and haunting, but Dolion doesn't push us into the throng a second time. Instead, he keeps his hands on my waist, his fingers just framing the knife at my back, and smiles at me like he has a secret, his pale blue eyes a constellation of stars. The sun illuminates the single freckle on the curve of his right cheekbone. My lips curl into a smile that echoes his. He bites his lower lip as something familiar passes over his face. He leans close, breath ghosting over my mouth. I close my eyes in anticipation of his touch.

And then the screaming starts.

Chapter 17

Dark forms block out the light as the dancers scatter from the street. A loud screech fills the air as the unidentified beasts plummet from the sky. Dolion disappears, as do Kyra and Kynna. I don't waste more than a second on Dolion abandoning me, more focused on whatever new danger we're in. I reach the girls just as Elara does, and together we corral them underneath the olive tree.

Between the leaves, I can see the beasts: a dozen giant birds, with wings that glint in the sun like metal and sharp snapping beaks. The few festival attendees who didn't hide are screaming as they flee from the screeching birds that sweep over the crowd as if searching for something. Mina stands beside me as we both peer upward. For a minute, I wonder if they're Keres, the winged death spirits I thought I saw in the trees when we arrived in Crete. But the Keres can't kill, they only feast on the flesh of those who already died violent deaths. And the Keres have humanoid features, unlike these monstrous creatures. It's this same fact that tells me these aren't the Erinyes here to drag oath breakers into the ground. Though the Erinyes *will* attack, they look like winged women, not beasts.

"What are they? Why are they after us?" Thyia asks from my other side.

"They're birds," Diomede says.

Chrysa scoffs, but her voice wobbles and she inches closer to Thyia. "Yes, thank you, Diomede. We couldn't tell they were birds."

"Don't snap at her," says Eriphyle, squeezing Diomede's hand.

"They're man-eating birds," Mina says, not taking her eyes from the sky. "Papa Simo—my mama's father is from Prosfora, he told me about them. They're native there."

Chrysa shutters; it's unclear how much is an act. "Elara grew up with those? It explains so much."

Elara doesn't respond; she's already halfway up the tree and dropping branches she's torn off. By the time she hops back down, she has a pile of thick sword-like sticks at her feet. "They're not hunting, not when they screech that way. They've selected their prey and are attempting to find it. They must be targeting one of those people out there."

Only Eriphyle moves, dropping Diomede's hand to grab the largest stick from Elara's stash. Elara turns to the others, ignoring me.

"These sticks will do for now, but if you can, find something metal to pierce their skin. They are metal borne and will snap our branches soon enough. Other than that, they die like anything else."

The other four girls nod in varying degrees of acquiescence and pick out their sticks as my eyes widen in alarm.

"You can't be serious," I say faintly. These children shouldn't be fighting monsters. At least not monsters they hadn't already been forced to fight.

Elara holds her branch like a sword at her waist. "We don't sit and wait for death. We meet it head on."

A gnawing worry grows in my stomach. "You meet death you're pledged to meet, like the Beast. This is running after danger."

Elara juts out her chin. "We're the Collected." Then she ducks and rolls out from under the tree's canopy, her focus never leaving the sky. Eriphyle dashes after her followed by Diomede.

I snag Thyia's sleeve and block the remaining three from leaving. "You can't agree with this," There is bravery and there is folly. A good leader can recognize the difference, and these girls are walking into what could be a bloodbath that shouldn't involve them. "If you must help, there are other ways. You can gather the wounded, direct the guard, wrangle a trap even."

"You know I'm the last to agree with Elara," Chrysa says softly, like she's speaking to a child. "But this is what we can do."

"We were trained for this," Mina says, squaring her shoulders. Gone is the little girl from a few days ago who cried on the ship. In her place is the warrior that her Island forced her to become.

I tighten my grip on Thyia as hysteria tints my voice. "Not for this, this is not for you. There must be an army, the Palace guard, anyone else."

"We're expendable," Thyia says, more matter of fact than I'd ever have expected from her. *Where is the girl who fears the dark and flees from the spiders Chrysa placed in her breakfast chair?* Thyia gently brushes off my grasp and the three crouch in unison and leave the canopy's protection. I can just hear Chrysa ask Thyia what expendable means before the squawking birds drown out their voices.

The thing in my stomach grows until it's clawing at my skin, threatening to burst free. My hands cover my mouth as if to keep that feeling inside. *Is this how Father felt, when I pushed against his guidance and made my own foolish choice?* I trudge to the edge of the canopy and back twice. The military still hasn't arrived, not even a guard. The street is empty of almost everyone but the girls.

The ground shakes, and I nearly lose my balance. Thyia falls, the only thing that saves her from a bird's sharp beak. Eriphyle helps her stand and together they strike the closest bird. A clang rings out and it retreats. But the other birds keep coming, and even the retreating beast returns after making a loop around the girls' circle. Diomede's stick has snapped, and she's using a chair to attack the two diving for her head. Elara's is gone as well, but she's broken half a javelin from one of the bronze statues leading into the stadium and slashes it at the sky. Every few seconds a straggler bursts from a hiding place under one of the market stalls or under their own tree to rush from the birds' lunging attacks. But... the birds are no longer targeting anyone else. They're intent on the girls.

My eyes fall shut. The shoes and shifts were to train the birds on us, evidenced by the birds' focused search the moment they arrived in the street. For those who jeered and don't want the Collection to 'end as intended,' the birds will do what the geas won't allow them to do.

When I reopen my eyes, the dozen birds no longer gleam in the sunlight. Clouds cover the sky and thunder rumbles from the mountain behind the Palace. *Does Zeus' darkening sky reveal his displeasure or is he offering a sign?*

Movement from down the street pulls my attention. A man runs from stall to stall, but the birds ignore him. He must realize their disinterest as he soars from behind the overturned flower stall and zips down the street, carrying something over his shoulders. As he passes the tree, the last of the sunlight glints off the long cylindrical object. It's Periphetes' club. *My* club.

I let out a quiet groan. If I didn't already regret every step that started with laughing at Lyra before, I would now.

Once I place my illusion to appear invisible, I chase after the man holding my club. The earth rumbles again, another earthquake, perhaps a message from Poseidon this time. I've no idea whether he supports the brash plan Zeus inspired. But it knocks the man off balance, and he loosens his grip on the club. I shuffle up behind him to yank it from his fingers. The surprise I hoped for lasts long enough for me to get my hands around the handle, but then he turns and tries to wrench it back. His brows furrow but he doesn't otherwise react to grappling with a club that looks to be moving on its own due to my magicked invisibility.

During my brief period outside the protection of the tree, two birds left the flock and now glide towards me. They must still sense me somehow. I hiss under my breath. I've never had to create an illusion for a sense other than sight, I don't even know how. But the birds' spiky beaks distract the man and his howl of fear overwhelms my shriek of frustration until I can hug the club and race for the tree's canopy.

The sky opens, the dark clouds making good on their threats, first raining quietly then thundering against my skin, each drop splattering hard enough to cause a prick of pain. Through the haze, I can just see the birds attacking the girls, but they falter from the storm's assault, arcing and falling at an angle, instead of keeping their aim on their prey. The heavy rain showers their metal bodies, creating a symphony of clangs. Their squawks don't lessen but change, no longer the cry of the hunt but the screech of irritation. *Noise is their weakness.* Thank Zeus for the knowledge.

The ground rumbles again, another good sign as the bird targeting me only slices off a lock of my waterlogged curls instead of carving into my neck. I scramble under the overhang of the olive tree. Two birds dash after me, but fear hoists the bronze club above my head and swings it against the metal wings of the beasts before they can do any damage. The swipe doesn't do more than daze them, but the clash of metal-on-metal rings through the space and both birds squawk and flee.

Faster than I thought I could move, I snag a branch disturbed by the birds' flight, folding it and the club into my illusion. Though the beasts can see me, Athena's studies taught me that even one extra second hiding from their sight can be valuable.

My chiton tears, exposing slick skin to the sharp raindrops, but at least now I can breathe.

The ground shakes anew and I stumble, slipping in the rain slicked dirt. Poseidon *must* be on our side, as my near fall stops one of the searching birds from impaling my shoulders. Twice is coincidence, three times intentional. I finally make it to the girls, who stand back-to-back in a circle. Elara has bludgeoned one and impaled another, though not without getting a wing-tip slice to the cheek. Chrysa's cheek bleeds too, and blood trails down a rip in Diomede's sleeve to her wrist. After swallowing the last of my fear, I smack the stick against my club, the birds scattering above us screeching angrily.

"Noise," I shout over the din, never pausing in banging my makeshift instruments. "You need to scare them off with noise."

"Is that Thalia?" Chrysa says, spinning in place, searching for the source of the sound.

I drop the illusion. Only Mina shows surprise at my reveal. Chrysa looks envious, and a little intrigued by the trick. Thyia and Diomede offer only brief recognition before returning their focus to the sky. Eriphyle and Elara act as though I haven't appeared by magic.

"Make noise," I repeat as the flock plunges back towards us.

"We're not giving up," Eriphyle says, scowling. This time, instead of only looking to Elara for approval, she also glances at Diomede as well.

Elara grunts and hands me her metal rod. "We're not. But she's right," she says begrudgingly. "All creatures will avoid pain and discomfort. If we make enough sound, only the most determined will keep attacking and we can dispatch them." She takes my stick and aims it at the sky. "By the Gods, if you vomit near me again, Heir, I will beat you with that club when we finish."

Panic has me laugh at the situation. "Just hit the birds, you can complain later."

Eriphyle gives her branch to Diomede and grabs the broken pieces of Elara's from the ground. The two clack their sticks in a discordant symphony. Elara smacks any birds that get too close, and Mina and Chrysa alternate between hitting their sticks together and clanging them against the birds. The rain falls harder, blinding both us and the birds until I can't see the rod and club in my hands. The girls have all but disappeared in the gray. But the deluge adds to the cacophony, each raindrop clinking against their metal skin until the birds retreat. We don't realize it until the sky transforms from a haze of gray to a sickly green, proving the Gods *were* behind us and our actions today. The rain reduces to a mist, and we're left standing in the puddles.

Chrysa drags Mina and Thyia into a joint hug. Diomede leans into Eriphyle, beaming at the sky. Even Elara looks triumphant, her lips quirked upward.

Another earthquake rolls through the street, and we steal back under the olive tree.

When we're all corralled and my heartbeat slows to manageable levels, I inspect them. "Is everyone okay?"

"Do you care?" Thyia asks, but curiosity, not accusation, colors the tone.

"She's starting to like us," Chrysa says. She attempts a smirk but winces when it pulls the wound on her cheek. Diomede rips a clean strip from her remaining sleeve and presses it against Chrysa's face.

"I'm trying to protect you," I say, frowning. That's the point behind my presence on Crete.

"And show off her magic," Eriphyle mutters.

Mina sits on the muddy ground and stares at her feet, shock painting her features. "They were after us," she says.

"We know," Elara says, but it isn't the snarling tone she usually employs.

"Will they come back?" Chrysa asks her.

Eriphyle applies pressure to the wound on Diomede's arm while Thyia watches.

"Unlikely," says Elara, her own bloody cheek clotting. "Whatever led them to us will have washed away in the rain." She turns to me. "That wasn't a terrible idea, Heir."

"Next time, make us all invisible though," Chrysa says, falling to the ground beside Mina.

"I don't think it would have helped, they saw through it," says Mina, leaning her head on Chrysa's shoulder.

"And she'll want to keep it a secret, it's too dangerous otherwise. The King would harm her for it," Thyia adds, combing her fingers through her hair. Elara and the others stare at her and she shrugs. "Avgo is known for passion, and passion has many forms. Rage is simply passion under duress, and that's the only passion King Minos has."

"For that and for his hair," Chrysa says. "He probably spends more time on it than you, Thyia, to get it looking like spun gold. Though yours looks like the birds built a nest in it now."

Horrified, Thyia runs her hands through her matted locks.

"I'll help you untangle it, Thy," Diomede says.

"I'm going to find a caretaker," I tell them. We've done our part, more than. It's time to return to our roles as the Collected, and not battle-weary bird beaters. "Stay under the tree."

"You're not in charge," Elara says but everyone, even Eriphyle, groans. Elara huffs and leans against the slick tree trunk but doesn't bicker again. I leave the rod by her feet and take my club with me.

As soon as I'm out from under the tree, I replace my illusion to avoid meeting anyone else. If Minos or any of his lackeys were near enough to catch my magic, we would have seen them aiding us with the birds and protecting the King's assets.

The street remains empty as I trudge towards the stadium. The Palace is behind it, meaning it is the most likely place that Dolion and the others ran to. Luck remains with me as I find him under an overhang down one of the side streets leading away from the arena. But he's not alone, he holds up another man by his neck, whose feet dangle inches from the ground. Though I'm under an illusion, I still duck around the corner out of sight.

"What were you thinking?" Dolion growls, slamming the man's shoulders into the stone.

The man shakes his head as best he can. "You said it was time to be active. No more whispering in the dark but bringing hope to the light."

"Yes, through the plans made by people smarter than you."

The man spits blood on the ground. Dolion doesn't flinch as it splatters on him. "Just because I don't waste my off hours with that seer doesn't mean I'm stupid," the man says. "This was the plan."

"Who?" Dolion shakes him again. "Who told you *that* was the plan?"

"I came up with it," he snarls. "It does what we want. No Collected, no Collection. It's impossible!"

Dolion laughs bitterly. "Only until another seven years passes. That's not what we want. We need a permanent solution, you imbecile."

The man juts out his chin, wincing when it presses his head back into the stone. "The Gods saw, Dolion, they wouldn't have interceded otherwise. They *must* know now."

My heart thuds loud in my chest, I'm almost surprised they can't hear it. Dolion's grip tightens. "They know the Collected was in danger, but not why or how. No 'impossibility' to point at the right target. You did *nothing* to move our goal forward."

"But—" He slumps in Dolion's hold. "Damn."

"Instead, you put excess attention on us. If I'd known this was your plan when I got you access to the Palace—" Dolion cuts himself off and shakes the man again. "You're lucky you didn't ruin everything. Where did you even find those monsters?"

"They were up the mountain," he grunts. He gestures to his neck and Dolion drops him with a sigh. "I was trying to be helpful, you know. You've been interpreting the plan your own way too. It's not like wooing one of them is much different from what I did."

"Manipulating someone's *heart* to sway the outcome differs from outright killing them. And now, who knows what your damned birds will do. Not to mention Leocedes running out into the arena and getting himself killed." Dolion says, leaning against the stone and crossing his arms around his chest. "She has questions, ones I won't be able to answer even if I wanted to. She barely talks to me over her fear. Now she'll hide away again, and we'll be trying this again in another seven years without an heir's skills on our side."

They both lower their heads as I curl my hands into fists, squeezing until my fingernails dig deep into my palms. Blood roars in my ears and I miss whatever else the man says to Dolion. He leaves and Dolion rests against the wall with his eyes closed. Before I can think through what I'm doing, I stalk down the alley to confront him, dropping the illusion in my anger.

Dolion's eyes fly open at the wet slapping sound my ruined tunic makes on the ground. The relief in his expression looks genuine, but the deceitful are wily.

He sputters. "You're here! You're well, I wondered with the birds. And you found the club! What luck. I stashed it when we arrived, but someone took it. How happy I am that it was y—"

"What's your game here?" There's no need for a mask to cover my emotions, my frigid countenance comes naturally now.

"Game?" He smiles wide, though his eyes twitch.

"Yes, your game with the Collection, with me. Your *goal*." Once I start, the words flow like a raging river. "You say you want to help me succeed, that you're closer to getting your 'due' than ever, but then I find you're in league with the man who attempted to murder us with man-eating birds. You give me silly little hints that have no bearing on my acts in the Labyrinth, except to almost ruin everything. What is 'success' for you here? My death, *all* our deaths?" I force away the tears threatening to break through the ice. "Because you may be unaware, but that's already the endgame of the Collection. We die. I don't need you helping things along."

He blinks, his mouth agape. "Thalia," he starts, placating.

"No," I spit, stalking closer until we're chest to chest, pointing my finger at his throat. "Tell me. Are we on the same side?"

"The geas," he croaks.

I shrug; my concern flew away with the birds his friend set on a group of teenagers. "You've almost activated it before. I won't stop you this time."

His mouth opens and closes twice, his frost blue eyes blown wide. "I can assure you your death is not my aim. It would actually be counter to my goals."

I press my index finger into the dip of his throat. I can feel the faint beat of his heartbeat through the tip. "Are we on the same side?"

"As much—" He coughs, his face turning red. "As much as we can be. I do like you, Thalia. I still wish to pursue—"

I cut off his continued lies. "Are you trying to stop the Collection?"

Veins pop in his neck, spiderwebbing up his face. Something cold like guilt slides down my back like the ice I'm projecting in my face, but I ignore it.

"Yes." His voice is no more than a croak.

The confirmation does little to soothe the hackles of fear and despair trailing along my skin. "Why?"

"For her," he rasps.

That I understand, even if I must swallow the disappointment at finding his attention false. It isn't like it matters, not with death staring me in the face in a few days.

But I have one last question for him, one that sprouted at Hecaline's fearful demand and bloomed when the man willingly swallowed his tongue. "What is the boar?"

His eyes water and a hacking cough starts in his throat. "He's... important," is all he can say before his eyes roll back in his head.

I step back and wipe my hands on my tunic, as if I can wipe away the unease at what I've demanded of him off my skin. "I understand secrets. I understand having goals that might put you at odds with others. And while we may desire the same ends, we are *not* a team. I will not be used." I lift my chin and drop the club with a clang. "You should find a better hiding spot for that. Assuming I live, I may want a souvenir."

Without waiting for a response, I turn on my heel and march away from him, my heart pounding. At least I know his interest in me was all part of his duplicity, though I can't imagine how it helps. And his duplicity doesn't matter, it *shouldn't* matter. Angry tears I held back pool in the corner of my eyes, and I scrape them away.

He wants to stop the Collection, which means we're aligned. But in nothing else. His guile doesn't matter, I'll *make* it not matter. The puzzle is all that matters. I'll stop the Collection, save his damn boar, whatever that means, and I'll return to Standia as the heir it deserves. Then, he can choke on his revenge alone.

Chapter 18

A still pond ripples as a single drop of red blood lands on the surface. There's a creature at the bottom, looking up. Two bones flash in the light. The creature blinks its bright eyes slowly until the blood hazes the pond and only darkness remains.

Chrysa drags me to training the next morning, after pouting at me most of the evening. She knew something affected me yesterday when I returned from visiting with Dolion, but she didn't ask, and I didn't volunteer.

Learning what they know of the Collection is as valuable as anything in any book. After all, it was Chrysa's notes that mentioned the boar, which is the only thing that lessens the pull to Orion's study. They take me to a small grove just outside the Palace, leading up the mountain. But by the time we arrive, I've exhausted their knowledge on the Collection.

"It's a sacrament," Diomede is saying as we enter the small clearing. "The Beast is a symbol of our misdeeds from the Island Wars, and the Gods demand we work together to defeat it and show the King how penitent we are. Once the Collected do so, they deserve to return."

Chrysa raises her eyebrows in my direction. After I quietly explain what penitent means, she asks, "So the fact that *no* one has returned?"

"They didn't come together as brothers in arms, and were justifiably killed," Diomede says with a shrug.

Mina turns green. "Are you saying we *deserve*—"

Elara stomps to the opposite side of the grove. "It's a waste to worry about why it happened, what matters is how to win it. Now, who intends to challenge me today?"

Eriphyle looks conflicted, her dark eyes flicking from Elara and Diomede. Quietly, she asks, "Does Prosfora explain the Collection differently?"

Elara's eyes widen, likely because Eriphyle didn't immediately follow her command. "It's a skills test," she finally says. "The winner dispatches the Beast and gains glory for their Island."

Chrysa repeats her question, "And that no one returns means no one deserved glory?"

"No," she snaps, losing all patience. "It simply means no one of sufficient skill has competed yet."

"Until you," Chrysa says, snorting. Elara juts out her chin but doesn't deny it. Chrysa eyes Eriphyle. "What does Petalidi say?"

"It's like Prosfora's," she says, biting her lip and wincing in Diomede's direction. "It means glory for the winner alone."

"With failure meaning punishment no matter the version, either by not being skilled enough today or because of the acts of long dead men," Chrysa says. "How fun for us. I'm *so* glad I volunteered."

"I always wondered why they pick the youngest," Mina says as she braids her short curls into messy pigtails. "Even though we age-out, it seems like they always pick the younger girls anyway, even if it's a blind lottery."

"We're vestal," Diomede says with a gentle smile. "That's part of the sacrament."

Eriphyle's golden skin loses all color. Chrysa looks ready to tease but Thyia interrupts.

"We're expendable," she reminds us. "We've no children or positions, and we've lived the shortest, meaning our families may not mourn as deeply as our elders."

"So, it isn't about the most skilled, but the least likely to be missed," Mina says, frowning like she's learned something painful.

Thyia shrugs. "Avgo believes similarly to Gerenia. This is not something to be won, but a sacrifice for our brothers and sisters from the other Islands and for our families who are left behind. They will live on because of our sacrifice, like Aphrodite's."

The already low mood in the grove sours. Each appears caught in their thoughts and they start to stretch, the conversation ending.

Maybe a combination of interpretations is right, I think while I inspect where they've been hiding since our arrival. The steep incline can't be good for practicing, but I only know that in theory. They've cleared the underbrush, which is piled near one of the trees marking the boundary of the space.

A combined punishment and a skills test, a *logical* skills test that is, seems an odd thing for a God to demand in exchange for aid. And it doesn't explain why Minos goes to such lengths to keep it quiet. Perhaps I've been wrong from the start, and Minos didn't need the aid of the Gods to defeat the Islands. There is *some* debt that the Collection pays, he admitted as much my first night here in that private room. *But if not in winning the war, then what?*

I look at Elara, who is running through a series of moves found in pankration, a combination of wrestling and grappling. I'm only vaguely familiar with the art because Standia's records confirm it was a skill for young boys and my ancestors couldn't find trainers who were willing to train us when the Collection changed to demand only women. Eriphyle is mimicking Elara's movement. Though she moves less smoothly than Elara, she appears no less skilled. I consider what I know of their two Islands.

Prosfora had more soldiers than almost all the other Islands combined, and Petalidi held the same distinction for weaponry.

The Islands were divided in fighting both each other and Crete, but Crete's military needed to be *enormous* to conquer all the Islands without divine aid. And so far, I've only seen a handful of guards but no army. Without Poseidon's direct influence keeping the Islands at bay, Minos would need a standing military in case the Islands rose up again. There aren't enough Cretan volunteers available otherwise.

I should have asked Father why Standia had never attempted to overthrow Crete's rule, whether it was by choice or by compulsion. My rashness in leaping into the Collection on a day's notice has longer reaching consequences than I expected.

I call out to the girls. "Why are you not training near the armory?"

Mina wrinkles her nose. "There's an armory?"

I mentally revisit the map I'd found of the Palace grounds. There were no depictions of the interior, which given its twining hallways, is unsurprising. I crane my neck to the side to orient myself. "According to the plans, it should be just around that bend."

Chrysa and Mina trade glances, the prospect of an adventure bringing identical excited smiles to their faces. "Let's go!" they say in unison.

"We don't have time to waste exploring," Elara says, fisting her hands on her trim waist.

"One less person training just means one more person for you to easily beat," says Chrysa. She, Mina, and Thyia stand beside me. Diomede joins us, followed by Eriphyle, who looks back at Elara and shrugs.

"Hunting a building is our best option when we cannot hunt the Beast," Eriphyle says.

"There's a chance there might also be unprotected weapons," Diomede says, slipping her hand in Eriphyle's, whose golden cheeks flush.

"I wouldn't think cheating is part of a sacrament," Thyia says, cocking her head.

"Didn't you say bringing weapons made everything unfair?" Chrysa's eyes flash. "Elara looked ready to spit at you when you did."

Diomede smiles beatifically. "No, the sacrament is us arriving with nothing but ourselves and preparing to meet the Beast. Finding weapons *together* once we've arrived would surely honor the Gods in proving we are united under Crete."

"That sounds convenient, but I don't care," Chrysa declares. "Maybe we'll need to break in, and Thalia can practice picking a lock."

"I want to pick a lock," Mina says as the six of us trudge away from Elara's fuming form.

According to the map I found, the armory is attached to the back of the Palace like a barnacle. If it is anything like Standia, it should have two entrances-one from the exterior and one from inside the Palace. After a few minutes' walk, where Chrysa and Mina act as though *they* are leading us to the armory and not me, we find it surrounded by ancient trees. From the thick under-brush and overgrown greenery crawling up the sides, it appears as though we're the first to come upon it in a long time.

More interesting is the single derelict building just beside it, unconnected to the Palace but close enough to the armory to be meaningful. I'd say it is the remains of a set of barracks, but time's ravages make it too difficult to tell. Most of the bricks decayed and crumbled long ago. Soldiers would likely congregate here to train and provide defense during a siege. But for Minos to overcome the Islands, he'd need space to train and house *thousands*.

Thyia clutches the neck of her tunic. "These are the only barracks? Even Avgo can house several hundred if the need arises."

"Maybe the others were destroyed," Mina offers.

"Unlikely," Eriphyle says gruffly, peering around the area. "There would still be an iron framework or the remains of a foundation if they existed."

"What does it mean that there's only one?" asks Chrysa.

"That they didn't need an army," I say. That I've confirmed the purpose for the bargain struck, to win an unwinnable war against our Islands, I keep secret.

Diomede hesitates before we get too close. "Perhaps we should leave."

"You *want* to go train with Elara again?" Mina asks, brows raised.

"Elara is unobjectionable," Diomede says mildly.

Chrysa snorts at the bland praise.

"I meant because of the plants," Diomede says as she points to the bushes at the base that stretch past the nonexistent rooflines, stepping forward. Eriphyle's quick grip keeps her in place, but it doesn't appear Diomede intended on touching the plants, whatever they are.

I peer at the creeping vines and shrubbery. They're beautiful in contrast to the ruins: winding leaves ending in cup-shaped flowers that are so dark a purple they look almost black, violet flowers that look like buttercups, star-shaped blooms on spindly stems. "What are they?"

"The great and smart Thalia doesn't *know?*" Chrysa says, pitching her voice sarcastically.

I restrain rolling my eyes. "They aren't plants we cultivate on Standia. If they were, I'd identify them for you."

Chrysa hums. "Excuses, excuses."

"Some of it is fine," Diomede says from behind the cage of Eriphyle's arms, pointing. "Medicinal even. That's belladonna, there's hellebore." She shivers. "But the purple ones... that's Cerberus' spit. The Gods don't like this place."

Or *someone* doesn't like it. But I remember that story: the drool from Cerberus, Hades' canine guardian, dripped through the earth and out bloomed monkshood, known as aconite. I've never seen these plants outside our apothecary book, but they didn't look like the illustrations. Either the book or Diomede is wrong. If she's right, they're all poisonous. "Are they wild or cultivated?"

Diomede shakes her head sharply. "No one cultivates Cerberus' spit."

It's harder to keep the eye roll from forming this time, but I manage it. Of the plants she listed, aconite has the most medicinal uses.

Giving the herbal threats a wide berth, we creep through the remnants of the doorway, a bare space choked with rubble and debris. Only two walls still stand, and cobwebs hang from the corners. Thyia takes one look at the spiderwebs that are still dewy from the morning damp and scampers back outside.

"Too bad there's no door," Chrysa says, wrinkling her nose as she steps over the crumbled remains. Dust dances in the air, catching the occasional glimmer of sunlight that pierces the gloom.

A musty, almost stale, scent permeates the area near the remains of the door, like the stench of the Labyrinth but worse. Mina sniffs, looking more rabbit than girl. "What's that smell?"

"Hemlock," Diomede says, drifting closer to a stringy green plant covered in tiny white flowers. "This looks like it's been cut recently."

"Well, this place looks and smells as good as my and Thalia's room," Chrysa declares.

Diomede pales, her milky skill looking almost spirit-like. "I'm terribly sorry, Chrysa. Had I known your and Thalia's space was so poorly outfitted, we surely could have sought alternative accommodations."

"She's kidding," I say to Diomede as I survey the broken walls. "Our room is likely the same as yours."

Chrysa and Mina inspect the space as Chrysa snorts again. "Yeah, that. It's more like a metaphor for being horrible, because of, you know, the imminent death." She glances at me and waggles her eyebrows, repeating 'metaphor' as though I should be proud. A smile pulls at my lips.

She doesn't wait for my reaction because she and Mina discover the remains of an iron bunk. Together they heave what looks to be part of the wall off the pile of broken bricks that hides it. Any other beds must be buried beneath other piles of the collapsed ceiling or already rotted away. But no matter how many beds are missing, the size of the room wouldn't support a large army, perhaps only a few dozen soldiers.

Chrysa hops onto the iron frame. "Just as comfortable as our beds though," she says. She finishes the joke with a shriek as the frame crumbles under her weight.

Mina gets to her side the quickest, and she and Diomede pull her from the cracked frame. There's red on her arms and over her eyebrow.

Diomede rubs at Chrysa's arms and the red smudges like a stain. "Are you hurt?"

"The only thing bruised is my pride," Chrysa says, wetting her fingers and washing away the rust the iron bars left on her face. My smile stretches, I made the same joke to Lukas only days ago.

"I doubt anything can injure that," Eriphyle says from where she sits on one of the crumbled piles. Diomede frowns and glides to her side.

Chrysa's eyes widen with glee. "Well, this trip is already worthwhile, if it has Eriphyle showing she has a personality."

Diomede looks like she isn't sure who to scold. She ends up glowering at Chrysa. "That isn't very kind."

"Are we going to the armory?" Thyia calls from outside the crumbling facade.

"Spiders," Chrysa mouths to Mina, who grins and the two tiptoe towards the webs near the back. "In a minute, Thyia," Chrysa says in a sing-song voice.

Diomede exhales and looks more put-upon than before.

Their ability to find pleasure in the mundane only increases the determination under my skin that we get out of this alive. "We're going now. No spiders," I add apologetically.

"Spoilsport," Chrysa hisses. Mina echoes her but all four dutifully leave the barracks' shell and we turn back to the armory as a group.

This building is less time-worn, the three walls surrounding the Palace intact. No door greets us, but there's another rectangular shaped opening. I walk through first, and a spark of electricity pings against my teeth.

"Wait," I urge the girls, holding out my hands to block them from entering. A buzzing feeling pricks against my fingers. I still have my tongue, so the geas isn't the terrible kind, but there's some kind of magic on the entry. "There's a geas boundary here. Be careful with what you say or do inside."

Tentatively, they all follow me inside, each taking careful steps, even Chrysa. When we're all inside and no one fainted upon entry, I inspect the armory. It's as small as I expect, if only to match the size of the barracks, with empty shelves covered in dust. Vines and moss crawl up the worn bricks, intertwining with remnants of shattered shields and what look like pieces of corroded weapons. A handful of racks, now skeletal frames, line the walls, their contents long pilfered or claimed by the relentless corrosion of time. Or perhaps they were always empty.

I trail my fingers over one of the grimy shelves. At one point, it might have held long spears, but there's no way to tell. Crete used to require soldiers to provide their own armor and weaponry, but records say Minos put a stop to that. It was a symbol of his wealth, an ancient transcript reported, that they could outfit their soldiers. But maybe it was a ruse, as he had so little army to equip. Maybe it wasn't a symbol of anything but his lies.

I turn to the girls, who haven't moved from the entrance and are uncharacteristically quiet. "What do you think?"

"Nothing," Mina says, blinking repeatedly.

"Yes, there's nothing," Diomede says.

I drop to my knees to peer at the bottom shelf, where I'd hoped to find the remains of a stash of swords. "There may be an old bow back here."

"There's nothing," Chrysa repeats. Slowly, I turn to face her. The others nod in agreement until they're all blinking, and their faces go slack.

"Nothing," they repeat as one.

The geas.

Quickly, I bustle them from the building, shooing and pushing them through the entrance and back into the overgrown grove until we're out of reach of the armory and its malicious magic.

"That's weird," Chrysa says as she leans against a tree near the aconite bush. "My skin itches."

Relief pools in my stomach that the geas didn't do something else to harm them, that it just affected their sight in the armory. Why I wasn't affected is a question for later.

"Perhaps—" I begin, but Mina interrupts.

"Where's the armory?"

"Yeah," Chrysa says, crossing her arms around her stomach. "I'm all for avoiding training, but I thought you'd show us something."

Thyia cocks her head and stares at me, confused. "Didn't you say the armory was here?"

The flow of relief mutates into dread. "It is," I say slowly. They look at me as though I've said the grass beneath our feet was orange.

With trembling fingers, I gesture to the building behind us. "There. We went inside, there was a geas line." My eyes fall shut. "And that must be what's happening now, you can't remember entering."

Diomede leaves Eriphyle and places her hand on my forehead. "Are you well?"

"She can't be, not if she's started imagining things," Eriphyle says, frowning, her focus narrowed to where Diomede touches me.

"I'm fine," I assure Diomede, who nods and returns to Eriphyle. "Do you—do you remember entering the barracks?"

They all stare back owl-eyed and blink in unison, standing stiller than statues. Were I not already fearful for their minds, I'd be frightened for myself in the presence of six living-specters. Finally, as though someone de-molded them from their sculpture casts, they move again.

"What are you *talking* about?" Thyia's voice raises. "There are no barracks here, Minos' army lives on the fourth floor of the Palace, the western wing." She bats her eyes teasingly. "If not for the prohibition in visiting, I'd have tried to meet a soldier."

That is absolutely untrue but I've no time to react other than letting my jaw fall open in shock, as Chrysa laughs.

"Are you trying to find a *husband*? If you live through the Collection, that is," she asks with a grin.

Thyia shrugs. "Love and passion are powerful. With the right amount of attention, a soldier might have saved me."

Chrysa looks horrified while Mina looks contemplative. "How would that work?" Mina asks.

"Do not consider such things," Diomede says, brows raised.

Unease threatening to spill over and drown me, I snag Chrysa's forearm and shake it. "Where did this come from then, if not the barracks?" I point to the rust smudge from the iron bed frame, my voice shrill.

Chrysa blinks again. "I must have run into something."

It feels as though all the blood has left my body. "And the dirt at my knees?"

"You're not the most graceful," Diomede says, wincing like she's caused me mortal harm at the implied insult.

"Chrysa said you trip over the air when you try to get out of bed," adds Mina. Chrysa nods in agreement.

"We should return to training and let Thalia figure herself out." Eriphyle says. She curls her arm around Diomede's waist to direct her back the way we came.

The others follow, whether because the geas is pushing them to leave the area or because they want to get away from the terror that must display on my face.

"Be careful, Thalia. If you lose your mind, you won't have any other skills to offer in the Labyrinth," Chrysa says. She smirks but confusion still swirls in her green eyes.

"That isn't kind," Diomede says as they all leave the grove.

Their feet crunching on the grass almost drowns out Chrysa's response, but I can just hear it before they retreat too far. "It's how I show affection."

I gracelessly drop to the ground and cover my face. Minos' magic is worse than I could have imagined.

Chapter 19

I run in and out of the armory three times, but I still remember it and the ramshackle barracks. After the third time, I can *just* see a spiderwebbing net of gold along the walls out of the corners of my vision, physical evidence of the geas magic over the building. Unlike the door in the Labyrinth, which showed me the illusion of a blank wall, this one doesn't reveal what the girls saw. Tangles explode everywhere I look; there's no way I can unravel this one. Before I consider attempting anything, something flutters in the trees above and I swear I see a flash of wings and white, gnashing teeth.

I flee to Orion's study, in search of the books that may save us. But instead of studying, I stare at Orion's covered desk ignoring the many books he's laid out for me. None of them will explain the geas we encountered. And that a geas can manipulate minds more than voices is harrowing. Everything I've learned is suspect, if Minos can make someone physically forget an event that's occurred.

I cover my face with my hands again. That's not even considering the possibility that the girls had it right, that there was no armory, and I was losing *my* sanity. It *might* make sense, if I'm the only one who—

"Are you well?"

Orion's voice pulls me from the spiral of my thoughts. He stands behind his chair, still all covered in black.

I remember our last conversion, and his offer to provide me with a safe space. "I could be better," I tell him as my voice catches. Why someone whose face I can't see inspires more trust than anyone else I've met is probably a character flaw I should examine after stopping the Collection.

He slinks into his chair. "Because of the Festival?"

I blanch. I'd almost forgotten about the murderous birds, though Dolion's deceit has kept my blood simmering nearly all day. "Gods' teeth, how was that only yesterday? No. While I certainly wasn't expecting the birds, that was manag—"

"Birds?" He's leaning forward, dragging his scarred hands towards a book and clutching it tightly. It's his hands that give away his feelings. Head angle helps too, the subtleties of body language giving away what his facial expression otherwise would. I wonder if others attempted to read me so, to learn the tells that my illusions couldn't hide.

"The man-eating birds, but we handled them," I explain to soothe the unease evident in the set of his shoulders and taut grip on the book. "They were intent on us and attacked us." He stiffens at my answer, and I frown. "What did you mean if not them?"

"There were earthquakes and storms. I hop—assumed at least one of the Gods had positive opinions on your introduction, though I suppose that was too much to wish for. Zeus has never..." His fingers tighten on the book as he cuts himself off. I wonder if there'll be fingerprint indentations when he releases it. "How did you dispatch these birds?"

A spark of fear flares through my mind and I swallow the lump the memory creates. "I found some metal, and we used it to frighten them until the rain became too much for them and they gave up."

"Clever," he says, releasing the book and dropping his shoulders. "Without bloodshed too. That's... good. Surprising, but good."

I try to shrug nonchalantly, but my cheeks heat from the praise. "We must all use what we have."

He hums, the sound trickling over my skin like cool water. "You shouldn't have needed to use anything. That is an oversight I will rectify," he finishes darkly.

I wonder what control he has over such things.

He places his hands on the table, they're tense like claws. "If the Festival isn't the cause, what ails you?"

"There's a—" I pause. Innate trust only goes so far, the rest must still be earned, not with the taint of Dolion's duplicity painting my encounters with those that claim to be allies. "The topic I wish to discuss is sensitive."

He leans forward again. "I told you this is a safe space, Thalia. Of that, you can be sure."

"But safety is relative. I may consider something a secret and tell my friend to keep it safe, but they may believe sharing my secret is the safest path."

"Clever and pragmatic," he says, and my flush deepens. "Perhaps you could tell me the topic and together we can discover if we have opposing beliefs on whether its... sensitivity must be kept secret."

That's the best assurance I'll get. After controlling my blush, I pitch my voice low, as though Minos can hear through walls. To be fair, given the new information on the geas, he very well could. "What's your position on the Collection?"

Orion's fists clench as he ducks his head. "I wish for it to be successful."

I purse my lips; another half-statement, like Dolion's. "But what does that *mean*? Do you want it to continue on, or would success mean ending it?"

"Ending, of course," he says, his neck cracking as he raises his head. Were his face uncovered, his expression would likely be shocked.

There's no strain in his voice when he answers, nor evidence of the geas. I chance another question. "...But what would ending it mean?"

"That—that one of the Island women—that they were agreeable and met—" He clears his throat. "My apologies. There are things I cannot say until the Collection occurs. It wouldn't be fair, you see. But ending the Collection would be a boon, to the women, the world, and—" He swallows audibly. "And myself."

"Does the end mean death to any of the Collected?"

He stands with enough force that his chair topples to the floor. "There should be no death from the Collection!"

Before I know I'm doing it, I reach over the table to grasp his clenched fists.

He looks down at my hands before slumping like a puppet with its strings cut. "I am sorry again, Thalia. I hope I didn't... alarm you."

"You didn't." Except that I believe we are aligned. And with the edges of the puzzle only just filled in, I need all the information I can get.

"I wish I could say more but fairness holds my tongue, you see," he says as he gently shakes off my grip and fixes his chair.

Fairness and *something* else. We both reseat ourselves and I lean forward, intent.

"But your apology brings me to my issue. What do you know of the geases Minos uses for the Collection?"

"There are many," he says, cocking his head to the side. "I'm told the citizens are under one, something placed at birth through their bloodlines. And those of us in the Palace and thus more connected to the Collection are under another. Don't doubt my sincerity, Thalia. I would not hide information from you if—"

My breath catches. "Yours is different?"

He crosses his arms around his muscular chest. "Mine is specific to my own circumstances."

"And if I were to ask you exactly what happens in the Collection and *how* to end it, could you tell me?"

He shakes his head. "In that scenario, the geas attached to the citizens and I are similar. I cannot tell you how to succeed."

That's what I assumed, and I shut my eyes in defeat. It would be too easy to find someone to explain it all. Unless I want to throw myself at the mercy of Minos and demand he tell me. Outside how suicidal that might be, it would also tell him at least one of his geas boundaries doesn't affect me, a fact I must keep hidden for my safety.

When I reopen my eyes, I stare at Orion's clothed torso. "What can you tell me about geas boundaries?"

His forearms flex, muscles rippling in a stressed pattern. "What geas boundaries?"

I gesture wildly around the room. "The ones on the fourth floor here, though I've not found them yet. The ones in the Labyrinth forcing us to enter it. And the one in the remains of the armory that makes you lose your memory."

Something cracks on Orion's side of the table. One arm of his chair broke, and he holds the wood in his hand. "There is magic forcing you into the Labyrinth?"

"Of course." I huff a frustrated laugh, ignoring his feat of strength. "*You* want it ended without bloodshed. You should understand why we wouldn't willingly run to our doom." I think of Elara. "Some girls are probably amenable, but any rational person wouldn't gleefully run to the center given the risks awaiting us there."

"Indeed," he says stiffly, dropping the broken wood to the floor. "As you can see, I'm no help on the matter of geases. You're better off finding someone else to speak with." He stands and offers a sharp bow. "I must depart. You may remain in this room for as long as you like."

The speed at which he attempts to flee threatens to give me whiplash. Before he can enter the doorway behind the bookshelf, I catch him and grab his forearm. "Don't go. If my questions upset you, it wasn't my intent. I apologize, I seem to do that a lot lately."

He sighs and ducks his head. "It's fine. That realization was—it felt as though—I'm simply... invested in the Collection."

I wince. There's more than one reason I stay quiet under my mask. "I understand."

I release his arm and he turns. This close, he towers over me, with my head only coming up to his covered chin.

"I meant what I said about geases, Thalia. I have limited information beyond the basic. Minos' minister keeps all such information, most likely under lock and key." He ducks his head. "It wouldn't do for others to learn how they're undone. Unfair, you see."

I ball my hands on my hips. "What's unfair about knowing exactly what we're being forced into?" He flinches and my stance softens. "I'm sorry. I'm doing it again."

As I turn to return to my seat, I glimpse the room behind him. It's a modest kitchen, with a low fire and a table with a single chair. With his secretive and solitary lifestyle, it's likely he can't partake from the Palace's large kitchen in the courtyard. Within it are two more doorways, one directly across from where I stand. Behind it is the corner of a misshapen bed and piles of books teetering around it, a string unwound and trailing out of view. The bedroom looks identical to what I saw at the top of the second entrance to the Labyrinth, the one I thought might belong to the Keeper of the Beast. "Is that your room?"

"Yes." There's a question in his tone, but I ignore it as my mind considers these additional facts.

From my vantage point two doors away, I crane forward to take in the piled books, the things I should have realized mirrored what I found in Orion's study. "Are you the Keeper of the Labyrinth?"

This time, I don't stare at his cloth covered face, but watch his hands. They twitch at my question.

"I suppose that's as good a title as any," he says. "Or as good as I may admit right now. Why do you ask?"

I return to my chair at his desk. "I happened upon your room when practicing in the Labyrinth."

"Did you make it to—" A shocked inhale comes from beneath the cloth as his voice intensifies. "You entered the second elevator?"

"Your 'always go left' advice proved valuable," I say, ducking my head. Exploring a stranger's space without permission is easier when you don't have to *admit it* to the stranger. "Apologies for my curiosity in your private space. I'm not sure where my impulse control has gone."

"No, but that you found it, and could enter it. That's—never happened before. I can't say I mind the intrusion," he says warmly. "Nor do I object to you feeling safe enough with me to act as you have."

A smile blooms from his kindness, though he's downplaying how far I overstepped, given that I've stolen into his room and prodded at his personal feelings. I quickly change the subject. "You being the Keeper explains your investment in the Collection and why you'd want it to end. I'm glad we have that in common."

He inclines his head in agreement.

"And I can understand why our unwillingness to enter the center would bother you," I say to better dull the discomfort between us. "The fewer women that enter, the less likely the Beast will be dispatched."

He scuttles closer to the desk. "The Beast?"

"Yes, although you probably have a name for it. The monstrous being we're supposed to either kill or let kill us, depending on what version of the story you hear. Though I'm hopeful I can end it without our death at least. I recently learned the skills we've been told are necessary for the Collection might be detrimental, and that maybe we should be *saving* the—"

Orion interrupts with a hacking cough. As he holds his hands to his throat, he attempts another bow, but the warmth is gone from his voice. "I am sorry, Thalia, but I truly must leave. I have duties related to the Labyrinth and must care for my throat. If you'll excuse me." And he leaves through the door as though chased by the Beast we were discussing.

Chapter 20

As the sun sets that night, the Palace walls shake from the foundation. Poseidon wants to tell us something, but I can't guess what. Maybe if we're lucky, he'll leave Olympus and come to Crete. His presence could delay the Collection until I fill in some of the missing parts of the puzzle and can prove Minos' oath breaking.

"I'm going to bunk with Mina and Thyia in case the ceiling smashes in," Chrysa tells me as we settle in after dinner. "Do you want to come?"

I slip my fingers under my pillow, feeling for Orion's book I'd hid when she arrived. "I'll stay here. Besides, five in one room would be too much."

Another earthquake rolls through the Palace. Dust drifts down from the ceiling.

"Diomede thinks the earthquakes mean the Gods are mad at us, so *she's* sharing with Eriphyle instead." She smirks. "Maybe tomorrow she can confirm whether Eriphyle has a personality."

I smile wanly at the joke she doesn't remember making earlier that day. "She'll tell you to be kind, I'm sure."

Chrysa laughs. "You're right. Anyway, yell if the walls fall." She leaves the room just as another quake hits, shaking her into the door before it slams shut.

My smile fades as I pull open Orion's book a second time.

"*Why did they* all *attack first?*" he writes over the section about the former Collected. *To save themselves from death by Beast*, I imagine responding. I trail my fingers over the dozens of names there, finding Serai's name added in ink near the bottom. My stomach churns at the clinical way their deaths are listed. The newer names overlap the earlier notes that continued his first question, *"Did none of them care about the crown?"*

What crown, I wonder. *Is it a victory crown for the winner or something else? And did they not want the crown, or did a geas force them to* believe *they didn't? Or is the crown—*

The walls shake again, lurching me from the bed. I take it as a sign. After stashing the book, I sneak from our room. If the geas boundaries don't work on me, perhaps I can break into the minister's rooms while he sleeps and find out more on how they work and whether they are influencing the Collected. I'd never consider such mischief on Standia, but maybe I'm not limited to being that Thalia anymore.

As I turn the corner from our hallway, I run into Dolion. His thick shoulder slams into my chest and I must swallow a pained scream to keep the others from leaving their rooms.

"Where're you headed, Hero?" He smiles wide.

I momentarily forget the pain in my chest in favor of my growing annoyance. "That's none of your business."

He leans against the wall, blocking my exit. "We may not be a team, but we can work together."

I exhale and smooth my face of any expression. "That is nearly the literal definition."

"I see the constipated look is back," he says, roaming his eyes over me. "Pity."

"You lost any ability to comment on me the minute your attention proved false," I say, lifting my chin.

"Were you upset about the attention? Because it wasn't false." His hand snags on one of my curls and he tucks it behind my ear.

My jaw drops in the combined motion of shock and outrage. I know what I heard. "Don't patronize me. You're using me to get vengeance for your lost love."

His hand remains in my hair, and he drags it back to my neck, fisting my curls. I restrain a shiver. "You keep talking of being used. In what way have I used you? Attempting to help you? Giving you hints?" He pitches his voice low and deep, letting it trail over my skin like a physical touch as he arcs my head back. "When I tried to kiss you?"

"Exactly." I'm ashamed to say I'm a little breathless.

He releases me to cross his arms and look at me through his long lashes. "Nothing stops both from being true."

The ground shakes again, knocking me backward, which has the benefit of giving me a little clarity from Dolion's soft touches. "Even if you are speaking honestly, we met less than a week ago, Dolion. If the choice was getting your vengeance by stopping the Collection or saving my life but the Collection continued, which would you choose?"

"They aren't mutually exclusive," he says, clenching his jaw.

I heave a heavy sigh, remembering why I let the hope of him wash away with the rain. "Just let me pass, Dolion."

Silently, he steps to the side. Before I turn the corner, he calls out, "The guard has doubled, since the King and his entourage have left. Thought you might like to know."

I falter before shaking it off and leaving him at the hallway entrance. When Dolion is out of sight, I confirm I'm alone and place my illusion. No reason to risk it, and the familiar action lets me focus on something other than Dolion's declaration. Better to worry about the geas and my inevitable death than the fickle attention of a man.

Moments later, I regret leaving him so abruptly, if only because I don't know where to find the minister's rooms. Eavesdropping on the first full day here told me the King's retinue live on the second floor instead of in the residential buildings, so I begin there and let the twisting hallways take me in a circle. I open every unlocked door. Most rooms are empty, but I can only hope those with occupants assume my invisible entry and exit is the wind or a consequence of the earthquakes.

I know I'm in the right place when symbols scrawl over the door frames, labeling the staff who should live within. A dozen empty military commander rooms come up first, followed by various advisors, and finally, the minister's room. A hard quake has already torn the door partly off its hinges and I celebrate my good luck as I slip inside.

A single window illuminates the middle of the room where a desk stands, leaving the rest in darkness. Presumably the minister's bedroom is through a door the darkness hides, though I hope I don't need to search there. The longer I'm here, the more likely I could be discovered. I fumble along the wall, looking for a candle.

"Who's there?" says a masculine voice in the dark. I stiffen and press myself against the wall, no matter that I'm hidden under my illusion.

"I can hear you breathing," the voice says.

Holding my breath, I tiptoe backward towards the door.

"Refusing to breathe while moving doesn't save you," they say, sounding amused. The rich depth of their voice is familiar and warm. "It's any sound at all, you see."

That phrasing pings something in my memory. "Orion?"

The voice inhales sharply. "Thalia?" A scraping sound echoes in front of me, Orion moving in the dark. "What are you doing here?"

I shuffle sideways, using his movements as a guide. "Looking for information about the geas boundaries."

"I suppose I gave you the idea," he says, huffing. With no other senses to distract me, his voice sounds deeper and drags like honey over my skin, smooth and syrupy.

"Why are you here?" My fingers trip along the wall until I find a lantern on a table, banging my hip into the side. I fumble for the handle while stifling an oomph. There was a lit candle in the hall I can use to ignite it. "Hold on, I'm getting us a light."

"Don't," Orion hisses; I freeze, releasing the lantern. "Leave the light. I'm—I'm uncovered."

That explains why he sounds different but will do me no good in my quest for the minister's knowledge. I stoop to the floor searching for the dropped lantern. "I'm clumsy at the best of times, Orion," I tell him. "I can't safely wander around in the dark. Let me light a candle, I won't illuminate it towards you."

Silence answers me. For a long moment, I wonder if my suggestion upset him so much that he left, rather than remain uncovered in the light with me.

Finally, he sighs. "No light. But come towards my voice, I'll keep you from harm."

I could leave and return with my candle lit, but I offered him a safe place too. *Oblivion*, he'd said. He'd rather see oblivion than himself. I owe him respect, not only because of the help he's given me.

I reach outward towards the desk reflected by the scant window light. Only the slight rustling sound coming from his long kilt tells me he's even still nearby. He remains hidden in the dark and there's no confirming whether I'm muddling towards him. I move hesitantly, feeling as though I'm wading through spilled ink. Before I get within reach of the desk, I hit Orion's outstretched arms. He grabs my wrists and tugs me away from the light. Either he miscalculates my distance, or he didn't understand the extent of my clumsiness as he pulls too hard and I strike his chest with my shoulder, careening back towards the light to stay standing. His hands go to my waist to stabilize me, spinning me towards him while mine land on his bare chest.

The scars I've seen on his hands repeat on his chest, the marks distinct under my fingers. His skin feels rough like leather, but strong, as the flesh doesn't give against my hands. I'm unsurprised, the figure presented under his black cloth was one of strength and muscle, the hard marble frame of a sculpted God's body, one found in the statues surrounding the Palace. I knew he was taller too, after standing so close to him this afternoon, but in the dark, I'm slight and petite compared to him. As the least fit of all the girls, not feeling like the frumpy one is... nice. It hasn't consciously bothered me, not when I know my skills have value too, but it's like a headache. Sometimes you don't realize the dull ache was there until it fades and there's no pain. The absence of it tells more than its presence.

"You feel different," he says. I wonder if he's thinking the same thing I was, how soft I am compared to the others, those warriors who can probably kill a man with a single blow. "Like a spark against my skin."

No, I've just forgotten my illusion. It speaks to his godly ancestry that he can feel it. I release it but don't drop my hands. "Better?"

I feel rather than see him nod, the slight movement of his neck just above my head. Under my hands, I find ridges in the skin of his chest, his shoulders, a raised scar on top of the wrinkled flesh that travels up his neck. I attempt to map it with my fingers to determine its extent, but he nudges me back until I'm no longer touching him.

The dark hides the heat of my flush, one of embarrassment and shame at practically caressing him, all because I wanted to picture him in my head. "I'm terribly sorry for—"

"No, you've nothing to apologize for." His own fingers at my waist seem to move deliberately away, slowly and with intent.

Or I'm still riled by Dolion's declarations and finding attention where there is none, and Orion is simply confirming I won't fall when he releases me. Still, my fingers tingle where they were pressed against him.

"It is I who should apologize for subjecting you to that," he says, his voice soft. "Saving others from seeing and touching me is another reason for the cloth. I didn't expect to meet anyone here, you see."

Without thinking, I blindly reach for him again, snagging his fingers in the dark, unwilling to let him think my questing touches were out of revulsion. I know what it's like to experience the unmet expectations of others and be found wanting. He allows my hands in his and doesn't withdraw as I squeeze them. "You didn't subject me to anything, Orion. There's nothing wrong with your skin."

"You're too kind."

"No, I'm not. If I were, I would have realized I made you uncomfortable. I simply wanted you to know." I try to withdraw my hands, my touch again forced on him, but he keeps them clutched within his. "I'm sorry. For now and for what I said and did earlier today."

"You did nothing earlier, except share your thoughts, which I requested," he says, shuffling us from the center of the room. He walks backward, leading me. "And it is for your comfort that I withdrew."

Another earthquake rumbles; I trip. Against my will, I strike his chest again, my face and neck pressing into the space below his collarbones. A masculine scent curls towards me, but I shuffle backward before I can determine what it was.

"My comfort only seeks yours." But the *Gods* certainly seem interested in continuing my intrusion in his space. "Though I can't say I'm not curious about what you look like," I add apologetically.

He directs one of my hands forward until I grab the edge of a bookshelf, something I can easily recognize in the dark. The other hand he remains holding, his fingers flexing. "Well... I am a man."

A laugh bursts forth involuntarily. "Yes, and?"

He hums. "And I have hair that is the color of the bark of a cypress. The King controls its length, but were I able to choose, it would be as long as the trees are tall."

Cypress trees, often symbols of Hades, are also symbols of mourning. I give him a small squeeze of reassurance as I wonder what he mourns. "Why does he demand short hair, if you can say?"

"Fear," he says.

"Ah. And your eyes?" I press, eager to better form my mental image of him.

"The blue-green of the ocean right as a wave crests."

There's poetry in his description and I smother a sigh at the image I've made of him. "Thank you." I don't want to make him uncomfortable by pushing too hard. "For indulging me when I didn't have the right and letting me familiarize myself with you. It was very kind."

He guides my other hand to the shelf. "I'd hope you realize you can be familiar with me," he murmurs.

I bend until my forehead touches the cold wooden shelf, warmth spreading over my cheeks, but not from embarrassment. "So long as I'm not *too* familiar."

A huff of breath, one close to my face, hits the air. "What if I suggested a trade? For each private thing I share you must as well."

The answer comes with little thought. Diplomacy demands fairness. Friendship demands it, and I've nothing to lose, not if I'm dead in two days. And I might be able to work around the geas, if I'm clever enough. "I believe I'm two ahead of you, if we include all of today."

"I am content with one revelation, so long as I can choose what I learn tonight."

I can't very well complain, not when I've taken much from him now. "Very well. Do your worst," I say, teasingly.

He lowers his voice, no matter that we're the only two in this room, and I feel the heat of him as he bends toward me. "Who told you of your task in the Collection, and what, exactly, were you told?"

My brows raise. "That isn't a secret."

"It is still my wish," he says, his tone serious.

I drag my fingers over the shelf, feeling the spines of various books he led me to. "We've always known. Seven of the youngest daughters from each Island must travel to Crete and into the Labyrinth, where they'll encounter the Beast, a monster that emerged sixteen years after King Minos won the Island Wars. What happens next is a mystery, but as none have ever returned, my family assumed it was a death sentence."

Something cracks in front of us, like a log hitting a fire. I spin to survey the room, but the darkness tells me nothing. "Is someone there?" I ask.

"No, we're alone," Orion croaks. "You must have been frightened when you were chosen, if that was your belief."

"I think I forgot to be scared," I say, blinking back the memory from only days earlier but what feels like a century ago. "I was full of this righteous confidence that I could show up, with no preparation and stop the Collection. That's why I volunteered."

For better or worse, the confidence remains. Though, I'm afraid it might be because allowing myself to give up is conceding that I'm not up to the task, that I'm unworthy.

"You volunteered?"

Another quake rolls through the room. Flecks of plaster from the ceiling land on my face and I stifle a sneeze. "I did."

"You don't seem the type to leap without considering the consequences, especially if you believe you must battle the 'Beast' in the center." He brushes off the dust from my face, gently dragging a cloth over my skin. Without light, I don't know where the cloth came from, or how he knew I needed it.

"Can you see in the dark?"

"Is that your next question?" He sounds amused. The cloth rustles as it returns from whence it came. "Because I would be entitled to another as well."

I take a deep breath, one clear of any dust. "Only curiosity. But thank you. And I'm normally not... rash. I think through everything, hence the mask." My lips purse. "My friend joked that the storms might have affected me, since I was acting out of character by volunteering on such little notice."

"Zeus would certainly not have pushed you towards volunteering," Orion says darkly. "Minos is *his* son."

I'm not so sure—I remember the storms aiding us with the birds yesterday, and what Dolion's accomplice said. Zeus *could* interfere, no matter that the decision was my own. But the growl in Orion's voice keeps me from arguing. "You never answered my question about seeing in the dark," I finally say. "If you can't, I fear neither of us may find the information we seek."

Orion leans close, dragging away the book my fingers rested on. "This one has relevant records," he says, dropping it on the floor. He pulls others down. Before long, he has a small pile at our feet. "Perhaps we could meet in my rooms tomorrow morning and share what we've learned. Now that you've mentioned geas boundaries, I find myself intrigued in knowing more." There's a waver in his voice at the suggestion, like he expects to be denied.

"I can't. I would," I say, grasping his bare shoulder and squeezing. He shivers beneath my hand, highlighting the ridges on his skin. "Tomorrow is our last practice run of the Labyrinth. I should probably try to find the center at least once, assuming I can't figure out how to end it."

"After tonight, I can confirm you're closer than you think," he says.

My neck snaps upward, as though I can see the truth in his announcement, no matter the darkness. I dig my nails into his skin. "Truly? Can you tell me more?"

The ground shakes, but only Poseidon knows if it's in support of Orion's declaration. "Not unless you find an escape clause in one of the minister's books," he says wryly. Gently, he removes my hand from its tight grip on his shoulder. "I *can* tell you I've already given you a hint, though I might be chastised for giving to you what I'm not to others. But... I have hope. And I hope you can enter the center for your... meeting."

I kneel towards the books he's gathered, using my hands to guide me to the floor. Orion follows and places two volumes in my lap. My mind revisits what he's just said, but I catch no hidden meanings.

"There was an accident," he says idly, pulling me from my thoughts. "When I was young, I was scarred by a fiery thread." I jolt in surprise at the sudden confession, but he's not finished. "I had to be submerged in water, but the damage was done. As I age, the scars lessen but they will never disappear."

"That sounds painful," I offer, unfolding my tunic to hide the books within. At least the dark hides the skin I accidentally bare too.

Orion hums as though his pain was irrelevant. "And now I have another personal question."

That forces a startled laugh from me. "You could have just asked me without the trade. I might have shared anyway."

"I've lived a long time knowing the necessity of things being fair. This is how I make it fair." He pulls me to stand. "From which Island do you hail?"

I lift my chin; that's the easiest question he could ask. "I'm heir to the Island of Standia."

"That is... wonderful," he says on an exhale. "It is very nice to meet you, Thalia, heir to the Island of Standia."

In my head, I create a face to match his scant description. Full lips with an upturned nose and deep-set eyes, or wide lips that rest in a frown with a curved nose and hooded eyes. Whatever he looks like, I want to see the smile that now fills his voice.

I make it back to my room under my illusion, leaving before Orion and placing it when I'm back on the first floor. Once inside, I eagerly pull the books he entrusted to me.

They are two slim handbound volumes, more like a folder stuffed with parchment than a book. Inside are notes from more than simply the current minister, spanning centuries. They appear to be organized by subject, with the first labeled GEAS and the second labeled COLLECTION PREPARATION.

My fingers itch to read the second folder, wondering whether Orion gave it to me by intent or accident. But I dutifully read the GEAS notes first, hoping to learn what happened today, and whether I can break the enchantments like I unraveled the illusion in the Labyrinth.

The first part of the notes is a gruesome record of each magical creature slaughtered for Minos' gain: centaurs, fauns, nymphs, and pegasi. Like Orion's book that lists the Collected, the detached way the ministers describe their experiments—like learning that centaurs' blood is less potent of magic than nymphs—turns my stomach. If I can stop the Collection, next will be honoring these creatures' lives. Maybe Hecaline and I can start a movement, starting with her boar.

I bow my head to my chest at the thought. Dreams are for the idle; I must earn my freedom before hope is possible.

The next section of the notes details the geases, and I greedily inhale the knowledge. As Orion said, citizens must undertake strict speaking geases, ones that attach to bloodlines. Only when a new family, unrelated to any Cretans, arrives does the geas need to be applied. And someone under a geas can never speak the prohibited phrases, not without punishment, not even to those who *also* have the forbidden knowledge. Tick marks line the page, under headings of "citizens," "Governors," "Palace," and "B." I never noticed Father behaving as though he couldn't speak of the Collection, but maybe he's partly immune like me, and our ancestors cleverly failed to disclose it to Minos. "B" must be the Beast. How odd a monster would need to be prevented from speaking.

Besides speaking geases, there are dozens of others: ones like in the Labyrinth that punish if an act isn't completed, ones that have prohibitions and act as locked doors against access. Others are like we found that morning, which scramble a person's mind and force them to no longer see the truth of what's in front of them. But the most distressing are the geases that force someone to behave in a certain way, described as 'behavioral modifying magics.' It would compel anyone who crosses the geas line to act a certain way, against their will. Ice drips down my back at the thought of all the terrifying possibilities. The notes offer no counter either, though if you're arrogant enough to assume you can't lose, perhaps one isn't needed. *Or*, my naïve optimism hopes, *they've never considered one.* Minos is unaware that geases conflict with something in my ancestry, or else I'd never have been eligible. This could be another limitation leading to Minos' downfall.

With the claws of unease dragging over my skin, I turn to the second book Orion provided. COLLECTION PREPARATION offers only a single page with few lines.

The first line is almost unreadable. I can only catch *"men not preference—could brea—imp—return to women candidates."*

I already knew men had been originally Collected as well, an oddity; that they weren't 'preferred' and that's why they were removed is something new.

"Women candidates should be chosen from the youngest," the next faintest script writes, providing some clarity on the choices

of candidates. "*Attempt to ensure their selection from the commonest families.*"

A different handwriting scratches through the last line. "*Too conspicuous. Must appear fair. Use influence over Islands to remove candidates from academic classes and concentrate education on combat related skills only.*"

A third hand closes the page. "*Divisions to remove intellectual curiosity and seeking only the youngest appear successful. None will accept when they meet him, they wouldn't even consider any option outside attacking. Minos pleased. To further ensure success, begin examinations of magical creatures to prepare for future contingencies.*"

I slump back on my bed and stare at the ceiling. A crack spiderwebs from the corner over my half of the room, mimicking the crawling path of my thoughts.

It isn't only that physical skills aren't needed, they're a detriment, and a deliberate limitation, one that cannot be conspicuous. To avoid Poseidon's eye, and any evidence they weren't fulfilling their end of the bargain. But what benefit is there in keeping your candidates ignorant for the Collection? And, given Orion confirmed I need to get to the center to stop it, what *are* we supposed to 'accept' when we meet the Beast?

The time has come to share this with the others. They need me to guide them on the logical parts of the task but... I need them. To guide me to the center.

The ground shakes again and I pinch my eyes shut.

"If you wanted to just *tell* me how to finish it, that would be appreciated," I say aloud.

Unsurprisingly, no one answers.

Chapter 21

The ground still trembles the next morning at breakfast. Chrysa and Mina share a chair when the constant rumbles caused Mina to careen from her seat one too many times. Chrysa loops her arm around Mina's waist, and they share a plate of fruit.

"Today's the last Labyrinth run," Mina says conversationally.

Chrysa nods. "By this time tomorrow, we could all be dead!" She says it with the same amount of cheer as every other day.

"Or we'll all work together to defeat the Beast and return to our Islands as heroes," Diomede says, looking each of us in the eye as though attempting to impress her will upon us.

Chrysa snorts. "Not with Elara on our team. She'll kick you in the throat and then use Eriphyle as a club to beat the rest of us and take on the Beast alone."

"Why me?" Eriphyle asks. Diomede shifts closer to her, and they hold hands beneath the table.

"Because I wasn't going to volunteer myself for the story," Chrysa says.

Thyia rests her chin on her folded arms. "I wish we had another day to practice."

"It wouldn't matter," says Elara at the other end of the table, leaning back in her chair and crossing her arms. "We're ready or we're not. Whatever skills Avgo gave you will have to be enough."

"I wish you'd said *that* before," Mina says, pouting. "We could have slept in and explored Crete instead of training. Since this is our last chance to experience it."

Diomede pats her on the back with her free hand.

"Avgo's training is better than you think," says Thyia to Elara, not lifting her head from her chin. "It may be the Island of love and passion, but Aphrodite was a warrior-protector too."

Elara looks skeptical, a sneer forming.

I clear my throat. It's time to involve them in what I've learned. "Actually, I've come across some information that might be helpful on that count."

Conversation stops as they all peer at me. Glancing back at Kynna by the door, I lean forward and gesture for them to do the same. "I found some writings that say the task in the Labyrinth isn't physical, but something like a puzzle, and that we need to 'accept' the Beast somehow, not fight him when we get through to the center."

Not a sound can be heard as they all stare at me with varying levels of surprise and disbelief. After a few moments of confused silence, the table explodes with sound, all narrowed to insulting me.

"God's breath, Heir. How stupid do you think we are? We'd play around as though there's a problem to solve, wasting time, while you sneak to the center and kill the Beast yourself," Elara says, scowling.

Eriphyle grunts in agreement. "It explains the chase she led us on yesterday, talking about some invisible armory. Just to give us less time to train."

"No," I huff. "I'm not conspiring to win in your stead. I'm saying *none* of us should try to kill him but figure out what will actually let us succeed in the Collection." I try not to let my irritation show. "You'd understand that if you used your brains for once." Apparently, I'm unsuccessful.

Chrysa wrinkles her nose and gives me a sidelong glance. "Is this another part of your campaign to get me to read so I can think the way you want me to? Because you're moving away from funny and back to completely stuck up again."

"You can't read?" Diomede's voice is shrill, sounding wounded by Chrysa's confession.

"No," Chrysa says, jutting out her chin, as if daring anyone to call her lesser.

"It's okay, Thalia, we won't let you die," Mina says, almost kindly. "We'll protect you since you're bad at anything useful."

"Over *her* dead body," Elara mutters.

Fire builds in my stomach. I've sacrificed my future for this, and they won't even *consider* that I could be right. "I'm serious. There's something going on here, and it isn't as simple as running into the Labyrinth in a kill-or-be-killed game," I snap, losing my patience at how little faith they have in me. A small voice that sounds like Mother's says I have done little to earn their faith, but I swallow it. "If you want to survive the Collection, you need to listen to me."

"It is rather convenient," Thyia says, the reasonableness in her voice only annoying me more. "You've done so poorly in the Labyrinth and are the least skilled of us, but somehow you've discovered a way for you to be the best."

"That's true," Mina agrees.

I shake my head, my hair fluffing as an outward manifestation of my anger. "I should have expected this. Of course, you'd not want to admit your own deficiencies. You're still children who view this as a game."

Elara shoves back from the table to stand. "I haven't been a child for seven years, when they first put a dagger in my hand and told us only half would leave the arena alive."

"If we live, remind me never to visit Prosfora," Chrysa mock-whispers down the table. The joke doesn't reach her eyes, which are now narrowed in my direction.

Lips pull back from my teeth. *Didn't I save them from Periphetes, from the birds?* It was wit not brawn that helped us then. "Fine, clearly, I'm giving you too much credit. They spent years manipulating your lessons so when you're presented with a problem that strength doesn't solve, *obviously* you wouldn't think to act logically for the first time in your life."

The ground quakes. I'd like to pretend it is from the force of my anger and not Poseidon trying to give me a message I may not want to hear. Elara snaps her fingers. As though they practiced it, the others stand in unison, each glaring at me.

Something like regret curls down my throat but I bite my tongue. I'm not wrong. Let their anger cool and I'll try again when they can behave reasonably.

They're marching towards the door when Kyra appears and stalks towards Kynna. Her normally dewy face is flush. They angrily whisper to each other before Kynna turns her attention to us.

"Today's Labyrinth practice has been postponed."

Elara stomps forward. "Why?"

"That doesn't concern you," Kyra says, looking down her nose.

"It concerns no one more than us," I say from my chair.

Elara scowls in my direction. I can already hear what she intends to say, but Eriphyle's question overtakes her.

"Will we have time to practice again?" she asks.

Kyra's expression hardens. "I don't know."

Diomede slips her hand into Eriphyle's. "Will we still complete the Collection tomorrow, even without our third run? I would hate to disappoint the Gods," she adds, biting her lip. Chrysa rolls her eyes behind Diomede's back and Eriphyle shoots her a glower.

"I don't know," Kyra repeats, glaring at Diomede and Eriphyle's joined hands.

The heat from our recent argument bleeds into my question. "Is there anything you do know?"

"It isn't kind to take out your anger on our caretakers, Thalia," Diomede says, frowning. "They don't deserve your ire."

"Just let it go, Di," says Chrysa, crossing her arms around her waist. "We deserve to know if we're dying tomorrow or not."

Eriphyle looks ready to hit Chrysa in the mouth, so I step between them to disengage the conflict. "Thank you, Chrysa," I murmur.

Both Chrysa and Eriphyle step away from me with matching sneers. Before either can say more, Thyia speaks.

"Where's Dolion?" she asks, peering out into the hall.

"Yeah, by now, he's usually acting like *Heir's* lapdog," says Chrysa. I restrain a flinch at the venom in her tone.

"That doesn't concern you," Kynna says, but her voice trembles in a way Kyra's didn't. "We will give you more information when we have it. Go, you're free for the day."

The girls travel in a tight pack out of the room and down the hall. Only Diomede looks back at me and sighs before they head out of sight.

Kyra has her arms around Kynna as she murmurs something that makes Kynna shake her head. When they realize I'm still standing there, they pull apart.

"You need to find something to do, Thalia," Kyra says, almost tiredly.

I lift my head and fix my posture, mimicking a confidence I don't currently feel on the outside. "Is Dolion well?"

Given the recklessness he's displayed so far, his scheming could have created the problem in the Labyrinth. *That's the only reason I want to know*, I tell myself.

So much for not lying to myself.

"It doesn't matter," she says, but Kynna squeezes her forearm.

"We don't know," says Kynna. "If we find out we'll tell you."

"Kynna!" Kyra exclaims.

Kynna looks back at Kyra and something unspoken passes between the two. Finally, Kyra nods begrudgingly.

"We'll tell you," Kyra says. She slants her gaze towards the walls. "But you should find something to occupy you today. The King returned this morning, and the earthquakes are not improving his mood."

Armed with Kyra's warning, and unwelcome wherever the girls may have gone, I snatch the folders from last night and return to Orion's study.

He's not there when I arrive, so I sulk at his desk, remembering the anger I inspired in the girls, remembering the anger of my own, as I rest my forehead on the wood.

I can't recognize the woman who reacted that way. *Where did my mask go?*

"Should I assume you didn't find the center?"

Orion stands at the doorway, the minister's folders wrapped in his arms. His question douses my anger better than any of the rain from Zeus's storms.

I turn until my cheek lies on the cool wood. In front of anyone but Lukas, I'd never behave this way. Maybe it's the risk that I won't live past tomorrow that makes things like 'appearances' seem unnecessary. "It was canceled," I say listlessly. "Or rescheduled, that hasn't been explained."

He drops the folders on the desk as though they burn him. "But you're entitled to practice."

"We practiced twice." I unfold my shoulders to shrug. "Does the bargain demand three tries before the official one?"

"No, only that it is fair." He inhales a sharp breath. "You know of the bargain?"

Whatever feelings still swirling within me from my argument with the girls are quickly forgotten. "Are you confirming there *is* one?"

He flexes his fingers. "Apparently, I am. I'd assumed the geas prohibited it." He drops his head. "I'd never even attempted to check it."

I stand and take his hands in mine. "Orion—knowing the bargain can tell me how to break it. Is there anything else you can tell me?"

"Break it?" His hands squeeze mine a touch too hard. "I don't want to break it. I want to end it, by fulfilling the terms. I want my chance."

"Chance for what?"

He shakes his head. "That must remain secret until tomorrow. I'm already risking much by continuing to meet with you. But hope is difficult to kill."

"And we aren't?"

He drops my hands and steps away as if in shock. I match him step for step, the heat from my earlier argument easily rekindling.

"I'd fulfill it too, Orion, were I not fearful that it might kill us," I tell him. "You would seek to continue the bargain at the expense of our lives?"

There's a shifting in his figure, almost like he's shuffling from foot to foot, but his feet remain planted on the floor. "If it ends, there will be no more Collected."

"But what if it doesn't? Or if it is stopped but only *after* someone dies?" I ask, tipping up my chin.

Carefully, like he expects to be refused, he reaches for my fisted hands. He rests my fingers atop his palms, the muscles twitching. "As I told you yesterday, death has never been the aim."

I huff. "It may be unintentional, but it still happens." From what I've learned, it *shouldn't* happen. But intent is meaningless when powerful men play games.

"I know, and I do not discount that risk. But this is the best chance in centuries. And I will promise you that if it doesn't end tomorrow, I have enough information to bring to Poseidon to at least warrant a discussion as to the terms."

"Before or after we have our brush with mortal peril?"

He runs his thick thumbs over the backs of my hands. It's almost too soft, like a kiss of wind and not the solid touch of a person. "Thalia, please trust me when I say I do not want you harmed. You will not die in the Labyrinth."

I stare at our hands. "And the other girls?"

"Not once in my many years have I ever willingly sought the pain of others. Did you learn anything useful from the Minister's notes on geas?"

It isn't an answer, but I'll allow the subject change, for now. I know I'm close to the answer; there are only a few pieces missing from the puzzle that will show me the full picture. "I did, though with what I now know and Minos back in residence, your willingness might not matter."

The light ministrations he's giving my fingers stop. "Minos has returned? We must restore the notes before they are discovered. And then I will lead you to a safe place to speak more."

Before I can do more than nod, he gathers the folders I returned and hides them somewhere unknown on his body.

He shifts on his feet, sounding almost bashful when he asks, "Would you like to learn one of the Palace's secrets?"

A door I'd seen in his room leads to another dark hallway that he guides me through. This one doesn't lead to the Labyrinth but connects to a warren of tunnels throughout the Palace, bypassing the most confusing twists in the exterior halls, cutting the distance between Orion's rooms and the Minister's on the second floor in half.

If Chrysa had been there, she'd joke that the dank corridors were worth the reduction in stairs. I frown at the thought; I should have approached them differently, instead of speaking down to them. The list of those I disappoint keeps growing and now includes myself.

Orion directs us through the winding tunnels without hesitation. Oiled rope, acting like an elongated lit candle, lines the walls, just below the ceilings. But still the sparse light does little to keep me from tripping over my own feet. Soon, he meanders down a short hallway that ends in two ladders, one that ascends into the ceiling, the other plummeting into darkness below us.

"Wait here," Orion says as he descends the lower ladder.

I do wait, for a few minutes at least. But the pull of what could be beyond that ladder is too great to ignore for long. Tying my skirt behind me, I climb up. The rungs end just after the ladder ascends into the ceiling, taking me to a small, enclosed space. There isn't even space for me to step off the ladder. Thin cracks of light appear overhead in three directions, as though I've appeared inside the lid of a wooden chest.

I peer through the cracks that illuminate a room above me. It's a kind of parlor with a wicker couch and several chairs. I *am* inside some kind of chest, in the corner of a room that looks almost familiar, like I've seen it from the edge of my vision or in a dream.

A snarl sounds to my left and I duck away from the crack.

"Where is he?" My eyes widen when I recognize the speaker. *How often does Orion eavesdrop on Minos?*

"He's supposed to be here," Minos snaps.

Or maybe Orion meets with Minos for Labyrinth related business, I mentally amend.

"I—I couldn't find him to, ah, to advise him, sire." That's the minister's stuttering. At least Orion can return the notes without fear of discovery.

I hear skin hitting skin, and the minister whimpering. I wince in sympathy.

"Your excuses do little to soothe my ire," Minos says venomously. "It is as though you *wish* to follow your predecessors to the gallows."

The minister whimpers again, shuffling into my eyeline. One cheek is vibrant red. "Of course not, sire. My apologies, sire. I am thankful to serve under your crown."

Minos grunts, walking in front of the crack. He looks haggard, his tunic askew and golden braid unruly. "My crown. That is the concern, isn't it? And with Poseidon and my own Father no longer blind to the damned Collection."

Zeus and Poseidon are *watching*. Good, perhaps that means I'm as close to ending it as Orion seems to think I am. I press my face closer to better see and hear. The floors quiver with another earthquake, dropping dust onto Minos and the minister's heads.

Minos stares at the ceiling as though it offended him. "As if any of them are worthy of it. Had I better foresight, I would have made the challenge more difficult. As if anyone would *desire* to sit at his side."

"It is ineffable, sire," the Minister says.

"Indeed." Minos lifts his shoulders, letting one hand wrap around his braid. It looks otherworldly in the light, like a sparkling golden star. "Find the simpleton and demand his presence in my rooms at once. He may believe his time is coming, but my dynasty remains never ending."

Chapter 22

I scuttle back down the ladder just as Orion returns from his solitary quest. He drags us further into the passageways until we pop out from the northern side of the Palace.

We duck through the trees, avoiding the city, almost sprinting away from the Palace walls like we're being chased. I scurry after his gait for several long minutes. When the city is at our backs, Orion slows and matches my speed.

"We no longer need to avoid exposure," he explains.

My mind creates a dozen reasons before I indulge my curiosity. "Are you not allowed out of the castle or..."

Leaves crunch under his feet as he answers. "I am, but I rarely leave. Or I do so in the evening when there's less of a chance of being seen."

"Why are you hiding?"

He gestures to himself, as he did when we first spoke to each other. "It invites attention."

My brows furrow. "If you never take the coverings off, could you not do so now and blend in as just another citizen?"

There's only silence in response, before finally, "No." Despite the curt response, he doesn't sound offended.

Emboldened by his answer, which is probably unwarranted given my conversational blunder that morning, I continue, "At some point, you'll need to remove it. Figuratively or metaphorically."

My hypocrisy tastes bitter.

"Tomorrow, at the Collection," he says, his voice sounding like a knife's edge. "I will bare myself to you."

I duck my head; all my training and I haven't figured out how to stop pushing. "I wasn't demanding anything, Orion."

"I know," he says, angling his broad shoulders towards me. "But for the first time, I'm happy about the possibility."

"Assuming I live," I begin, but his grunt interrupts me. "Assuming I live, I would see those parts you keep hidden," I finish, repeating what he'd said to me at our second meeting.

He nods, and we continue walking in companionable silence. Soon, the sea grows in front of us. Bright sails dot the horizon; ships like the one that brought me here. But instead of continuing towards it, Orion guides us deeper into the trees. I let out a soft sigh, and he cocks his head.

"Do you miss the sea?" he asks.

"We haven't been gone long enough for me to miss it," I say. But still a longing built. My life was surrounded by the sea, even if I rarely entered it. The tallest floor of our home, where my room is—was—looks out onto the sea. Most of the duties Father allowed me to help with involved sea trade. And the malleability of water was something I always envied.

His fists clench and release. "I haven't visited the water since I arrived in Crete when I was sixteen years old, just before the Collection began," he says, his voice oddly intent.

It isn't a secret, not like the ones he's shared before, but I offer him something in return. "I spend little time outside my duties, but I've loved the idea of the sea. Instead of discovering the world through books, I could uncover our world myself."

He stops, not unlike a deer watching for a hunter and my focus narrows to his trembling form. "Perhaps you could reintroduce me to the water someday," he says quietly.

"Of course." My face warms. "Assuming I live."

He flinches. "Assuming you live."

We walk another half hour before the land we tread through seems familiar, particularly when we begin the walk up a small hill.

"Where are we going?" I ask as I trip on another hidden tree root, my clumsiness amplified by Poseidon's consistent quakes.

Orion cups my elbow to save me from falling. "A friend's. She will provide shelter. There are spells within her home to keep any of Minos' spies from entering."

I regain my footing, but Orion doesn't surrender my arm. It's that fact that keeps the knot of discomfort in my stomach that formed at his response from growing too large. "Are you and she close?"

"As close as we can be under the circumstances." He hooks his arm around my waist and hoists me over another possible stumbling hazard. "She doesn't leave her home, and I only visit once every decade. If not for the age difference—" He laughs, a rich sound that lingers against my throat. "If I weren't the elder, I would consider her my favorite maiden aunt."

The knot in my stomach loosens. "I look forward to meeting her."

He releases my waist but keeps one hand connected to my forearm. "Now it's your turn."

"This is turning into less of a reciprocal trade of secrets and more like a child's get-to-know you game," I grumble, but I don't get the chance to further respond. Another tremor rolls through the earth and I stumble, rolling my ankle. Orion's grip keeps me standing, but only barely, and it does nothing for the white-hot spear of pain that bursts from my leg.

I squeal just as something scuttles away from the underbrush. Orion whisks me off my feet, rushing us under the canopy of a nearby tree. He sets me down after clearing any undergrowth that might hide a prickly animal. I lean against the rough bark as he kneels before me.

"What happened?" The question comes as he peels the fabric of my chiton that's twisted around my leg upward towards my knees.

"I think something bit me," I say, biting my lip to keep from crying. The pain has ebbed, present but blunted, though the shock remains.

Orion bares my ankles and locates the source of my dramatics, a red circle just above my right ankle bone. "Oh, Mother," he sighs.

I sit up, watching his hands, shoulders, any part of him that might give reason for his resigned tone. "What? What's wrong?"

"A scorpion stung you."

"Will I be alright?" I can only imagine what might happen if I can't walk tomorrow. Elara would leap over my hobbling form before I even get the chance to explain what I know.

He rests his hands on his knees. They don't flinch or flex. "You may lose your leg," he says gravely.

"Fantastic." I lean back against the tree, stinging tears forming in my eyes. I close them to trap them inside, hiding them with my anxiety. "Just in time for the Collection tomorrow."

"Thalia, I apologize. I was teasing you."

My eyes pop open, several tears spilling forth.

Orion holds his hands aloft in a yielding position. "It was a joke."

Roughly, I scrape the wetness away. "It wasn't funny."

"I realize that now. I thought you knew and were jesting with me by asking. Scorpions on Crete are bothersome but not venomous." He tilts his head, a conciliatory gesture.

"Why would I know that? It's not like I took any of the survival classes." I wrap my arms around my chest. My stomach begins to hurt as guilt curdles within. *Would one of the girls have seen it and avoided its sting?*

He sits up on his knees, like he's about to leave. "Again, I am sorry. The pain of the sting will fade in another minute. Then I can take you back to the Palace and leave you be for the rest of your time here."

A sliver of hope dies at the thought. I reach for his hand to keep him in place. "No, it's fine. Please. Don't leave."

Now his fingers flex. "If you're sure."

I yank on his hand as if to pull him to me, but he doesn't budge. "Yes, I'm sure. I'm overreacting. It's been a difficult few days."

"I understand," he says. "Give it a minute and we can keep going, if you are sure remaining with me is your wish." It's a question no matter that he didn't phrase it that way, but whether there's a deeper meaning within it is unknown.

I twist my ankle. The stinging has receded further, even the ache from rolling it has dulled. "We walked all this way and I have nothing else for me at the Palace." Another set of tears threatens to form, thinking of the fight with the girls this morning. "But distract me until the pain ends. Why would it sting me? I wasn't bothering it."

He drops back to the ground with almost supernatural fluidity, taking my ankle back in his hand and rubbing the skin above the sting. It isn't the distraction I had in mind, but I won't complain.

"For the blood flow," he explains quietly. After a minute of staring at my foot, he says, "You probably didn't realize it was there, but it considered you a threat. Any beast will protect itself to avoid pain."

"So will humans and Gods," I reply.

He huffs a laugh before speaking in a voice as soft as a whisper, saying, "It is possible that Gaia was testing you. What you might do to one of her children when it encounters an inadvertent threat."

My neck snaps upward to stare at his clothed face. Gaia's children... like Poseidon's child and the dynasty they would take from Minos. The child whose name is half-smeared in Orion's book, the "Bore." I shudder out a breath while the realizations form. "I think I can stand now."

He helps me up, keeping one arm looped around mine as though he's my escort, and we begin walking again.

"You never reciprocated my secret," he says.

I pull myself from my woolgathering as I continue connecting pieces of the puzzle and shake my head at him. "I don't think telling me you consider your younger friend to be a maiden aunt counts as a secret."

He inclines his head towards me, and I swear I feel the heat of his gaze even through the dark gauze. "I've told no one before, and it matters to me. Both make it a secret."

Something warms within me. "I have ten aunts," I answer. "So many to keep them under the age of eligibility for the Collection. Terribly inefficient, now that I think about it, as one would always be the youngest," I continue, frowning. I shake away the logical issues the Collection created. "Three of them wish their husband had been the heir, two wish my grandfather had allowed them to be the heir, four are so unassuming I forget they exist, and the last—" A smile forces its way forward. "The last is a traveling minstrel."

"Truly?"

I nod, the smile fading as I remember why she travels. "She was the youngest daughter. When she aged-out, she left the Island, never staying in one place too long, always afraid Minos might change the age cut off and call for her one day."

Orion's hand grips my forearm, not tight enough to hurt but enough that I can feel the heartbeat thumping erratically under his wrist. "Youngest daughter?"

"Those eligible for the Collection," I say, raising my brows.

"I wasn't aware only the youngest were requested." It sounds like he speaks through clenched teeth.

"The youngest and most uneducated." My eyes fall shut in shame; the vision of their physical resilience runs through my head. "That's not fair. The youngest and least qualified for any *cerebral* skills. They are all quite proficient in physical feats. But give them a puzzle and they'd tear it in half before solving it."

My distaste for their limitations must appear in my tone as a stifled exhale comes from under Orion's cloth, like he's disappointed. Like the expression he might offer me now would mirror the girls' faces from this morning, where underneath the anger was hurt.

"It shouldn't be a surprise," I say, pulling my arm from him to wrap it around my waist. I glance around the foliage, confirming we're alone. "The notes you left me last night confirmed it was the aim, choosing the youngest and removing them from non-combat related education. Only brawn was sought for the Collection, everyone knows that. They focused on survival and physical skills. *I'm* the deficient one in that respect," I finish, repeating Thyia's truths, never truer than with the scorpion a minute ago.

"You aren't deficient," he says firmly.

I know, I think but don't reveal, knowing a little better what the Collection entails. Each hint fills out the bargain and how to fulfill it. *But will I make it to the center without them?*

Orion clears his throat, pulling me from my sharp thoughts. "My favorite color is blue."

I heave out a laugh. "Mine is red."

Orion keeps up a constant barrage of random statements—he has no siblings from his parents, he prefers night over day, the burns sometimes still ache—that I respond to in kind, until the incline deepens until we arrive at a familiar windowless hut.

"Is this... Hecaline's home?" I ask when we approach the door.

Orion's back muscles ripple under the cloth and he turns towards me. "You know Hecaline?"

The door opening steals my answer. "Is it time, my star?" she says, peering out from the crack, her milky eyes unfocused.

"Not quite, Hecaline, but soon," Orion murmurs. "May we come in?"

Hecaline widens the opening and steps aside.

"My star?" I ask Orion as we step through. Her home looks no different from a few days prior, except a new carving made its home above the ouroboros snake on her wall: a crudely chiseled boar.

"It's after his true name," Hecaline answers.

"Orion is my true name," Orion says in a tone that tells me this is an oft repeated argument.

"Not on this plane," says Hecaline. "Who did you bring with you, my star?"

I step forward. "It's Thalia, ma'am. We met a few days ago."

"Thalia, Thalia. Do I know any Thalia?" She directs the question to Orion, who is guiding Hecaline towards her mat.

"You called me Alis once," I offer as I follow them.

She cackles as she drops elegantly to her knees. "Alis, she said. Spirit-born of Athena playing like she's a child of earth and sea, when we all know she's a sky made mortal. Did you hear that, my star? She thinks *she's an* Alis."

"She thinks she's Thalia, Hecaline. That's her name," he says.

Hecaline pats the mat next to her with one hand, a near perfect mimicry to my last visit. She extends her other hand and I join her before she makes the same complaint she made last time too. Because I expect it, I don't flinch when she runs her fingers over my face. At least this time, the dirt is only on my knees and not my cheeks.

"I know you," she says, lips pursing.

"Yes, we met before. You offered us shelter from the storm when we arrived."

As if I didn't speak, she snaps her attention to Orion, who stands at attention beside the stove. "Too distracted to notice my hair, my star? I did it to favor you."

Both Orion and I inspect her from our respective vantage points. The short black hair I remember has lengthened, now long enough that she can braid and wrap it around her head like a tangled crown. If she loosened it, it would be as long as Minos'.

"Don't let anyone see that," Orion says seriously.

Hecaline waves a weathered hand. "Don't let anyone see, he says. As if I don't know my mind. I will cut it, as it must be cut, as *all* must be cut else his game is up. It was only for you and your girl. Besides, none who can visit me will betray me. At least not yet."

"Thalia isn't my 'girl,' Hecaline," says Orion, stuttering. I get the impression he's blushing under the cloth. "She is one of the Collect—"

"Hero!" she warbles, the volume of her voice rattling my ears. Even Orion jolts from the sound. "Dolion called you *Hero*. That's who you are."

My cheeks heat and I avoid looking at Orion. "Yes, but as we've said, I'm Thalia. That was a silly nickname of his."

She pats my knee. "Words have power. That boy has made, and will make, certain *silly* decisions. I'd call them stupid, but what do I know?" Her teeth bare in a sharp smile. "I'm just the seer."

"Who is Dolion?" Orion asks.

"A caretaker," I explain, eager to change the subject from Dolion and his actions.

"You remember, the son of Cleades and Philea," says Hecaline. "Spoke the word on Perry's ship."

Orion ducks his head, his voice sounding hoarse. "Friend to Lasthena of Avgo. I remember."

I remember seeing Lasthena's name in the book Orion gave me, one of the Collected listed before Serai's time. It must be Dolion's lost love, and someone who Orion dealt with in the aftermath of the Beast's violence. Though I expect a pang of annoyance or hurt at the reminder of Dolion's duplicity, it doesn't come.

"Don't mope," Hecaline says. "Without Lasthena's death, Dolion would not do what he will. His path is necessary for the next stage."

"A useful death is still a death," Orion counters, putting words to my thoughts.

She shakes her finger in his direction. "But the blame rests with only one man."

She lets the words float in the air around us for a long minute. Does she mean the being in the Labyrinth, or Minos? Or Poseidon?

When the silence grows uncomfortable, she asks, "Now, my star, if it is not yet time, why have you come?"

Orion splays his hands. "We need a private place to speak. The King has returned, and the walls have ears."

I suppress a shudder. With the blood coating them for their magic, it might be a literal statement.

Hecaline smiles, inclining her head towards me. "The King has returned but the blood remains. You did not need to sojourn here, not when you could create privacy." She grabs my face again before either of us can comment. "Have you not told my star yet, deary? Of whose blood pools in your veins?"

My gaze slips to Orion. How much easier it would be if I could see his face. "He knows I'm the heir to Standia."

Hecaline shakes her head. "Of course, he knows that. But that is only part of why Zeus swayed your heart to volunteer. Does he know the rest—the skills in your blood?"

"Minos would know if I used it," I begin, though I've never used an illusion to cover sound. And then my mind recognizes what she's said.

Orion realizes it faster than I do, as he slams to his knees by her side before I can consider what to say. "Do you mean to say Zeus interfered?"

"No, I mean to say Zeus convinced her," she says, like she's surprised we're unaware. "Have you gone deaf in your years, my star? You heard me, Thalia, yes?"

I stutter out a sound that could be yes or no. Orion inhales a deep breath.

Hecaline purses her lips. "Did you imagine you volunteered on your own?"

"I—I *joked* about the possibility of godly aid," I say, a shiver making its way through my body. "But it was my mind that pushed me forward."

She pats my hand as pity fills her milky white eyes. "You might have gotten there, deary, but Zeus needed your words faster than your soul would have offered them."

I force a single breath in and out to keep myself calm. I think of the dreams, of the storms that created the itching under my skin that only faded when I boarded the ship. It's one thing for me to tease about the idea getting put in my head, but it's another to learn that the first choice I made for myself was not a choice at all. But letting myself react to it is for after I've solved the puzzle. Or after I'm dead.

That thought only pools more dread in my stomach.

"The bigger issue," she continues, as though she hasn't up-ended my worldview, "is what Zeus expects in exchange for it."

I press my fingers tight to my throat, to better hold the panic within. So much for reacting *after* the Collection ends. "What—what would he expect?"

"It's a bargain, deary. He's done something for you, you'll do something for him."

"Is stopping the Collection not enough?" I demand. Anger is always a better friend than fear.

She pats my hand. "You benefit from that act just as much. No, I see he will want something else from you." She tilts her head towards Orion. "From both of you. When you come together."

"Hecaline," Orion starts softly, interrupting what is sure to be a meltdown from me. "You know I trust your sight. But Minos is Zeus' child, and he's never directed his gaze towards us before. If he had, perhaps I'd not have spent centuries trying to rationalize the fairness and been able to—" He cuts off hoarsely.

"And you wish the decision would be free from influence," she says in a voice just as soft. "I understand, my star. I know how long you've waited. And I'm sorry to tell you you'll likely wait longer."

I feel as though I'm intruding on something private, as the two gaze unseeing at each other. And I've missed something in the riddles they speak. Hecaline pats his hand, and he flinches.

"You know my throat is bound more severely than yours on such matters," she continues. "But... the earthquakes are not simply Poseidon's."

Orion hisses a breath through the cloth before shifting from his knees to sit. "Thank you, Hecaline. If you don't mind, Thalia and I came here for a purpose."

She inclines her head and ambles to her cot in the corner. "Wake me before you leave, there are things I still wish to say." Then she closes the curtain, leaving us in mock privacy.

Orion stands and prepares tea, just like Dolion had during our first visit. For several long minutes, his puttering about is the only sound in the room. Even my breath has quieted.

"I thought you might need a moment. In the years I've known her, Hecaline has never offered a prediction reassuringly," he says as he hands me a cup. The heat is nearly unbearable, but I keep a tight grip. "As the… Keeper of the Labyrinth, I know what it's like to be a playing piece in the game of a higher power."

"Oh?"

"My father." He drops beside me, resting his twitching fingers on his knees. "Those with power always want more of it."

I smile wanly, having thought similarly before. I stare at my cup, wishing we were back outside, playing our silly sharing game. "Are you close with your parents?" I ask, trying to avoid the unpleasant revelations Hecaline threw at us both.

"I don't see my mother as often as I would like, only when I can spare leaving the Palace." The cloth at his neck flutters like he's tensing the muscles there. "I've not seen my father since arriving on Crete… for the first Collection."

"What do you do between Collections that you can't visit?"

His shoulder twitches. Not a shrug, but some kind of flinch. "I wait."

I return my gaze to my cup. The steam curls upward like a vine, like those that grew in Standia.

"My mother named me Orion," he blurts. "My Father has a different name for me. What some consider my true name, as Hecaline announced. A type of star."

A type of star. There are thousands in the sky, forming constellations. But I don't have time to run through my memory, not when I feel the weight of Orion's stare on me. If a masked person who reveals nothing could sit expectantly, he does. I nod, knowing what he's after now. I'm not the only one avoiding what we've learned. "You know Thalia is the muse of comedy," I finally say.

She's the child of Zeus and another Goddess, one of nine who could have made up more islands but didn't want to sacrifice their powers. Given the yoke Crete has around the Islands' necks, she probably chose right.

His head dips in agreement.

"My parents chose it hoping I would emulate her, that I would lead my people with laughter." My eyes flit to Hecaline's curtain, but it remains closed. I force the true secret forward. "It's no doubt a benefit that my opportunity to rule might die in the Labyrinth. At least it avoids the inevitable disappointment when I can't."

"Why do you think you can't?"

I shrug; there's too much to get into it now. A good ruler would have handled this morning's argument better. A good ruler would have solved the puzzle by now and stopped the Collection without more ceremony. A good ruler might not have been played like Hermes' lyre by Zeus.

Orion leans forward, resting his palm on my crossed knee. The heat of him is comforting. "Do you wish to rule?"

"There's nothing else for me," I say.

He cocks his head. "Thalia also means to flourish."

I make a sound of acknowledgement. The Muse flourishes, and Hephaestus' nymph child Thalia was known for the same. Failing to flourish into the heir I wanted to be still leads to disappointment.

He leans back, withdrawing his hand, his posture rigid. "But if names called forth truths, the Collection would have ended years ago. Perhaps we both need to realize we make our own destiny."

"Easier said than done," I mutter to my teacup.

"Did you learn anything about the geas?" Orion asks.

The conversation segue doesn't allay my bad feelings. "Yes. As I suspected, there are geases that can manipulate one's mind. But worse is that it can manipulate someone's actions. They may not understand why or how they do something, but the magic can take their free will." And now it's confirmed that the Gods can do the same, and even I'm not immune from that.

Orion inhales a sharp breath, sucking in cloth. "Do you mean to say they could spell someone to do something they'd never intend?"

"Yes. And never realize why, or that it wasn't their own mind pushing the act."

His head falls into his hands as a distressed sound comes from under his cloth covering, almost making me jolt in place. He's slumped as though praying, but the keening sound denies any fealty being paid.

Blinking away my dark thoughts, I tentatively touch his knee. "Are you well?"

One hand covers mine, his muscles trembling. "It just explains—I've always hated my—the confirmation."

"It's the line," Hecaline yells. "Did you hear me, Thalia? That's the line."

My gaze shifts from the curtain to Orion and back as my mind races at what Orion has revealed today and what I've discovered. The pieces continue to form and slot snugly into their proper places. "The line... for the boar?"

She bursts out from behind the curtain and jauntily returns to her pallet, sliding beside us. "The boar, Alis?" She takes my other hand and places it on Orion's other knee. "Why, he's in the Labyrinth!"

Of course! My lips twist in triumph just as Orion recovers himself and breaks our connection. He dabs at his eyes, though the act is useless over the mask, and leaves Hecaline's hut.

When we're alone, I turn back to Hecaline. "You know my name is Thalia."

She blinks owlishly. "I know exactly who you are, deary. You're the mortal child of the sky, who can join the child of earth and sea."

Chapter 23

Orion returned to Hecaline's hut only to imitate the block of marble I compared him to the night before. Like the muscular statue whose figure I thought he borrowed, he failed to react to any part of our continued conversation. Instead, each sliver of information I could offer him ran off his back like water. He also gave little in the way of helpful information to me, but the notes he'd taken from the minister's office weren't too relevant to my task here. Those that were relevant he was spelled not to speak about, anyway.

He said nothing during the trip back from Hecaline's, no more reciprocal conversations or even pleasantries. We marched in silence in the dark. I couldn't tell what he was thinking under the cloth, but his shoulders were raised towards his ears. It was early in the journey back that I realized I missed hearing the baritone of his voice sliding over me like silk.

We finally enter the secret tunnels inside the Palace. He remains mute as he escorts me up and down winding tunnels and ladders. When our trek levels out, and we must be near an entrance close by the hallway holding our rooms, he pauses. A small doorway, one which is only as high as my hip, appears before us. But he doesn't move to open or try to direct me through it, he simply stands, his head cocked towards the floor. The rise of his chest is my only warning he's going to speak.

"Will you wait a minute?"

Before I answer, he sprints down the tunnel and out of sight. I hug my stomach while I lean against one of the bare walls.

I'm nearer to the solution than I should be considering how I've floundered. After my chat with Hecaline, after the long silent walk with only my mind for company, the puzzle is nearly complete, more colors filling into the picture. Only a few pieces haven't revealed themselves, corners that need to be slotted into place. But corners are never required to capture a puzzle's image, just the full view of it. If I just had a little more time...

But maybe knowing three quarters will be enough to save us. Tomorrow I will make my stand with all that I've learned.

Orion reappears with a book. "I'm going to bring attention to Minos' acts, his potential breaches," he says softly. "With the evidence I now have, the Collection must end."

An unexpected and inappropriate pang of disappointment pulls in the space behind my chest, but I smother it. That it *ends* matters, not that I ended it. Though it still feels as though yet another choice is taken from me. "What about the hope you wanted," I ask. "And your wish to only stop the Collection after you've gained it?"

His fingers twitch along the book's spine. "The risk is too great."

He's right, and I know it. Tomorrow, I'd welcome it. But after today's realizations, I wanted to claw back my control somehow, be the one to use my mind and finish what I started. Or, at the very least, bring it to Poseidon's attention myself. Still, I force a smile on my face. "Thank you, Orion, for attempting to protect us."

Quick as lightning, he cups my wrist, pulling a shocked gasp from my chest. "Always," he says, his voice intent. "I will always seek to protect before causing harm."

I slip my arm from his tight grip. "I believe you."

"I hope so." He drops his head, looking at the book. "It means this will be our last time together. As soon as I reveal the fraud, the ship will return to deliver you to Standia."

Another pang hits then, disappointment swirling with something else, lost opportunity perhaps. This man might have been my hope, if I'd let him. But much like the small opening I provided Dolion, it was slammed shut. I clasp his covered forearm. "It was good to know you, Orion, even under these circumstances."

He holds out the book. "For you. To remember me by."

When I take it, he starts down the tunnel without another word.

"Wait!" My voice rings out in the small space, surprising even me in its intensity. He turns back slightly. "I wasn't speaking idly when I said I was glad to have met you. I know enough of the bargain to know it's difficult being involved in the Labyrinth. Even as its Keeper."

He dips his head.

"But... thank you." I flounder as my face heats. "Thank you for letting me... drop the mask. It means something to me that I could, that I'd have this chance. Now."

As quickly as he left, he returns, stalking back down the hallway. He gathers me into his arms, not like last night when he loosely held me but tighter. His arms wrap around me as he lifts my feet off the floor. The book falls to the floor. Grasping at his back, I drop my head into the crook of his neck and inhale. Finally, I can scent what's been only dragging at the edges of my subconscious: he smells like wood smoke and honey and the salt of the sea. Again, Lukas' image flits through my mind, even as I burrow my head deeper into the cloth. Kissing Lukas didn't feel as intense as this, as this simple embrace from someone that's not quite a stranger and not quite a friend. From someone who is something different but lives in the same controlled world, one without choices and freedom. From someone who might have been something to me, if the choice ever arose, my own unwritten future.

"Be well, Thalia," he rumbles against my mussed hair. And then he releases me and leaves a second time.

After bending to pick up the book and scraping at my eyes, I tuck the gifted tome in my belt and breathe deeply. I can still smell him on my skin. In a different world, I might invite Orion to Standia, and show him my home as he's attempted to show me his.

Swallowing the impulse to run after him and do just that right now, I drop to the floor to shuffle through the little entryway. Darkness greets me when I crawl out into the hallway. The hinged door closes, blending into the deep ocean blue wall. Above it, in the sky-blue gradient, is another double-sided triangle. I trace it with my fingers before shaking my head.

The hallways are still empty, and I find my way to my room with little trouble. A single candle is lit next to Chrysa's bed, which is empty. Her bedding is also missing. I exhale heavily at the sight.

"Thalia," a deep voice says behind me. Not Orion's, not the smooth melody from under black gauze. I suck in a gasp as I spin towards the sound. Dolion leans against the wall, hidden behind the door, his hands pressed against the stone like he's afraid he will be dragged from it.

My hand goes to my chest in alarm. His presence washes away the maudlin feelings that settled on my skin. "I thought you were a specter for a moment," I say. "What are you doing here?"

"I—I made a mistake," he breathes. His eyes are wild, his breath erratic.

"Dolion—"

He jolts forward, too fast for me to step away from him, and grabs my hands. His olive skin is pale and clammy. "I pushed too hard, I—I should have been less obvious."

"Calm down." Any lingering annoyance disappears in the presence of his fear. I direct him to my bed, and we sit side by side, my hands still held tight in his. "What happened?"

"I was—I was working on the—the plan. We're so close, and I wanted to make sure there were no surprises."

I've never seen him so rattled. I shake off his grip and instead press my palms to his cheeks, breathing in and out steadily until he mimics my actions, as I've done at home when Lukas fought with Argon. "What did you do?"

He licks his lips, not meeting my gaze. "Deianira has always liked me. It began before I left Crete. I thought, perhaps, I could use it to learn more about the regime and, and—" He stops speaking.

My hands drop from his skin, scalded, and I stand. This must be the silly—no, *stupid*—decision Hecaline mentioned. "God's damned teeth, Dolion. And she, what, realized you were using her feelings and kicked you out? You've only yourself to blame if you've lost your position as a caretaker."

"No," he whispers. He tucks his trembling hands in his lap. "She didn't realize it, not until she wanted me to... be with her. I couldn't do it, I couldn't—" He inhales a shaky breath. "When the guards threw me from her rooms, they saw my tattoo."

"What tattoo?"

Slower than dripping honey, he drags a hand from his lap to the edge of his chiton. He lifts the fabric over his thigh, baring more olive skin thatched with dark hair. The fabric rises at the same speed as my blush, which begins on my cheeks and tumbles downward. Finally, he reveals the skin at his hip and raises his gaze to my face.

On his upper thigh, right at the juncture where his leg meets his hip, is a tiny black image of a double-sided triangle, the same mark in the hallways, the same scarred tattoo on the man from the Festival arena, the same sketch in Orion's books.

I know the answer but I ask anyway. "This isn't a criminal's mark, is it?"

Dolion shakes his head. My hand reaches forward as if to trace it, the symbol of—but I pull it back to my chest. The puzzle's answer doesn't matter anymore, not if Orion alerts Poseidon.

"I evaded the guards," he says, covering the tattoo with his kilt again. "There are so many hallways it will take them ages to locate me. And when they do…" He trails off, clenching his jaw.

I take my place back on the bed. "Why did you not leave through one of the entrances?"

"I don't know." He stares at the floor, his voice tight. "All I could think of was finding you."

I drop my head into my waiting hands. "Dolion," I speak into my skin.

"We're friends, Thalia. I wanted that comfort if tonight's to be my last night alive."

My hands fall. I won't quibble with him on our friendship now. "Surely you won't be killed."

"It's a traitorous symbol. If Deianira tells her father, killing me might be my best option." His expression is bleak, his face pale. "It was—" *stupid* "a poor decision to etch it onto my skin. But I wanted something tangible to have, to remind myself of what I'm doing."

"I'd think a broken heart was enough of a souvenir," I mutter uncharitably under my breath. Shame drips down my throat at the words. "You could stay here until it's safe," I offer.

He inhales a sharp breath, but I keep my gaze on the floor to avoid whatever expression lives in his eyes.

"Chrysa's bed will be empty," I continue. "And I have information that the Collection won't take place tomorrow."

"Won't take place, meaning they'll be over? And Minos will no longer be the k—" he coughs just as an earthquake rolls through the room. We both tilt our heads back as if we can see Poseidon in the room with us.

"I don't know what will happen after, whether certain titles will change or stay the same but for the lacking Collection every seven years," I admit, speaking in code that I hope he understands. "The… requirements for the… change won't be met, as the Collection will be cancelled beforehand.

He scowls. "That's not good enough," he says, pursing his lips. "Remaining in this state, no matter that's there's no Collection, isn't good enough."

My head drops backward. "What do you want from me, Dolion? You want the Collection stopped; I'm trying to stop it." This isn't my favored outcome either. I'll go home not having proven I could do it, instead hoisted on the back of a breached bargain discovered by another.

"I want vengeance," he all but snarls. "I want exaction."

It's just as I expected, vengeance over the risk of my life. Dolion blinks as though surprised at his vehemence.

"I need to speak with… others," he says, clearing his throat and standing. "I appreciate the offer, but I need to leave the Palace to report on what you've said. We might still have an opportunity for *change*, if the Collection is gone, especially if you remember my riddle. But all the entrances are guarded."

Orion's tunnels might suffice but that isn't my secret to share. I frown, at him for what he needs me to do, at me for doing it anyway. "I might have a way to get you out, but you'll need to run. Minos can sense when I use it."

"Your illusions?" he asks with wide eyes.

I stand in alarm. "You're not supposed to know about them," I hiss, pointing a finger at his chest. "Who told?"

With his escape planned, Dolion's fear dims. He offers a smirk, one that pinches in the corners. "Thyia can be quite chatty."

I fist my hands at my waist, annoyance reappearing. "And you just took advantage of her, like you take advantage—"

"Are you jealous, Hero?" He moves beside me, crowding close, the grin turning hungry. "You needn't be."

I need the illusions just to stop all this damned blushing in front of men. "I'm not. I'm simply worried for the many women you're manipulating," I say primly.

His expression falls. "Only Deianira, Hero."

"Yes, well. We need to get you out of the castle." I shuffle backward. "Once I place it, you need to run. The magic in the walls tells him when I use it in the Palace. I don't know if he can track you through it."

"I understand. You're a good friend."

I roll my eyes, glad the intensity has seeped from the room. "We're not friends."

He rolls his eyes back at me in a dramatic, and frankly unnecessary, manner. "Whatever you say, Hero."

Before I place the illusion, I stare at his towering form, still too close to me. "Why *did* you think seducing Deianira was a good idea?"

He drags his calloused thumb down my cheek. "Because people in love do desperate, completely irrational things. They'd betray their best friend—their father, in this case—for it."

I inch away from his touch. "You should use your time in hiding to consider better tactics in the future. You'll have all this free time without the Collection."

He follows me, cornering me against the wall. "Maybe I can visit you."

My chin rises as I remember what I wish I had offered to Orion. "Standia welcomes all visitors."

"Including me?" His breath mingles with mine.

"I may live to regret this but, yes. Including you."

His blue eyes sparkle like the sun reflecting off the sea. Brighter than how Orion described his eyes. My stomach swoops when I think of them both in the same span. Before he can say, or do anything else, I place the illusion, letting it fall over his skin like a blanket.

He looks at his hands, which he braces against the wall to either side of my shoulders. "I can't see them."

I roll my eyes again. "That's the point. But you need to run. Whenever possible, go left. It will take you from exit to exit."

He smiles. "Thank you, Thalia."

And I know what he's planning to do, I can see it in his expression, his face holding the same intensity it had just before the birds attacked. The scent of Orion on my skin stalls my reaction but not for long, not long enough to tell Dolion he is unwelcome. Because maybe he is and maybe he isn't, because if Orion is wrong and my almost-there solution to the puzzle isn't enough, I could die tomorrow, not having experienced *any* of the hope and possibility I never realized I was missing living in Standia.

And so, he kisses me hesitantly, a brush of his lips over mine. My own magic from the illusion sparks against my skin. That must be the only reason bubbles build in my stomach as he repeats it once, twice, innumerable times. He smiles into it, kissing the corner of my mouth. Gently, I push him away.

"You need to run," I tell him.

He nods, the smile not dimming. "Good luck, Hero." And he dashes through the door.

When it slams behind him, I touch my lips lightly. It was *nice*, pleasant. Not powerful but comforting, like the gentle lapping of water on a shore. Like Lukas' but softer.

I slump onto my bed. It jostles the book still tied to my waist and I yank it out. It isn't another book to help me with the puzzle, but a poetry book. A book of *love* poetry.

I bite my slightly swollen lower lip, no doubt imitating a toadfish. If I'm wrong about everything, and I die tomorrow, at least I won't need to deal with any of the emotional fallout.

Chapter 24

The earth and sea fold into each other, melding into a single compact star. It leaps into the air to hang next to another star, dimmer than the first but no less brilliant. The night sky blackens as some unseen force pulls the two stars away from each other. The remains of the earth swallow the universe.

I meet the other girls for breakfast on what should be our last morning here. They're still ignoring me. And reminding myself that I will return home soon and won't need to spend time with them again does nothing for the rocks shuffling around in my stomach.

"I can tell you're intentionally ignoring me this time," I tell Chrysa when I slip in the empty seat beside her. I plunk a peace offering in the form of a pomegranate on her plate.

She shuffles her chair farther from me, even as the corner of her lip pulls upward and the pomegranate vanishes into her lap. The earth rumbles, as if cheering me on.

I glare at my plate to shore up my nerves. I can do this; I'm an adult and an heir. "I shouldn't have spoken down to you or assumed you didn't understand the gravity of the Collection. I thought I was helping you."

Elara harrumphs and I chance a peek at them. Diomede looks ready to talk, but Mina and Eriphyle's hands on her arms restrains her.

"You're right, I don't have any of the skills you have." I huff a bitter laugh. "And maybe mine aren't all that great anyway, since I haven't even found the center. But you must believe me that there is something else going on. I've been working on stop—"

"Collected." Kyra's crisp voice interrupts my speech. "You are to come with us."

The others rise while I remain seated, rooted in place. *Did Orion speak with Poseidon and end the Collection as he promised? Or did Minos learn of the plot and now will punish us all?*

"Thalia, up," Kyra snaps.

"Where are we going?" I ask faintly.

"To the Labyrinth," Kynna says from behind her. The girls stare at me with varying expressions of annoyance and confusion.

I stand and follow them as though taking my place on the gallows. Maybe Orion decided to chance it, that the possibility of hope—of his ward's success—was too great to ignore. Or maybe he hasn't gotten through to Poseidon yet.

We enter the elevator and descend into the depths below the Palace. Earthquakes shake the suspended carriage, but its magic keeps us aloft. I wrap my arms around myself, content the dark hides my fear. I shouldn't have abandoned my search last night; I should have continued researching and analyzing until I knew for sure what would happen. *What if I can't get into the center?* I'll never even get the chance to offer my solution.

We shuffle from the elevator silently, cramming into the antechamber and waiting for Kyra and Kynna to open the door and send us to our fate.

"You will have extra time to practice," Kynna says when she opens the door.

My neck isn't the only one that snaps towards her at the announcement.

"This isn't the Collection?" It takes a second to realize it was my trembling voice that asked.

Kynna shakes her head.

"We get another chance to practice?" Elara asks eagerly. She glances around the room and washes her face of feeling, returning to the stiff-lipped girl we've come to know.

"It must be fair," Kyra says, her full lips tight in the corners. "You will complete the Collection tomorrow. Now, go."

Kyra and Kynna make shooing motions at us.

Elara is first through the entrance, disappearing around a corner. Diomede nods to Eriphyle, who takes the permission given and chases after Elara.

"Come on, Thy," Diomede says, hooking elbows with Thyia. "We'll meet them in the center." And they follow the others.

When just Mina and Chrysa remain, they both face me. Chrysa crosses her arms at her chest, and a second later, Mina mimics her.

"You were saying?" Chrysa asks snidely.

I peek at Kyra and Kynna, who still wait in the antechamber.

"We're to watch the entire time," Kynna says, answering my unasked question.

I turn back to Chrysa and wince. "Will you show me the center? I can explain on the way."

"If you beg for forgiveness," Chrysa says.

"On my knees," I promise. "Offering my weight in pomegranates."

Her responding smile gives me hope things will work out.

"So, it's all a game, just not how we thought?" Mina cocks her head like a flustered bird.

"Yes," I say as the two direct me to the center of the Labyrinth. "It isn't about killing the 'Beast' but accepting it. It's all tied in to how Minos won the Island Wars." I squint along the walls of the Labyrinth, looking for the visible gold web of magic that might reveal whether Minos is listening. "He only gets to keep his crown for a short time, I think that's the purpose. He's a regent until the king shows up."

Chrysa turns back and smiles hungrily. "We could be rulers?"

"No, I don't think so," I say apologetically as Chrysa's face falls. "The ruler of Crete would be the child born of the union of Poseidon and Gaia, Mother Earth."

Mina blinks. "Who's that?"

Orion's covered form flashes behind my eyes but quickly flits away. He's the Keeper of the Labyrinth, not its occupant. The child I seek is someone yet unseen, someone possibly terrifying, if he's known in the Labyrinth as the Beast. I return my gaze to Mina and Chrysa. "The Borealis."

Chrysa groans. "Thalia, come on. You can't just say the Borealis all serious-like, with a title and everything, as if it means something to us."

But Mina gasps. "The boar Hecaline was talking about, and that man from the Festival!"

I squelch the sliver of frustration that she figured it out so easily when I was walking around assuming Hecaline forgot my name for a week. I shouldn't have doubted Hecaline's canniness, no matter how doddering she appeared.

"Fine," Chrysa says, stopping at an intersection somewhere that I hope is near the center. I've attempted to memorize the route but there are too many turns. "But still—who is the Borealis?"

I lean against a wall and lower my voice. "Do you remember the notes I read from your friend back home?"

She nods.

"And how they thought the Beast was a boar?"

She nods again, but slower this time.

"I think they misheard, or it got mistranslated over time," I explain. "The Beast *is* the Borealis."

She wrinkles her nose. "And we're supposed to accept it, what, as our true King and keep our fingers crossed it won't murder us first?"

"Assuming the Collection won't be stopped today, I might have an idea about that too-"

Voices echoing around a corner interrupts my next reveal. Before long, Thyia and Diomede come into view.

"We've been waiting ages," Thyia complains. "What's keeping you?"

"Thalia says Minos isn't the true king, and the Beast is, but it's really the Borealis and the entire point of the Collection is for us to accept it as our ruler before it kills us," Mina says in a rush.

Diomede turns paler, which seemed impossible, while Thyia clutches at the neckline of her tunic.

"Thank you, Mina," I say after taking a calming breath. "It's slightly more complicated than that, but that is the gist."

Diomede recovers first. "We should tell the others," she suggests.

Chrysa rolls her eyes. "Do we have to?" Raised brows from Diomede has her pout. "Fine." Suddenly, she beams. "But dibs on telling Elara she's not winning anything."

The center isn't far from where we stopped, and the foursome guide me around a few more turns until we arrive at the center.

It isn't much to look at, though I'm not sure what I expected. There is an entrance and an exit, across from each other. The floor is the same scuffed brick as the Labyrinth, the walls the same polished marble. The rotting smell Chrysa mentioned after our first practice wafts through the fetid air, the faint scent of death I feared I'd recognize in the antechamber.

"No," says Elara, her sharp chin rising. "I won't."

"You don't need to," Diomede says gently. "You can stay behind us while we meet him."

"And leave you with the glory?" She scoffs. "No, I'll be first in and first one to pounce on the Beast."

"Don't be bullheaded," Eriphyle says.

Elara looks betrayed, but she shouldn't. Anyone can see that Eriphyle has found someone else to follow.

"If you try to kill him while we don't," she continues, lecturing Elara on strategy I didn't think she understood. "He could go after us all."

Elara shrugs unconcerned. "Then he goes after us all, and the strongest wins."

"They've always said 'meet,' Elara," I explain sharply. "Not *kill*, not *fight*, but meet. We meet the Beast, and then must accept him, *join* him."

"They've never called him a Beast either, did you notice that?" Thyia asks from behind me. "It's always 'he' or 'him.' Even from the caretakers."

I hadn't noticed that. Both Elara and I frown, but for different reasons.

"If we're lucky," I say when I turn my attention back to Elara's snarl. "It won't matter, and my contact will have reported the breach in the bargain to Poseidon and he'll shut it down." A soft tremor rolls through the ground as if in response.

"Or the Erinyes will," Diomede reminds us. "If Minos truly is an oath breaker."

Elara growls. "The breach being us wasting our lives training when we should have been sitting inside with a book and stuffing our gullets with snacks as heirs to an Island?"

"Elara!" Diomede cries. "That isn't kind."

"But it's true!" She growls and looks like she'll leap on me. It takes all my years not to flinch from the fury emblazoned on her face. She turns to the others, almost pleading. "Why are you all so willing to forgive her for what she said yesterday? We were in agreement!"

"Because I want her to be right," Mina says softly by the entranceway. "I want to go home and see my mama. I don't want to be expendable. I want to live."

"Me too," says Chrysa, standing beside her and slipping an arm around her waist. "Not the going home part, but I want to decide my fate. I spent too long pretending to be someone else. I'm not ready to give up being 'me' yet because you decided your glory was worth me losing my chance."

Unbidden, tears pool in my eyes but I blink them away. Again, it comes down to choices.

"It's cowardly to back down from a fight," Elara says, giving her attention to the other girls who haven't yet stood against her. But Diomede only offers a serene expression, Eriphyle mimics Diomede, and Thyia stands like a caught doe, graceful but afraid.

I tilt my chin and imagine myself staring down a dissenter in Father's Council House. That's all Elara is. "No, it's clever. It's wordplay and we're doing exactly what we're supposed to when Poseidon made the bargain."

"Coward or clever, either is better than dead," says Thyia, her voice wavering.

"I know it's only been seven days; you are so much smarter than I thought you were," Chrysa says.

"Chrysa!" Diomede says with a shriek.

"It's a compliment, Di," Chrysa snaps back.

I ignore them. "Elara, please. Give me five minutes. If the Collection goes forward tomorrow, just wait five minutes before attacking."

"A lot can happen in five minutes," she says, tipping her chin.

"We can hold him off while Heir does her thing," Eriphyle says.

Diomede stops chastising Chrysa and agrees with Eriphyle's offer, beaming at her with pride. "We'll stand together as a team."

"And if I'm wrong—" I exhale. "If I'm wrong, I'll sacrifice myself first, letting you make up for the time you lost." I shift on my feet, the knife living in the holster at my back cold against my skin. "And... I'll give you my knife."

They all bark their reactions. "You have a knife?" "That's not fair!" "We could bring knives?" It all overlaps so I can't tell who speaks.

"Yes," I shout above the din. "I have a knife. It was my father's ceremonial knife I brought from home. I've kept it with me."

"All I did was smuggle in a few notes," Chrysa says, crossing her arms, but delight pulls at her cheeks.

I smile wanly. "And Elara can have it. She can even be first to strike the Beast—the Borealis. But *only* after my five minutes."

"Does she get to decide that for us?" Eriphyle whispers to Diomede, who nods indulgently.

Elara sniffs. "I'll think about it. But you're interrupting my practice time." And she turns away towards the back entrance.

The others recognize the conversation's end and begin doing whatever it is they do to practice in an empty space without a foe or weapons.

I glance at Mina who smiles shyly. "Can you help me understand what I'm seeing in here?" I ask her, swallowing my pride. "You're the huntress."

She steps away from the wall. "Sure. What do you want to know?"

Everything. "Something must happen here, else the girls would return home. The Borealis surely wants the crown, if the Fates say it's his. Killing the people who could give it to him seems irrational." Unless Minos killed them after they failed to 'accept' the Borealis, but that *also* seems unlikely. What better way to keep the populace behind you than by using teenagers likely traumatized by your opponent? Killing them would simply be wasteful. "Can you deduce anything?"

Mina bites her lip before pointing to the corner between the two entrances. "There's where it happened."

Together we step towards the area. It's the only place in the center with large stains on the walls and gouges in the marble and brick.

"Is that dried blood?" I ask, squinting. Mina nods.

"This is the only place with evidence of a fight, like someone was cornered. But look at how the inner corner is completely clean." She points to the space, a large column without stains. "There are no blood stains there, not even a splatter."

I tiptoe closer. "What does that mean?"

"I think the Beast, the Borealis, was there. That's where his body stood. He was cornered and only attacked when he was surrounded."

My brows raise. There's further evidence that violence wasn't his aim, and why Orion must feel personally responsible when his ward kills. *Any being will avoid pain,* he'd told me. "It wasn't him cornering the girls?"

"No, or else there wouldn't be one big clean spot in that shape, it would be littler ones for more of them or none, since they'd probably be moving around."

One more step forward and it feels like lightning against my teeth and crawling over my skin. I hiss and shuffle back again. "That's the line."

Diomede and Eriphyle wander over. "What line?" Diomede asks.

"The line for the boar," Thyia says, joining us in the corner. "Don't let him cross the line. Save the boar, Alis."

"Oh, that's where you got Borealis from," says Chrysa from behind me. "It took you six days to figure that out?"

My expression flattens. "Right. But look." I place my hands in the air and press them forward until I hit the geas boundary. "This is the line, a geas boundary. I imagine if he crosses it, he'll act erratically, start attacking when he wasn't before."

"Geases can make you do things too, not just lose your tongue?" Mina asks. The others look green at the thought.

I nod, unwilling to open the discussion of the armory now when I've finally got them on my side. "Death has never been the goal. He is corralled into this corner by seven Collected who mistakenly believe they must kill him. When he crosses it..."

Each girl considers what I've told them as I step away from the line of magic that makes my teeth itch. I put my hands out to map the line in the air. "If the Collection goes forward, until we figure out how to accept him, keep him from this corner."

"And what if he attacks from a different corner?" Elara calls.

"Then you'll have my knife and corpse to distract him with," I say blandly.

Elara nods, appeased.

As a group, we return to the antechamber before Kynna calls us back. Somehow Diomede convinces Elara to remain with us on the journey back, instead of jogging off on her own. They chatter a little about what I've said, what they plan to do tomorrow, things they miss on their Islands, while I walk in front of them. Alone, set apart as the heir again.

Before I get too maudlin, voices reach us. We're only one turn away from the antechamber. Shockingly, a finger to my lips quiets the girls immediately.

Perhaps I should have been more forthcoming earlier. I could have avoided a lot of angst and disagreements.

"How soon until you call them back?" a weary voice asks.

I look at the others in confusion until Thyia whispers, "Deianira."

I'd forgotten to tell the others about Dolion and Deianira. Her presence, after learning of Dolion's deceit, can't be good.

"Whenever you wish, Lady," Kyra says, sounding more respectful and fearful than she has before.

Deianira huffs. "No, no. Follow your routine for now. We must act as though all is well."

"Then only a few minutes remain."

"Good," Deianira says firmly. "I need her—them—to attend the luncheon at once. Tonight is my last—well, suffice to say I need them."

"Of course, my lady. They will wash and dress and be ready for the luncheon within the hour."

"And you'll advise them of the change?"

"Yes, my lady. That they will be directed to the center upon entry tomorrow."

"Good," Deianira repeats. "Less chance for shenanigans from the remaining girls that way."

There's a brief pause before, "My lady?" That's Kynna now.

"What?" Deianira asks, annoyed.

"We had an update." A shuffling sound vibrates back to us, like Kynna is scuffing her feet. "Two of the girls have developed a close... friendship."

The girls shoot bewildered glances at each other until I gesture to Diomede and Eriphyle. Had it been any non-romantic form of friendship, Kynna would have reported a mix of the six of them.

"Like yours?"

"Yes, my Lady," Kynna replies.

Now only Mina looks confused until Chrysa whispers in her ear and she raises her dark brows.

"There's something else," Kyra says. "Another of the Collected wasn't born—" She's cut off with a sharp grunt, as though someone elbowed her in the stomach.

"Please pardon Kyra, my lady," says Kynna. "That is nothing of consequence to the Collection. All *seven women* are prepared for this evening."

Chrysa's shoulders slump slightly, as though she knows what Kyra was about to reveal. I reach for her wrist and squeeze. When I try to remove it, she snags my hand and holds it. I offer her a reassuring smile while Mina hugs her other side.

"But the other two," Deianira says. "Are they being discreet?"

"They do not flaunt the change in their association. Likewise, they do not venture out in public or leave the Palace. No one but us should know," Kyra answers.

Deianira huffs a laugh that sounds bitter. "Yes, but one cannot hide from the gaze of the Gods, even inside the Palace, no matter how my Father attempts to do so. It is a small mercy they cannot enter. We will not remove the girls yet, not so close to the end. It would... complicate things when we are attempting to prove this Collection, like the others, is ordinary in all respects. One missing Collected will already bring attention. But advise me of any other changes that might make the... bargained outcome impossible."

"Why does it matter?" Diomede mouths.

All but Elara and I shrug. Instead, Elara scowls down the hall like she wants to burst through the door and leave, while I consider the question. Why *would* their relationship matter?

"And our arrangement?" Kyra asks quietly.

"Your names will remain off the betrothal lists," Deianira confirms.

Both caretakers sigh. "Thank you, my Lady," Kynna says. "And now it is time to call them back."

Chapter 25

After Chrysa and I put on the crisp white peplos Kynna and Kyra delivered for the luncheon, we all corral in Eriphyle and Elara's room to discuss what's coming. Elara doesn't want us there, but, as Eriphyle pointed out, it would be easier to trap Elara in her room than force her into another's.

Eriphyle, like the others, continues to rise in my esteem.

"Something might happen at this luncheon," I warn them. "They don't know we've realized the game or that Poseidon will soon know of the treachery, but this is their last chance to impede us. Please... just be aware."

Elara huffs, laying alone on her bed and looking at the ceiling, like we're not there. One finger plays with the new shoulder clip she was given, a jeweled version of the original brass trinket we wore for the Festival of Poseidon. We all received new shoulder clips to match our shimmering robes, ones that look like gold thread was used at the seams.

"If everything is supposed to be normal, then nothing should happen," Mina says, crowded on Eriphyle's bed with Eriphyle, Diomede, and Chrysa. A pearl makes up the moon on Mina's new clip, a stunning display of wealth. Even my golden owl clip now boasts chalcedony for eyes, instead of eyeless sockets.

"This isn't normal," says Thyia from her place next to me beside the door. The leaves on her rose clip appear to be formed from actual emeralds. "Kynna told me this is the first pre-Collection luncheon they've done."

"Why would she tell you that?" "When did you have time to ask her?" Both Mina and I ask simultaneously. Thyia answers us together.

"Right after we left the elevator. I wanted to know if I needed to dress myself in a specific way. She said King Minos has never met with the Collected after the first night."

"It's a pageant. A play," I realize. "He's putting on a show for Poseidon. The luncheon, our new clothes, the jewelry. 'Look how well I treat the Collected,' 'they're in no danger.'"

"'We didn't kill the rest of them, it's all that awful Beast's fault,'" Chrysa adds.

Elara flicks her gaze towards me. "We still don't know that Heir is even right, and this isn't some scheme to win, holding me back for five minutes."

"If five minutes is what it takes for you to lose, then you don't deserve to win," Eriphyle says under her breath.

The air sucks from the room. Elara stares at Eriphyle as if she has two heads, while Diomede frowns.

"It's about working together," Diomede starts, but Chrysa's sharp laugh covers it.

"I knew you had a personality. You've got some bite underneath that bulk."

Eriphyle smirks just as Diomede turns her ire towards Chrysa.

"So, if it's a show, then we're even more safe," Mina says as the others squabble.

I shake my head. "Deianira is planning something, most likely against me. Remember? The Collection must go on as normal with one less Collected, she said."

Mina wrinkles her nose. "How do you know it's about you?"

"Because it has to be about her, the oh so special one," Elara says under her breath.

"Maybe it's because of Dolion," Chrysa suggests. Diomede has angled away from her with crossed arms.

Thyia sighs. "Poor Dolion."

"What do you mean 'poor Dolion'?" I ask Thyia. What I wouldn't give for an illusion to hide the probable blush on my cheeks. "Wait, no. It's not about Dolion. It's about us being close to the answer."

Elara stands, cracking her neck. "The answer only *you* know. The one only *you* could figure out. Even if they don't want us to win, they'd still choose the one who had the best chance of winning."

"You mean you and winning means killing the Borealis," I say flatly.

Elara nods and smirks, like she's daring me to argue again.

Instead, I sigh. "Fine. It might not be me, it could be any of us. But one girl will be targeted, which means everyone needs to be careful at this luncheon."

"You're not in cha—"

Chrysa groans. "Good Gods, Elara. Find another taunt. You're becoming a—what's it called when you're a joke of yourself?"

"A caricature," Eriphyle says.

My brows aren't the only ones raised at her immediate answer.

"We'll be careful," says Thyia, returning to the topic at hand. "But... do you suppose they'll let us keep these clips?"

The luncheon is in a large banquet room off the first floor kitchen that opens into a courtyard. It isn't like the symposiums we sponsor back home—no games and entertainment here—but an over-the-top parody. The hall boasts towering pillars, each intricately carved with grapevines and scenes of bacchanalian revelry. The ceiling is ornamented with a mural depicting a joyous dance of nymphs and satyrs, ironic given Minos'

actions towards them. It's likely a meanspirited joke of his, seeing the beauty of those creatures he murdered.

The room is set for fifty, but only nine will sit at the table: the seven of us, Minos, and Deianira. The caretakers (minus Dolion) and various other staff, including the minister, position themselves around the long wooden table. Elaborate centerpieces of gilded olive branches and cascading vines decorate the tables, intertwining with golden candleholders and aromatic herbs. Hanging lanterns crafted from iridescent seashells and precious gemstones cast a soft, radiant glow over the table.

Draperies of fabrics embroidered with golden thread frame the windows and doorways, billowing gently in the breeze that carries the scent of the nearby gardens. Like the rest of the Palace, the walls are covered with Cretan symbols. From a distance, they could be Poseidon's tridents and bulls, but up close, the trident's middle prongs have been gouged out leaving it a two-pronged bident. And the horns of the bulls have been rounded to look more like a ram's. Both symbols of Hades. I wonder if it's a hint at the death Minos wishes upon us or his own secret revenge against Poseidon.

Minos no longer looks haggard like he had when I was spying on him yesterday, but regal and sporting a self-satisfied smirk. He wears the bull head around his waist again, but his golden braid isn't choking it. Instead, it's wrapped around his head like a shimmering crown before falling behind him. Another hint perhaps: that Minos will not relinquish his crown unless it is cut from him.

But Deianira looks worse than she sounded in the Labyrinth, wrinkled and twitchy, with eyes that bounce from the walls to her plate. I slide into the bench directly across from her to better watch her, followed by Diomede, Eriphyle, and Elara. Mina, Chrysa, and Thyia take their seats on the other side, lining the table beside Deianira. The only downside to my positioning is that I'm also directly diagonal to Minos.

But if Minos wants this Collection to remain normal, or as normal as it can be with the Borealis unknowingly murdering his possible sponsors, *he* won't misbehave at this luncheon. Deianira is who we must watch out for. Minos must surely believe that tomorrow, he'll gasp and clutch at his chest as another set of Collected die, bemoaning 'those poor girls,' sympathizing that 'I had a feast with them just yesterday, I can't imagine what made them react so,' and playing the conciliatory rube to Poseidon. Maybe he'll try to use it to convince Poseidon that the bargain is impossible.

I smother a smirk. Minos is in for a surprise.

The ground rumbles, another rolling earthquake. The lanterns above us shake and a single seashell lands on Chrysa's plate. Mina quickly grabs it and stuffs it somewhere in her skirts. Minos' eyes twitch before he banishes the reaction.

When we're settled, he snaps his fingers, and nine servers appear from a hidden door holding platters. They drop the overstuffed portions in front of each of our plates, a pungent array of meats and cheeses, the best meal we've been served here. Chrysa and Mina don't even serve themselves; instead, they drag the platters on top of their plates. I muffle a smile, so does Diomede. Warm and flaky bread comes next, the yeasty smell strong and mouthwatering, followed by large carafes of wine. In this, I'm reminded of home, of the overabundance Standia offered to its people. Before we can serve ourselves the dark burgundy wine, Deianira stands and grabs the nearest server. Quickly, they remove the carafes and our individual cups. Minos directs a sharp gaze her way, which she avoids by glaring holes into her platter of meat, but the servers' return halts any questions Minos might have wanted to ask aloud.

They've restored our cups now already filled. Instead of the flowered centerpieces and roasted meats, a musty smell wafts upward. It's similar to the scent outside the armory, where we found the poison plants.

The hemlock had been cut, Diomede said. But they don't remember that conversation. Deianira angles away from us as best she can. Beside her, Mina's nose twitches and she looks ready to comment on the odd scent until Chrysa's hand disappears from the table. She jolts, her knee banging into the underside; Chrysa must have pinched her.

"Poison," I mouth to Diomede beside me. She nods and the message travels down our end of the table. Mina takes a long whiff from her cup and shrugs.

Minos lifts his goblet and bares his teeth in something resembling a smile. "I would raise a toast. Not to Poseidon, may his reign over the sea continue everlasting, but to our Collected. Indeed, you young women are a credit to your Islands."

Chrysa mutters something under her breath that I don't catch. Minos' speech is a far cry from the pompous declarations he made at the Festival of Poseidon. *Gods, was that only a few days ago?* But he thought himself untouchable and now must play a role. I smother another smile behind my expressionless mask. He doesn't realize that he's already lost, that Orion is telling Poseidon of his treason. By tomorrow, he'll crumble, just like the lives of so many he's damned. He'll lose his crown, and someone else will take his seat.

Deianira shifts, but Minos isn't finished. His attention flits around the room and he appears to speak through gritted teeth. "Intelligence, beauty, strength, these women have it all. Any of them is worthy of their permanent place at this table."

I inhale sharply as more pieces slot into place, into a puzzle I thought I'd already solved. Diomede rests her hand on my forearm, likely imagining I need reassurance. I do, but not in the way she must think. Minos' cagey language can't hide what we already know: that his crown is on the line, but even if the Borealis takes his crown, we have no place at his table. The only permanent members are the King's family. His children. And his spouse.

As Minos continues droning on, I realize the last piece I was missing. Chrysa was right: one of us would be a ruler.

They removed male candidates for the Collection not because they're allegedly stronger and would, thus, *defeat* the Borealis or fight him for the crown but for something simpler: because a woman will sit by the Borealis' side at this table. *They will* join *him*, Hecaline said, and *come together*. They are entitled to their permanent place, as the King's family. Only women are chosen because the Borealis prefers women, making the inclusion of men too easily exposing Minos' scheme to keep his crown and why the rules changed. Which is why Diomede and Eriphyle's relationship could threaten the Collection, because they would be unavailable. Which means to defeat Minos... someone must accept the Borealis and agree to be his consort, to take their place by his side. That's what Minos meant yesterday with the minister; he must have assumed no woman would agree to become the Borealis' wife.

Nausea roils in my stomach, threatening to surge into my throat. I close my eyes for the count of three. Visions of green sails burning in a fiery blaze dance behind my closed lids.

When I reopen them, Minos has finished, and cups are raised. I can indulge my disappointment and worries in my bedroom, after I've survived Deianira's sloppy scheme. I lift my cup, raising my brows at the other girls. They lightly shake their heads; the mustiness isn't in their cups. It's only in mine, though Deianira's focused stare at my mouth makes it an easy tell. The nausea at the possibility of losing my freedom ebbs, knowing that if becoming the Borealis' consort is required, it is my responsibility; the poison is proof why I'm the only one who even has a chance. Squaring my shoulders, I tip the lip of the goblet and place a tiny illusion on the liquid before any can breach the seam of my mouth.

Minos twitches at the magic he must feel but doesn't otherwise react. I swallow a smirk instead of the poison, glad for the spiteful feelings rising within me, ones that drown the panic at the knowledge of the last piece of the puzzle. Better to think of Minos' lacking future, rather than my own. Let him experience this discomfort at knowing foreign magic is present that he can't control. His unease is only a modicum of what we must bear.

A server fills his plate, and he jabs his thumb into a slab of meat. Deianira bats her server away, still watching me. I take another pretend sip.

Chrysa hisses across the table. Minos and Deianira shoot glances her way, but she blinks guilelessly, or as guilelessly as she can appear, until they look away. Then, wide-eyed, she mouths to me, "You drank poison?"

"Magic," I mouth, my pleasure at Minos' discomfort waning. Instead, my own crests, firm in the knowledge that whatever happens at the Collection won't be ideal for my future plans. I can only pray Orion spoke with Poseidon already.

Chrysa clears her throat and nods at me, like we're in on something together. "Thalia, you're looking flush," she shouts. All eyes in the room converge on her. I consider placing another illusion to duck under the table and avoid whatever *this* is.

"Yes, and sick," Mina adds, sounding like an actor that needed to find another career choice. Deianira flinches as Mina leans over her to better inspect me. "You should go back to your room."

"We'll help," Chrysa says, standing and reaching over the table like she intends to pull me across it. She slaps my cup down the table, liquid splattering over my and Deianira's platters until the cup bounces to a stop on top of Minos' plate. The few remaining burgundy wine drops fall onto Minos' half-eaten bread. His nostrils flare and a scowl burns over his face.

Chrysa frowns, unashamed. "Well, that's not great."

Watching Minos try to keep calm as the remains of his luncheon went up in metaphorical flames would have given me a sense of malicious delight, had I not been at the center of it. Deianira rushed from the room screeching that no one should eat the wine-tainted meat while Minos stared after her with the rage in his expression barely hidden.

We were bustled out after Minos loudly claimed the luncheon was a wonderful meal and that we should go forth and continue enjoying his hospitality until the Collection tomorrow.

Perhaps he thinks Poseidon is blind.

"You only drank a small amount; you should be fine. Thank the Gods, the worst will only be intestinal distress," Diomede says after trying to tuck me into my bed. We congregated there after Kynna and Kyra dropped us off. "Just wait until my Governor hears all the blasphemous things Minos is doing in the Gods' names."

I resist her unneeded aid, batting away her hands. "I didn't drink any. But don't forget Deianira when you're complaining to your Island. They're both undermining a valid bargain with the Gods."

Elara rolls her eyes and leaves the room. We watch the door close behind her mutely. An earthquake aids it along, banging the wood against the stone.

"At least Deianira has made her move already," I say. "She would be desperate to try something else. We should be safe until tomorrow."

Thyia bites her lip. "Are you sure? Desperate people will do desperate things."

A heavy silence pervades our small space. I attempt a reassuring smile, though their expressions tell me I failed. "If she does,

I'm still certainly the target, so you'll be fine. And Minos won't dare try anything, not when he's trying to keep control over the Collection. But remember, the Collection shouldn't happen tomorrow. My source has all but confirmed that, so simply lie low until tomorrow when Minos's treachery is exposed."

"What if the Collection *does* happen tomorrow?" Mina asks from her place on Chrysa's bed.

If it goes forward, my future is all but gone. Accepting the Borealis as King in place of Minos is one thing, but agreeing to sit at his side is another. Heir Thalia, spirit-born of Athena, will be renamed and remade.

But that's not what Mina needs to hear. If only I'd gotten better at comforting them. "If it does... then wait for me to have my five minutes with the Borealis."

"And let the Erinyes take Minos where he belongs," Diomede adds with vindictive glee. Eriphyle squeezes her side, smiling like a predator.

Chapter 26

"We're going to all stay together tonight," Chrysa says, sitting on her empty bed. "You should come."

I duck my head to hide a smile. They spent the few remaining daylight hours after the farcical luncheon outside. Using Orion's tunnels, I snuck out and joined them for as long as I dared to shore up tomorrow's plan, assuming Elara doesn't change her mind, assuming Orion doesn't stop it. But I kept the last piece of the puzzle hidden.

"I'll come say goodnight. But I'd like to do one last review to make sure there's nothing I'm missing in case the Collection goes forward."

"Your books," she says, turning smug when my mouth opens in surprise. "You know, if you don't want a Karavian to go through your things, you shouldn't leave them out."

I snag them from their hiding place, confirming the two hadn't been lost or stolen. "They *were* hidden."

"Under a pillow doesn't count." She leaps from the bed before I can react and grabs the top volume from the small pile, Orion's poetry book, and opens it to the front page. "My dearest Thalia, it is with great affection that I leave you this book."

"It doesn't say that." Flushing, I try to snatch it from her grip, but she sidesteps me and stands on her bare pallet out of reach.

She makes a face. "Of course, it doesn't. I can't read, remember?" She clears her throat and continues, "If you were less of a bore, I'd leave you flowers or candy."

"Anyone that would leave me a love note would *like* that I read," I mutter, crossing my arms and waiting for her to finish. There'll be no chance of that for me now, unless the Borealis' moniker as the Beast is only because of his figure and not a hint at a monstrous personality.

"But the heart wants what it wants. Love, Dolion." Chrysa wrinkles her nose just as my stomach drops. "Where is Dolion, anyway?"

Using her distraction, I take back the book, and busy myself straightening them. "I'm not sure. I know he left." I can only hope he made it out of the Palace without harm.

"He wasn't that good a caretaker, but he was nice," Chrysa says, frowning.

I shrug. In his way, he was both and neither. He had his own goals and didn't care how he accomplished him, though I can't fault him much for that. And that he was only tossed from Deianira's room after attempting to exploit her was good luck.

Pity it revealed his allegiances. At least, if the Collection occurs, my pseudo-sacrifice might bring him, and many others, some comfort.

She hops to the floor. "Bring pomegranates if you come."

"I'll try," I say to her back as she leaves the room. I finger the books when I'm alone, trying not to let myself fall into a depression.

It's probably best that the Collection won't occur tomorrow. It is the safest option. And gives me the ability to return to Standia as heir, and not a corpse. Or the consort to the mysterious and unlucky Borealis.

Particularly since only I should wed the Borealis. I can only imagine Queen Elara.

I shake off my unease. No matter the outcome tomorrow, this is my last night in Crete; I need to make the most of it. I snag the history book Orion lent me and follow Chrysa into the hallway.

As Chrysa ambles left towards one of the other rooms, I duck right. Kyra and Kynna's soft voices come from down the way, and I race towards Orion's secret passageway to avoid being seen.

I shuffle in the darkness of the hidden tunnels until I amble around a corner and find a lit lantern, one Orion must keep available for his secret jaunts. Tipping it over and onto the thin line of oiled rope that hangs in long loops above me lights a spark that illuminates the halls. I begin my search for Orion's room.

It takes longer than I expect to find the entrance that would lead to his rooms, but it allows me to recede into my mind and further convince myself of the necessity of what I plan to do. Twice I arrive in dead ends, other shortcuts to secret places in the Palace. On another night, I'd nose around to discover more, but dawn won't wait for my curiosity.

But curiosity follows me anyway, as after I crawl up another ladder, one I hope takes me to the top floor. Just ahead is the thin line of a doorway and I gently press it open.

The grating tones of Minos' voice greets me, and I careen back into the tunnel.

"You imbecile! What if she'd died?"

"I thought—accidents happen." That's Deianira responding. They must be speaking of the poisoning attempt. "It wouldn't come back to you. Your hands didn't do it, nor mine. The servants placed the poison."

"No, you thought to maneuver above your station, as though I need your protection!"

"But I couldn't let her compete," Deianira says, her voice wavering.

"Do you really think the Collection is the end of this? Did you forget what I received from the bargain? He cannot remove it, not without stealing it from my head."

"No, Father, I—"

"You're lucky I prepared for this day. But now I'll need to wade through that damned cave again. I have a mind to make you do it and then feed you to the Keres."

The voices soften as they walk farther from the door, wherever it may lead. I turn back and find another ladder to the fourth floor. Finally, I recognize the thin light leading into his bedroom just ahead. After taking a bracing breath, I knock on the door. The light extinguishes.

"Orion?" I whisper into the cracked doorway I can't see but can only sense is there. "It's Thalia."

A small gust of air is the only evidence that it has been opened until a familiar scarred hand grasps my forearm and pulls me forward.

"Thalia?" His voice is gruff, but smooth, uncovered. "This is a surprise. I intended to find you before dawn."

I smile faintly as he pulls me deeper into his rooms. "Yes, I wanted to-"

"The Collection will go forward tomorrow," he says.

Something pinches in the spaces between my ribs, but I can't tell if it's relief or fear. I'll get my chance tomorrow, but at the expense of my identity.

His voice breaks as he continues, "Poseidon wants to see it for himself. Words can't explain how sorry I am."

He stops us in what must be the kitchen, or else I'd still be tripping on piles of books. "Orion, it's alright. It makes sense that he'd want confirmation. But that's okay. I know what to do now."

He grabs my shoulders, rattling my bones with the intensity of his grip, though it doesn't hurt. "You must leave. Now. The moment Minos' deeds are shown after the Collection, he'll be confirmed an oath breaker, but you aren't safe. I've contacted allies who will give you passage but you must leave at once."

It takes but a minute to consider the idea and disregard it. It is still not a true choice, not when I'm being forced to take it. And without a choice, I will stay here and do what I planned to do. I cover his hands on my shoulders until he releases the crushing grip. "No, Orion. I can't do that, especially not without the girls. Didn't you hear me? I know what to do. I'm staying."

"But... the center and the geas boundaries... and the bargain and Minos, and... and the crown." He sputters out thoughts, nonsensical to anyone but me.

My thumbs brush against the muscular and scarred skin of his forearms in a gentle rhythm. "I know what I must do."

He hisses through his teeth. "And you're accepting? You'll... join..."

"Yes." The word comes out more as an exhalation than anything else, something forced. I'll do it, but I won't like it, not when I'm losing so much, not when the risk of disappointing more than Standia is so great.

Orion bundles me in his arms, just like last night, but this time pulling me even closer. My feet remain on the ground as one hand clutches the skin at my neck and the other rests against the fabric of my low back. Greedily, I take the refuge he gives me, no matter that my practical side knows I should question him more on Borealis found in the center. On my future King.

Except when I realize that his entire chest is bare, all other thoughts stall. This embrace is nothing like last night's when he was clothed, nor is it familiar to the one the day before when I tripped into his chest. This is charged, like lightning, like fire. His skin burns against my body, his short curls tickle the skin behind my ear.

"You're unclothed," I gasp into his neck. My eyes fall shut in embarrassment. *Brilliant deduction, Thalia, no wonder you barely solved the puzzle.*

He withdraws, stepping out of my reach. "I shouldn't have—"

"No." I'm quick to reassure him. "Please, I could use the comfort of a friend."

He steps closer, the heat of him revealing his nearness, and places his hands on my hips. "Am I a friend?"

"Yes." There's no chance for more now. Whatever desire for it, from him, from *anyone*, will drown in the sea along with my heirship. But now is not the time for regrets. I lay my hands on his chest, drumming my fingers against the skin as a silent question.

"Please," he murmurs, tightening his grip at my soft waist.

A shiver runs down my back to settle in my stomach. Were I a different person, I might take it as a plea for something else.

My fingertips glide up his brawny chest, over the smooth skin at the apple of his throat, uncovering the flutter of his pulse. He stills, as motionless as when I first met him. I don't linger on the vulnerable dip of his throat, my tactile expedition focused on refining the picture of him I'd created. His squared jaw leads to a sturdy bone structure. A wide nose perches over full lips, the skin surrounding them slightly rippled with what must be supple scar tissue. Wavy hair, like mine, curls just below his ears. The visual of him forms, adding in the details he'd allowed earlier. My hands return to his chest.

"Thank you." My voice is a little breathless, flush from the trust he'd given me and the idea of continuing my exploration.

"I said I would bare myself to you a—" He clears his throat, the geas still active. "When it all ended."

I lean my head against his chest, snatching liberties I would never consider taking but will because of what tomorrow will bring. "I know. But everything will have changed then."

"For the better," he says. He makes it sound like a guarantee, but it isn't. "If you are accepting tomorrow."

That all depends on the being behind the Borealis moniker. "Possibly. Hopefully, though I feel as though I'm giving up my freedom for it," I mutter.

"You wanted to rule," he says, but it's a question so I treat it like one.

"*Standia*, as the Governor, not as his wife. And because it's expected of me, and what I was born to do. I was willing to sacrifice it to help my people in the Collection and prove my worth to them, but not... not change my purpose."

"You could do both," Orion suggests tentatively. "There's no requirement that you relinquish your heirship. Being a woman of the Islands was—" He cuts off with a cough. The geas must have activated. "That was Minos' proposal when Poseidon suggested it. It sounded altruistic, a way to keep the Gods' powers in check and appease Gaia," he says, implying the last term of the bargain, and connecting the dots I'd left separate. Minos could hold the crown of Crete until the Borealis and an Islander could rule together. That's why acceptance as consort is important. Orion huffs darkly. "Now we know it was all part of his scheme."

"It was a good idea. My own circumstances involved betrothal for a similar reason," I say, thinking of Argon's ambition. "I was lucky it was to my best friend, someone I knew and trusted and would certainly come to love, if I'd let myself. But now, it's..." I trail off and exhale. *It's to a stranger.*

He recoils, almost dislodging me. "You are not *required* to do anything, Thalia."

"There's no choice here, Orion."

"The boat—"

My lips twist. "The boat isn't a choice either, but another forced outcome. Just like the Labyrinth. At least in the Labyrinth I can do something good."

He releases me and deliberately puts further distance between us. "Why did you come tonight, Thalia?"

I shrug, useless because he can't see it. "I wanted to see my friend one last time."

"Yes, your *friend*," he says, an emphasis on the last word that sounds bitter. That might haunt me for a time, following me just like Dolion telling me his attention wasn't false, these two possibilities that might have been something had things been different. At least I'd kissed Dolion, and Lukas, before the doors shut and my future remained unwritten.

"May I—" The words form and float out of my mouth before I realize I've said it. I bite my lip, holding in the rest of the request, one that would do nothing but bring regret. Neither probable death nor impending engagement is an excuse to slake my curiosity in kissing a third man. I extract my book from beneath my belt, using it as the excuse for why I cut myself off. "I also wanted to return your book."

"I—I shouldn't have presumed," he says, taking it from me. "I'm sorry."

"What?"

"You've been very clear that we are but friends. That's all I can ask for." He clears his throat. "No matter what tomorrow may bring. I'll return the book of verse and we can go forward as though I never off—"

I blindly reach out, grabbing his wrist. "No! You can see in the dark, but I can't. I meant to bring the history book, the one you lent me. I want the poetry."

He shuffles backward, but I follow. "Thalia, it's alright. I understand."

"I'm not trying to make you feel better. Your gift means something to me. It's a memento of your friendship." *A memento of an unwritten future of my own.* I tug on the book. "Please, let me get the other one."

"Thalia," he sighs. He puts up a token fight to keep the book, but finally surrenders it.

I clutch it to my chest. "I'll be back. I'll be quick. It will be as though I never left. We can continue our game until sunrise. I believe I'm still at least one secret ahead of you. We should even it up before dawn."

Determination delivers me back to our hallway before too much time passes and I duck inside my room undetected.

Dolion sits on my bed, standing when I enter and reaching for me. "Thalia, thank the Gods."

Though relieved, I duck around him, too intent on my quarry to let him distract me. "Thank the Gods for *you*, Dolion, that you're well. But I'm in the middle of something. The offer to hide in my room remains, if you need it, and we can talk tomorrow after the Collection."

He snatches my arm, keeping me from avoiding him again. "I need you now," he says, voice weak. "Please."

That's when I truly *see* him. He looks worse than last night, preternaturally pale with sweat dotting his brow. Dust covers his cheeks, a long line of something rusty red and flaking drags across his forehead, and a scratch mars his sharp cheekbone.

I reach out, stopping short of touching him. "What happened?"

"That's not important." His gaze flits upward, something wild pools in his eyes. "But what happened after. I—I don't know what to do. I tried to speak to Hecaline for guidance, but I couldn't get inside. I even tried praying to the Gods, but they remained elusive as ever."

He ducks his head, fingers flexing against my arm. "Thalia, I need help," Dolion pleads even as I glance at my bed, where the history book hides. "I have the chance for—for something I've only imagined. But the choice is... difficult."

I don't have time for this, so I offer him a flippant response. "Will it make you happy?"

"Yes." The force behind the word could knock down a wall.

"Then do it. Life is short, Dolion. Even for the Cretans. We get few good choices in this world, why not take them when they come to us?" It's something I might have told past-Thalia, had I known where I'd end up tomorrow.

He sucks in a trembling breath, still looking distraught rather than relieved. "Are you sure?"

"Yes, and I wish you luck with whatever it is. But I'm busy now," I say, attempting to turn back to the bed, but his iron grip keeps me in place. "We can speak more tomorrow after the Collection."

"No, no. The choice involves you. You must come with me."

I scowl at him. "Had I known that, I would have told you no."

He flinches, dropping my arm as though burned and wrapping his hands around his neck. Gone is the cocksure man who toyed with danger, willfully risking his tongue and life to earn closure. Now, he looks lost, broken, a little boy needing help to gain some happiness.

My shoulders slump. It was much easier when I could pretend I cared little for my comrades here. "Alright, I will. Just... one minute."

I withdraw the poetry book from inside my tunic and straighten the bent edges. The spine cracks, the front cover fanning open and revealing letters in Orion's penmanship. I glance at Dolion, who still stares at nothing. I'll give myself this, read Orion's words once, just in case, before going off on whatever dire quest Dolion has for me. It *is* my last night of freedom. I'm allowed a little selfishness, a little reminder to carry with me. I expose Orion's inscription.

Ink blots decorate the space before the words, betraying the length of time he must have considered what to write. Below it,

> *If I'd ever been given the choice, I would have chosen you.*
> *Your child of Earth and Sea,*

Orion
Borealis

The book falls to my bed. My hands tremble as I cover the soft gasp attempting to spill from my mouth. *How could I have missed that?*

Dolion now stands at the door, one arm held out for me. "Thalia, please." He looks too nervous and distraught for someone who seeks his own happiness, but I don't have time to add that worry to my list.

Gently, I deposit the poetry book with its less shocking brother. *I'll be back,* I promise it. *I'll correct our misunderstanding.* I square my shoulders and let my heir mask cover the anticipation buzzing at my skin.

"I do have somewhere to be," I tell Dolion as I march towards him. "So, I can only indulge you with this for a little while."

"I understand," he murmurs as he holds open the door for me, gesturing with a quivering hand.

As soon as I walk through it, my head explodes in pain.

And then darkness.

Chapter 27

Consciousness comes slowly, filling the edges of my vision with light. Blearily, I blink and straighten the crick in my neck. The light I'd seen wasn't consciousness calling, but the bright blaze of an oil lamp in my face. Behind it, Dolion's face bleakly stares down at me.

I sit up with a groan. It feels like someone walloped me in the head. Dolion scurries away as soon as I move. Distantly I recognize the sound of a heavy door opening and creaking shut, and the turning of a lock.

I claw my way past the haze that threatens to keep control of my mind, a sign of some form of head trauma, surely. I know little of medicine on a good day. Even if I *wished* to diagnose myself now instead of discovering exactly what's happened, I likely don't have the knowledge. A wall catches me when I lean backward to avoid falling back to my side. I'm sitting on a thin wooden bench that's pressed against a stone wall. Beside it are three other identical stone walls, all windowless and wet. Chains covered with arcane symbols hang from them, and through my mental haze I can see splashes of gold magic wrapped around the iron. Mildew crawls up the sides of the stone, a gray color that tells a story of disinterest, that the prisoners within merited no comforts, not even protection from the sickly damp. The floor is strewn with straw while the air carries a chill, and the faint scent of earth mingles with the acrid aroma found at the center of the Labyrinth. The smell of blood and sweat, perhaps. A wooden door bisects the wall across from my bench, with a barred window. Dolion stands on the other side of it, one hand clutching the lip of the window that reveals his body from stomach to head.

My lips smack together, clearing away the dry cotton-like feeling within. "What did you do, Dolion?" The words are dragged from my mind to my mouth, rasping and slow.

He holds the oil lamp closer, illuminating his sweating face. The rusted iron line on his forehead remains, but the dust and blood from his cheekbone have dribbled towards his neck from the damp. "You just need to wait in here until the Collection ends."

Perhaps it's the shock that dulls my reactions. Or the head trauma. Whatever the reason, neither pain nor frustration, or even futile sadness, rises within me at the realization that another choice has been taken from me. Not even curiosity builds at wondering *why* it happened. Resignation might be the closest emotion I'm experiencing. But otherwise, I've been hollowed out.

Dolion presses his forehead against the bars. "I had to, Thalia," he whispers, as though I demanded he confess. "Once the choice was given, and you agreed."

A spark of something flickers through the empty abyss of my thoughts and mind. "Don't blame me for this." I barely recognize the sound of my voice.

"He—Minos—Zeus and Poseidon are aligned, but Ha—" He cuts off with a gasp. I might have wondered what geas he's under now, but my mind remains quiet, uncaring. "They'll work together, Minos and H—him, that is. He just needs time for—for it to happen."

I stare at the bench. A former occupant has scratched crude designs into the seat: hatch marks to track the days, several squiggles that could be winding snakes, and a double-sided triangle. "What of your vengeance?" I rasp.

"This *is* my vengeance," he breathes. "Minos promised me—he—he promised he would demand Lasthena's soul in exchange for my help. She—she could come back."

It's a memory that ignites a kindling within, a realization that I was right, no matter that I didn't want to be. The flint threatens to set the hollow chasm ablaze and with each word, another ember inside me lights, filling me with righteous anger. "You never answered when I asked what you would choose if given the chance for your vengeance at the expense of my life," I say through clenched teeth. "They 'aren't mutually exclusive,' I seem to recall. Isn't that what we said?"

"I did, Thalia," he says, his voice pleading. "I will get Lasthena, but you will still live. Minos promised. Nothing changes."

He'd warned me of this, I realize dimly. *Love makes people irrational, betraying everything*, he'd told me. Something thick threatens to choke me, only freeing my throat when I let out a bitter laugh.

"And you believed him?" I gesture around the cell, the quick movement giving me a headache. "You think he'll let me live, even if it's as a forgotten specter here? No one has ever returned from the Collection or been seen again. I can assure you I will breathe my last breath in this forsaken Palace, and it will be soon."

I'm not afraid of the prospect at this moment. Anger consumes everything in its path like wildfire, obliterating those feelings I might want to hide behind a mask, most notably my continued anxiousness and self-doubt. How ironic it is that I gain my assurance only when I feel wronged.

He shakes his head. "You'll be safe, Thalia. I promise. With—with Lasthena back, we will begin again. We'll get you out, and you can help. We can use the time to prepare for the next Collection, when we win it. It will only delay the plan for a few years," he says, like it's a consolation.

"And what of the others?" Concern for them is the only feeling my anger doesn't immolate. "Those girls liked you, *trusted* you. Unless they are hidden in nearby cells, they will die. You know this." I stand woozily, but I swallow the rising nausea. It slides the knife's holster over the dips of my low back. Dolion forgot to remove it or didn't think he'd need to. "You chose your vengeance, your happiness, at the expense of them, at the expense of everything."

The oil lamp cracks as he swings it into the bars, wrapping his fingers around them, as though he's the prisoner fighting to be on the other side of the door. "It—it is a necessary sacrifice. For now. The Collection needed to continue. Minos needs the—the outcome cannot happen now."

"Perhaps that can be part of their eulogies. If they are given burial rites and not tossed into the sea like garbage," I spit. The image dulls the anger, creating bleak regret in its place. I shouldn't have continued to underestimate them. I should have told them the *entire* story and let one of them become the consort in my stead. Now, five minutes will pass, and Elara will incite the bloodbath that will kill them all.

Cold fire fills Dolion's eyes. "I was willing to die for this cause. Lasthena did die. Sometimes sacrifices must be made."

"There's a difference between a sacrifice you make and one made of you," I hiss, fisting my hands on my hips to disguise the subtle movement of undoing the folds of my robes. I haven't considered whether, or how, to use the knife. But I must leave this room. And he said it: sacrifices must be made, no matter that thought curdles in my stomach.

"Don't you dare lecture me, Thalia," he says, jutting out an accusing finger. "I've devoted my life to this cause. But you—you swanned in here as the little miss perfect heir, hiding behind a frigid mask and only minding when it affected you. You never cared a lick for the Collected before."

My chin rises as I square my shoulders, swaying only slightly. "And you did? You who are so selfless to now destroy the lives of many all for a long dead woman?"

"If you'd ever allowed yourself to be vulnerable enough to fall in love, you'd understand. You'd do anything for them."

"And you don't patronize me, Dolion. You'll find no sympathy from me for your selfishness."

He scowls. "Of course, you think it's selfish. That's why I—" He cuts himself off.

"That's why you what?"

The fire within him snuffs out. "That's why I abandoned the plan to seduce you. Had it worked, you'd take the necessary steps in the center. You'd want my happiness enough to sacrifice your own. But you think of no one but yourself."

I rear back as if slapped. "Do you even hear yourself? You think I'm selfish and thinking of only myself when I'm willing to accept the Borealis, and you're the one sacrificing us for your lost love. May the Erinyes take you, and Hades keep you," I curse.

He sighs. "I made only one oath, Thalia. And that was to Lasthena, which remains unbroken. I'll be back this afternoon," he says as if it should reassure me.

"Wait!" I shuffle closer to the barred window, abandoning my plans for the knife. There's no chance for it now. "When is the Collection?"

He stares at me for a long minute, a kaleidoscope of emotions flitting over his face. There's nothing handsome in it now. I can't even remember why I'd thought he was. Finally, he turns away and mutters, "It's now."

He starts down the hallway, taking the lamp with him. Before he disappears from sight, he glances back at me, the rust stain on his forehead gleaming red in the dim light. "You'll see. It will all work out."

I'm not sure if he's trying to convince himself or me.

There's no time to panic now, not if the Collection has already begun. When it's over, when I'm out, I can indulge in all the hysterics I'd like. But now, I must act. I lock everything behind my mask and think through a plan. There's the leverage idea again, the one I attempted with Lukas the day of the Scrimmage. But after sliding my hands around the bottom edge of the door, there's no place to hook anything to make the lever.

I lean my stinging head against the door, resting my cheek against the iron bar as my fingers search for the keyhole. Chrysa's teachings didn't stick; I merely watched in mute irritation as she shoved a dinner knife inside the locking mechanism and wiggled it around until it popped open. It shouldn't have worked; the opening was for a thin rod not the wider edge of a blade. But it's my only hope now.

I rip my knife from its holster and shove it into the thin hole, wrestling it this way and that. The sound of scraping metal overtakes my frustrated breathing, creating a symphony of failure. Flakes of rust sloth off the lock, fluttering onto my wrists. At least, I tell myself it's aged dust and not tiny insects I can't see in the dark. The fear makes me shudder and, somehow, the knife wiggles just so.

The mechanism snaps, the lock opens. I lean against the bars again and let myself laugh. After all my planning, it comes down to luck. And at least I didn't slice my hand open.

After shakily replacing the knife in its holster at my back, I try to open the door.

It won't budge. I shove my hand through the barred window, scraping at the skin. The sting has me cry out in pain, but I won't yield, reaching and clawing until I can slip my wrist through the space and search for the mystery keeping the door shut. A slab of wood lays perpendicular to it, a secondary bar to freedom. I scratch and dig, trying to get under it, trying to get a handhold to lift it free, but it doesn't work. Grunting, I pull my hand back inside, holding it against my chest. The pain pulses in time with my heart.

I slink to the floor, shuffling backward until my back hits the bench. With Poseidon's gaze focused on the Collection, maybe he'll recognize that a Collected is missing. Maybe he'll realize his son isn't bloodthirsty on his own and save the girls before Orion kills them. But then I remember Deianira's words, that the Gods can see inside the Palace but not enter it. Poseidon could send the Erinyes after Minos for his oath breaking, but the girls' lives are surely forfeit.

My hand throbs, but the darkness hides the extent of the damage. Defeated, I place an illusion over my other hand, using the golden sparks to lightly illuminate the space. Purple blossomed over my wrist, leading into thick red scrapes along the fingers and meat of my palm. At least the pain in my hand distracts me from the dizziness of my head. At least I'll still be alive until the afternoon, something I can't say for the others.

But after all this, I'm defeated by a block of wood.

I thought I'd known better, thought I was better. Maybe Nephele *should* have come, she could have gotten the door open at least. I shift to sit on the bench, ducking my head. The golden net over my hand highlights the scratches on the wooden base. This time, seeing the double-sided triangle makes me wince. But the carved snakes... the snakes remind me of Standia.

I drop the illusion and rise. I can't simply give up. I'm the heir to Standia. We understand duality: that everything with an ending has a beginning. This must be the steel Father mentioned. Brawn isn't a sign of a weak mind. But failing to recognize that brawn has its place is.

I kick at the space just above the knob hard. Something creaks as I ricochet backward, tripping until I slam on my backside. The pain smarts, there'll be another bruise there soon, and I swallow the bile that rises in my throat from my aching head. Still, I stand again. The girls did this every day for years. I can manage it for the few minutes it takes to break through the wooden latch on the door. But I won't risk falling and breaking my leg, not when I've a Labyrinth to search.

Angling my shoulder, I shove into the door a second time.

This is for Chrysa. I run into it again.

This is for Mina. I hit it again.

This is for Diomede. Something cracks.

This is for Thyia. My shoulder throbs.

This is for Eriphyle. I switch shoulders.

This is for Elara. Something snaps.

This is for Orion. I hit it again.

And this is for me.

The door gives, bursting open and showering me with splinters of wood. I lose my balance and fall to the ground, injuring the other wrist which starts swelling.

Swallowing the pain, I hobble up the stairs.

The stairs lead to a hallway on the Palace's first floor, but nowhere I recognize. I start running, my breath gusting out of my chest from the strain and earlier blows to my shoulder. Luckily, I'm alone in the hallways. More aches bloom as I skitter into walls when I make sharp turns. My eyes dart from side to side, searching for a double-sided triangle that would mark the entrance to Orion's tunnels. I find one that leads to another storage room, like the one Dolion dragged me to on my first night here. I banish Dolion from my mind as I shove boxes aside and find a door into the tunnels. It feels as if no time passes as I race through the darkened hallways, climbing and twisting until I finally find Orion's rooms. As expected, he isn't present. I burst into his bedroom and through the entrance into the Labyrinth, golden sparks raining over me as I cross the geas on the threshold. They don't slow me, but the tongue swallowing may be delayed. It won't matter so long as I can accept Orion or explain how it's done.

When I descend the elevator and enter the Labyrinth, I can only hope I'm not too late.

Chapter 28

The Labyrinth is quiet. I pray it's because I'm a stadium's length away from the center, surrounded by winding stone walls and not the more sinister alternative. My energy lasts me through the first three corners, flagging around the fourth, just in time for a guard to appear on the other side. He looks nothing like the dozen men I've seen surrounding Minos, wearing the battle regalia of a bronze breastplate, shin greaves, and holding a long spear like a walking stick. He stays utterly still, acting as a physical barrier to continue forward.

Though I'd already slowed to a crawl before coming upon him, I hold up my arms to show I'm not a threat. "Please, I must get to the center. I'm one of the Collected." My breath gusts out in low pants.

The guard doesn't move except to breathe, his eyes looking through me.

"It's important that I attend." Surely, he knows that. Although, he isn't as gaunt as the other guards, so perhaps he doesn't see the problems with Minos as King. Or, just as likely, he's magicked into remaining in that spot. I shuffle closer. That prompts a reaction, as he aims his spear at me, though his feet stay planted to the floor. The movement reveals a flash of gold along the tip. Squinting, I can just see the golden illusion magic over the spear. The spear isn't real.

My lips thin. Of course, this is a physical demand. *I understand, Zeus, Poseidon, whomever. Brawn good, logic unnecessary.* It's not like the prison cell didn't already prove that.

I ready myself to barrel through the illusion, hoping I'll knock into him and run before he can get back up and chase me, assuming the geas will force him. With a burst of energy, I dash forward, cutting through the illusion of the spear. I let my continued anger at Dolion and my circumstances propel me, angling my least injured shoulder towards the guard. But I run right through him as well. He flickers until the entire illusion collapses, the guard and spear, as I've passed the area where it is active.

I give the Gods watching a tiny acknowledgment for letting this be easy. If I'd had to dismantle that illusion with my head feeling like it does now, I would probably pass out.

I keep moving. More guards appear but disappear when I run through them. Near what must be the center, a pile of rubble blocks the hallway. It's not an illusion, and I inwardly praise myself for remembering to check. Even so, I must dig through the rock until it crumbles forward enough to offer me passage.

My fingers split as I rake through the rubble. Minos may have thought these physical challenges would stop me, but he's underestimated my stubbornness. Or he's trying to run out the clock.

I dig faster.

Minutes—and more scratches—later, an opening appears that I can squeeze through. My shoulders catch, the space too small for me to fit through, and I swallow a frustrated scream. Wriggling madly, I slip through, stumbling to the floor and slamming my scratched palms on the ground. If I were still worried about appearances, I'd flinch at my ripped clothes and defeated posture. But the success I'm after is more important than looking like an 'appropriate heir' now.

The hallway leads me around several more corners until it ends at a dead end. I halt and rest my clenched fists against the stone. No golden illusion reveals itself, no matter how long I squint at it. It's a regular stone wall, blocking me from the other side.

I can hear Deianira's venomous voice and her unknowing revelation from our last practice run: the guards weren't to stop me but to keep me from straying off the path to the center. All I've done is put myself farther from the goal.

Blinking away tears of frustration, I start back the way I came when I hear something muffled on the other side of the wall.

"We're supposed to work together. What about what Thalia said?"

Someone growls. "Damn her. Eriphyle, if you don't move, I will hit you."

"Wait," I shout at the wall, beating my scraped palms against it.

"Thalia?" I still can't tell who says it, but it doesn't matter.

"Yes, it's me." The words come out in a cry. "I'll be right there."

"Did he kill you? Are you a specter?"

"I don't think he's killed her, he's quite tame for a beast."

"If she was, she'd walk through the walls. Use your head." That's Chrysa, surely.

I lean my head against the wall. "Just—don't do anything. Keep Orion from the geas corner and I'll be there as fast as I can."

I end up lost again. I tried returning to the second elevator to restart but couldn't find it. As I stumble down hall after hall, my head hangs low at the realization that I may have lost my chance again. *How long will Orion and the others wait for me?* Orion can't do more than imply the solution that will stop Minos, and I kept that information from the girls yesterday. At some point, it will be too late.

It isn't until I'm half crawling around corners, listening for the sounds of the girls' whining complaints in the elusive center, that hope appears in the form of another person.

A real person, that is.

The minister sits huddled in a corner, curled into himself. Before I approach, I confirm there's no magic over him. It's him, alone and sniffling. But that isn't to say a geas doesn't have him in its grips.

"Minister?"

His neck tilts upward with a crack, staring at me like he's seen a ghost. Given I'm on my knees on the floor with my robes in tatters around me, he might not be far off in his assessment. "He's killed you," he breathes, clawing at his bare head and twitching. "He'll be coming for me next."

"I'm not dead." *Not yet anyway.* "What are you doing here?"

He shifts his gaze from side to side, like a caught mouse. "Punishment," he hisses.

I stalk forward as fast as my shuddering limbs will let me. There's a sharp red welt on his cheek. "Do you follow Minos willingly?"

He curls tighter into a ball. "I'm—I'm bound to him. We're all bound."

A less exhausted Thalia, one mindful of interacting with nobles and heads of state, might react more reasonably, or think through what he's saying and holding back. But that Thalia is likely still unconscious in the prison cell. I crouch in front of him. "Get up. I need your help."

"He'll kill me. And when he finishes you off, he'll come for me. He'll come for anything in these halls."

"He won't kill you, assuming you mean the Borealis. We've handled that." I hold out my hand impatiently. "I assume you know the route to the center?"

Sweat glistens from his pale forehead as he stares at my dirt and blood-stained fingers. "You've accepted him?"

"Not yet." I bite my tongue at the slip, something he didn't need to know. "Can you get me to the center?"

"Will you protect me in exchange?"

"As best I can until Minos is deposed," I promise. My thoughts are slow, but not so disjointed that I'd willingly agree to something I can't fulfill.

A few nervous tears leak from his eyes as he nods, before rattling off the directions to the center. When he finishes, I hold out my hand again.

"No, I'll—I'll stay back. Just in case." He averts his gaze, staring at the floor.

I straighten my back, a painful move, and scowl at him. "If you've sent me the wrong way, I will be back. If not me, the Erinyes."

"I didn't," he stutters. "I swear."

I start down the direction he gave, before stopping and calling back to him. "If you don't follow him willingly, find somewhere safe for the next day or so."

I don't wait for a response.

I have no memory of how I find the center. I know I follow the minister's directions somehow, but it's as if I'm asleep while doing it. But finally, *finally* I stumble through the center, my arms outstretched and ready to stop whatever I might find and help Orion take his mantle as King of Crete.

But I can't see Orion anywhere. Instead, the girls stand lumped together in a warrior's formation, Elara at the center. But—no, Chrysa and Mina aren't there: they're huddling together in the corner. They're standing on top of the geas line I showed them, acting as a physical barrier keeping Orion from crossing. They both bare their teeth and wield fisted hands even though I can see them trembling.

Across from them in a hulking figure, a creature that's half man, half beast. The bottom half is covered with a black chiton, but his upper body is naked, baring skin that would be honey gold if not for the gray scars littering it in a winding, slithering design. Atop his thick neck is something monstrous, like a distorted version of a boar's head, with two curved horns and a long snout. I can only see one eye, but it looks like a black marble, one without an iris or pupil. I rub my eyes in case the head blow affected my vision, but the creature remains solid in front of me. My muscles scream as I lower my arms, the pain I'd buried bursting out at the sight of my mistake.

I must have—I must have been wrong. It can't be Orion. I've seen the shape of his head under the tight gauze and felt the soft curls at the nape of his neck. There is nothing to indicate he's part animal. The Bea—the Borealis turns to me slowly, his mouth opening and braying out nonsense. His eyes look feral, filled with something wild.

"What happened to you?" Diomede says.

Only now can I see she's got one hand on Elara's elbow, holding her back. The Borealis has his hands up as if in surrender.

"Who cares what happened," Chrysa snaps from the corner. "Where have you *been*?"

"I was tied up," I murmur, staring at the Borealis. He angles his neck towards me and his stomach muscles tense. First Dolion, then the dead end. Now this. *What else was I wrong about?*

"For real or meta—like a metaphor?"

"Metaphor. I wasn't tied up, but I escaped a prison cell." I explain it almost idly, like I'm talking about the weather.

My concentration is fixed on the Borealis' strange, monstrous face. *It makes little sense.* The pieces fit together, the scars on his chest—those that follow the lines I mapped with my fingers, they even look like they could have been created by wrapped fiery thread. *How could I have been wrong?*

"Oh, Thalia. That's terrible. Attempted poisoning and then imprisonment," Diomede says, yanking on Elara's arm. The Borealis snuffs, his arms reaching for me, that look in his eye burning brighter. I flinch just as Elara lurches forward and the Borealis immediately raises his hands in surrender again. *Could it be Orion's bestial brother, the* second *Borealis, and all the signs should have pointed me there instead?* I shoot a glance to the rest of the center. *But where is Orion?*

"We waited for you," Thyia says. "Elara wouldn't wait any longer."

Elara snarls at the Borealis, whose attention doesn't waver from me. "Where's my knife?" she demands. The Borealis jolts, his neck snapping to bray at Elara.

"Accept him, or whatever you're supposed to do," Eriphyle says. She's holding Elara's other arm. Elara jerks but can't slip from Eriphyle's clutches, though Diomede stumbles forward from the movement. Thyia grabs another part of Elara's arm to support her.

"Accept him or don't, just keep him away from this corner," says Chrysa, her voice wavering. "He hasn't attacked yet, but if anyone can provoke a murder, it's Elara."

Mina laughs, sounding almost hysterical.

"I already told you, Chrysa, he's quite calm," Thyia says almost reprovingly.

The Borealis' black eyes pierce through me as breath gusts from his beast-like nostrils. He huffs, braying something again, but quieter this time, and ducks his head. The movement illuminates something along the curve of his horns. Something gold, like a net. Like an illusion.

I start towards him again, focused on where I can see the golden magic. He stares at me until I'm close enough that I could wrap my arms around him if I wanted. He brays again, even softer now, a plaintive communication I can't understand.

I'll fix it, I want to tell him. *I won't make another mistake.* But instead, I ask, "Orion?"

He nods once, snuffing out something. The hope that fell like a rock into my stomach rises once again. There's still a chance.

"Thalia, not to press you, but could you hurry? Elara is a bit stronger than we are," Diomede says, almost stumbling again. She and Thyia cross their ankles together as a brace.

"Not stronger," Eriphyle says.

"She's just determined to win," Thyia adds.

"Yes," Elara agrees. "With *my* knife."

The matrix of magic is simpler than that of the armory but more complex than the second Labyrinth entrance, golden thread wound closely together to form a mask over Orion's face. The increased headache as I work is one small drop added to the sea of my pain, the flood held back by sheer determination to finish what I've started. But the strands unravel under my mental fingers as like I'm cutting through water. I almost laugh at the thought.

Everything slows down as I unwind the illusion, and Orion's soft bleat is the only sound I hear. Things happen in the background like a silent theater performance: Elara continues shoving at the others, knocking Thyia to the side where she careens into Chrysa and Mina's corner. Diomede must loosen her grip to help Thyia because Elara is partly free and runs towards Orion as fast as she can, only faltering when Eriphyle yanks her back like an animal on a too-short leash. They grapple on the ground as Diomede shouts something unintelligible while Chrysa looks to be egging them on. Mina leaps onto Elara's back and the two fall forward. Eriphyle snatches Elara's legs and pins them down. Time speeds up when I untangle the last of the golden string.

Then, like the air is sucked from the room, everyone pauses. Orion's brays transform into words as the pooled netting falls from his head.

"Please," he repeats in a whisper. "Please, not again."

My hands cover my mouth as his gaze focuses on mine. The man in front of me *is* a man, no longer half beast. The scars present on his torso also cross his face, thin lines below his lips, over his nose and cheeks, one bisecting his eyebrow, all slightly shiny and grayer than his honeyed skin. They're haphazardly placed, as though the fiery thread was loose against his sharp-boned face and thick neck. His lips rest in a down turned position, framed by grooves on each side of his mouth, while his nose looks like it might have been broken and poorly set. His hair, the cool brown of the trees, and his eyes, the blue-green of a cresting wave, are as he described, both traits from his parents, the Gods of Earth and Sea. I traced those features only hours ago, but he's more real than I could ever have imagined. He's the most striking man I've ever seen.

He says nothing; I say nothing. The center is still but for our soft breaths. Even Elara is silently looking at Orion from her prone position on the floor with shock.

"Well, shit," says Eriphyle, breaking whatever hold we're all under. Diomede balks, about to reprimand her.

Chrysa creeps from the corner. "Are we good? You're not going to go murder us anymore?"

Orion flinches. "I never was. The cloth must have muffled my words." His deep voice rumbles against my bones. It's no different from when he's spoken uncovered in the dark, but so much more, now that I can see the corner of his lips quiver, the twitch of his nose, the emotion swirling in his eyes. I'm nearly giddy imagining speaking with him and *seeing* his reactions rather than guessing them by his gestures.

Though, the giddiness could also be the head trauma.

"We're fine now," I tell Chrysa, taking one of his hands in mine and squeezing.

"We could hear you," Thyia says, interrupting my mental celebration. She stands wide-eyed beside Chrysa, no longer guarding the corner. "We simply couldn't understand you."

"You don't look like a monster anymore, though." Mina is quick to reassure him from her place on Elara's back.

Orion's mouth ticks into a frown and he pulls away, stepping backward from all of us as though to hide.

All but Elara shouts and he halts.

"Stay in the middle. That corner has a geas that will take your free will and make you a danger to us," I say, my arms outstretched. "Mina wasn't insulting you, she meant it literally. Your head looked like that of a boar."

His fists clench just as his jaw does. "I knew something was there, though my mind thought it was my usual cloth covering. Not... not a mask," he says, frowning.

"We'll find something to cover you with." I touch my chiton tunic, but it's covered in muck, and what looks like smudged rust. A look at my arms and fingers tells me it's dried blood.

Thyia bites her lip. "Why?"

He glances at her before returning his gaze to me. "It can wait."

"Your comfort is important." I spin to the girls, looking for the cleanest cloth. "Diomede, would you—"

"No, Thalia. It can wait," Orion says. "We must leave the Labyrinth. You need medical care."

"And to get far away from the murder corner," Chrysa says.

But it can't be finished this easily. "Has Poseidon seen enough?" I ask. "I can still accept—"

Orion interrupts me. "It's enough. The mask, the geas line you mentioned, what I've gathered myself—the bargain is surely breached."

"Then you were right," Elara says from the floor. Mina scrambles off her as Eriphyle releases her legs. Both offer her a hand up, but she refuses.

I dip my head, but don't deny it.

"If I know Minos, he will try to wiggle his way out of it when Poseidon arrives. We must be there to meet them," Orion says. "We'll wrap your wounds and then bypass him in the throne room."

"No, Minos has warded against any Gods' entry," I explain. "And there could be any number of new geas boundaries within the halls. We need to leave the Palace entirely."

"But the only way out is past Kyra and Kynna," says Mina.

I glance at Orion, who nods and I answer, "Not quite."

"Is Dolion back?" Thyia asks at the same time Chrysa demands, "Are you keeping more secrets?"

"Come," says Orion, cupping my elbow. "Let us leave this place."

The story comes out on the ride back up the second elevator and through to his rooms.

"I, for one, wouldn't have minded being Queen of Crete. It's the first step in becoming the ultimate ruler of all creation," Chrysa says as we take turns descending a ladder in the secret tunnels. "Imagine all the power. All the jerks on Karavi would pay."

"Which is probably why Thalia didn't tell us," Thyia reasons. Standing next to the oil lamp, she can't hide the blush on her cheeks as Orion lifts her from the ladder onto the floor below.

"That's not why," Elara says. She was first down the ladder and is leaning against the wall with crossed arms.

"Choices, right?" Mina says as she follows Thyia. She springs from the ladder and almost collides with Diomede, who is just finishing wrapping a bandage around my wrist. There's nothing to be done for my bruised shoulders and legs. Or the possible concussion, but both Diomede and Orion said it was lucky I didn't break a bone. All the energy I used to get to this point seeps from me. I can't even hold myself steady.

"That's not it either," Elara says. "She didn't think we could do it."

The already quiet tunnel turns silent, as all eyes focus on me, even Orion's. I busy myself fussing with one of Diomede's other wrapped bandages.

"That was part of it," I admit. "I want you to have choices to do what you want, though I didn't think you'd be up for leading a nation. It isn't a simple choice. You're sacrificing so much to take that position. And what if you failed and were no better than Minos?"

"I'd be better than Minos, at least," Chrysa says under her breath.

"Even with all my experience and background, even I..." I cast my gaze downward, the dim light hiding my fears. "Even I can't completely commit to it, not when I'm still unsure if I can do right by *Standia*, must less Crete."

"You never had to," Orion murmurs. He replaced the cloth over his head and I already miss the sound of his uncovered voice and the expression in his gaze.

"I thought I did. And I thought if anyone had to, it needed to be me." I glance at each of the girls, but the tunnels are too dark to catch their expressions. "But I know I've done you all a disservice. I've assumed you had limitations because you didn't live how I did."

"But you were the one with limits," Mina says. "Because you'd have died in the Labyrinth without even finding the center."

"We all would have died," says Chrysa. "Thalia would just have been first."

"You're right." I bow my head, blinking away my shame. "I was the lesser in the Labyrinth. And I thought you all were the lesser outside it."

"Not anymore?" Eriphyle asks.

I shrug. "I couldn't have escaped from that cell with only books."

"Actually, you could," Chrysa says. "This one time—"

Elara pushes off from the wall. "Can we go? I'd rather not spend my last time on Crete listening to Heir whine."

Orion bristles beside me. "From what I'm told, you would have died without her."

"And now I'll go back to Prosfora a failure. Better dead than that," she snaps, stalking down the tunnel.

"Seriously," Chrysa mock-whispers to Thyia. "I am never visiting Prosfora."

"After three left turns, there is another ladder down. Then, two lefts and a right and two more ladders down," Orion says to the remaining group. "That will take you to an outside exit."

They take the hint and start down the tunnels. Only Chrysa turns back. The dim light illuminates her waggling eyebrows.

"I wanted a minute with you," he explains when Chrysa finally disappears. He fists his hand against my back, gripping the sweaty fabric of my chiton. "Once we advise Poseidon, there's no telling what Minos might do. You should all hide at Hecaline's until he's deposed. When it's safe, I'll get the seven of you on my allies' boat."

"I can't speak for them, but I won't be hiding. I want to finish this. I've come too far to leave now."

He drops my chiton. "It isn't as simple as telling Poseidon, Thalia. Minos received certain benefits from Poseidon that can't be taken except by force. Benefits my throat still cannot speak of.

And with what you've told me, he could have other geases active we are unaware of."

"Then we handle it together. I can unravel illusions and walk through geas boundaries, you can pin him and call the Erinyes to take him away, if Poseidon can't do anything. You have the godly blood for it. And—" I swallow a lump of nerves. "Worse comes to worst, we'll fulfill your side and I'll accept you."

"I wouldn't ask that of you."

I touch his chest. "It's alright."

He jerks away. "Don't. It's more than simple words, you see, an act you can't come back from. It's no choice, like you said."

"It's *my* choice though, that's the point," I spit before the annoyance fades away and weariness replaces it. "I didn't know it was you when I'd said that. That was the piece I was missing. I didn't realize you were the Borealis. When I realized it, I was somewhat... relieved." I let out a tired laugh. "I can't say it's the perfect choice, going from Thalia the heir of Standia to Thalia the consort of the Borealis. I still... I still don't want to lose myself. But it isn't as damning as I may have implied last night."

"I won't have you sacrifice that," he says firmly. "Not for me, not when I'm a monster."

I approach him cautiously, like a skittish animal. "Giving that up *is* a sacrifice but one I'm willing to make for you, if we need it. You, Orion, the man who is most certainly not a monster."

He drags the gauze off his face, revealing anguished eyes and thinned lips. "Look me in the eye and tell me I don't appall you. I know how unappealing I am, you see. You needn't flatter me."

I owe him a reasoned answer, not something flippant so I spend a long minute studying his face. It's simply an unintended benefit that I get to look upon him more. No one would ever say he's conventionally attractive. Not because of the scars, but because of the sharpness of his features. Though, no one would call me conventionally attractive either. The only negative his scars offer are in creating his self-consciousness. With his open expression, I don't see them as anything but a part of his face: a part of the kind, and clever Orion I've come to know over the past week. But he's so much more than his appearance.

Except I don't say any of that. Instead, I cautiously approach him, arms outstretched. "May I do something?"

He nods, trembling. I cup his cheeks, the scorching skin soft under my hands, and stare into his bright eyes that flick from my lips to my cheeks and higher. My heartbeat thumps heavily, too loud in the quiet of the tunnels. His pupils blow wide, eclipsing the lambent blue, making him look more Godlike than ever. The soft pressure of my fingers pulls him closer to my height until his face meets my own. I've never initiated this on my own, but I know what to do, and what I want. I close the distance until our lips touch.

He makes a noise low in his throat as he drags one hand to my back while the other cups my head, holding me and keeping my jaw steady as he licks into my mouth. I wrap my bandaged hands around his neck, slipping my fingers into his soft curls. Before I realize it, I'm pressed against the wall, standing between his legs. It isn't nice like with Dolion or soft like with Lukas. There's nothing comforting in this contact. Instead, it's a heat, something that steams against burbling water, not a pleasant warmth but a blazing inferno. It pools through my limbs and out into the cavernous tunnel, combining with our heaving breaths as we explore each other's mouths. *I might have missed this,* I think through the haze of lust spiraling in my chest. *I might have let him hide from me until I returned to Standia.*

That thought jars me into remembering where we are, and what is still to come. Slowly, I withdraw. He doesn't chase my lips but remains close, breath gusting against my cheek. "I'm not appalled," I whisper, licking the taste of him from my lips. "The opposite."

He smiles broadly. A dimple appears on his right cheek, outlined by two faint scars. "Shall we find your friends?"

I grin back. "And watch Minos get dragged to the Underworld."

As we travel through the tunnels, Orion keeps his hands on me as if afraid I'll change my mind and run from him in fear. Or fall to the ground with fatigue. I can't honestly say which.

We stumble from the tunnels, not encountering the girls who must have found their own way out from the Palace walls. The exit deposits us to the south, close to the guts of the armory and the thicket of trees surrounding it.

"Hey Thalia," Chrysa shouts from somewhere hidden in the bush, the usual bravado in her voice quivering. "Did you forget a secret?"

When we find her, monstrous winged women hold all six of them in place, Hades' Cerberus by their side. And before them, Minos, offering a gleaming smirk.

Chapter 29

S un filters through the small grove. The Keres, for that must be what the beasts are, look like nightmares made flesh without shadows to hide them. Though their naked figures are female, spider webbing black veins crawl over milk pale skin that stretches tight against a skeletal frame. Leathery wings like a bat's pull tight against their backs, the spiked tips curling over their heads like horns. Their sinuous limbs are capped by clawed hands and feet. Pupil-less eyes as black as a raven's wing stare unblinking outward, each revealing white teeth with elongated canines.

Six stand in a row with their arms wrapped around the girls, their hands winding up to hold the girls' throat and cover their mouths. The pose could be romantic, a sensual embrace from a lover, if not for the fear on the girls' faces. Diomede has turned green while Mina and Thyia tremble in the Keres' grasp. Even Eriphyle, who looks childlike in the Ker's embrace, has turned pale from fear. Chrysa won't stop wriggling, forcing the Ker's claws to squeeze tighter along her face. Only Elara looks unaffected by the sharp claws digging into her cheekbones.

At their side, Cerberus growls. Seated, the dog still reaches my shoulders, with skin the color of cremation ash and eyes the color of blood. All three heads focus on something within the trees, as if watching for invisible threats that may come upon him. Behind him, leaning unconscious next to a tree, is the minister, who no doubt told Minos of what I'd revealed, either willingly or not.

"You stupid child," Minos chides. I bristle, only to realize he's not looking at me but Orion. "All you needed to do was run through the motions again, like we do every seven years, and things would have remained pleasant. Indeed, I was willing to remain merciful, to let you live and sacrifice only a few citizens, but you have forced my hand."

"Your honeyed words have proved duplicitous," Orion says. He slips in front of me, half covering me from Minos' glare. "Poseidon knows of your breach. The bargain is broken, you see. You have nothing."

Minos laughs, his hands snaking to his hair before aborting the gesture at his shoulders. "You think I need Poseidon? Come now, Orion, you've always been naively foolhardy but never willfully dense."

It's a testament to his arrogance that he meets us with no guards. A single ceremonial blade, like Father's, like that in a holster at my back, is tucked into his belt. He must not think he needs them. Although... the Keres may be here because they expect bloodshed, but Hades doesn't loan out his guardian Cerberus to just anyone.

"You agreed to a second bargain," I realize, adding up the remaining clues: the symbols of the Underworld so subtly decorating his banquet hall and the Festival grounds, the continued teasing demand for fairness, to entice Hades even if fairness was a lie.

Minos regards me with a flippant look. "I'm finished bargaining with the Gods. This is a partnership. He protects me."

"You'll need protection from more than Poseidon," Orion says, clenching his fists. He stalks forward but Cerberus' growl halts him in place.

"Don't tempt me, Orion. The Gods may be blind to your true pacifism but I know you wouldn't hurt a fly unless I magically forced your violence," Minos says, grinning viciously.

Orion flinches at the reminder. I place a bracing hand on his shoulder and step out from behind him. "He didn't mean himself," I snap. "He meant Zeus."

Minos turns slightly pale before rallying and scowling at the sky. "That threat is less effective when he's failed to interfere before," he says. "Poseidon may be blinded from my actions as he hides in the depths of the sea, but Zeus has no such excuse. He's seen my clandestine meetings with his foul death-dealing brother over the past decade."

"The Erinyes then," I say. Hades doesn't command the Erinyes; they live near his domain but are entities unto themselves. One of the Gods—Orion even, with his two godly parents—simply needs to call them with blood, and Minos will be out of our hair.

Minos blinks, a singular admission of his fear, before waving an indolent hand. "They do not worry me. A good king prepares for all contingencies."

"A good king wouldn't break a bargain with a God." My voice is low.

Cerberus growls behind me.

Minos inspects my rigid stance as disdain crawls over his face. "Even Poseidon, who has seafoam between his ears, and that lumbering oaf beside you would someday realize the bargain was worthless. Thinking someone would accept and join that monstrous thing. They should have given me the crown without condition, not forced me into this farce of a bargain. Not when the only reason for it is Gaia's supposed demands. She has allowed me and the rest of the Kings without consequence thus far."

My brows raise. I'd forgotten that part of the book. Gaia wants her son to rule over the entirety of her earth, not simply Crete. Deposing Minos is only the start.

Minos' disdain turns to self-satisfaction. "And in the Gods' conceit, none ever considered how anyone would take it from me, if this misbegotten bargain had ever been fulfilled. But I tire of this. Let us finish what the Labyrinth didn't." His pinched face tightens as he snaps his fingers and the dog leaps forward, arching across the air coming right at us.

Before I can even react, Orion shoves me hard and takes the brunt of Cerberus' attack. My neck cracks to the side as I fall to the dirt, the swaths of bandages Diomede applied the only thing keeping me from reopening any wounds. Pained whimpers pull from my throat as I attempt to rise while Orion and Cerberus grapple. Bone snaps against bone when the dog's skulls crack into Orion's ribs. His hands brace on Cerberus' throats, but that still leaves one jaw of gnashing teeth free. The ground shakes, Cerberus' teeth only just miss snapping Orion's ear off.

"Thalia, run!"

That's Mina's shrill shout, muffled from behind a Ker's hand. But surely, I can do something. I'm no warrior, but I toss illusion after illusion onto the two, flickering their images. It does nothing for Cerberus, his noses trained for the hunt. Orion appearing larger, invisible, or even smaller: none of them keep Cerberus from his battle.

"Do the thing," Chrysa cries. A glance at her shows blood on her teeth, where she's bitten a Ker. "Accept him!"

"Orion, I'll—" I start, unsure of the words needed but determined to accept him. He'd said it wasn't simple words and my heart pounds in my ribs as I search for the right phrasing. "Orion Borealis, I—"

"No," Minos growls. "We can deal with him after. Get the girl! She's his only hope now."

Cerberus drops Orion's bloody arm and hones his dangerous focus on me. He snarls as I scramble away from his sharpened teeth, grasping for the knife at my back. I never get the chance to remove it from its holster, as Orion rushes toward Cerberus, clutching his torso and dragging the two of them into the trunk of a thick tree. Cerberus whines, snaking his necks towards Orion. One jaw bites the space between Orion's shoulder and neck and Orion grunts. I can hear the girls' muffled shouting. Orion's neck remains bared, twitching.

I rise on shaking limbs, grabbing the knife. Even I know the dog could tear out Orion's throat in that position. Orion smacks them both into the tree again, but the dog won't release Orion's skin, keeping Orion's neck tilted upward. Instead, one of the remaining heads slams his skull into the space just below Orion's jaw. He gurgles and then falls, landing on the ground with a thud, burying Cerberus' lower body beneath him. Cerberus breathes heavily but doesn't uncover himself. Instead, he lies on the ground, as if waiting for more instruction.

Heedless of the danger, I fall into an illusion, cloaking myself in a golden net to appear invisible, skittering to Orion's side. He's alive, just unconscious. Cerberus' gaze tracks my movement.

"Find her," Minos demands. "I feel her magic, she is still present. Kill her while the oaf still lives. Then this farce will finally end. The others can become carrion feed."

Cerberus shuffles, dragging his lower half out from under Orion, then angling back on his haunches. A sharp, high-pitched whistle fills the air and both of us flinch. My hands cover my ears as Cerberus' three heads shoot towards the trees once again, the source of the sound. No one else reacts as we do, though Minos looks irritated, but that began at my disappearance and not from the whistle. As quickly as it began, the whistle stops, fading until only Minos' snapping commands can be heard.

"Well? Idiot animal," he says with a stony expression. "Your master has demanded you obey me!"

Cerberus ignores him, returning to the Keres' side and laying down as if in repose.

"You insufferable—" Minos stalks to Cerberus, brandishing his knife and looking like he intends to attack Cerberus into obeying him. Cerberus rises back onto his haunches until he stands, towering over Minos. He growls, letting one thick glob of drool drip from his middle mouth and right onto Minos' head. Minos shudders and covers his head protectively, the skin on his forearms bubbling with burns from the corrosive spit, before remembering he wasn't alone. He shuffles back from the Cerberus with as much pride as he can muster, turning his commands to the Keres.

Minos orders them to strike the girls and then sniff me out, but they stay eerily still. An inappropriately timed laugh threatens to spill from me; had Minos been more well read, he'd know the Keres are not killers, but watchers. That they are holding the girls is probably only at Hades' request. Minos will never convince them to bring harm. No, they'll wait until someone else has killed us and slurp up our remains.

Unless I can stop it. I stare at Orion's still form. His chest rises and falls but gives me no clues on what to do now.

"Orion Borealis, I accept you as King of Crete, and as your consort," I whisper into his ear. Nothing happens. I trace my hand over his face, half covered by his cloth mask. One closed eye is displayed, the skin below his eyelid purple with burst blood vessels. More blood dots his torn shirt, scratches from Cerberus' claws. It's extraordinary luck the bite on his shoulder looks to be clotting now, even as the edges bubble like acid.

Minos is now standing in front of the Keres, his hands on his hips, roaring with impotent rage.

Quickly, I start again. "Orion Borealis, I am Thalia, heir to the Island of Standia, and one of the Collected and a child of the Island. You are a Child of Earth and Sea, and the Fates owe you this damned crown. I'm accepting you as my King, in all definitions of the word." I gently kiss the dirty cloth covering his lips.

Still, Orion remains unconscious, and Minos doesn't react. Frustrated tears threaten to form as I rest my forehead on Orion's bloody chest. I should have asked Orion exactly what we needed to do, or if we even *can* when he's not conscious.

But even if I figure out the words and fulfill Orion's part of the bargain, Minos has implied he'll keep what he has unless taken from him by force. Minos also claimed Erinyes cannot take him, leaving me at a loss on how to defeat him, not with Hades as his partner. There must be some other way.

Something flickers in the corner of my eye, like the gold magic of illusion but more fluid, akin to silver mercury. My head pops up just as Cerberus' six ears flick in that direction, confirming it isn't a trick of the light or another sign of head trauma. The mercury forms an amorphous shape of a man.

I *know* that shape, and I know who can appear invisible. I press my fingers to my lips and then to Orion's uncovered cheek before rising silently and limping towards the being. Minos still snarls at the Keres behind me, spewing vitriol at them for losing me, at the girls and demanding they tell him where I might have gone.

I chase the being through the trees, shuffling and stumbling as fast as my sore limbs will allow me, until finally, he stops underneath a cypress and removes his invisibility. Before me stands Hades, holding his horned black helmet.

"Clever Thalia. It has been many moons since one of my niece's blood saw through the magic of my helmet. It is only for your pedigree that my guardian did not flay the flesh from your bones," he says.

His voice curls like smoke against my skin and I can't help shivering. He's as tall as Orion, but with piercing blue eyes and knife-sharp cheekbones half covered by a thick black beard. His skin glitters like the moonlight with black hair as dark as an abyss that swoops over his angular forehead.

I fall to my knees, both in fealty of his godliness and out of exhausted fear in his presence. If my 'pedigree' saved me from a mauling by Cerberus, perhaps it can save us all now. At the very least, I won't continue assuming I can do this on my own. "Please, don't do this. Don't side with Minos."

He stares at me, cocking his head like a predatory bird. "You are missing several chapters of this book, girl. I am not siding with Minos. I am on no one's side but my own."

"What do you get out of this, then? You can't care about Minos' ambition. And as one who deals in fairness, you can't be blind to his treachery towards your brothers. He is not to continue ruling, that's the bargain. By letting him undermine the deal, you're *aiding* Minos in oath breaking, in defying Fate!" My mouth spits the words before I consider who I'm shouting at. But I can't cower before him. I'm the only one free to speak the words, and there are no other options before me now.

To my surprise and relief, Hades doesn't take my insolence as an insult. Instead, he smirks. "Fate can be so fickle, child. As are the Moirai."

The Moirai—the sisters of the Erinyes, close allies of Hades, and the ones decreeing Orion should be king. "What of them?" I ask, my voice nearly shaking.

"You shouldn't be here, not according to your thread. You were pushed," he explains, confirming what Hecaline had already revealed. "Though the imbalance of *your* fate is not my concern. But balance is what I demand. As for you, you should run. Return to your Island and fulfill the fate set out for you as a lackluster, but generally competent, Governor, with your three boy children begat by your childhood friend. Your fate is still possible, so long as you abandon this path now. The concerns of the Gods are not for you."

The bare rendition of what my life would be, what I'd expected it to be just a week ago, doesn't distract me. "Letting Minos do this isn't balance," I snap. "Those girls are entitled to full lives. That should be their fate. And Orion is owed the crown by the Moirai. It is not for Minos."

"Threads can unspool," Hades says cooly. "*Surely,* you've read something to that extent," he finishes in a mocking tone.

My fists ball at my side. "So, you may manhandle destinies, changing Orion's course, but no one else can. What have you offered the Moirai to have them abandon their will?"

He remains silent, not giving me more information, not that he would, not that I should expect a God to indulge me. He lifts his helmet as if to replace it on his head.

Minos' voice carries; he's shouting invectives now. *Who knows how much longer Orion and the girls will live?* I don't know why Hades wants Minos to succeed, or why he'd object to Orion taking up the mantle. Nothing I've read can explain that. But I have read enough, and know enough, to try one last argument.

"He is an oath breaker," I begin, intent on discovering the bargain with the Erinyes that keeps them from eviscerating Minos. If I discover that, perhaps I can appeal to Hades and renegotiate. He can get his balance while the Erinyes handle Minos, *without* Hades needing to act. "What part of the partnership keeps the Erinyes at bay?"

Hades freezes just as the helmet grazes his hair, his crystal-shard eyes dropping to the earth.

No. Not the earth, but to the area below it.

The realization washes over me and my jaw drops. "They don't know, do they? They're blind to him, else they'd have come the minute the breach was revealed." My mind races. I think of Father and how he handles dignitaries, before summoning Lukas' confidence and Argon's guile. "Are the Moirai blind too? You've yet to answer what their sisters think of Minos' fate being altered so."

Light sucks from within the tree's canopy as Hades seems to grow taller. Shadows lengthen along with him, and the ghost of a strong wind drags through my messy hair. His teeth are now fangs and vulture wings sprout from his back. I blink and his visage returns to normal, but his teeth remain bared.

"Are you threatening me?" he asks, his silky voice low and menacing.

"I am reminding you that I am well read." I also know the Moirai, the Erinyes, *and* the Keres are sisters, but only the Erinyes are violent. I raise my chin, though I'm sure it trembles. "It can't be a threat, because I'm not intending to do anything about the knowledge."

"Yet," he says dryly, the shadows vanishing as quickly as they appeared.

My shoulder lifts as an admission. "I do want you to withdraw your support."

His gaze slides over me as he breathes out low and long. "You would expect a favor from me?"

"No. A bargain," I say, my heart jumping in my chest. "If the stories are even half right, you wouldn't want to support an oath breaker, so you must get something out of the partnership. Make it fair. Withdraw support from Minos and get your balance some other way... through a bargain with me."

"It is the height of arrogance to assume you have something I want, girl."

Blood leeches from my face but I don't flinch from his dark glare. The mask slips on easier now, hiding my quivering limbs under the guise of confidence and competence. I imagine I'm Father on his best day, but instead of negotiating with the citizenry, I'm seeking a deal with a God. "There must be something."

"How idly you offer," Hades drawls. "When you know this is not a bargain you can set aside, like that with your little minister."

I wince behind the mask.

As quick as a flash of lightning belonging to his brother, Hades grins, something tender that sends fear careening into my stomach. "I will withdraw support as you requested. Minos will no longer have my protection or my soldiers."

The hair rises on the back of my neck, and I swallow twice before I can speak again. "And in exchange?"

He splays long fingered hands. "There is something I want. And I intend to get it. There will come a time when you will be expected to do something, something you will desperately desire. The need for it will overtake your thoughts, an you will feel as though you might die if you don't do so. When that time comes, when that feeling crests and you intend to act—don't."

"Just '*don't?*' How will I know when, or what?" I ask, wincing as I know what he'll say.

"You'll know."

There is much to be desired in a bargain like that. It is one that could leave me questioning every act I take in the future, though that isn't new.

Before I can otherwise answer, he leans close and runs one fingertip down the edge of my jaw. "Would you rather I demanded your death? The death of your mother, your brother, your true love?"

I take a fortifying breath. "But the Erinyes must take Minos."

Hades raises whip thin brows. "Such a demanding thing. Fine. I will advise the Erinyes, but you must remove his invulnerability. I will not have him spending eons playing in the River Styx after the Erinyes tire of him when his soul should remain in Tartarus."

"Remove his invulnerability?" I stand dizzily. "Is that not part of withdrawing your support?"

He smiles like a cat. "That's part of the original bargain with Poseidon. I will not break my brother's oath for him."

Another piece of the puzzle I thought I'd solved, the thing that gave him his crown also gave him invulnerability. *Great.* "How am I to do that?"

But Hades doesn't answer, slipping on the helmet and fading from sight. I can still see his liquid outline walking away.

"Hurry, girl," he says as if standing right next to me, his voice rattling inside my head, even as his form gets smaller in the distance. "Soon it won't matter if I'm no longer aiding Minos. Not if your goal is to keep your comrades alive."

Chapter 30

I race back from where I came, just in time to see Cerberus melt into the earth and the Keres release the girls one by one to shoot into the sky. Minos stares at the disappearing Keres, stunned into silence.

The minute Mina is free, she rushes towards Minos. Her foot stops a few inches from his chest and she springs backward, knocking her neck back from the pressure. There must be a physical shield keeping her from harming him. But still, Minos turns his attention from the empty sky to Mina's falling form. He juts out his fist and connects with her splayed throat. He cradles his hand as Mina drops to the ground, clutching her neck. Tandem pained groans roll through the space, from Minos and Mina. Chrysa slides to her side just as Diomede reaches Minos and pulls back her hand to strike him. Like before, she can't connect with his skin and her hand slams backward like on a taut string. This time, Minos doesn't retaliate, but simply stares in smug fascination as Diomede tries again and again. Eriphyle, Thyia, and Elara watch silently.

I creep behind Mina and Chrysa and drop to the ground.

"Are you alright, Mina?" I whisper. Neither girl reacts aloud, but Mina minutely nods.

"What's the plan?" Mina asks from the corner of her mouth. "Taking his crown and then kicking him to the Underworld?"

At some point, I want to say. But the step before it is a millstone around my neck. "I can't accept Orion while he's unconscious, though Minos is invulnerable anyway."

"So, no plan," Chrysa hisses. "Great."

"Hades and his soldiers are gone," I offer. They both laugh quietly, ducking their heads to avoid Minos' gaze.

Minos must be bored with Diomede's unsuccessful attacks as he withdraws the ceremonial knife and aims it at her. This prompts Eriphyle and Thyia to burst towards them. Only Elara remains where the Ker had held her. Diomede grabs the blade's handle, but Minos slices her wrist, and she hisses. Minos does too, covering it with a low laugh, though he squints in agony and blood appears on his own wrist.

My eyes widen in realization. Whatever makes him invulnerable means we can't touch him. But he can't hurt us, the Collected, not without causing himself the same pain.

"That's what I thought," he says hoarsely. "Now, let us talk like reasonable people."

Eriphyle and Thyia avert their course towards Diomede. Thyia rips a strip from Eriphyle's chiton to cover Diomede's slowly weeping wound, while Eriphyle glares at Minos hatefully.

"You think a knife worries me? I forged something larger before I could walk," Eriphyle says, raising her fists. "See if such a blade can cut through my skin."

I stare hard at Minos, as if I can see what gift Poseidon gave him. "There is some way to remove his invulnerability," I murmur, more to myself than Mina and Chrysa. "I just need to think."

Even though Eriphyle can't touch him, Minos still flinches at her jolting movement, his free hand flying towards his hair. It glints in the light, like gold. Like magic.

"No, no," Minos says, holding the knife out handle first. "The knife isn't for me to use on you, or even you to use on me. But for you to use on each other."

Eriphyle falters, confusion swirling in her eyes. "Us?"

"There must be a victor," he says with a winning smile, his confidence only belied by the tremors in his hand held aloft.

"The Collection is no more. We must have a story to tell the Islands. Why not one of you, the ultimate warriors, defeating the monster in the center and returning home a winner?"

"It's his hair," I hiss to Chrysa and Mina. "That's what I was missing. His hair makes him invulnerable." All the signs were there, every hint, even Dolion's damned riddle. "I just need to get close enough to cut it."

"We can't get his knife," Mina protests.

Chrysa pulls her up to stand, angling her head to continue speaking without detection. "She has one too, remember? On her back."

I follow, rising on shaking limbs. "And he can't hurt us without hurting himself. That's why he wants us to finish each other off."

"He really should have brought guards," Mina mutters, wrinkling her nose. "I can jump on him and surprise him while you-"

"No, I'm the only one he can't see coming." I glance at Orion. He's undisturbed but still unconscious. "Stay with Orion, just in case. He's the only one that Minos might harm without consequence. I have an idea."

"...A *good* one?" Chrysa asks, one brow raised.

I don't begrudge the lacking faith, but it isn't as though I've had *bad* ideas so far. Though I won't risk secrets again. "I'm going to sneak up on him and slice off the braid."

"That's barely an idea," Chrysa says.

Even so, they slink towards Orion while I shuffle to Minos' side. One hand plays with the folds of my chiton, until my fingers slip through a rip in the side, one large enough to drag the knife through without catching on the fabric. I don't withdraw the knife yet, I'll save that until I'm closer to Minos, in case I trip and miss and the magic forces me backward since I can't physically touch him. Better not chance it.

"But we'd know it wasn't true," Thyia is saying to Minos as I stalk forward. Minos may believe she's considering it, but I know her a little better by now. She's toying with him, her own weaponized weakness.

Minos still thinks he has the upper hand; it's the only explanation for why he hasn't run for aid from his puny guard. As Deianira proved, they, at least, can affect us with some intent to harm.

"Simple magic, my dear. A little blood and you'll have no memory of anything otherwise." He surveys the three of them and smirks shakily. "What do you say?"

The illusion falls as soon as I get within reaching distance of Minos. It must be part of his invulnerability, which thwarts any invisible sneak attacks too. He jumps backward, not from the magic but my presence, and a spark of vindictive glee runs through me at the slight surprise and fear he displays, overtaking the disappointment that I couldn't slice off his mane without being seen. My illusions may fail in close proximity, but magic isn't necessary to win this battle.

"You thought you could come upon me and cause me harm?" He narrows his eyes. "I've managed every contingency, idiot child."

I want to boast, to tell him Hades abandoned him, that I've discovered his secret, and his game is over for good. But instead, I say, "How about just me?"

Elara makes an annoyed sound from behind me, stomping forward and shoving between Eriphyle and Thyia. "You'd be the winner?"

"No," I say, one eye on Elara's stiff form, the other on Minos. If she ruins this for us, it will be *me* complaining for centuries in the Underworld about it. "You all win. You can all be spelled, but I can't. So, spell them all and just kill me."

Minos flicks his attention between us. "I intended on your death regardless," he says, twitching.

I step forward as he steps backward. Even so, he re-angles the knife towards me, but I'm desperate enough to disregard it.

"Then kill me first." My fingers close around the handle of my knife still at my back.

"Thalia," Diomede says. "Are you sure?" Behind her, Chrysa and Mina look like they want to inch forward but I sharply shake my head.

"I have no issues with it. I'll even volunteer to help strike the fatal blow," Elara says, grabbing my upper arm and dragging me closer to Minos. For a minute, I fear she'll snap my neck.

"Now, wait a minute," I spit, trying and failing to plant my feet. "Minos should be the one to kill me."

If she bungles this, I will haunt her until she joins me in the Underworld and then pester her until her ears off.

She scowls at me, her angular face hawkish in the late afternoon light. "Don't you worry a *hair* on your royal head, *Thalia*. You want death, I'll give you death." And she switches arms, half hugging me from behind and dragging me forward. She slips her hand through the rip in my chiton, her icy fingers sliding over mine to the holster.

I still for a minute, not long enough for Minos to notice. She's never called me Thalia, and I realize what she intends. "Brutes all of you," I say, letting her take me to his side, as though I've given up.

"That is how they were bred," Minos says, smiling. "Centuries of selection, to create such a woman."

When Elara gets closer to him, she inclines her head in a bow. "I would take your knife. So it may kill her and not my own hands."

I try to keep the surprise from my face. Her fingers are already curled around *my* knife but perhaps I've misunderstood her plan. Minos studies her, dragging shifty eyes from the top of her mussed black hair to the tips of her split toenails. "From where do you hail, dear child?"

Elara's cheeks twitch, no doubt restraining a sneer at Minos' endearment. "Prosfora, sire. Born from the Island of Ares."

Minos smiles faintly. "Of course, my brother of war. He would relish death at his hands, and not from something as base as a borrowed weapon. Especially from a willing subject."

Elara lets the sneer come now, shuffling me closer to him but keeping the hand holding the knife hidden against my back. "She is not worthy of such a death. A knife is good enough for her."

Minos laughs, tossing his head back. His braid slides towards down his shoulder as he looks back at her. "Then take it, child," he says, placing the knife in the flat of his combined palms. He's still overly arrogant and doesn't even look concerned.

Elara smiles, the first genuine one I've seen. "Thank you, sire."

She reaches for his knife with her empty right hand. As soon as her fingers close around the shaft, she shoves me aside and slices forward with her left. The knife flies, cleaving through the braid at his neck. A bright flash follows it, but Elara doesn't release the knife. Instead, she lets it continue slashing, hitting the base of Minos' throat and splitting the skin. There's no time for Minos to react beyond gasping in surprise, before blood arcs from the wound, splattering Elara and me.

Minos falls, hitting his knees first and then slumping onto his stomach. He gasps once, twice, three times, and coughs. And then, silence.

We all watch mutely as blood pools on the surrounding ground. Something darkly satisfied roils through my stomach at the sight.

Elara is the first to speak, as she cleans the knife on her chiton, casting her dark eyes to mine. "No vomit this time, Heir?"

I'm still stunned into silence, but the guilt I'd expected never appears. Neither does any disappointment—that it wasn't me to finish the deed—rise. But *something* does: three ghostly apparitions pull from the earth, growing into winged women. We all freeze like statues in their presence, as though our stillness will keep them from noticing us.

Unlike the Keres, the Erinyes' skin is burnished bronze and smooth like oil, and their eyes a stunning green that cry blood. Snakes writhe where their hair should be, hissing and crawling around their shoulders and bare breasts, dripping venomous slime down their naked forms, flecks that burn the earth where they land. They crouch around Minos' body, laying hands on it with clawed fingers, until something pale and amorphous drags from beneath his skin. They move too quickly for me to inspect what, but I can guess it's Minos' soul they're snatching to torture. Something screams, not us and not the Erinyes, but quicker than I can blink, two of the Erinyes drag the white smoke back into the ground. The last Erinys looks at us, her snakes flicking their tongues, before she, too, vanishes back where she came.

Minutes of silence pass, our breaths returning as life cycles back into our veins.

"What were those?" Eriphyle asks, her focus pinned on Minos' corpse.

Diomede drops to her knees with a gasp. "Those were the Erinyes."

Eriphyle joins her, rubbing her back. I tear my gaze from Minos' soulless body to Orion and stumble to his side. He's still breathing, thank the Gods, deeply enough to confirm he's alive, but remains unconscious. I rip the cleanest piece I can find from the tattered remains of my chiton and tie it around his face to cover him.

Beside us, Mina presses her hands against her cheeks. "And the King is dead."

"What does that mean?" Thyia asks, her own fingers clutching at her neck.

Chrysa giggles, a nervous sound. "That none of us will question Thalia any time soon, that's for sure."

I heave a breath. "The King is dead. Long live the future King, Orion Borealis." I let out a laugh, staring at Elara, still holding my knife and looking like a spirit herself with the sun haloing her body. "And long live Elara, winner of the Collection."

Epilogue

Orion recovers in the privacy of his rooms. He remains unconscious after his battle with Cerberus, as Cerberus' spit is as potent a poison as the plant named after it. Minos' invulnerability meant he didn't employ any healers, and he let the rest of his attendants manage their ailing health without magic. Diomede has been busy playing mock-healer, using the scant skills she picked up on her Island, with Mina and a few palace workers trailing behind her to learn as much of the craft as they can. Mina and Diomede will return to their Islands soon, though I hope a member of Diomede's Governor's family, a spirit-born of Apollo, will visit Crete once we're ready, as it needs healing magic.

While Orion is unavailable, I attempt to keep the country from falling into further disarray, with the girls as my 'Council.' That may sound overdramatic, but Elara took her victory seriously and transformed it into 'guardian of the Collected and Borealis.' She continues to report unrest and the possibility of insurgence at any moment, from those agitators who wanted Minos' reign to continue. Chrysa tells me she's overreacting, but better be safe than sorry, especially where Gods and Cretans are concerned.

Orion's lacking presence didn't help matters. The citizens *knew* Minos was no longer King and their geases fell, but Orion hasn't shown himself. Neither has any wife, meaning it's unclear to the populace if Orion even *is* king. No messengers have been sent to any of the Islands either, as that could bring forth another conflict before Orion is ready. And that's before we even consider the rest of Gaia's demand, that Orion rule over all earth. Holding Crete is only the first step.

Even though Poseidon never came to check on the breached bargain and mete his own justice, Deianira still fled with half the guards, those apparently loyal to Minos. The rest have accepted Elara as their new commanding officer. Knowing the chills her stare can provoke, and her new penchant for wearing Minos' ceremonial knife as a pendant on a necklace made from Minos' braided hair, I'm unsurprised they are indulging her. Fear of her retribution tempered my behavior, and that was when she didn't have any true authority. That she likely has more combat training than any of them certainly helps her credibility.

As soon as things settle, I intend on returning home, to report on what's occurred and be present for the next steps in our political relationship with Crete. Orion will need allies on the Islands certainly, though my stomach begins to hurt each time I think about leaving.

A month after Minos' death, Mina finds me in the throne room hearing a report from Chrysa and Eriphyle on Hecaline's recent visit. Chrysa sits on Minos' throne while Eriphyle and I stand around her. As a meeting room, it is the most private, because the illusions stick easier here than anywhere else. In between courtly duties, I practiced applying my illusions to other senses, and I managed to silence the room to anyone not inside the walls.

"She said something about the earth cracking," Eriphyle is saying.

I slide a glance at Mina by the door before frowning. "Did she say anything else?" I have a vague recollection of her mentioning the world cracking once before, but the memory is too slippery to hold.

"Earthquakes," Eriphyle offers. "She said it was related to the earthquakes, but they were different somehow."

Not Poseidon's earthquakes, that I remember.

"You know Lina, she's all about puzzles," Chrysa says, smirking. "Maybe this time you'll figure it out before we all almost die."

I roll my eyes and she laughs. "Next time, let me know when she's here," I tell them. "With Minos gone, I know she has more freedom of movement, but she never stays long enough for me to speak with her." It's like she's avoiding me.

"We don't want to take you from your vigil over Orion," Eriphyle says gruffly.

"She *says* she'll be back soon," Chrysa adds. "Something about her 'star' shining bright."

I straighten my back. "*Orion* is her star."

"About Orion," Mina says, skipping forward. "He's awake."

I sprint through the halls until I arrive at Orion's study, barreling through it into his bedroom. Perhaps I shouldn't have, but I had his bed fixed when he remained in one of the healing rooms. Now the bed dwarfs him, rather than the other way around, and sheets should be soft and supple against his skin.

As soon as he bares it again, that is. No one but the healers have seen him uncovered since the day of the Collection. My own skin has only recently been exposed to the air, once the cuts finally sealed and the bruises faded.

Thyia and Diomede are sitting by Orion's side in the two chairs he once put in his study for us to share, chatting quietly.

They both stand and leave when I appear, but not before Thyia beams and pats Orion on his covered wrist. His hand twitches, a slight flinch, but she doesn't notice.

When they slip through the doorway back into the study, Orion tilts his head towards me.

"Hello," he says.

My mouth opens but no sound comes forth. *How do I greet the man who risked his life for me, who might be* king *if not for me, whose entire life was upended because of my actions?*

"Are you well?" he asks quietly.

His voice prompts me into action, and I sit on the edge of his bed, shaking my head. "I should be asking that question of you. How are you?"

He slowly shuffles to a seated position, the covered muscles in his arms and shoulders bunching. "This is not the worst I have felt when waking up abed."

"I imagine not," I say, reaching out my hand for him. I let it stay aloft, to not force my touch on him, in case he's changed his mind.

He quickly grabs mine and squeezes my fingers gently. "I am glad you remained. I wanted to see you."

"Of course. I couldn't leave without seeing you awake again."

He releases my hand and with trembling limbs, unravels the cloth over his head. I make a slight protesting sound, but I can't deny I want to see him, *truly* see him again.

"Now you can," he says when the cloth lies on the bed between us. "Thalia, I—"

"Where are my two?" A loud voice echoes down the hallway.

I leap upward, pushing the cloth back into his hands to veil his face again.

He shakes his head. "It's only Hecaline."

As if his utterance called her, the door to his study bangs open. For weeks, she vanished anytime I was near. And now, I finally have a minute alone with Orion, she appears. The Fates *are* fickle.

Hecaline shuffles through to his bedroom, stopping at the doorway. "I am a harbinger of doom, my star."

I suck in a breath and Orion grabs my hand again.

"Hecaline," he admonishes. "Thalia doesn't understand your humor."

She shakes her staff at us. "Deny me all my fun. We never even got to the joining."

Orion's cheeks darken, though I can't tell if it is from embarrassment or annoyance.

Hecaline shuffles to the edge of Orion's bed and sits down beside me. "And it's my *humor*, he says. I *do* have portents to share. But my star is not yet king. Crete must accept him now, since the magic hasn't come together. And then the rest must follow."

Orion doesn't react like this is a surprise. It makes some sense: Minos' line is ineligible, and Orion hasn't met the terms necessary to become the King of Crete without citizen approval. Even with the bargain breached, he needs an Island consort at his side before they accept him under Poseidon's terms. I lick my lips, and offer, "I can still—"

But he cuts me off. "I am willing to prove my worth to Crete in another way," he says. "And follow the Fates' decree. An Island consort was the demand for Minos and Fath—Poseidon, you see. Not the Morai or Mother."

Relief tinged with the tiniest bit of regret chases through me. "They *must* accept you," I say. "By all rights, you are the next king. With or without a... bride. I am sorry to have—"

"No, Thalia," he says firmly. "It isn't your fault. In fact..." He casts his gaze at Hecaline, who watches us with her blind eyes as though we're her favorite play. "In fact," he repeats, lowering his voice. "Though our... acquaintance has been short, you are my closest companion, aside from Hecaline. I appreciate everything you have done. And hope... we can further our friendship."

My cheeks heat even as I swallow a lump in my throat. I must return to my life and responsibilities in Standia. But Orion and the girls have become more important than I could have imagined, and being pulled away—back to my usual life—sounds... awful. "I did plan on staying for a short time... to help with the initial transition, should you wish it."

"I would welcome your presence as long as you are willing." He squeezes my hand. The look in his eyes—mirroring the hope that burns within me, that hope for my own possibility, some potential future—makes me want to stay until the stars fall from the sky.

"Welcome, he says. Of course, she's welcome," Hecaline says. "She's needed, how about that?"

We both glance at Hecaline, though her blind gaze focuses on me, so I respond. "What do you mean?"

"What I've been saying since you arrived," she says. "The earth's going to crack. You're expected to keep it together."

The room trembles as thunder rumbles in the distance, and the walls shake with the force of a rolling earthquake. Stacks of books crash to the ground and lit candles topple beside them. I leap to my feet to stamp out the flames.

Hecaline cackles as the lights snuff out.

Author's Note + Bonus Content

Thank you for reading *Threaded Secrets*, the first in a new romantic fantasy series loosely based on ancient Greek mythology.

If you're interested in more of my writing, check out my website (**kmalady.com**). You'll find a free prequel 'novella' that follows each of the six girls right before they become part of the Collection, giving you more details of their histories and personalities.

You can find other fun information there about my other projects, like *The Ascend Trials* (a romantic YA portal fantasy all about subverting tropes), *Kneeling Kingdoms* (my upcoming standalone high-spice fantasies), and more!

Upcoming Sequel

E mbark on a journey beyond the Labyrinth's depths in the spellbinding sequel to *Threaded Secrets*. Thalia and Orion face an unforeseen challenge as they grapple with the consequences of their choices. Bound by ancient bargains and guided by the whims of the gods, Thalia must navigate the complexities of love, duty, and the looming threat of the earth cracking. As earthquakes fracture the very ground beneath her island, Thalia seeks answers from the depths of the Underworld, where old bargains may unravel and new alliances form. Join Thalia on a quest that will test her resilience, unravel hidden truths, and challenge the bonds that tie gods and mortals alike in *Threaded Destiny* (working title), the second book in the Threads of Fate series.

COMING SOON